The
DREAMHEALER

Shane Briant

For my beautiful nieces Natasha and Rosalind, my nephew Toby, and all my gorgeous great nephews and nieces.

ACKNOWLEDGMENTS

Many thanks to Scott Citron of Scottcitrondesign for my fabulous cover design.

I'd like to thank everyone who helped me deliver the sequel to 'Worst Nightmares.' They've been wonderful enough to keep badgering me to write the sequel.
Laura Blake Peterson, my amazing literary agent at Curtis Brown, who supports me without question – regardless of GFCs.
Jeffrey Bloom.
The Hotel Buci, my favourite Paris boutique hotel.
Melissa Brooks.
Nick and Sheelagh Hippisley Coxe – I'm afraid I treat their house as my own!
Steven and Marti Nalevansky, simply for being my friends.
Beau, Amanda and Josef Nalevansky – ditto. Rupert, Lizie and Hervé. Virginia Bates. Freddy. Giblet. And of course, my beautiful Wendy.

THE SET UP

1.

The music began in his mind as the smallest possible sound wave. So slight that it was possibly less than one sound byte. A wild animal would have heard it long ago, but it took Josef much longer to fully comprehend.

Within a second his signature piano piece became unmistakable – one so often requested of him by the great concert halls of the world yet seldom granted. 'Opus Clavicembalisticum', a solo piano piece composed by Kaikhosru Shapurji Sorabji in 1930 – one noted primarily for its length and extreme difficulty. The longest piano piece in existence, it's duration close to four hours, depending on tempo naturally, it remained still one of the most technically demanding solo piano works in existence.

Josef Kafni was one of an elite few international soloists who had truly mastered the piece. It often came to him in his dreams. It was his tour de force – his showpiece.

Yet this night something felt different. Very different.

He could feel the barest sensation of muscle spasms in his left arm, his head was swimming as he began to break through the fog and mist that often separated the unconscious mind from the conscious.

Yet was he still dreaming? Yes. Surely.

But where was he?

Josef found it supremely difficult to open his eyes. It was an experience he'd often had as a child growing up in Prague;

dreaming he'd awakened; yet still experiencing some terrible childhood nightmare, unable to move or scream.

The strident piano chords began to build in his head, the volume ramping up in successive waves, each splashing higher than the previous one.

Yes! He was indeed playing his signature piece, but he had never played this extraordinary piece as well! Possibly once at Carnegie back in 2006? Yet now everything felt curiously so very different. Where was he? Why could he not see the keys, nor feel them. Why could he not move? What was happening to him?

His fingers had an effortless will of their own, requiring scarcely any muscle contractions whatsoever to carry them across the keyboard at such breakneck speed. Such dexterity was humanly impossible! It was a miracle!

It was only as the famous intertwined lines moved towards their multiple speeds, each one superimposed over the other, that Josef broke through into consciousness and became aware of the true horror of his situation.

For it was not *his* rendition of Sorabji's masterwork that was pounding in his eardrums, but John Ogden's masterly version – perhaps the finest performance of the work ever. And Josef was not lying in his Fifth Avenue apartment bed, vainly trying to waken from what seemed like some glorious yet heart-stopping dream, he was actually part of an horrific nightmare world in which he was lying supine on a surgical gurney in a windowless cell!

His torso and legs were also strapped to the gurney, both his arms extended at 30-degree angles from his sides. Each was strapped to separate metal extensions attached to the sides of the gurney. Trolleys packed with an assortment of surgical instruments, swabs as well as bottles of fluids and syringes stood on either side of the gurney. A metal stand held a drip that fed down to his arm, attached by a catheter to the flesh at the crook of his elbow.

A brilliant operating light shone a harsh beam

downwards, directed at his right hand.

His eyesight was at first a blur. But as it began to clear he tried to focus on a man at his side, dressed from head to toe in olive surgical scrubs. He was wearing specialist spectacles with a bright light shining down between the lenses. He was busy working on the fingers of Josef's left hand with a scalpel, slicing the skin of each small bone open as if he were delicately filleting some very small fish, such as an anchovy. The room, which looked more like an underground tomb, measured scarcely more yards than a luxury hotel bathroom.

To one side of his gurney stood a pedestal that shone with a bluish light. It slowly became apparent to Josef that atop stood a laptop computer; it was the screen that radiated the blue light. But what was looking at on that eerie screen – it resembled a hooded figure standing on a chair. About to be executed? Hanged?

Josef wanted to scream yet couldn't. Instead, it was his brain that silently screamed. He tried to fill his almost empty lungs but failed – it was as though his entire body had been anesthetized. Yet he could feel his left hand. Yes! So very acutely.

As the surgeon's scalpel skimmed into the sinew, separating what remained of the tissue that still held the metacarpal of his forefinger from the trapezium, the pain was like a million needle lances ripping through his nervous system. It was like nothing he had ever experienced before – as keen, extreme and pure as Yehudi Menhuin playing a harmonic on an E string.

There was the slightest pause in the music as Ogden lifted his fingers from the keys for the first time during the piece. Then the music raced on, continuing with the double action of fast-paced stabbing chords.

The music was now deafening. It filled the room with an audible ferocity akin to a drill being inserted in both Josef's ears; the drill bit held close to both eardrums. Josef knew it would ultimately deafen him, yet he was quite powerless to alter his fate.

It was only then that he became aware that his right hand fingers were still playing along with Ogden; dancing along in a world of their own.

Bewildered, Josef turned his attention to his right arm and immediately his heart stopped still.

His right hand had been completely separated from his arm at the wrist. The veins and arteries had been tied off neatly to avoid too much blood loss, and each finger had been surgically removed, each tiny bone skinned and scraped free of all flesh or tissue; the bones placed like a jigsaw less than half an inch from where they would have still formed part of his arm.

The bones were the pure white.

They lay on a gleaming white cloth.

It was only then that a second man, also dressed in surgical scrubs, entered Josef's field of vision. He walked up to stand close to Josef's head, crouching slightly, smiling. There were earplugs in both his ears – there was no way this man was going to suffer hearing loss himself! As the man stared down at him, Josef could tell that he was actually relishing the abject panic and horror being inflicted on the world famous pianist through the tiniest vibrations in the bones that were being skinned.

"Good evening, maestro. Welcome to the land of the living," the man said. The skin around his eyes creased in an easy smile.

"For now, anyway..." he continued, his voice like slow-moving crude oil. "My friend here," he said, gesturing to the man who was still busy working on the bones of his left hand, "is a qualified surgeon. He knows his business. You are in good hands." He laughed lightly. "My small joke." He looked down at Josef's severed right hand. "I say! It looks absolutely magnificent! A future collector's piece, I'd say."

Josef couldn't take his eyes off the separated fingers of his right hand. The white bones had been fanned out precisely, like a museum exhibit in London's Natural History Museum.

The music was now so deafening that Josef felt it might soon cause his head to explode. Prior to his concerts he'd often quipped that the harmonies now pounding his eardrums were should "bite like nitric acid". At this moment, those words held a particularly grizzly relevance.

Of course the real horror was that the receptors in his brain stem were still giving him phantom stimuli; the barest muscle sensations in both his arms informing some place deep in his stem that it was *he* who was playing the Opus Clavicembalisticum – when Josef knew full well it was Ogden!

"Good work, Jean," the second man said, turning his attention to the surgeon; tapping him on the shoulder as he examined the handiwork.

The surgeon jolted briefly at the touch; then looked up from his work to focus on the second man. He'd been startled – he too was wearing earplugs.

They locked eyes with each other for several seconds, then the surgeon broke the silence. "Will you kill me too?" he asked; his voice the barest reed. "I mean, eventually? How can I be sure you won't?"

"You should be thinking of your wife, Jean. Not yourself. Tut tut! Do as I say and she will live. That's enough for now. Surely."

The second man nodded towards a computer screen that was set on the stand close to the surgeon. It showed a young woman – one could only tell because of the bulge of breasts through the upper clothing – a noose was hanging around her hooded head, her hands were bound behind her. She was standing on a bentwood chair, finding it increasingly difficult to maintain her balance. The room she was in was in every way the same as the windowless surgery where Josef lay.

"The sooner you finish, the sooner I will cut her down, Jean. I have no reason to kill *her* – she has not seen me. So consider *her* future rather than your own."

The surgeon stared blankly. "So you *do* intend killing me."

"We shall see, Monsieur Ballon. We shall see," the second man cooed. "But hesitate one more time and you both will die."

The surgeon hurriedly returned to his work, made one final cut, then selected a different, preferred, surgical instrument from a wooden box. He then began scraping the bones clean.

Waves of horror and agony coursed through Josef's body as the phantom concert continued in his brain like a mad fandango.

Finally the surgeon began to lay out the fingers of Josef's left hand in a decorative arrangement, similar to that of Josef's right hand. It was as if he were conducting a very odd autopsy.

"I have never seen fingers so slender and delicate," the second man muttered to himself. "They are superb. Quite magnificent."

He turned to the surgeon. "When the amputation is complete, tie off the blood vessels, or whatever they are called. Properly, though. He must not die. I will not make a murderer of you. Does that make you feel better about what you do?"

The surgeon did not reply, but his expression, even under the facemask, betrayed relief. He returned to his work with renewed care, staunching any flow of blood.

The second man again crouched down close to Josef's head. The music was swelling to its violent climax; the piece was almost at an end now.

"A music critic once told me this, but I feel sure you'll know this quotation..." the second man whispered softly into Josef's ear. "'*the occasional excursions into tonal regions of this passage provide massive relief.*' An interesting observation, though possibly not so in your case."

He turned back to the surgeon, placed an arm around his shoulders and talked to him softly, so that his patient could not hear.

"I reiterate. I do not want this man dying on me. Am I absolutely clear?"

"Very clear," the surgeon replied stonily. "But I cannot guarantee there will be no infection. These conditions are appalling."

"I have done everything possible. I have given you the necessary equipment to sterilize the equipment. Now finish things off properly and bandage my patient. Then we will go visit your sweet wife."

The surgeon continued with his post-operative clean-up work.

As he did so, the second man yet again bent down close to Josef's ear, this time so that it was the *surgeon* who could not hear.

"Sadly my friend, in a short while we must leave you alone. I have errands to do. I have to make sure this man's wife is safe and sound; after all, I made a deal, and I honor all my deals. We will leave you to your music. It is on a continuous loop. Wunderbar, eh? I wish I could have seen you play in person, but you've been overly long in America recently. Anyway, you'll have the pleasure of listening to a *real* master until I return. I feel sure you don't consider yourself in Ogden's league. No matter. I am off! I have some games to play."

So saying he injected more of his wonder drug of choice – Succinylcholine – into each of Josef's limbs. It had been his favourite drug for some time now. A precise dose was a must; any more and one risked heart failure.

Twenty minutes later the surgeon was finished, and the second man opened the reinforced steel door.

Josef strained to see through the opening but all he could

make out was a dark corridor.

"Oh, by the way, my friend here has been kind enough to tie off the blood vessels at your wrists in an attempt to make you as comfortable as possible. You will not die. We shall return soon, to check your condition. Oh, and relieve any pain!"

He beckoned the surgeon. "Come, Monsieur Ballon. Let's see your wife released."

The surgeon pulled off his gloves, cap and mask and walked to the door. As he reached it, the second man gestured him to go first. "Please…"

The second man held up a syringe for the surgeon to see. "I am sure we won't be needing this today, Jean. I think we understand how we stand, don't we?

The surgeon 's eyes flicked to the syringe – he knew he could try his luck, but the odds were not good.

The second man, known to Interpol as Nick Hoyle, followed the surgeon into the black corridor, locking the door behind him. He had embarked on a fresh era of horror, and he felt he was doing himself justice.

2.

A strong south westerly was blowing hard, whipping up a mist of moisture from the Pacific that billowed like a thin cloud around Dermot Nolan's face. But neither the chill nor the spray registered – he wasn't simply *lost* in his thoughts, he was *bereft* of any. He'd been sitting in his wheelchair for over an hour in a mentally numbed state on the cliff top staring out into the ocean, oblivious to the fact the earth was continuing to spin on its axis, that there'd be his favorite pot roast waiting for him when he returned home, that his wife Neela loved him with an enduring passion.

A gull swooped down low, flashing across his field of vision, bringing him sharply back to reality. His right hand clenched the wheelchair's brake as he considered his options; to release the mechanism would cause it to roll forward, ultimately propelling him into oblivion; to leave it as it was would confirm his life of emptiness.

The thought of eternal peace was so tempting. The months in rehab, the chronic pain, the black dog depression and the despair that had gone along with it had shrouded his every waking hour, as a vampire's wings might in the night. Worst of all was the total lack of any recall. That was the hardest pill to swallow. What had happened?

He'd regained consciousness in the ECU – come back from the very rim of eternity – to find himself lying in a hospital bed, hooked up to an impossible numbers of life-saving machines.

Blip, blip, blip.

The relentless sound of a monitor thrumbed in his brain as he came to. What had happened? Where was he? More to the point, *who* was he? And who was the woman sitting in a chair at his side, reading a book?

She was beautiful.

Her dark hair cloaked her lean, structurally perfect face. The eyes looked kind, yet thoughtful. Yet there was an all-pervading veil of sadness about her aura.

Had he undergone some terrible illness? Was this woman his wife? His lover? Could she be his sister? He preferred to think of this beautiful woman as his lover. That she loved him. It was a blessing that someone did. He wasn't alone in his nothing-world of monitored sensations; one which held no reality.

"Honey?"

The word came out of the breeze, like a pin prick.

He was back on the cliff-top. The beautiful woman he'd seen that day in the ICU ward was at his side, a baby in her arms, a Cairn terrier on a lead at her side – one he'd been told bore the name of 'Scary.'

The breeze had picked up. A giant tanker was making it's way to harbor, as yet well out to sea.

The beautiful woman smiled. "It's getting cold, darling. Let's go home, shall me? Dinner's ready."

The woman, Neela, kissed the top of his head. Dermot uncurled his lean fingers from the brake lever and held out the hand to her. She held it in hers, squeezing, then lifted his palm and placed it on his daughter's warm flawlessly chubby cheek.

Neela watched as Dermot's face flooded with joy as he stared at his little angel. He'd been told he was her father. Perhaps life would one day regain some semblance of normality.

Neela had always known Dermot's recovery would be a very long road. For weeks he hadn't even known who she was. Then when the synapses of his brain had finally begun to function, it had come to him in an instant. She was 'Neela' – the love of his life. The baby in her arms was their daughter, Virginia. Yet everything else remained a mystery; a former life shut out of his conscious mind by a granite wall of emotional self-protection.

Ever since regaining consciousness he'd insisted on sleeping with the lights on. Darkness was anathema. The psychiatrist had advised, despite the protestations of the investigative authorities, that he be asked no searching questions regarding 'the incident'. He should be allowed to rest; to find his own way back to the present.

Neela understood that it was most likely that Dermot had no desire to come to terms with what had happened to him. The shrink had agreed. Re-living the horror of his abduction and incarceration might drive him into an even deeper psychosis. The remembrances should be allowed to surface in their own good time, rather than be stimulated too forcefully.

Of course, this strategy did not sit well with the detectives charged with the task of setting straight the exact circumstances of Dermot's abduction. The torture. The coffin. Enquiring minds at the LAPD needed to have Dermot clearly state who had placed him in his sarcophagus. Such a statement from the victim himself was essential; though there was absolutely not reason to believe that anyone other than the most obvious suspect was guilty of the crime. It was a formality; but nevertheless paperwork that needed to be attended to. Police work was all about the paperwork.

At that early stage of Dermot's rehabilitation, Detective Hansen, at the North Hollywood Precinct, knew he was a long way off a face-to-face interview with the victim – Dermot's mental mechanisms of self-preservation had closed the vault doors to remembrances as tightly as possible, locking the past away, so as to cling to sanity.

It had taken several months to raise Dermot's body weight to an acceptable, yet still very meager, level. There had been an almost catastrophic degeneration of bone and muscle tissue during his time lying flat on his back in his coffin. Survival, after all those months, had been no less than a miracle. The day they lifted Dermot's unconscious body from his grave, there remained the barest muscle tissue clinging to his bones. An elderly Jewish doctor, on duty at Cedars Sinai hospital the night Dermot was unearthed, was graphically reminded of the terrible photographs taken of Jews who had failed to survive the liberation of the Nazi concentration camps; so shocked he'd spontaneously burst into tears while treating Dermot.

Now, eight months later, still well under an acceptable weight, his limbs were just able to function properly. The doctors had recommended that Dermot continue to use his wheelchair as often as possible; the bones in his legs desperately needed time to regain some strength. But he was making progress; now capable of eating solid food.

Back home from the cliff-top, Neela turned the key in the lock, walked through the living room. While she continued on up the stairs to the nursery to change baby Virginia, Dermot wheeled his way into the kitchen, opened the fridge and spooned some dog food into a bowl. Scary had obediently remained by the door. When called inside, the dog wagged his tail, licked Dermot's hand and began to eat.

Dermot reached for the fixings of the ritual evening margaritas. *Mr. and Mrs. T* mix; the busy man's miracle helper.

"Esther called while you were out," Neela called from upstairs, where she was now putting Virginia to bed.

"Any messages?" Dermot asked.

"No, she was simply checking on you. She loves you."

"Doesn't look as though any of the houses have bitten," Dermot muttered.

His literary agent, Esther Bloom, had been doing her best to resurrect his career. Not such an easy task because of Dermot's former notoriety; more particularly because of the shame of plagiarism. Added to which Dermot was still being blamed for being 'the man who had known where all the bodies were buried but had never granted closure to the families.' Of course, when word had spread of the horrific retribution 'The Dreamhealer' had meted out on the once bestselling author, to some extent the public had forgiven Dermot.

Esther felt now was the time to start Dermot's career afresh; there was a slim chance that the literary world might also be in the mood to forgive Dermot his previous misdemeanors and accept him back into their community. It wouldn't be exactly easy to sell Dermot's essays, but she saw it as a personal challenge. She'd try.

Initially she'd suggested a series of one-on-one interviews with high achievers in the arts community; a series she'd suggested should be titled 'Pinnacles'. It would be a modest start.

The first two interviews had already been conducted and written – the subjects, Josef Kafni, the concert pianist, and

Galina Yablonskaya, now being celebrated as the new Margot Fonteyn. Dermot was working on the third interview, involving world famous neurosurgeon, Bernard Dutont. Esther's idea was to offer the interviews, either singly or as a series, to the *New Yorker*.

Dermot's house on Cliffside Drive was small yet comfortable, purpose built by an architect who'd developed motor neuron disease late in life and had been confined to a wheelchair for the final fifteen years that preceded his death. Finding this particular house had been happenstance, since most houses on Point Dume had been out of Dermot's reach financially. The one he and Neela had found was built of wood and more resembled a weekender than a principal residence. However, it was all they could afford. Their former house in downtown Los Angeles, in Linley Place, had achieved such notoriety that few people felt comfortable buying the property. No one relished buying the house belonging to the missing ex-Booker Prize-winning novelist who had been discovered buried alive in his own garden. It was hardly romantic. And since there was no possible way that Neela and Dermot could ever go back to live there, it was ultimately sold for the land value alone. The house was demolished by a developer, and a small block of units was built in it's place.

"Is Virginia asleep?" Dermot called up the stairs.

"I think so, not sure. Her eyes are closed. I've changed and fed her. I won't be long."

While Neela was upstairs, Dermot raised himself out of his wheelchair. He could quite easily support himself on his legs – the wheelchair was simply a convenience when he felt the need to venture outdoors to relax and gaze at the ocean and be alone with his thoughts. It was a time when he could attempt to come to terms with the past and present.

"I wish I had Vig's capacity for tranquil sleep," Neela said as she returned to the living room.

Dermot smiled, handing Neela her drink. "I wish for the same thing every day."

"Have you fed Cheesecake?" Neela asked. Cheesecake was a fat irascible cat with a constant propensity for aggression; an angry fur-ball who'd agreed to a shaky truce with Scary the terrier. She was an urban mouser and had never gotten used to being a Malibu pussycat.

"She'll come in and eat when she's ready," he replied.

"How was today, darling?"

Rather than answer glibly, Dermot considered her question carefully. "It was a good day. No demons."

Neela wrapped her arms around his neck and kissed him gently.

"Time the healer?"

"Time the healer," Dermot repeated. He had decided not to confide in her just now that the detail of the horrific months interred beneath the ground was suddenly returning thick and fast to his conscious mind. It was as frightening as watching the tide recede on a Pacific Island, knowing that within the hour a Tsunami would be thundering in. He needed time to come to terms with each new recollection. He was hoping for several small waves. One single one, flooding his whole new world would be too much to bear. And there was another thing that deeply disturbed him; he had remembered the face of the man who had placed him in his grave. He could see the face now.

Where was Nick Hoyle now?

3

Commandant Gassin was tempted by the ganaches with the orange and balsamic vinegar chocolate but feared the strong flavor might not appeal to his granddaughter Solange. She was only five years old.

Depite Gassin delayed window shopping, the counter assistants were thoroughly professional. They knew there was nothing more annoying than to interrupt the languid process of selection. The expectancy was often as sweet as the eating.

Gassin was leaning towards the delightfully elegant box entitled *Bonbons Arts Premiers*. The chocolates were shaped into heads, faces, *les artifacts primatif.* Some were dark chocolate, some milk, and others were delicate swirls. He knew the vision of these beautiful chocolates – there were so many shapes to choose from – would be a fantasy for any young girl. And the flavors! The Borneo Mogodar, milk chocolate so very delicately flavored with passion fruit, the Chancay Sensations, black raspberry flavored, and the Danse Magar Chloe with delicious praline leafed through dark chocolate. Pierre Hermé's chocolatier in the rue Bonaparte in Paris were to Thierry Gassin what the Trianon restaurant had been to Marie Antoinette in late eighteenth century Paris. Gassin was still a small child at heart.

As he drank in the myriad rich aromas of the shop, his cell phone vibrated in his pocket and he knew it was decision time. He settled on two packages; the box of *J'aime les Macarons*, a delicious assortment of macaroons he knew to be Solange's favorites, and a box of *Bonbons Arts Premier*, Pierre Hermes personal homage to the worldwide origins of 'chocolat.'

Having given his order to the sales assistant, Thierry Gassin walked out the front door to answer the cell phone on the sidewalk.

There had been a time not so very long ago when the call might have been his darling wife Adelise; but a drunk driver had cheated them both of what were to be the travels of a blissful retirement – voyages they'd been mapping out over many a glass of pastis. Africa, Nepal, China – dream destinations. Adelise had been the driver that evening on the Avenue Daumesnil; he the passenger. They'd lain in the wreckage face to face, just inches apart, for three hours as the

Sappeur Pompiers cut them free; the firemen concentrating their efforts on the man – since they could see the woman was already dead.

While they used the cutting tools, Thierry had prayed, begging he might die with her in the wreckage, but his God would not allow that.

He now felt Godless, yet not alone. He had a son, Auguste, a principal at the Conservatoire de Paris, and a granddaughter, Solange, who would soon be opening the box of mouthwatering macaroons to celebrate her fifth birthday.

Thierry raised the telephone to his ear and turned up the volume – his hearing was not what it once was.

"Gassin?" a voice enquired.

"Georges?" Thierry replied. He at once recognized the voice of an old friend at the Quai des Orfèvres; Paris' equivalent to Parker Center.

"*C'est moi.* I'm sorry to call you on your day off, Thierry. I know it's a special day. Solange is five?"

"Correct. You've a fine memory. Every year you remember all our birthdays; Solange's, Auguste's, mine. You know you can call me any time you wish. However, I hope today you don't intend asking me for anything more than the advice I can give over the phone."

Thierry Gassin was the Commissariat Principal of the sixth arrondissement of Paris, and head of La BAC, the local police force. He was based in the SARIJ off the rue Bart, one of the many Paris investigation judiciaries. The station was open to the public seven days a week. Thierry's rank was Commandant, yet he could have risen far higher had he chosen to 'play the game' with elements within the police force who had few ethics.

The 'Crim', the celebrated if not a little notorious 36 Quai des Orfèvres, was not so far away from the rue Bart. It was the home of major crime in Paris, close to the Palais de Justice on the Isle de la Cité. This was where every aspiring career Parisian cop dreamed of working. This was where one's rank could rocket upwards in a very short space of time. This was where the famous ex-cop Olivier Marchal had worked before becoming the new prince of French crime films. This was where the toughest cases were investigated; bank robberies, assassinations, gang wars. Those who worked here were a law unto themselves, a cadre often 'off the limits'. They were crime-busters, who by reason of the burden of work often drank too much, didn't sleep enough and occasionally found it difficult not to slide into the path of corruption.

Gassin had found himself at '36' after a brief spell with a department that dealt almost exclusively with drugs; nicknamed *Les Stups*. But his heart had always been in solving homicides. So after a short time with the dope boys he'd asked for a transfer to '36'. And because he'd demonstrated he was indeed a brilliant homicide investigator, the transfer had been immediately granted.

However, after five years of backbreaking work, he crossed paths with a cadre of corrupt cops and had been confronted with two options; leave '36', or inform on his fellow officers. Since he'd recently married, and a baby was on the way, he decided not to risk putting his family and career at risk – he was no *Serpico* at heart. Gassin took the first option and his stellar career stalled.

Yet he wasn't bitter about the way things turned out. The whole structure of the Paris police force had recently morphed into a quasi-military organization. The '*Maigret* days' were long since gone. The only things he missed were the big murder cases – he no longer headed up these celebrated homicides now that his patch was 'the burbs'.

"Thierry, my friend, I'm afraid I shall *have* to disturb your day," Georges continued. "But you know better than to blame me. This comes from the top. Barbier."

Gassin was surprised to say the least. Commissaire Divisionnaire de Police Barbier? Jules? His tough former mentor?

"I know what you're thinking," Georges continued. "Surprised? Me too. He asked for you by name."

"I would have thought he'd forgotten me by now."

"No, not at all. The Lachaise beheading case? Remember? He fought like a tiger to keep you at '36' after you headed up the case and finally closed it?"

"Yes, I heard. But why does he need me now? Aren't there enough clever *flics* at 36?"

"He wants to see you. Today. In his office."

Gassin took a long breath, noticing through the clear glass of the shop front window that the sales assistant was trying to gain his attention, holding up twin parcels of chocolates.

"Today's not good, Georges," Thierry replied. "Solange expects me."

"Don't be foolish," Georges said good-naturedly, "Barbier also expects you. At 2 p.m. I wouldn't be late. Unless you're ready to retire."

He wasn't. What would he do if he did? Sit and reread Manchette novels in his small apartment in the rue Dauphine? Watch the last Marchal movie? Or the fourth season of *'Sur Ecoute'* – the T.V. show Americans knew as *'The Wire'*? His present job was a pleasure; he answered to no one on a day-to-day level. Very occasionally he was interrupted by a call from a superior at head office; Le Place Louis Lépine. This was clearly such a time.

He glanced at his watch and sighed. Who knew, he could possibly be finished by 4 p.m. and still make it to the party.

"Please tell the Commissaire I shall be there."

Georges laughed lightly. "No need."

4.

Dermot held baby Virginia by her arms so that the tips of her feet only just made contact with his knees. She was burbling with joy. Dermot had been free of the wheelchair for several months now, and was beginning to feel less of a cripple. Neela was reading aloud from an article in the American Literary Review, her expression almost as happy as her daughter's. Scary was asleep on the sofa and Cheesecake was looking up at the dog, debating whether or not to bite the tail that hung over the lip.

"Nolan's new series of articles in the New Yorker, 'Pinnacles', brings new meaning to what has for countless years been dry, elitist and cliquish rhetoric. The series appeals to Everyman as much as to the musical, ballet and painting cognoscenti. Quite simply, Nolan is brilliant. There is no bombast here—simply the fascinating exploration of genius in the arts, in every field imaginable."

She paused to see Dermot's reaction. But his attention was still focused on his daughter.

"Pretty gratifying, considering you're the closest thing to a musical yahoo I've ever met," she said with a wry smile.

Dermot's first three essays had already been published, all becoming talking points in New York, Boston and Chicago literary circles.

"Hey, easy. They're merely the insight of an interested amateur; it's hardly professional criticism. That's the whole fucking point," Dermot barked.

Virginia looked up at her father with a look of bemused intensity. Was Daddy cross?

Neela didn't respond to Dermot. She let the magazine drop to her side, walked over to him, and began stroking the soft fluff on Virginia's head. She knew it was always better to give Dermot time to apologize for his outbursts. It usually didn't take too long if she remained silent.

"I'm sorry, darling. I really am," he said finally, in the barest whisper as he closed his eyes.

"Honey. Be happy. You've rediscovered yourself in a surprisingly difficult genre. It's not just the Review; I'm applauding you. In fact *everyone* is applauding you. So be happy."

"Don't get me wrong, I *am* delighted."

Neela held out her arms and Dermot passed Virginia over to her.

"How about a glass of wine?"

"Why not?" Dermot replied, cracking a smile.

Dermot stood, reaching for a walking stick that was lying propped up against the side of the sofa.

"Quite an irony, wouldn't you say? *He* never needed a cane. Now, thanks to what he did to me, *I* do."

He poured white wine into matching glasses. The silence in the room was suddenly palpable. Virginia again started to burble happily – she had no inkling of how both of them felt.

Since the moment Dermot had been plucked form his pseudo-grave, Neela had done her best to rebuild their lives and move on emotionally. She appreciated that Dermot was doing his very best too. However, for him the task was almost superhuman. How many she ever comprehend what lying several months in a coffin might do to one's sanity?

Like the five stages of grief, Dermot had been forced to work through his own private torment. The same rules applied; denial and isolation were absolute when he'd regained consciousness. That was natural since he'd remembered nothing. Then very slowly, as his strength returned, so had the first vestiges of his memory. That's when anger had kicked in; in a big way. He was angry; with God, the world at large, at his physical condition, the way others had treated him during the months he'd been falsely accused of serial killings, as well as bitter about what had happened to him. There would never be any forgiveness for his tormentor. Yet he never mentioned his nemesis by name.

Then the bargaining period had begun as he tried to rediscover a meaning to life, as well as forging a belief system – as much for Neela and Virginia's sake as for himself. Though never a deeply religious man, despite being brought up in a staunchly catholic atmosphere in Ireland, he'd always considered himself at worst a lapsed believer. Now he wondered how any god could have left him to suffer in such a way for so long. Why had his desperate prayers remained unanswered for so many months?

So began the next stage of grief – the bargaining. If God would keep his wife and child safe, he'd do his utmost to put all thoughts of rancor and vengeance aside in an attempt to build a better life for them all; one free of bitterness.

This had been the hardest bargain to keep. He knew Hoyle was out there somewhere. It was simply a matter of time before they met up again. Somewhere.

Dermot's psychiatrist had warned Neela to expect the fourth stage – depression. Yet despite the pills, coupled with her intention to allow the waves of depression simply wash over her, Neela found dealing with Dermot's sullen mood swings was harder than she'd ever envisaged. She longed for the return of the initial stages of the healing process, when he'd so desperately needed her by his side; needed to have her hold him, tell him everything would be fine, wipe away his tears, feed him and allow him to cherish his darling child.

"Of course the greater irony is that now that I have a hatful of ideas for novels, no one wants me to write. It's as if I'm a literary leper. Must be the first time no one wants to commission a former Booker Prize winner."

"Honey, you *know* the reason they won't commission you just yet. I keep telling you, time will be the healer. Give people *time*."

"Sure," Dermot replied coldly, "I'll give them time. But

how long? A few years? And meanwhile I'm the dullard magazine essayist."

"Dermot, writing for the New Yorker on a regular basis is what most writers only aspire to, let alone achieve. It's not only Esther that thinks you'll receive awards for the series. They're fabulous. Incisive. Insightful."

Neela pulled Virginia close to her heart and began rocking her – as far as she was concerned the conversation was at an end; she hoped Dermot wouldn't carry it further. But he did. He allowed two minutes of prescient silence to pass, then ranted on.

"How could Dan have done this to me? It's unbelievable."

Copies of his notorious best selling novel *Worst Nightmares* had been withdrawn by Dan Wasserman's publishing house following his arrest for the serial murders; despite massive worldwide sales, Wasserman had ultimately bowed to universal ethical pressure. In America, political correctness was everything. Had Wasserman been the sole arbitor, he'd have left the books out there in the marketplace; after all, what greater publicity could there be for a book, than to have the author charged with the serial killings of thirteen people, and then have the final melodrama played out live on court TV? If the author were to be found guilty it would be a publishing bonanza! For though Dermot could not profit from his crime, yet Wasserman could.

Of course, deep down Wasserman knew the moral integrity of his publishing house, Fischer & Grothe, would ultimately be called into question if he didn't act, so he halted all reprints.

It had deeply wounded Wasserman to know that he was sitting on the rights to the most notorious novel of his time; the worldwide sales figures had been the most astonishing in the past ten years.

For weeks the publisher had mulled over his problem – he was sitting on the rights to a literary gold mine. Yet one he couldn't publish! Then one afternoon, while in bed with his much younger Thai lover the scales had fallen from his eyes.

A biography!

The inspiration was solid gold. He could commission a hack to write Nolan's biography! True genius! He knew it would be incorrect to ask Nolan to write his autobiography; he suspected the author would refuse anyway. But if someone *else* were to write a blow-by-blow account of just a five year period in a Booker Prize winner's life, concluding with the discovery of the author lying in his own grave; *that* would be dynamite! And the joy was that Wasserman had the rights to the literary integrity of Nolan's novel. He could justifiably allow sections of *Worst Nightmares* – if not all of it – to be included in the bio-epic! A ghostwriter could use the material as he saw fit; as 'illustrative notes', or subtly disguised as 'research material'! And best of all, Wasserman could offer a miserly fee to an in-house hack, knowing most would jump at the opportunity. After all, it was a gimme that the book would be an instant best seller.

Wasserman could take the moral high ground by including his instructions in a watertight confidentiality clause in the contract. These would outline exactly how the book should be structured; as an investigative piece, delving into the moral issues associated with serial killings, one that would also include the continuing thoughts of some celebrated psychiatrist who would analyze the motives the fugitive killer, Nick Hoyle. The hack would be instructed to detail the psychological elements of Hoyle's descent into moral depravity, counter-pointing it with Nolan's own; one initially caused by depression and despair, ultimately fed by greed and personal vanity.

Wasserman had debated between a flat $200,000 fee, and a one per cent royalty. He'd settled for the former but had found it surprisingly hard to attract a decent hack writer. Ultimately a little known B grade movie screenwriter by the name of Ken More had been offered the job and he'd leapt at the opportunity.

"Who the hell is this jumped up Ken-fucking-More monkey, anyway?" Dermot muttered more to himself than to Neela. "What a dumb-ass name. No body of work. A twenty-three-year-old screenwriter of schlock horror movies. Jesus H!"

Neela wasn't about to inflame Dermot further with argument or comment.

"It was good of Esther to come and bat for me. That's loyalty for you," Dermot continued sarcastically, reticent to snap out of his sullen mood.

"There wasn't a thing she could do about it, honey. You know that. Dan owns the rights; he can allow anyone in the world to use the material. You have no veto. He lost a lot of money when you were charged – this is his way of saving himself."

What Neela had said was as true. Yet Dermot had a point too. Despite Esther arguing that the young New Zealand writer was hardly a man of sufficient literary stature to write the story of her client's life, she was reluctant to forgo her share of the royalties due to Dermot when the new book, '*Diary of an American Madman*' hit the world's bookstores.

"Well maybe the kid'll get a piece of the action that came my way. Some serial über violence. That man's still out there somewhere. Hoyle might take offense. Who knows? What kind of karma would *that* be!"

Neela turned to face Dermot and took his hand. "I know you don't mean that, honey. Ken More was just doing his job. He needed the work. And think of all the good it'll do those starving kids." Dermot had insisted any royalties due to him personally would go directly towards the Hunger Project.

"I wonder what genius came up with the title. '*Diary of an American Madman*'? Gogol would turn in his..." He stopped himself, he'd almost revisited his own worst nightmare. "It's not even clear who is being referred to. Who the hell is the madman? Me? Or him? Hoyle."

Neela rose and touched Dermot's cheek lightly with her delicate fingers. "I'm going to check on Vig. I'll be back. Okay?"

Alone, Dermot had no one to argue with. Despite this, his dark thoughts continued. How could things ever be the same without closure? With his nemesis out there, free as a bird, how could he ever move on?

Closure. Another irony. He hadn't cared too much about bringing closure to the families of Hoyle's victims, had he? Because it had suited his own purpose – to have brought the families closure would have signaled the end of his novel, and all the money and fame. Of course later he'd deeply regretted his depraved behavior.

Yet now he knew precisely what it was like to have no closure. The past was the past; move on, that's what his shrink had advised. Well, he simply couldn't do that!

What the hell were the police doing to find Nick, anyway? Had they made any progress at all? Were they waiting for him to strike again so that his trail would run hot again? Were they confident that Neela and Vig were safe?

So many questions.

He had to know the answers.

5.

Commissaire Divissionaire Barbier rose from his seat as the door opened and Commandant Gassin stepped into his office.

Befitting a Commissaire, the room was five times the size of the cramped space that served as a working area for detectives under the eaves at the Directorate of the Judicial Police Prefecture of Paris – 36'.

"Thierry," Barbier opened, with a warm smile, walking around his large desk holding out a hand. "It's good to see you again. Been some time, no? Do sit down. Is there anything I can ask my assistant to get you? A coffee perhaps. Evian water?"

"No, thank you, Commissaire. Nothing."

Barbier sat, as did Gassin.

"We go back a long time, Thierry. In the privacy of my modest office, please call me Jules."

Modest? Thierry wondered how many of the hardworking *flics* would agree with Barbier's description. It was probably twenty paces by fifteen. The walls were wood paneled, the furniture antique and expensive, the framed watercolors original and signed. But Thierry didn't begrudge Barbier the spoils of reaching very close to the top. He deserved it; he was a diligent administrator, and as far as Gassin knew a clean cop.

"I've often wondered how you'd adapted to the quieter life in the suburbs, Thierry. I mean no disrespect, but I always picked you as someone who might have been sitting in my seat one day. Why did you make such a choice, I wonder?"

How could Thierry answer the Commissaire's question? Because he hadn't been prepared to put his life and career in the hands of an internal affairs investigation? A probe that would have enquired into the corrupt practices of three cops, all of whom were still in the force, now much higher up the ladder than himself.

"I never regretted my move, Jules. Though at the time I appreciated the incentives you offered me to stay, I had a family to consider, and at heart I'm a quiet soul."

"And a brilliant investigator," Barbier added. "The Lachaise case. Inspired work."

"Thank you."

Barbier pressed a button on his desk and within seconds the door opened and an intelligent looking woman of around thirty opened the door; shortish hair, dark suit, harsh features and prescription glasses. No bimbos here, Gassin noted.

"*Une thé Anglaise, s'il vous plaît, Marie. Earl Grey.*" Barbier glanced at Thierry. "Anything to drink?"

"No, thank you. Just now, nothing"

The assistant smiled crookedly – she had a crooked face – nodded, and closed the door.

Barbier stood and turned his back on Thierry, looking out over the Seine towards the left bank.

"My detectives need your inspiration, Thierry." Barbier was loathed to admit he personally needed Thierry's help; better to suggest his detectives needed 'inspiration.'

"I'd be happy to help in any way," Thierry replied, deliberately substituting the word help for inspiration; he suspected the flics at '36' had hit a brick wall on some case. A new perspective was perhaps needed?

Barbier turned and sat himself in his vast chair, eyeballing Thierry. "You have that certain…" he hesitated for a moment, "How shall I say? Instinct? I've always preferred to think things through logically – facts, clues, evidence, forensics; they're my strong suit. But you have a sixth sense about criminal mentality that I've always admired. That's why I was sad to let you go."

"You'll make me blush soon, Jules," Thierry quipped wryly.

Barbier continued as though he hadn't heard. He didn't smile. "I would like the benefit of your special instincts about a matter that cropped up two days ago."

"It would be my pleasure."

Barbier paused, as though he found sharing this

particular information somewhat difficult. "What I am about to share with you is confidential. For the moment, it is between you and me alone."

"Of course, Commissaire," Thierry replied, using his title to signify that he understood they were now talking formally, rather than between friends.

"A parcel was delivered to me at my home two days ago. As you'll know, few people outside of the force are aware of my country address. So, to that extent it was a personal, as opposed to an official, delivery."

Thierry nodded.

"It was a package that measured approximately fifty centimeters square and was quite heavy. Naturally my staff set it aside, informing me that the sender's name and address were not written anywhere on the parcel. I arranged for my people to take it away to a more a secure environment.

"Within the hour, I received a call from the bomb squad. They told me it was not an IED, but suggested I should visit their section personally because they felt sure I would prefer not to discuss what they had discovered over the telephone – you see. my home line is not yet completely secure."

The door opened and Marie brought in a cup of aromatic tea for her boss. As she opened the door to leave, Barbier called to her. "Please, no interruptions whatsoever until I say so. Thank you, Marie."

She nodded and closed the heavy door.

Barbier reached down, opening the bottom drawer of his desk and pulling out what looked to Thierry like a polished wooden box with a glass top.

"It's quite beautifully presented – if such things are possible of being presented '*beautifully*.' He laid the box on his desk and gently pushed it towards Thierry, who leant forward.

It was the closest thing Thierry had ever seen to an articulated display of animal bones – the kind he used to view in the *le museum national d'histoire naturalle* as a child; the Natural History Museum in Paris. The elegant mahogany box looked store bought, yet was both elegant and strong. Through the glass top Thierry could see the bones of a human hand – the left – each bone dry and staked by small metal clips to the base. Each tiny bone was separated from each other. Thierry noticed that the lid of the box had been prized open and the smallest bone of the middle finger – the distal – was missing. As a natural history exhibit of a human hand, belonging to someone long since dead it was, as Barbier had correctly observed, quite beautifully presented.

"Have you any idea why anyone would send this to you, Commissaire? Do you collect such artifacts? Some people do, I know."

"No, I do not, Thierry. I think you should read the note that was enclosed with the box."

He passed a sheet of folded paper that was lying under a paperweight on his desk. Thierry opened it up and read. *'Commissaire. By now you will have enjoyed looking at my exhibit and will be wondering why I sent it to you. So let me get straight to the point and feed your by now intense curiosity. For this is my delightful new game—one I recently invented; one which will bring me much pleasure. You see, the bones of this hand were once attached to a very prominent countryman of yours. World famous, as a matter of fact.*

'The game goes like this. Should you be able to identify the hand, I shall set my hostage free—he, or she, will live. You have one week. Don't let this celebrated hostage's worst nightmare become yours, Commissaire. Beware."

Thierry took his eyes off the letter and was silent for a few moments while he took it all in. Then he looked up at Barbier. "Have forensics begun to...?"

Barbier cut him short. "They are presently working on the bone which is missing from the case. But there are obvious problems with DNA. First up we have no idea with whom to match any sample; secondly there is no tissue left on any of the bones; there's just the bone material to work with. This makes matters harder. So it would seem that I may have to play this man's obscene game of attempting to correctly guess who this hand once belonged to. Either that, or risk a madman deciding to kill again."

"If indeed he killed the *first* time. Amputation is one thing, a 'kill' is another. And the author of this note may or may not be a male."

"All true. Let me just add that two highly skilled pathologists have already taken a look at these bones and both have concluded that the death of the host body in all likelihood occurred, if it occurred at all, only days ago. A week at most."

"Isn't neo-forensics wonderful. That we can be so sure of something so precise."

"Not wonderful enough, perhaps." Barbier paused, and sipped his Earl Grey tea. "So, I need the benefit of your instinct before I make any decision. I ask you bluntly – in your opinion, is this threat credible, or simply a stunt."

Gassin took his time in replying. This was a hard question. Instinct was one thing, but in Thierry's case a decision of any kind was invariably an adjunct to at least *some* body of evidence.

"I'm sure it is not a primary concern, but my guess is the author of this note is challenging you personally. He is indicating that you personally will be embarrassed if you fail to guess the identity of the celebrity to whom these bones belonged."

Barbier said nothing – it was plain to Thierry that it was the personal issue that was paramount at this moment in time.

Gassin filled the silence. "There are some disturbing elements in this note, Commissaire."

"I wonder if we agree upon which? Continue."

"The language. It's a well-crafted intelligent letter. But that simply goes to show that the author has an education; nothing more. Whether this is a prank is anyone's guess. Which brings me to the next element. Is the host body alive or dead? The author of this letter has gone to a great deal of trouble to present the bones of the hand properly, and if your experts say the body to whom they belonged possibly died less than a week ago, then unless the author had the hand removed from a living person or a corpse we have not yet found, the bones would have had to have been accessed from a morgue."

Gassin looked up at Barbier and let the words hang in the air.

"I already assigned a large team to this very matter," Barbier replied as he set down his cup. "Intense investigations yesterday revealed no missing hands, neither in morgues, nor hospitals. All bodies have both accounted for."

"Then one might have to lean towards the theory that the host body is still alive, or has not yet been discovered. Of course this doesn't necessarily mean a murder has been committed."

"Surely it's more likely the host body is deceased," Barbier cut in, "than to conclude that the author of this letter stumbled across a corpse in the Bois de Boulogne and thought to himself *what a wonderful joke I can play on the Commissionare Divisionnaire*. Why would he bother to keep the host body alive?"

It was a good point. While Thierry was debating it, Barbier continued. "There's something about this letter that bothers me more than anything else. You have not drawn attention to it. Possibly deliberately? I find two words deeply disturbing. It's the reason I called you in today. It is the reason I would like you to head up a team I have assembled to get to the bottom of this within the time period referred to in the letter."

"The mention of *Worst Nightmares*?"

"You have it in one, Thierry."

6.

'Big' Detective Sergeant Jim Hansen was keeping a watchful eye out for Dermot Nolan – he was due any minute now – as he pumped the ten kilo hand held weights up and down with the ease a child might have lifting a bag of candy.

As the count reached three hundred, he let both arms drop and lowered the dumb bells to the floor then sat down at his desk.

Seated opposite him was a new partner of several months standing, Chick de Groot; tall, lean, a mop of unruly dark hair. Chick was busy with notes for a murder book.

Hansen pulled a desk drawer open and took out a jar of Novedex Xt; a testosterone booster supplement. He popped a few pills in his mouth, washing them down with pre-mixed Syntha-6, an ultra premium protein that was said to taste 'ridiculously' delicious—the flavor de jour was *Cookies & Cream*. Hansen thought it tasted like shit, but the results were worth it.

When Hansen's former partner, Detective Mike Kandinsky had been alive, Hansen was generally viewed by his fellow cops as 'one major ripped kinda guy.' That was then; now they could only stare at him in awe – he was like a character out of a comic strip.

As he chugalugged his protein drink, Hansen noticed Nolan enter the detectives' room. He saw the receptionist reached for a phone, so Hansen waved a hand and tossed the plastic bottle back into a drawer and exited his small office, walking into the larger detectives room at North Hollywood Division.

Hansen glanced briefly at Nolan's walking stick then

thought better about making mention of it. Nolan looked a shadow of his former self, yet from what he'd read about what had happened to him in the NYPD case notes, he should have looked far worse. By rights be should be dead.

Hansen held out a hand as large as a pork roast.

"Hi, Mr. Nolan. Good to see you again. And looking so much healthier."

Dermot looked down as his hand was enveloped in Hansen's – he lost sight of it completely until the huge detective let go. For a moment Dermot was lost for speech. Hansen had always looked ripped, but now he looked preposterous; a lot like Rabelais' fictional giant, a living breathing LAPD version of *Gargantua*.

"You're very kind, but I'm still not good. Getting there, maybe."

"Lucky to be around, I'd say," Hansen replied with a smile. "Why don't we go over to my office over there? We can speak more privately there."

"Sure, that'd be great," Dermot replied.

As they entered, Hansen placed a hand on de Groot's shoulder. "Hey, Chick, could you give us a few minutes? Dermot Nolan, Detective de Groot, my partner."

Dermot nodded and shook Chick's hand.

"Good to meet you, Mr. Nolan. Heard a lot about you."

He turned to Hansen. "I'll get us something to eat."

As de Groot closed the door behind him, Dermot sat. Hansen walked to his own side of the desk, slumping into his big chair. The wood groaned.

"Well, I think it's terrific you finally decided to come and see us. Don't get me wrong, I've been told what you've been through and I'm amazed at your recovery. But, well, it's not been easy making sense of it all without your side of the story."

Dermot was expecting a lot of small talk, and frankly wasn't in the mood, so he came straight to the point. "Does anyone know where Hoyle is? Is there a warrant out for his arrest?"

"Yes, there is. And no, we don't know where he is. Not a sign since the day we got word you'd been found alive. Fact is, it was me that called your wife that day. We had no idea..."

Dermot cut him short. "Is there an APB still out there on him? I don't know if you guys still call it that. Do you?"

"Sure, APB, Bolo, ATL. We got a few names for the same kinda thing."

Dermot stared blankly at Hansen.

"'Be on the look out,' 'Attempt to locate' – all the same kind of thing. He's on the database at the National Crime Information Center, and in the U.K. there's an All Ports Warning. And that's not figuring in Interpol! That's 186 countries! I tell you, it amazes me we haven't picked up the sonofabitch already."

"Yes, it amazes me too," Dermot muttered quietly.

Hansen picked up on his tone. "I know. Things appear easy in books and movies, but on the street it's not the same. Whatever they tell you, U.S. borders are as secure as a one-digit computer code. Crossing into Canada, Mexico? Piece of cake, if you have any smarts at all. But let me tell you..."

"Yeah, yeah. Everyone's doing their best. I know. I just want to know the status quo."

"The what?"

"Are people still assigned to tracking him down? Or is it becoming one of those cold cases where the attitude in the squad room is 'if there's any sightings we'll go into overdrive, but *meanwhile we got other things to do'."*

"That's not the way it is at all Mr. Nolan." Hansen's voice was tinged with disappointment. Right now..." He paused. "...your 'status quo', right?"

"Right."

"Well, we've followed up every conceivable lead. He's vanished. Gone to ground. But let me tell you, there's only so long a man can stay underwater," he continued, unaware of his mixed metaphor, "He can hold his breath, have the best scuba gear in the world, but ultimately he's got to surface."

Dermot stared off, wondering what he could say next.

"Tell me something, Mr. Nolan. Has something happened recently that makes you think he might have surfaced someplace? Or maybe is about to?"

"No. I just want to see him in leg-irons, that's all. I want him locked up forever. Until that happens..."

"I know, Mr. Nolan. It's tough. I know that." He shifted in his chair. There was a pistol crack from the woodwork.

"Don't make furniture like they did in my grandpa's day," Hansen observed, then continued, "tell you what though, now that you're here, how about I take a statement of everything that went down the day you were taken hostage. And then the rest. That'd be a tremendous help and might open new avenues of investigation."

Dermot looked at Hansen office wall, noticing a framed photo of his old pal Mike Kandinski. Hansen followed Dermot's gaze.

"Yeah, he was a good buddy as well as a great partner, Mr. Nolan. The best. If it hadn't have been for a mix-up that day, I would have been there with him. *For* him."

"If it hadn't been for me, he'd never have fielded that call," Dermot added in a whisper.

"Well, whatever. That was his job and he knew that. Doesn't stop me blaming myself."

Hansen said nothing for a few seconds as a mark of respect, then continued. "But hey, we gotta move on and clear up the case. Nail the slime-ball. So... you got time today? For a chat on the record? It'd be mighty useful."

Dermot looked up. "Sure, why not. I'll do whatever it takes."

Hansen rose. "Great. I'll just go set up an interview room and be right back."

As he opened the door a thought occurred. "By the way, you know how many worst nightmares-dot-whatever-it-is sites are up and running on the Internet?"

Dermot said nothing–he didn't want to know. But Hansen had never been well known for his diplomatic skills. "Thirty-four. In twenty-eight countries. We check 'em out daily. Every one of 'em."

7.

Since her father had brought her to France at the age of four, Galina Yablonskaya had achieved every one of her childhood dreams. All but becoming a mother. Galina considered marriage to the perfect husband a prerequisite for motherhood, but she had never found the time to look for one, let alone find him. Her life so far – she was twenty-six – had been devoted to the *Ballet de L'Opéra* in Paris. Often referred to as the new Anna Pavlova, because of her facial features, Galina had been made a ballet principal aged twenty-three. She'd been a stunning Masha in 'The Nutcracker', played the title role in Fokine's 'Firebird' to universal praise, and had been an explosive Gamzetti in 'La Bayadere'. She was riding the crest of a wave, and though deep down her wish to become a mother was still smoldering, her life had no time for such fancies.

While she waited for Mr. Perfect, she indulged in frequent love affairs – only those with no strings attached. While the public perception has always been that the icons of the ballet world seldom engage in vigorous sex on a regular basis, they do; the extreme physicality of a ballet dancer's profession tending to accentuate carnal desires.

Tonight, Galina was looking forward to a late night supper with her new beau, Patrice de Valloire; a middle-aged choreographer currently on loan from the Kirov Ballet. Over fifty, attractive in a brutal kind of way, yet very sensitive in spirit, he was a kind and gloriously accomplished lover. She anticipated that her few hours with Patrice would stand her in good sexual stead for an entire week.

Despite the rigors of her performance that night, or possibly *because* of them, she felt energized, potent and ready for any positions Patrice could suggest in bed.

As she approached her Mercedes, parked in her reserved parking space beneath the Opéra Bastille, she clicked a button on the remote control but for some reason the lights didn't flick on. It was so very annoying. She'd only taken delivery of the car at the Frankfurt Auto Show two days previously, so still felt a teenage thrill of joy each time she drove it. Right now she was suddenly angry – was there already a technical problem with her remote?

Thinking she'd forgotten to arm the security in her brand new silver Mercedes-Benz F700, she walked to the driver's door to pull it open. Sitting in and starting up the car, she let the engine run for a few seconds, placing her small Chloe clutch bag on the passenger seat. Then she engaged reverse gear and looked over her shoulder.

That's when she saw him.

Before she could even register surprise, the man who had been lying on the floor behind the front passenger seat, lunged at her, applying duct tape to her mouth, instantly wrapping it around the back of her head. Everything happened in a few moments.

Galina tried to scream, she'd left it a micro second too late.

She felt a sharp pain in her left arm and almost immediately lost the power to move her arms and legs. A hypodermic needle! This man had injected her with something!

Panic washed through her. What did this monster plan to do? Rape her there and then? Take her somewhere?

Her assailant leapt out of the rear door, pulling open the driver's door. Dressed in army fatigues, wearing a black balaclava, he pushed her across into the passenger seat and onto the floor. Within seconds the struggle had gone out of her and she was limp.

Where were the fuck is security?

Galina's assailant quickly scanned the parking structure. No one about. Perfect. He quickly pulled a hood from his pants pocket and pushed it down over Yablonskaya's head; if she saw his face he would have to kill her at some stage later, and that wasn't part of his 'game'. Having done this, he pulled off his own woolen balaclava and smoothed his hair with his hands.

Everything was going wonderfully.

As Hoyle slipped off the handbrake, he heard footsteps clicking close-by. He knew he'd have to be quick. The spectacular new Mercedes was itself such a star; everyone in the Opera Bastille would recognize it as Yablonskaya's. Time to get out of there fast, past the security guy he'd sedated on the way in.

As he reversed out of the parking space Hoyle spotted a woman about seventy years old walking directly towards the Mercedes. Hoyle swore. Bad luck. Most people had already left the Opera. Worse luck still that this old woman's car should be in the same area as Yablonskaya's. Just as well the windows were slightly tinted. Even so, it'd have been obvious to anyone that cared to look in that a man rather than a woman was driving.

As Hoyle drove the Mercedes past the old woman, he felt her eyes on him. It was just instinct – he didn't actually look at her.

As he slowly drove up the ramp he glanced in the rear view mirror and saw the woman had stopped just where he'd passed her. She was staring after the Mercedes, most likely wondering why a man was driving Galina Yablonskaya's car.

Hoyle didn't care. It could have been anyone. A friend? A secretary? Anyone. Hardly something that would make her grab for a cell phone to call the cops. Of course if he'd raced past her at speed to avoid being seen, she might very well have guessed something was very wrong and called 17 – the police emergency number. But the woman didn't matter; he'd soon be gone, the car dumped, and Yablonskaya would be his.

Less than two minutes later, he pulled up behind his Grand Espace Renault.

Knowing there'd never be a time of day when there'd be absolutely no pedestrians on the streets of Paris so near its epicenter, he'd come up with a plan. A car change would have to be affected quickly, the new Super-Merc would have stood out like hot coals on the snow. So the exchange car would have to be parked close-by in a quiet side street.

He gently pulled off Yablonskaya's hood, then lifted her through the passenger door, noticing she was still fully conscious; the dilation of her pupils were witness to the terror she was surely feeling.

Abductions were always such fun!

He pulled her to her feet, supporting her with both arms wrapped around her waist; leaning to his right so that her limp head rested on his shoulder. A casual observer in the street might think she'd had several drinks too many, and her husband or lover was taking her home.

As he opened the rear door of the Espace, an elderly couple passed by, giving Hoyle just a cursory glance. Aware they were looking, he spoke to Galina, making sure they heard him speaking softly and sweetly to the woman he was still supporting. "It's all right, darling. You'll soon be home. We can pick up your car in the morning. What do you say?"

The couple moved on, unconcerned.

Hoyle placed Yablonskaya in the back of the Espace and closed the door quietly. He then climbed into the driver's seat and engaged the gears.

Phase two of the game was about to unfurl.

8.

Gassin dipped his croissant into the last of his cappucino and nodded towards Renney, the morning manager of the Nestlé Bar in the rue Dauphine; he was ready for a ristretto. He was still feeling piqued at being hijacked by the Commissaire while he had so many duties to perform at the rue Bart. He hardly need to be summoned summarily to headquarters – he was content to be 'Master of the Suburban Cops', and had little ambition left. The last thing he wanted was to be heading up a team of young turks who worked out of '36'. Barbier's one concession was that Thierry didn't have to move into the Quai des Orphèvres full-time, but could remain based in the *sixième arrondissement* while touching base with his team twice a day. It wasn't such a hard ask, as it was not far for Thierry to travel.

He'd arrived at Solange's birthday party only an hour after it started. The chocolates were a big success with all the kids – adults were told they were off-limits to all but the under-sixes. And police commandants.

Gassin hadn't slept well that night and felt drained of energy.

Waking at 4 a.m. he found he couldn't get back to sleep, so he put his mind to work, making a few initial observations about the skeletal hand.

It was indeed likely he was dealing with a psychopath. The police laboratory had established that the hand had had blood passing through it less than seven days previously – it was a rough estimate. These were not old bones, they were fresh; it was possible to establish that without doubt. So it was logical to assume that he and his team were searching for a man or woman with sufficient surgical experience to perform delicate amputations.

The bones had been pared of skin and tissue in an expert manner, so it was again safe to assume that they were looking for a surgeon rather than a doctor; though it was conceivable the perpetrator could have been a doctor who at one time had *been* a surgeon. He could also be a retired surgeon, or a retired doctor with surgical experience.

Of course, that was what *most* detectives would have thought logical, and consequently determined as a fact. That was why Chief Barbier had been so keen to add Gassin to his team. Because Gassin never assumed *anything* as a fact.

As he drank his second coffee, he debated whether or not a psychopath could possibly have *kidnapped* a surgeon, *then* forced him to perform the operation of dismemberment.

The Lachaise beheading case had been similar in many respects.

The detectives who had been initially in charge had been too quickly convinced they were looking for someone with sufficient surgical skill to behead the Deputy Mayor of Chinon in such a clinically neat fashion. The head had been delivered to the home of the mayor's wife on a silver serving dish, similar to the banquet piece of John the Baptist. But the murderer turned out to be no surgeon, but the local butcher, a sixty-five-year-old man who'd once studied medicine at the Université de Savoie.

It had taken Gassin weeks to convince the pathologist

assigned to the case that it was conceivable that someone *other* than a practicing surgeon could have separated the Deputy Mayor's head from his torso in such an expert manner – someone who possibly had all his life been a 'wannabe' surgeon.

Ultimately there remained just fifty suspects on the list who could possibly have had anything to do with the crime. One had been the local butcher. He'd been placed on the list because the Mayor had at one time had a one-night stand with the butcher's daughter.

Big mistake.

No one even considered that Didier Fouchier, the Deputy Mayor's local *charcutier*, could have performed the surgical task himself – he was a simple man who would have needed to enlist the services of a surgeon to help him. And how could he have achieved that?

However, various slender threads of evidence, combined with Gassin's gut feeling, had led him to prefer Fouchier as his man; the single stumbling block being the lack of personal surgical expertise – the handiwork of the town butcher would be very different in terms of neatness.

Leaving no stone unturned, Gassin investigated every one of the fifty suspects, searching for a medical background. Then bingo! Fouchier's past at the University of Savoire came to light—he'd studied medicine forty-five years ago, but had been kicked out after three years. A retired University professor who had been Fouchier's surgical mentor recalled that the young Fouchier had the habit of dissecting animals in sequences other than those that were common practice. Apparently surgeons would, early in their careers, develop various quirks of practice that remained their life long 'signatures'.

"I'm not saying there aren't several ways to amputate a limb," the Professor informed Gassin, "but it's the *subtle* ways that a good surgeon approaches the task that are his 'signature.'"

Developing the habit of sequencing the process of an amputation in a way other than a textbook fashion could well have been one of Fouchier's early 'signatures'. That was Gassin's thinking.

Gassin passed this information on to the pathologist, and it soon become clear to the pathologist that in removing the Mayor's head the surgeon who had performed the decapitation had done so in a non-standard sequence. After beginning as any good surgeon would, midway through the sequence appeared odd to say the least. Either the surgeon had been inexperienced, or this was his personal style – his 'signature.'

That had been enough for Gassin.

However, a search warrant of both the butcher's shop and Fouchier's house revealed no surgical implements of a calibre necessary to perform the operation. Gassin was not phased; he persuaded his superiors that it was worth the time and expense of digging up two acres of Fouchier's garden. The medical equipment was soon found, and Fouchier confessed.

The notorious case was closed.

Gassin looked at his watch. It was ten to eight – time to walk to work.

As he strolled along, he put his mind to the case of the hand. Was he again searching for a surgeon? Or someone who once had studied medicine? Could the same deductions apply to this case as well? Was it possible that a surgeon had performed the task under duress? That element had not occurred to any of his team, and yet it was such an obvious possibility. He would assign someone to investigate all missing persons with either surgical or extensive medical experience. It was quite possible that some poor man – or woman – had been kidnapped and pressed into the grizzly task of severing someone's hand. Gassin hoped that this person was still alive. It was conceivable that the surgeon had been murdered as soon as he'd severed the hand?

He rose, smiling a goodbye at Renney – he had a tab.

Renney nodded back. *À plus.* See you later.

It was a decent walk to his office in the rue Bac, but not overlong. Gassin enjoyed the stroll every morning and evening, considering it his exercise for the day. It gave him time for quiet contemplation about any outstanding cases. He made it a habit always to carry a pad and a pen so that he could note down any ideas that occurred to him about current problems on his 'patch'. Quite often they were the best ideas of the day.

The hand. If this was a very sick game, then why a hand rather than a finger, or indeed a foot? Thoughts scudded through his mind. Had a famous person by the name of *Le Main* – the hand – gone missing? Was the psychopath referring to 'the hand of God'? Could it be some Mafia reference? Such as a horse's head, or a fish? Was the hand itself famous? Did it belong to a famous sculptor? A professional boxer? Even a surgeon – the idea of one surgeon amputating the hand of another might appeal greatly to a deranged psychopath. Every avenue had to be explored, yet he and his team had so little time.

As he passed the church of Saint Sulpice and turned towards the Rue de Vaurigard he pulled out his cell phone and punched in a speed dial.

"Antoine? C'est Thierry Gassin."

In his foxhole under the eaves at '36' Lieutenant Antoine Becaux answered. "Commandant Gassin! Good morning."

"I have a task for you. Feel free to share it with any of the team who aren't busy enough today. Tell them it's on my instruction."

"Of course, sir."

"Missing persons. I want to know of any surgeons or doctors that have gone missing in the past two weeks. Also, any who have taken extended holidays."

"Geographical parameters, sir?"

"All of Greater Paris, Antoine. I need the information by four o'clock. I'll be with you then."

"All of Paris, sir?" Antoine asked incredulously.

"All of *Greater* Paris. When you've finished that, extend the radius by ten kilometers. Then another ten. You understand?"

"Of course, sir."

"Oh, one more thing. When you're at Missing Persons, factor in anyone recently missing who uses his hands in their trade."

"But...the demographics..."

"I know what you're about to say. I am not including all workingmen, just people whose hands are their livelihoods— for example, a hand model? You see what I mean? Artisans, musicians."

"Yes, sir. Scultpters, conductors?" the young detective replied.

"Exactly."Gassin flipped his cell phone shut. It was a start. He knew he'd have to find answers quickly. The time frame delineated by this psychopath had been seven days. He now had four to go. He'd spend today on a different area of research; on the reference to 'worst nightmares'. He felt the answer might lie there – it was the last thing the writer had dwelt on. The final clue.

Those two words were the key.

9.

Neela could see that Dermot was in a very dark mindspace the moment she walked into the house. He was spoiling for an argument but she was in no mood to oblige.

"Seems they're doing sweet fuck all to find the motherfucker! They're all waiting for someone to call in info from Timbuktu or some other remaote corner of the globe to say *'Is this the guy you're looking for? Is this the serial killer? He's here on the beach sipping a daiquiri! Right now."*

Neela attempted a calming word. "Honey..."

"And while the various cops of the world sit on their hands, that slime-bag is out there somewhere thinking of ways of chopping up beautiful girls, terrifying old ladies, or burying children underground."

"Honey," Neela tried again only slightly more forcefully.

But Dermot was on a roll. "And if that wasn't bad enough, an eighteen wheeler turns over on PCH and I'm five cars back of it. Took me three hours and then some more to get home and tell you about it."

Finally Dermot paused for breath. Scary slunk out the back door into the garden; he didn't like being around his master when he was in this kind of a mood. Cheesecake just watched, intrigued.

"Can I get you something to eat, honey? It's way past lunchtime."

The thought of food and drink seemed to mollify Dermot. "Yes, that'd be great. Meanwhile I'll get us each a strong drink."

"I'll pass, but you go ahead," she replied.

Another red rag to a bull.

"Oh, I'm some kind of a lush and you're the sensible adult?"

"Not at all, silly," she replied mussing up his hair and smiling. "Hey, let's not argue." She paused briefly. "So, I take it the meeting with Hansen didn't go too well."

"Took me four hours to answer all his questions. *That* I have no issue with. It's the fact that they don't appear to have one lead that'll help track Nick down that bothers me. How is that possible these high-tech days? No records of him traveling anywhere? No credit card usage? Come on! How the hell did he manage to vanish at such short notice without sufficient money to live on? Tell me that? It's not as though he's some kind of James Bond with a selection of false passports and credit cards in false names stashed away, just in case."

Neela walked through to the kitchen. "Hey, come on through with me and we'll talk about it."

Neela began fixing the chicken salad and Dermot sat down at the kitchen table. "To fake his identity or leave the country, he'd need a passport in a false name. How many people do *you* know you sell counterfeits?"

"We're not Nick," Neela replied, reaching for the mayo. "We're not criminals with agendas. Remember, the man's a sociopath. He's extremely clever. He planned everything he did to us, as well as the people he butchered, with the greatest care. He made no mistakes. It was sheer serendipity that the municipal workers stumbled on you while they were drilling. That was a thousand to one chance."

It was true. It had been a miracle. And not simply at the eleventh hour but at one minute to midnight!

"So you have to think that Nick always had an exit plan in mind? Just in case?"

"I'd bet my life on it. If he could lay his hands on all the drugs and hardware he used to torture and kill his victims, he'd have no problem finding people that supply fake passports. There must be dozens of such people in Los Angeles alone. In America? A hundred? Who knows, maybe Nick researched counterfeiters in other states. Even abroad – remember, his art business took him all over the world. You surely can't imagine that the LAPD are capable of tracking down and interviewing every phony identity dealer in America."

"Why the hell not? Nick butchered a bunch of innocent people. He almost got me too. Might have had a go at you as well, only the cops showed up at the door with seconds to spare. What do you think the traces of sulphuric acid were for?"

Neela put down the bowl of chicken, her hands were suddenly shaking; Dermot's words had brought everything back in a microsecond – she remembered the abject terror she'd felt the first time she'd been told of the slumber shades and sulphuric acid they found under the bed."

"So you're saying he had a plan for such an eventuality? If they ever found me, he could simply pack a small valise and disappear? What about his appearance; there were photos on the television within thirty-six hours?"

"Maybe he was in South America or Europe by then. Asia? Australia?"

Dermot poured himself three fingers of Bourbon, then continued with his train of thought. "They take photos of people in most countries as they go through immigration, don't they?"

"I'm not sure about that. Maybe it's just here. No, I think it's Europe too."

As Neela served the chicken salad, Cheesecake entered and sat by Neela's side, squawking almost like a bird for food. Then the house phone rang. She picked up, glad of the interruption—she was still trembling at the thought of how close she had been to losing her eyesight; and very probably her life.

"It's Josef's agent calling from Paris," she said to Dermot, cupping the mouthpiece.

Dermot took the phone. "Mireille! Good to hear from you. How's Paris? I hear there's a heat wave there right now."

"Yes! It's incredibly hot considering the time of year. But that's no problem, I love the spring whatever the weather." She spoke excellent technical English but her accent was as thick as a MacDonald's quarter pounder.

"Has Josef had time to read my article yet?"

"I'm afraid I don't know. We haven't been in touch for two weeks."

"I hope he's not sick."

"Not that I am aware of. Didn't you read of the cancellation of the concert? Josef was to play at the Cité de la Musique ten days ago. The Chopin number 2 in F minor as a starter, followed by the Opus Clavicembalisticum. You know the pieces?"

"Of course. The Sorabji is a tour de force."

"Well, he never showed up. I'm telling you, it was embarrassing."

"Really? That's outrageous behavior. What excuse did he have when you spoke to him?"

"I haven't had that opportunity yet. I'm beginning to think his enormously taxing schedule finally took its toll. He probably snapped, packed his bags and went somewhere more peaceful. His apartment was empty when I went to visit, and Cecile wasn't there either. So she must have gone with him."

"Or she's also missing?"

Mireille laughed lightly. "Hey, I know you are a famous novelist, but let's not get too theatrical, huh? Kidnapped? I don't *think* so." She laughed shortly again, making the suggestion sound ridiculous.

"Besides, this isn't the first time he has disappeared to recharge the batteries. The last time he *did* tell me, and I was able to handle things."

Before Dermot could say a word, she added "And I believe a long time ago you did the same; didn't even tell Neela, and returned with a masterly book? *Devil and the Hindmost?* Am I right?"

It was true. Yet cutting a publicized concert was certainly very naughty, even for a maestro. Dermot couldn't imagine Josef letting down his fans quite this badly.

"You're not concerned for their safety, Mireille?"

"Not really. More curious than concerned, Dermot."

"Have you alerted the authorities?"

"Not yet. He missed a concert and has been out of touch for a few days. No time to call *les flics,* huh?"

More light laughter in Paris.

That seemed to be an end of that. He was curious now as to why she had called him.

"So, what can I do for you today?"

"You mean why did I call? You're so diplomatic! I just called to apologize for Josef not yet reacting to your wonderful article in the New Yorker. I know he'll be delighted... when he decides to come back to us, that is."

"I hope so. Keep in touch, Mireille. Let me know when you're back in touch with Josef. Please ask him to call me."

"I'm certain he'll call in a day or so. He has an engagement at Carnegie Hall in five days, so I can tell you his hijinks haven't made my life any easier. Anyway, I must get busy. Please give *bisous* to the lovely Neela."

"I will. Kisses to you too. Goodbye, Mireille."

Neela had been looking at Dermot throughout, roughly piecing together the conversation logically.

"What's this about Josef missing?" she asked.

Dermot filled in the gaps.

"Don't look so worried, Dermot. You disappeared yourself once."

"Jesus, I'm going to have that shoved in my face every six months as long as I live!"

"Not at all, I'm just making a good point. But I'm with Mireille – why would anyone want to kidnap Josef?"

"Usual reason. Money?"

"You'd think whoever kidnapped him would need Lucille in situ to pay the ransom, wouldn't you? Why kidnap her too?"

It made sense.

Neela pressed home her point. "There'd be no reason to kidnap them both."

"That's true," Dermot conceded. If the object had been a ransom there would surely have been a demand note. And Mirielle hadn't mentioned one. It was very odd."

"Surely he'd take his cell phone with him – wherever he went. That'd be a no-brainer. As would be telling his agent he was going to cancel the concert."

"Darling, that's the novelist coming out in you. People do quirky things every day and you don't immediately conclude that they've fallen off the planet, been kidnapped, or taken by aliens to another galaxy."

Dermot pulled out his cell phone, accessed his contact list, and pressed the call button. A minute or so later he pressed the end button.

"Nothing. It's dead."

"He probably doesn't want to be called. Maybe he's switched his cell off. Maybe the battery's dead."

"The phone would still go to messages. A dead cell phone means it's not working any more. It doesn't add up."

"Dermot, you have to stop thinking of new things to worry about. Let's try to move on and start a new life. We can't become obsessed with 'maybes'. The nightmare part of our life is behind us."

"Maybe," Dermot finally answered. "Maybe not."

10.

During his busy day at his office in the rue Bart, Gassin put aside all mundane tasks, and after clearing the paperwork he'd been obliged to attend to that day, he put his mind to what he now referred to as the *'Hand Case.'* This was the kind of conundrum that Thierry found as addictive as any crossword might be to the daily puzzler. There was no doubt in his mind that he could solve the riddle the madman had set Barbier; the only problem was the pressing time factor.

Firstly, he put his mind to the last phrase the psycho had written down, *Don't let this celebrated man's worst nightmare become yours, Commissaire. Beware.* Since it was the final line of the text, it was likely to have some special meaning. And one had to remember, this man was ostensibly playing *'a delightful game,'* as he put it. So, as with a cryptic crossword, every word most likely held special significance, over and above its dictionary meaning. He recalled reading the message for the first time. Two words seemed to leap out at him; *worst nightmare.* This immediately put him in mind of the Dermot Nolan serial murder case; how could anyone in the law enforcement not remember the *Worst Nightmares Serial Killings* case?

For months, these notorious murders had been front page

news in all European dailies, despite the fact that they had taken place in America. The subsequent murder trial of Dermot Nolan had become a *cause celèbre*. Nolan's worldwide celebrity, due to his novel *'Worst Nightmares'* topping the New York Times best seller list for a record number of weeks, together with the incredible brutality of the murders, had assured that. And following the withdrawal of all charges against Nolan, the final astonishing twist; the revelation that Nolan's childhood friend, now the new prime murder suspect, had somehow managed to kidnap Nolan and bury him alive in his own back garden! Nolan's worst nightmare had been served up to him in a most horrific way imaginable.

This was possibly the most intriguing case Gassin had ever come across; he appreciated how hard it would have been for the LAPD detectives to claw their way to the truth.

However, the chances of the *'Hand Case'* having anything to do with the *'Worst Nightmares Serial Killer Case'* were very slim. Was he clutching at straws? Possibly. It was simply that something had nagged at Gassin. The details of the Nolan Case were highlighted by the great pleasure that incriminating Nolan had given his one-time best friend, Nick Hoyle. There was no doubt Hoyle had relished putting people to death in the most depraved ways. The horrific nature of the killings hadn't bothered Hoyle in the least – they were simply a means to an end, revenge on Nolan. The letter sent with the bones had a similar flavor of the enjoyment. How could anyone call this kind of behavior 'a game'?

At four o'clock, Gassin informed his personal assistant that he was on his way to the Quai des Orfèvres and would be available on his cell phone only in cases of emergency.

On his way to the Quai, he briefly stopped by the Soleil d'Or on the Boulevard Palais for a *salade Nicoise,* with extra anchovies just the way he liked it, before carrying on towards the Préfécture de Police.

By 4.50 p.m the same day Gassin was seated behind a desk in a smallish room under the eaves of 36 Quai des Orfèvres.

Opposite him were three Lieutenants; Antoine Becaux, Franc Migget, and Gideon Simon.

"We continue to draw a blank throughout France regarding any John Doe missing a hand," Becaux began.

Becaux was possibly the smartest of the three lieutenants; Gassin could tell that almost immediately. He had blonde close-cropped hair and Paul Newman-esque pale blue eyes. Migget, by contrast, was Algerian in looks, had mahogany colored skin, was tall, slim and angular, with a prominent aquiline nose. Simon was neither good looking nor ugly; he was the quintessential Paris movie-cop. He was the kind of determined investigator who looked at every last shard of detail, then made a considered choice of how to proceed. The last of the three Muscateers, Gideon Simon, had ground his way to the top. A few years older than the his two associates, he'd made a name for himself in Marseilles, cracking drug rings, and then had been fast tracked to Paris.

"We've checked all mortuaries, morgues and hospitals," Becaux continued. "Also, teaching hospitals. This has led us to believe that we shall soon be looking at a fresh body; one that will be missing a hand."

"All right. What's the consensus of opinion, then? To whom does the hand belong?" Thierry asked.

Migget replied. "The person who wrote this note evidently appears to be enjoying a personal game at the Commissaire's expense. He tells us the hand belongs, or once belonged, to a *celebrated man*. The three of us agreed we should search for a celebrity who relies on their hands for their trade; without which he or she would be physically impotent."

Gassin nodded. It wasn't exactly rocket science, but they were brainstorming, so everything had to be said aloud.

"So, who's missing?"

Simon took over. "There's quite a list, I'm afraid, sir. The stumbling block is that a great many people simply go on holiday at this time of year and don't think of informing anyone where they are going. This problem is escalated by the fact that these days everyone who appears, or has at one time, appeared on television is considered a celebrity – even game show hosts. However, two people caught our attention. One was Didier Leroc."

"The painter?"

"Correct. We initially targeted only the most celebrated artists; at first restricting our search to Greater Paris. Leroc is currently nowhere to be found. His apartment has been empty for ten days. His agent has been unable to reach him."

A surge of frustration surged through Gassin's veins, though he did his best not to allow it to show. Leroc? It could be any one of a thousand people in Paris! Yet the three detectives were doing their best, given it was a practically impossible task assigned to them.

"On close examination of photographs of Leroc's hands, we came to the opinion that his fingers were not sufficiently similar to those delivered to the Commissaire. They were short and Mediterranean in character."

"So how many people remain on your list – missing, that is, without any particular reason?"

"Major celebrities? Twenty-two, sir. We are currently attempting to reach twelve surgeons, three sculptors and a pianist."

"Which pianist?" Gassin asked, intrigued – he was fond of classical music and his son worked at the Conservatoire.

"Josef Kafni."

"Really? *The* Kafni? Missing?" Now here was someone that would definitely fit the bill if they were dealing with a psychopath with a twisted sense of humor.

"That's right, sir. We brainstormed who might prize their hands more than other people and we came up with surgeons, pianists, sculptors, painters…'

Gassin interrupted, this was becoming a self-congratulatory speech. "How did you find out Kafni was missing?"

"For no reason that his agent is aware of, he never showed up for his last concert. She has been unable to locate him since, and it appears that his cell phone is no longer functioning. A dead battery is one thing, but a phone that is completely dead suggests it was possibly destroyed so that it renders a fix on location impossible."

"Is his agent concerned?" Gassin asked. "Is Kafni in the habit of disappearing arbitrarily?"

"Unfortunately, his agent informed us that he has done this kind of thing before—taking it in his head to split because he'd under undue stress. But he's never failed to show at a concert before. That's unacceptable behavior."

"Okay, find him. *Toute suite.* Time is against us. What about surgeons, and those with medical experience?"

"Again, we have a list," the detective replied.

Before Gassin could register frustration, Becaux carried on, as if to justify himself. "You gave us a brief to include all surgeons in Greater Paris, as well as doctors with some surgical experience. As you can imagine, there are many thousands of such people. This list is many pages long."

Franc Migget, to Becaux's left, leant forward as if he wanted to speak.

Gassin gave him the nod. "Yes, Migget? You have an idea?"

"Yes, Commandant. I suggest initially we target any active surgeons who have inexplicably gone missing, rather than attempt contacting every surgeon in Greater Paris. A call to each hospital in France would only take one man half a day to complete."

"Good idea. Please begin those calls when this meeting is

over. It's a shame you didn't kill two birds with one stone and ask after missing surgeons while you were asking about missing hands. But that's water under the bridge. Moving forward. One last thing we should have thought about yesterday. Where could such surgery have taken place? What equipment would have been necessary? Where could a non-professional access such equipment – that is presupposing our man found someone with the necessary expertise perform such an operation for him?"

He glanced at the third detective. "Simon, perhaps you can make that your task."

"Yes, sir."

"Try targeting our bordering countries. If I were setting up a primitive surgery I would source my equipment across some border, presuming any investigative team would begin by contacting French providers. So, Belgium, Luxembourg, Germany, etcetera."

Simon nodded.

Gassin and his three assigned detectives continued brainstorming for a further forty minutes, at which time the Commandant thought the lieutenants' time would be better spent on the phone searching for Kafni, painters, and surgeons, as well as contacting hospitals in the search for missing surgeons.

"I'll leave the three of you to to get on with the investigations. I'll be available twenty-four seven on my cell. Overtime is no problem – the longer you're prepared to work, the richer you'll be." Gassin winked. "And the more grateful I shall be. It will certainly go on your records. That's the incentive."

On his way home, he dropped by La Bar du Marché in the rue de Seine. As with the Nestlé in the morning, Gassin checked in here most evenings. He didn't much care for the décor, but this ugliness was amply made up for by his favorite waitress, Nicolette. She always welcomed him, kept his corner seat available from 6 p.m., and when the bar wasn't too busy occasionally joined him for a chat.

As he sipped a vermouth, Gassin wondered whether the author of the letter would keep strictly to his timeline. It was possible the man was bluffing, thereby wasting everyone's time. However, instinct told him he was dealing with a violent and single-minded potential killer. He determined making his own list of things to do in the morning. But right that moment he had priorities. Tonight he was preparing *confit de canard* – he was an excellent and dedicated cook, despite the very cramped conditions of his tiny kitchen.

Second on his list of 'things to do' would be to check on any current information concerning the whereabouts of the *Worst Nightmares Serial Killer* suspect, Nick Hoyle. Had there been any recent sightings in Europe? First thing in the morning he'd contact his source at Interpol and see what Pascal came up with. He'd also, as a wild card, check on the whereabouts of Dermot Nolan; though it hardly seemed possible that there'd be any more twists in this man's personal saga. Had he perhaps gone insane and was committing a crime himself? Unlikely yet worth considering.

What concrete evidence did he have? The bones and the note, that was all. Everything else was conjecture.

He had less than three days and nights to find someone who had amputated the hand of a celebrity. The police were expected to work miracles in solving crime, but this was verging on the ridiculous.

11.

Dermot had a good day for a change. While Neela was at work downtown at the Museum, briefly standing in for a colleague who had been taken sick, Dermot spent the hours at his desk scouring the Internet for information about art dealers. He'd fed and changed Virginia, who was now sitting in playpen just a few feet from Dermot's desk, bird happy, playing with her soft toys. It was convenient spot because he could keep her constantly in his peripheral vision.

She was the perfect baby, hardly ever any bother; she seldom cried unless uncomfortable, and ate everything she was offered by her parents.

During the night it had occurred to Dermot that if anyone could guess Nick's whereabouts, it might be some other specialist art dealer; one either working in America or Europe. After all, how else was Nick keeping in funds; it wasn't as if his pockets were bottomless?

Detective Hansen had already shared a great deal of the information the LAPD had garnered subsequent to Nick's sudden disappearance; he'd cleared his bank accounts same day as Dermot had been unearthed, in fact within an hour of the cops arriving to collect Neela. He'd sent the proceeds to offshore accounts which were in turn emptied and the money on-sent to numbered accounts. There had had two accounts in America; a checking account and a business account. The entire proceeds had amounted to just over two hundred and seventy thousand dollars. The manager of the California United Bank had been surprised by the request for the sudden withdrawal, but there had been no need for any cash withdrawal, so the process had been easy enough.

However, Dermot knew a quarter of a million dollars was hardly a sufficient sum to support a new life. Far from it. So he had to conclude that since Nick had been planning his cruel killing spree for many years, he'd put further money aside for an eventuality such as a quick escape, possibly in a Swiss bank account. However, there was no way of pressuring Swiss bankers.

Dermot had been told of the international photo campaign that had been mounted worldwide to snare Nick, and knew that none of the hundreds of sightings had led anywhere. So it logically followed that Nick had almost immediately slipped either north, across the border into

Canada, or south into Mexico. From there it would have been just possible to take some respite and consider changing his appearance dramatically – to match any fake passport he'd purchased earlier for just such an eventuality. With a passport depicting a man with a full beard, or possibly a shaven head, the world would be his oyster.

There was just one snag. His funds would be diminishing day by day, and at some stage he would have to replenish his accounts. Dermot couldn't see Nick robbing a bank – it would have been far too facile and obvious for Nick. And there would always have been a good chance that such an act would have lead to disaster; how many bank robberies went bad?

So Dermot 's current thinking centered on Europe, where Nick could end up dealing again under an assumed name with perhaps a different facial appearance. He even considered whether Nick had opted for cosmetic surgery, but a call to Hansen revealed that extensive investigations by both U.S. authorities and Interpol had turned up no leads whatsoever in that particular industry. Of course that wasn't to rule it out completely; there were shyster plastic surgeons all over the world who operated on American citizens on a daily basis, and most knew their clients were evading the police.

Dermot looked down at Virginia. She'd fallen asleep. He glanced at his watch – it was 5.10, and the late afternoon shadows were beginning to slant through the windows of the home office. His back was beginning to ache, and he realized that apart from the occasional playful cuddles he'd given Virginia, as well as the feeds and changes, he hadn't moved from his desk since 11 a.m. when he'd made himself a sandwich and popped a beer. Neela wouldn't be back for a couple of hours, depending on the traffic, and there was a tuna bake ready for when she got home. In the meantime a walk along the beach seemed a wonderful idea for them both, as well as ideal exercise for Scary, who'd spent the whole day sleeping in the front garden.

"How about it, Peaches? Walkies?" he asked Vig softly.

She opened her eyes and squinted at him, then smiled. It was times like this that broke his heart – he simply loved her to death. She still hadn't said the magic word 'Dada', but he waited hour by hour for that particular moment.

He reached out for the baby sling he'd hung on the back of the chair opposite, securing the waistband and hooking it over his head till the shoulder straps were comfortable. Then he lifted Virginia gently out of her pen and placed her in the sling so she was snug against his chest, her head a few inches below his. He finally placed a bright yellow beanie on her head and they both were ready to rock and roll.

As he and Vig stepped outdoors, Scary awoke from a dog-nap and began wagging his tail. Outside, there was no more than a gentle breeze, and the first thing he and Virginia saw was the Pacific sparkling in the distance.

Turning left out of the house, he began walking along Clifftop Drive towards the powered lift and staircase that led down to Point Dume Beach. The deep red flowers clinging to the cliff tops, combined with the lush green foliage looked magnificent. Virginia was staring up into the sky as the seagulls swooped low over their heads. It was great to be alive on such a day; the black dog of despair was absent, and Dermot was aware how lucky he was to *be* alive. As he and Vig drank in the sea air, Scary raced ahead of them, every so often returning to them as though rounding up sheep. Dermot no longer needed his cane; his legs had responded wonderfully to physiotherapy and he'd put on a deal of weight, most of which had been muscle tone.

As he stepped onto the beach, he pulled off his sandals and dug his toes deep into the soft sand. Scary raced to the ocean and started barking at the low waves.

Setting off towards the west end of the beach he couldn't help smiling, despite his investigative concerns of the day. Right now he'd put all thoughts of Nick's whereabouts behind him; he'd relish the beach with his 'best girl' and faithful mutt.

A hundred feet further on, he passed a middle-aged couple, walking arm in arm, marveling, as Dermot did, at how such a majestic beach could be so wonderfully empty. He adored the surprising solitude of Malibu and often wondered how on earth he could have borne the day-to-day frenetic life of downtown Linley Place.

As he stopped to look out at a beautiful sloop sailing past, way out to sea, he heard someone calling out from somewhere behind him. It sounded like a child's voice.

He turned, but initially could see no one; the beach was empty.

Then the call came again and he was able to track the source better, finally looking up the slanting cliff face.

Standing on a rocky outcrop was a young boy dressed in dark shorts, an amber T, and runners. He was aged about ten. Possibly younger. He was standing perfectly still with his hands clasped behind his back, like a kid at school being reprimanded by a teacher.

But it was a distictive feature of the boy that made the hairs on Dermot's neck stand up. His hair was bright red! No, more orange than red.

He felt a hard ball form in the pit of his stomach. The orange hair. It immediately reawakened a terror that he thought he'd put behind him. Orange hair like this he'd seen only once before – it had belonged to a very scary man who had called himself Albert K. Arnold.

"Dermot?" the boy called down to him. Dermot's blood ran cold. How on earth did this child know his name? More to the point, how could the kid have known he'd be walking the beach at this hour? Had he been waiting for him? If so, for how long? Then logic kicked in. Maybe it was a chance encounter?

It was bizarre, nonetheless.

Dermot began to walk slowly towards the boy.

Soon he could make out the child's features quite well.

He'd never seen this kid before.

"Who are you?" he called to the boy, in a friendly manner. Was he the child of a neighbor?

Instead of replying to Dermot's question, the boy simply placed a finger over his lips, as though shushing him, and smiled in an obviously teasing way that was quite chilling. There was something very creepy about the boy's stillness and demeanor.

When only fifteen yards separated them, the boy called out again. "Dermot? You need to know something! The game has begun!"

He shouted the final four words loudly like a gladiator in Rome about to challenge a lion. Finally, after a pause, he continued. "Catch me if you can!"

Yet still he didn't move.

Rather than scare him off, Dermot stopped still. "What do you mean? What game? Who are you? How do you know who I am?"

The boy didn't reply. He simply continued to grin, cocking his head from side to side in a playful gesture.

"Tell me what you want," Dermot continued, attempting to sound patient. "This isn't any game any more."

"Sure is, Der aot," the boy replied almost immediately. "It's a *cool* game. Wicked! But now you've gotten the message, I'm sooooo out of here."

As the boy turned to leave, he reached a hand up to his head and pulled at his hair. To Dermot's immense surprise, the hair came away in his hand.

It was a theatrical wig! That was why it had looked so distinctive – so unreal, almost fluorescent. The kid threw it upwards into the air, whooping and hollering, then turned and raced up the steep cliff.

As the wig floated in the air towards him, Dermot stepped forward, shouting. "No! Stay! Please! Please stay! I must know! Who sent you with this message?"

But the boy kept scrambling up the Cliffside.

"Hey, kid! Stop, when I tell you!" Dermot shouted, almost hysterically. He was beginning to lose it in a big way. Even Scary now understood something was very wrong and had run from the seashore to Dermot's side. But the boy continued to claw his way up the cliff face.

Finally, despite Virginia being strapped to his chest, madness overwhelmed him and Dermot started after the boy.

"Hey, don't do this to me, kid. I'll give you ten bucks! What do you say?"

The offer fell on deaf ears.

The distance between him and the boy was already thirty yards, but the surge of adrenaline caused by panic gave Dermot a power he never imagined he was capable of. As he climbed after the boy on the shifting shale, the question of Vig's safety was all but forgotten.

"How about *fifty* bucks, kid? Fifty fucking bucks! Just hold it right there and tell me! Who sent you?"

By now the kid was now on the ridge, looking down at him. "No way, man. Wouldn't risk it. That dude scared the livin' shit outta me. An' anyway, I made a deal!"

Dermot's feet were beginning to slip on the loose shale – he was hardly making any progress. But despite his precarious state, he was obsessed by the boy standing atop the ridge, staring imperiously down at him.

"Who sent me this message? Just tell me that, for Christ's sake!" he shouted, as he became subliminally aware that Virginia was just four inches from his face and now crying; terrified.

"Just give me a fucking name!"

"Okay, I'll give you a freakin' name. Just back off, man!"

Dermot crouched down, panting, just ten yards from the boy, stroking Virginia's head and cooing to her in an attempt to calm her.

"Arnold! Albert K. Arnold," the boy said, with a smirk. "That's who it was! Happy now?"

The words came as such a shock that Dermot feet skidded backwards. He tumbled on the loose shale, instinctively rolling to his right so that he, rather than Virginia, took the impact of the fall.

Instantly he sat up and checked his daughter. She was crying hysterically, the tears running down her rosy cheeks. There was one small graze on her right cheek, but was otherwise fine.

"Jesus Christ," he breathed, astounded by his impulsive insane behavior. "What the hell was I thinking, for Christ's sake? Shush, it's okay, sweetheart. Everything's okay. Daddy's here to keep you safe."

His words had a soothing effect, and little Virginia stopped bawling; her sobbing becoming a sniffle.

Dermot stood, this time making sure he had a firm foothold. Then he looked up the cliff one last time – the kid was gone.

"Are you in*sane!*" Neela barked as she bathed the graze on Virginia's cheek with a mild disinfectant. As far as Vig was concerned nothing had happened; she was again smiling and chuckling with joy. By contrast, Neela was ropeable.

"You tried to run up a sheer cliff face after some young kid, putting your own child at risk? I'm astonished! What the hell were you thinking?" Neela was doing her best to keep her anger in check; she knew there was nothing to be gained by shouting at Dermot, yet her heart was pounding so fact she could scarcely refrain from slapping his face.

"You're exaggerating, Neels," he replied contritely, though he knew she was within her rights to call him any name she wished. "I wasn't climbing a sheer cliff face; there's no need to exaggerate. I was just walking…"

"Up the side of the cliff which was angled at about forty-five degrees and had a shifting ground base of shale. If you'd fallen and Vig landed on her face she'd have disfigured her for life! So don't tell me I'm exaggerating!"

"But Neels. The boy said…"

"I don't give a flying fuck what the boy said." She held up a hand. "And I'm allowed to use the F-word until Vig can understand what I'm saying."

"Honey, Vig is fine. I fell down, she didn't. She has a tiny graze on her cheek. It's hardly broken the skin. So get over it; you've had your say and I've told you how sorry I am."

Neela wrapped Vig in her night suit then gently lifted her from the table and set her down in her Moses Basket where she usually slept. The joy of this basket was that it could remain downstairs while Vig was downstairs and could then be taken upstairs when they went to bed. Dermot remained silent, though Neela was aware of a slightly crazed look in his eyes; one he was clearly trying to choke back. Perhaps now was the time to cut him some slack. She walked over to him and wrapped him in her arms.

"You and Vig are all I have. You *have* to look after her, as well as yourself. And that means *whatever* happens."

"We have to talk about this, Neels."

"I know we do. I know. But first I'll get you a glass of wine. All I ask is that you try to calm yourself and don't shout while Vig is trying to get off to sleep. Okay, honey? Deal?"

"Deal."

Dermot sat down as she poured them both a glass of sauvignon blanc. "Are you absolutely certain about the words the kid used?"

"I'm *very* certain. First up he called me by name. Dermot. He called it out as a question at first, as if he was unsure of who I was at a distance."

"We've lived here quite a few months, honey. Why *wouldn't* the kid know who you are?"

"Oh, come on, Neels," the edge was immediately back in his tone. "Let's not get into these usual stupid arguments – like the ones that almost drove us both insane while Arnold's diary was ruining our lives. I don't *need* to examine every nuance to know what happened today, and you don't have to come up with a dozen plausible reasons for what the kid said. Enough of the Devils's advocate! He was wearing an orange dress-up wig, and he told me his name was Albert K. Arnold! As far as I'm concerned, that's the end of the story! One thing I know right now – we're back in our nightmare world, and I'm shitting myself. You'll have to excuse *my* language now because I'm waiting for Vig to learn the meaning of words too."

"Can I simply make one point?"

Grudgingly Dermot nodded. "Okay. Shoot."

"No interrupting?"

"Nah. Never."

"Okay. Well, people who live around Malibu know you live in Point Dume. Most know what you look like. A hell of a lot of them have read your book and were scared to death by it. Okay so far?"

Dermot nodded imperceptibly. "Well? Don't stop. Go on!"

"So they know what the bad guy in the book was called. Albert K. Arnold. They also know the old guy that delivered the manuscript had bright orange hair."

"So?"

"If you were a devilish kid and wanted to play a cruel trick on the author of the novel, the first thing you'd do is find a play-wig, then you'd dye it orange, seek the author out, then tell you his name was Albert K. Arnold? Just for fun!"

Dermot said nothing, deep in thought.

"It's possible," he had to admit.

Neela continued; she was on a roll. "It's much more plausible than thinking that Nick Hoyle's come out of the woodwork, and has hired a ten-year-old kid to tell you he's coming after you. I'm sorry, but I think that's ridiculous."

Dermot lifted the palms of his hands to his face and groaned.

"Look, I'd love to be able to see things your way, honey. But the thing is, you have no idea what it's like to be buried alive in a coffin for months, screaming, lying in your own shit, and eating rotting putrescent food scraps just to stay alive. You know damned well it's taken its toll on me emotionally, as well as psychologically."

"Of course I do. I'm here for you; and will be as long as you live. You've shown amazing courage. Just to…"

Dermot cut her short, as he took a deep breath – latent anger swelling yet again. "Yeah, I know. You can cut the hero crap. The thing is, I know what's happening, yet you won't accept it. '*Game on*'! That wasn't the kid suggesting I was about to play some damned game with *him*. '*Catch me if you can*' – those are the precise words that Arnold used when he sat down next to me in the Red Line all those months ago. It was as if the kid had rehearsed the damn words; as if he'd been told *exactly* what to say! It's him! He put the kid up to it. Nick! He's got something in mind, and he's drawing me out."

"If that's true, and I emphasize the word 'if', then I concede he *could* be trying to draw you out. But the last thing you should be thinking of is rising to the bait, or the challenge – whatever you care to call it. We never want to see that man again."

Dermot was silent, a wild look in his eyes.

Neela continued, scared for them all. "So now you're thinking you might try catching the bastard yourself? Don't be insane!"

"I have to," he replied.

Neela stared at him in shock. "You want to have it out with him *personally*?" She paused, catching her breath. "You can't be serious."

Dermot held his glass out for a refill. Neela grudgingly poured.

"Nick only did what he did because of something I did to him when I was a kid. I started this crazy game of his. It was me!"

"You made one mistake. You had a one-off fling with his wife, for God's sake – you didn't *kill* anyone! It wasn't right; of course not. But you and Giselle both realized you'd made a huge error of judgment. You knew that the moment it was over that night. Neither of you were thinking of the consequences then – you'd had too much to drink. As you said, you were *kids*!"

"Hardly kids, we were in our early twenites. But look, I hear what you're saying. The thing is, I need to end this conclusively. I've been waiting a long time for him to come and torture us again. I knew he'd either show up or send someone. That's why I bought a gun."

Neela stared at him – incredulous. "You did what?"

Dermot shrugged with a touch of annoyance. "Neels, it's just a gun. I have a license. Remember the terror when you thought those guys paid by Nick to scare in the elevator? You thought they were going to kill you? Well, if you'd had a gun then, would you have pulled the trigger?"

Neela looked down. "I'd like to think not, but maybe… yes, I would have. That's true."

"Well, then. I rest my case. It's in my nightstand drawer, to protect you and Vig."

Neither could be bothered to re-heat and fix up the tuna bake, so they froze it and discussed their next moves as they ate chicken sandwiches. Neela couldn't bear the thought of having to leave their new home, and Dermot was outraged that she could even consider it.

"He'd not driving us out. No way."

"Honey," Neela replied, "what if we were to go live somewhere such as Austria? I checked, *Worst Nightmares* was never published there."

"No. We live where we *want* to live. Where there's a good life for Vig to look forward to. That means here."

There was a hiatus. Then she spoke. "Are you going to tell Hansen what happened?"

"I already called him. The moment I got back in. But it's a weird thing; I was so fixated with the orange hair and that creepy wide grin the kid kept giving me that I couldn't remember a damned thing about what the boy was wearing."

"I can understand that, honey."

"Anyway, Hansen understood too. I told him what I could remember – that the kid was about four feet six, average weight, and black hair once the wig was off. Hansen told me he'd get the Malibu cops to keep a look out for the kid, but it's a hard ask seeing as all they've got to work on is a boy aged about ten or twelve with shorts and dark hair. For what it's worth, I'm seeing Hansen first thing tomorrow at North Hollywood. We'll see what he thinks then."

"Did you pick up the wig?"

An electrical bolt scythed through him. "Shit!"

Neela stared. "You left it there?"

"I was more concerned with Vig's well being right then. I thought she might be hurt. I wasn't thinking straight. I was going to go back and then it went clean out of my head."

"Well, go see if it's still out there on the beach. First, let me say something important." Neela placed her right hand over his on the table. She looked deadly serious. "Don't leave me again, darling. Never again? I simply couldn't stand it."

He squeezed her fingers. "I never will – that's a promise. Wherever I go – *if* I go anywhere – you're coming with me." He cracked a small smile. "Got to have someone to cover my back for Christ's sake."

He grinned at her, she laughed, and the tension was broken. The only audible sound was Vig snoring lightly. Then Cheesecake strode in and caterwauled for her cat fud and grits. Scary raised an eyelid for half a second then went back to sleep.

That night Dermot searched the beach with a flashlight for several hours before giving up and returning home. Maybe the kid had returned to pick it up later, or someone else had found it and taken it. The latter was Dermot's explanation of choice. The alternative was too horrific to entertain – that Nick had actually been there up close all the time, watching.

Dermot finally managed to get to sleep at around four in the morning. Two words kept reverberating in his mind. *Game on.*

12.

The room was approximately five paces in each direction. The walls were covered with lightweight metal cladding – a mixture of aluminum and some heavier metal; the kind used twenty years or so ago in the manufacture of cold stores.

This day, there was no meat attached to the hooks and gibbets that had once hung over rails running east to west across the ceiling. In one corner there was a camp bed with a small folding table next to it that operated as a nightstand. A portable lavatory stood in the opposite corner. An industrial light shone from at the top of the wall that faced the door; the heavy-duty glass protected by a web of metal.

It was cold, but not freezing. Even after all the years, the space still stank of stale meat products, in the same way as a butcher's hands ill smell of flesh no matter how many times they are scrubbed with carbolic soap.

Géraldine Yablonskaya lay on the camp bed in a fetal position, her elegant legs tucked up beneath her. She was cried out; her face cold and stained by dried tears and mascara. In truth she was barely recognizable as the '*New Pavlova*,' more resembling a common French *prostituées de pays*, or perhaps a clown. She had not the slightest idea why she was where she was.

When the anesthetizing drug had worn off, she'd found herself in the trunk of a car, her hands and legs bound behind her so she couldn't struggle, her mouth taped so she couldn't call out or scream. There was a hood over her head but she had no way to take it off. How long had she been in the car? She had no way of knowing, the vehicle was moving when she woke. It wasn't traveling excessively fast.

Finally, the car halted. Some moments later the trunk was opened and she was lifted free and carried somewhere by a strong man. She heard a door open and realized she was being carried inside a building and down some steps – she counted them; twenty. She was now most likely in a cellar or basement. Then her tormentor slung her over his shoulder as though she was a side of lamb, and she heard a key unlocking a much heavier door than before. It sounded like a big key, an old metal one. Then she was lain down on a sagging camp bed.

"I will now cut your hands free," a soothing voice said. "If you attempt to strike at me, you will regret it. Always remember, your life belongs to me until I decide to set you free. I can do as I wish,"

The gentle tone, counter-pointed by her current situation, terrified Yablonskaya. She'd recently seen a horror movie set in an Eastern European basement where people were tortured, and she couldn't help recalling the face of the movie butcher; he'd had such a pleasant sing-song voice yet the man was totally insane – it had totally creeped her out in the cinema. Now this man was talking to her in a similar vein. She was hard pressed not to pee herself with fear.

He first reached under her dark hood and pulled the tape from her mouth. He was surprisingly gentle when he did this. Then he cut the ropes that bound her wrists. Yablonskaya made no move to struggle; she knew now was not the time. She had no idea where she was, whether the door was locked, or how strong her kidnapper was.

"Now I have things to do," Hoyle cooed. "I suggest you attempt to calm yourself and get some rest. Tomorrow will be a busy day."

"What do you want of me?" Yablonskaya asked in a low tone.

The Dream Healer did not respond.

As she heard him leave, locking the door behind him, she began to panic. What was this man's purpose? Was he a sexual predator? Was she to be kept as a sex toy, like that Austrian girl who had borne her own father's children and been kept locked underground for twenty-four years? Was he a sadist? Would she be physically tortured as in the movie?

She began to shake uncontrollably, so she assumed a fetal position for comfort, clutching at her clothes to keep warm.

Time would tell.

In the silent corridor outside Yablonskaya's room, Nick Hoyle looked at his key ring, selected a second key, then stopped at the next door along the corridor. He inserted it and opened the door.

The room was identical to Mademoiselle Yablonskaya's. Clearly another chamber formerly used to keep meat or vegetables chilled or frozen, depending on the thermostat setting.

Sitting in an armchair on one side of the room was the surgeon who had amputated Kafni's hands – Jean Ballon. He looked up at the bearded man as he entered, but said nothing; he had not connected this bearded man with the photos of the *Worst Nightmares Serial killer* that the world had once seen splashed across the daily newspapers in France. How could he? Hoyle was clean shaven then.

Opposite Ballon was a low camp bed similar to the one in Yablonskay's room. Lying on it, with her back to wall, was the woman the young surgeon had been forced to watch standing on the chair, a noose around her neck, while he'd been performing his disgusting surgical work. She was his wife, Cecile. The chair she'd been precariously balancing on stood in the center of the room. Above it a noose hung down as a reminder to them both to behave. Madame Ballon was wearing a black hood, while her husband was not.

The surgeon looked pale, haggard and exhausted, yet was surprisingly calm. He was wearing a metal cuff around one wrist that secured him to the wall by a metal chain to a ring.

By contrast, his wife's body language was one of terror. Unlike her husband, she was not chained to the wall but free as a bird – albeit in a cage. She, like Yablonskaya, was curled in a fetal ball facing the wall, shaking like an aspen leaf, clutching at a blanket she'd been given.

There'd been no reason for the Dreamhealer to chain her; she had no avenue of escape, and Hoyle was easily capable of handling this scrawny woman should she decide to mix it with him. There was also a calming element in allowing the woman to sit with, touch, and, who knew, have sex with her husband. Hoyle had found it an intriguing thought. Was the human sexual urge strong enough to counter the terror of the prospect of immediate death?

"My opinion is that Monsieur Kafni was in good shape today," Hoyle observed. "Considering the shock to his system, both physically and mentally. It will be fascinating to see if he can ultimately come to terms with his new body. Sans hands."

The surgeon simply stared at him with abject hatred. "I did what I could," he replied.

"You did wonderfully well. No evidence of infection and a heart rate now returning to acceptable levels. You have scored quite a few brownie points in my book."

"Brownie points?" The surgeon was unfamiliar with the expression.

"I'm pleased with you. Put it that way."

Hoyle smiled.

"Will he be able to walk in two days?"

"You're going to release him?" the surgeon asked with some hope in his voice.

"Of course. I was rather hoping that if we gave him a few of the right shots he might even be able to run."

The surgeon's face darkened, what new horror was this man contemplating.

"I shall return shortly with some *nourriture,* as you refer to it in France," he told the young surgeon. "You'll be well catered for in my somewhat primitive hotel. Which would you prefer, white or red wine?"

Hoyle turned to Madame Ballon. *"Madame? Rouge ou blanc?"*

She didn't reply. She continued to shake. Monsieur Ballon stared at the bearded man – how could anyone capable of such unspeakable acts idly talk about the choice of wines for dinner?

"Still not adequately warm, *cherie*? I shall bring you another blanket at dinner time. I have to be honest with you, I didn't cook the food myself. However, there really are some marvelous products available at the local Champion supermarket. I chose some duck for tonight. I hope you like it. I merely checked in now to see that all was well with you both and talk to your husband about Monsieur Kafni's well-being."

"I have done what you asked me," the young surgeon said in French. "You told me that you would set Cecile free. Are you not a man of your word?" His tone was surprisingly calm.

"I am indeed!" the bearded man responded in fluent French. "However, let me remind you, I never told you exactly *when* I would release your wife. You see I have another task for you. Just be obedient, and all will be well."

"I shall not perform any more savagery for you."

"To take such an attitude would be a mistake," he said. "A grave mistake," he added, looking at the shaking form of the surgeon's wife, Cecile."

"You have allowed me to see your face, Monsieur. Does this mean you intend killing me when this terrible game of yours is at an end?"

"You have a fertile imagination, one nourished by too many movies." Hoyle chucked, though the surgeon was clearly correct in his analysis. However, it was to his advantage to allow this young man to hope he might survive his ordeal and finally be reunited with his wife outside his current grizzly confines.

"I could hardly have asked you to perform your skills with blinkers on, now could I? Hence the hood. Of course, I could have worn one, but they are so..." he paused. "Uncomfortable. Are they not, Madame Ballon?"

She remained silent.

"As to whether or not you will live, Ballon? I'll give it some thought. But the lovely Cecile's fate is in your surgical hands, plain and simple. You refuse my demands and I shall hang her—have no illusions about that."

The surgeon simply stared at the bearded man. Such unspeakable cruelty was beyond comprehension. While Ballon was a healer, this man was the exact opposite. While his life had up to now been dedicated to surgically restoring a normal life to his patients, he was now being morphed into a butcher by this beast. It was unbearable. Yet what choice did he have?

"I am not asking you to end a life, am I?" Hoyle observed, as though it was a reasonable thing to ask of the surgeon.

Ballon looked down. This was true, yet essentially what was the difference? Severing both hands of the world famous concert pianist Josef Kafni would be an emotional death sentence.

"Will you allow Kafni to live?" he asked.

"You recognized him? Well done! Shall he live? Of course! That's the whole point of this wonderfully entertaining game! He will be set free tomorrow; that I promise you. And as a gesture of good faith I shall bring in a computer some time after his release to prove it to you. I'll show you the footage of his release. How about that?"

That was some kind of relief to the surgeon. Yet would he ever be able to forgive himself for having done such a terrible thing to a man such as Kafni, simply because his wife's life was at stake?"

"I shall go fetch your *souper intime* – your intimate supper of duck and red wine. Who knows, a few *rouges* and you both may feel like a *siesta crapuleuse*; a little physical intimacy can do no harm. It may even serve to soothe the nerves." He laughed lightly. "*Siesta crapuleuse*, a lewd dissolute act of sex in the afternoon. How I delight in the French language!"

"You are a sick and depraved human being. You know that, don't you? You should seek help, for you are mentally ill."

Hoyle looked up as if debating whether or not this might or might not be true. "Quite possibly," he murmured finally, almost to himself. "But it is in the nature of human beings to have their dark sides. The majority of civilized humans; those with adequate money, sufficient friends, health and happiness, may never be forced to go there. But consider the third world, where starvation and misery is the norm; where butchering humans in the name of some revolutionary ideal is the every day act of child soldiers? That is where true darkness lives. *Quant a moi*? As for me? I had darkness visited upon me some years ago; first by my government, who sent me out to butcher their enemies, then by my best friend. I no longer see any light whatsoever. That is my burden. I live in a very black place and have become accustomed to it; so much so that I relish it." Hoyle thought for a moment and laughed. "I wonder, does this make me a modern day vampire of sorts?"

He walked to the door and opened it, turning briefly to look at Madame Ballon. She was still trembling.

"I shall bring several blankets. Cecile looks chilled to the bone."

She was, but not by the temperature.

13.

Gassin had suggested to his team that they dine together that night. It would be his treat. It was his way of showing his appreciation for the outstanding work the three detectives had performed so far, as well as a time for bonding – they'd put in long hours and had very little to show for it.

He knew from bitter experience that investigative work usually proved ninety per cent unproductive; a dreary task that had to be done in order to reveal the productive ten percent, ninety per cent of which was also useless. However, two days further down the track, at nine o'clock in the morning, the time frame designated in the letter came to an end, and Gassin was fearful for 'the man without a hand.' If that man was indeed still alive.

Gassin had chosen the restaurant Allard. It was one of his favorites and close to home. He'd always been a traditionalist when it came to food and the Allard was gastronomic perfection; it had a pre-war feel to it, both in décor and cuisine. His favorite dishes were the Bresse chicken with the sautéed ceps, and the duck with olives. Tonight he'd decided to introduce his team to the famous Allard duck—how was he to know that they would be sharing the same dish as the surgeon who had removed both of Josef Kafni's hands. Of course the Allard duck would be a far superior meal to the pre-cooked cellophane-packaged bird Nick Hoyle had bought at the Champion supermarket, and was in the process of microwaving only half an hour's drive away in the small village of Auteuil as Gassin and his lieutenants entered the restaurant.

Despite Gassin's generosity, the mood amongst the three French detectives was restrained. Analysis of the box had proved useless. No prints, no marks, no residue. The box itself was available worldwide on the Internet, and several hundred had been sold in the preceding month. The paper was copy paper available in any newsagency. The glue that had been used to affix the typeface cut from the International Herald Tribune was very ordinary, again available anywhere. The sections of the paper that had made up the text had been confirmed as belonging to the edition published the day before delivery of the box. So they had little or nothing to go on, barring their imagination.

"Medical experts assure me that such an amputation would not require a deal of equipment," Migget began. "This would be especially true if there wasn't any real concern for the well-being of the patient. If there was such concern, then infection would be the uppermost concern. Anesthesia would be imperative, and might well need a specialist, though I'm assured a competent surgeon could handle such a procedure. However, should he not be sufficiently expert, the body might well go into shock, thereby killing the patient."

Migget passed a list to Commandant Gassin; it contained details of all equipment that was a surgical necessity, as well as items that would be a luxury yet not vital."

As Thierry studied the list, Migget continued. "There are countless surgical instrument stores all over Europe selling most if not all of the articles on this list. Had we been looking for an ECG machine, for instance, we might have had better luck."

Gassin turned his attention to the second lieutenant. "Becaux. What about the surgeon? What have you found?"

"Here we have had more success. Several hours into our investigations – incidentally I recruited five assistants to help us out – we came across the disappearance of a young surgeon working at the Chesnay Hospital in Yvelines."

"That's that monstrous glass building, isn't it?"

"I believe so, sir. I have only seen photos. It appears that a man by the name of Jean Ballon, aged twenty-nine, has not reported for work for ten days. They've called him frequently on his home phone but there has been no answer. It appears that his cell phone is dead—not out of juice, but dead. As in no longer existing. Same as with Kafni."

"Someone destroyed his cell because they didn't want

anyone to be able to track him in this way? That's your thinking?"

"Exactly. So we visited Ballon's home to talk to his wife."

"And?"

"She is missing too. Inexplicably. We've talked to her family and friends, and it is quite out of character. As with her husband. He would never have simply walked away from his busy schedule at Chesnay.

"A sound surgeon?"

"Supposedly quite brilliant, sir."

The first courses were served. Gassin had suggested the *saucisson Lyonnais à cuire pistache*; Lyonnaise sausage with pistachios. All but Simon had followed his recommendation.

As they began to eat, Gassin continued. "So we have a surgeon who may have been abducted, or has simply disappeared off the face of the earth ten days ago. And we are still searching for Monsieur Kafni?"

"Correct," Simon added.

"So let us put ourselves in the mind of our psychopath. He wants to operate on a human being. It's a minor operation compared to heart surgery, so minimal equipment is required. Sterile premises would be ideal to fight infection. Heat is a breeding ground for micro-organisms, and we are currently in the grip of a heat wave. So let's think of cool places. Cold storage facilities. Basements are also cool."

"The saucisson is miraculous, sir," Migget interjected incongrously. It had clearly impressed him.

"I'm glad you like it. But to more pressing matters. I imagine you have sent out photos of Kafni and the Ballons on the Internet? The highest priority?"

"Done, sir. Every police officer in France will have seen

them by midnight."

"So now, my friends, we have to consider carefully. Is it conceivable that this missing surgeon, Ballon, is our psychopath? Is his wife a willing accomplice? Remember the infamous English couple, the Moors murderers, Ian Brady and Myra Hindley? They worked together. Or have Monsieur and Madame Ballon both been kidnapped? He to perform the surgery, and his wife as a hostage to assure compliance?"

Becaux replied. "I have spoken to ten of Ballon's personal friends; the consensus of opinion is that he is a man of great integrity, selflessness and charm. He would have to have the devious charm of Ted Bundy multiplied a hundred fold for it to be him."

"Good. I believe you, and we have little time. So, one way or another we must find our Monsieur Ballon. We find him, we find the man who orchestrated this nightmare crime. We may find Kafni alive."

A waiter refreshed their glasses with a Corton Charlemagne Domaine Bonneau du Martraym 2003 – fine wines were Gassin's single extravagance, and he could hardly drink alone.

Franc Migget studied the bottle in awe, it was a superb Grand Cru. One day, he silently promised himself, he would be a Commandant too and be able to indulge himself and his girlfriends in such a fashion.

14.

It was an unusually hot day for the time of year. As the sun beat down on the water, the ocean looked diamond studded and unbelievably calm. There was scarcely a breath of wind in Malibu. And if this vision wasn't beautiful enough for Dermot, the drive through Topanga State Park was almost as breathtaking.

However, Dermot saw none of the beauty that surrounded him. His mind was elsewhere. He was again in the iron grip of obsession. He'd hoped that there was one chance in hell that the so-called 'Dreamhealer', Nick Hoyle, would finally leave him in peace. Now he knew differently. Despite Neela's devil's advocacy concerning the boy with the orange hair, Dermot was certain that a second phase of torment was about to be unleashed by his one time best friend.

Surely the suffering Nick had already caused him was sufficient payback? For any human, that would have been *way* over the odds? But of course Nick was no longer thinking like a rational human; he was a deeply disturbed man, devoid of compassion – no longer capable of distinguishing good from bad, right from wrong. Nick was most likely as obsessed about taking further revenge on him as Dermot was obsessed with tracking Nick down and seeing his nemesis incarcerated, so that he could no longer threaten Neela and Vig.

As he fed onto the Ventura Freeway and started towards Van Nuys, Dermot became aware that he'd been checking his rear view mirror every few seconds since he'd left home. It slowly began to dawn on him that it hadn't been for the sake of road safety; a synapse in his cortex had begun pulsing messages to his cerebellum without his even being aware of it.

Was he being followed?

He swore at himself. What was he thinking? Was his mind still so scrambled by the trauma of his burial that he was again looking for doppelganger cars, as he had before he'd been charged with the multiple murders? Would he ever be free of such obsessions?

He smiled wryly – he was an ass even to be thinking such thoughts. There was no way Nick would take the chance of stalking him on the open road. In California? No. If he had any sense he'd be in some country with no extradition treaty with the States. If he were roaming Los Angeles, it was just a matter of time before he was spotted; his face had been shown so many times on the television. that even if he'd let his facial hair grow, and wore dark glasses together with a hat he'd run the risk of being recognized.

Dermot rolled his shoulders to take some of the tension out of his system, then turned on the radio, tuning in to KTWV – maybe some smooth jazz would soothe him.

He filtered off Ventura into the 170. He was half an hour from North Hollywood Precinct.

Apart from going over yesterday's events yet again with Hansen, what more could he ask of the detective that he wasn't already doing? The chances of finding the boy were minimal; there were thousands of kids living in Malibu. If Nick had found a boy, paid him, and brought him up from the city, the numbers were in the hundreds of thousands. Would he confide in Hansen that he had it in mind to search for Hoyle himself and become pro-active, rather than pretending nothing was happening and waiting for Nick to fulfill another disgusting agenda of horror?

Why not tell Hansen? If he went to Europe in an attempt to smoke Nick out, Hansen might be helpful enough to give him some phone numbers – Interpol, the French Police, the German cops – so he could hook up with the authorities in whatever country he decided to visit. It was worth a try.

Thirty minutes later he drew up outside the North Hollywood Division building in Burbank Avenue, found the last visitor parking space available, and walked to the entrance.

Hansen was sweating like a pig, and he knew it wouldn't be so pleasant on the nose for Nolan when he arrived. The air con was on the blink in his office and the fan he'd plugged it just wasn't cutting it. Of course the three hundred one arm push-ups he'd performed while waiting for Dermot to arrive hadn't helped the B.O. count. He pulled out a tube of Junior Mints and crushed a few in his left hand, then ground them around with his right like a mortar and pestle. Maybe the minty smell would disguise his body odor?

When Dermot knocked lightly on Hansen's door, his partner, de Groot, was at the filing cabinet, riffling through paperwork. Hansen held out a sweaty paw to Dermot, then had second thoughts and pulled it back. "'Fraid I'm real sweaty – you may prefer not to shake fists," he said embarrassedly. De Groot gave Dermot a polite nod and continued to file.

'Fists'? Well, if you were Hansen you didn't think in terms of hands and fingers – the detective's hand was like a bludgeon. So 'fist'? Yeah, that was just about right.

"Take a seat? Anything I can get you, Mr. Nolan? Water? Soda? Coffee?"

"Thanks, but nothing right now. And call me Dermot."

Dermot sat on the chair that Hansen had pulled up by his desk. De Groot sat at his own desk, preparing himself to listen and contribute as much as he could.

"So, anything new happened since we last spoke? Remember anything else about the kid?"

Dermot shook his head. "No. Nothing. It's the weirdest thing, isn't it? You fix on one single thing – the hair – and forget everything else?"

"You'd be amazed at how many rape victims can hardly remember a thing barring the outrage, pain and humiliation."

"I can imagine."

"I doubt it," de Groot mumbled barely audibly as he ran his slim fingers through his wild black hair. He'd been in an ugly mood all morning – his young wife hadn't been 'in the mood' first thing that morning, while he'd been very much in that particular zone.

"Whatever," Dermot mumbled back over his shoulder at de Groot, then looked at Hansen. "So, no lucky breaks finding the kid?"

"Nah. Nothing. It's a shame someone got to the wig before you did. With the description you gave me, I visited a few of the biggest hire stores in town and I eventually got lucky. Hollywood Toys & Costumes on Hollywood Boulevard. I went down there yesterday to speak to the manager just before closing."

"And?" Dermot was getting excited; his scalp was beginning to itch.

"Some old guy came in and hired it two days ago. A vagrant. Late sixties. Manager said if he hadn't paid the full deposit as well as the hire fee there and then, he'd never have let the bum have the wig."

Dermot was instinctively taken back to the day the man calling himself Albert K. Arnold had delivered the 'Diary' to his house in Linley Place. He'd been a vagrant too. A bum with orange hair. So, getting some old street guy to hire the wig made sense; that was the way Nick had operated in the past – just pay some idiot who you've never seen before to do what he'd rather not do yourself, someone who was so fucked up he wouldn't remember what Nick looked like.

"You thinking what I'm thinking?" Hansen asked.

"Sure, that's Hoyle's M.O."

"Yeah, it does kind of make you think that there's more to this than just some pain in the ass smart kid who wants to tease the fuck out of you," Hansen replied. He caught sight of an expression of disapproval from de Groot. "Don't mind my language."

"Any chance of fingering the old guy?"

"Yeah, why not? Who knows? We're giving it a try. 'Course there are a whole bunch of mindless old bums walking the streets of North Hollywood. But the manager gave us a decent description, and we've drawn up an identikit picture of sorts."

"So you agree with me now? You see Hoyle's hand

here?"

"Can I butt in one moment, Jim?" de Groot asked.

"Sure. Butt away."

"Well, it all comes down to degrees of separation. Mr. A asks Ms. B to do him a favor and ask Mrs. C to ask Mr. D to buy something. By the time we've found Mr. D, we're looking at the near impossible task of tracking back all the way to Mr. A. Sometimes we get lucky and there's just Mr. A asking Ms. B to help out. I'd say Hoyle is far too smart to put himself at risk so easily."

"But it does tend to suggest that he's back in the city – back from wherever he went to escape you guys?"

"Very possibly," Hansen replied. "But we can't be sure that the kid wasn't given the wig by some guy *other* than Hoyle who just doesn't like you much, knows where you live, and wants to scare the hell out of you."

"Oh come on, detective! The only man I can think of who bears me a grudge is Hoyle. I've never had an enemy in my life, barring him. I make friends easily. And I tell you something else, I get on really well with the people who make up the Malibu community. So what's more likely; that someone in Malibu wants to drive me nuts, and has gone to all this trouble, or that we're looking at Hoyle's handiwork again?"

Neither Hansen nor de Groot said anything. It looked as though both detectives were coming around to Dermot's way of thinking, and it pleased him a lot.

"Which means," Hansen replied, "that either Hoyle has somehow managed to engineer the wig hire and the prepping of the kid from abroad, through a third or fourth party, or that your instinct is correct and he's here right now."

"Or *was* in town a few days ago to set things up," de Groot interceded, "and he's gone back to where he came from, and is again hiding out some place."

"If he's come and gone, that's a help in itself, isn't it?"

Both detectives looked at him a bit blankly – what was Nolan thinking now?

"Check with immigration whether anyone looking at all like Hoyle entered or exited the country in the past few days." There was a hint of desperation in Dermot's voice.

"You really don't fully understand what you asking, Mr. Nolan," de Groot replied. "You know how many people fly into and out of this country every day?"

"A lot," Dermot answered.

"No kidding. It's a staggering number. U.S. airline carriers carry about seven million domestic and international passengers a year in the States. And remember there's the roads into Mexico and Canada to think of too."

"But we can try, can't we? After all, we're looking at a dangerous serial killer. He's on the 'Most Wanted' list!"

"He is indeed," Hansen said soothingly – the last thing he wanted was for Nolan to become hysterical in his office; he was very aware of the psychological problems that Nolan was still recovering from. "At every exit point in this country there's a photo of Hoyle stuck up somewhere. Believe me, the immigration guys aren't dumb. Figuring out if a guy with a wig and mustache is the same guy who was clean shaven when he robbed the Wells Fargo bank is meat and potatoes to these guys."

Dermot looked at Hansen, not mollified in the least.

"Which makes me think it's more likely Hoyle never left the country," Hansen continued "That he simply found some place away from everywhere to lie low until he thought it was safe to come out of hiding."

Hansen was wrong in his thinking. Very wrong. The man he was searching for was at that precise moment in France, planning to cut a piece off Galina Yablonskaya.

15.

Hoyle smiled. Though life was quite perfect, France so somehow so annoyingly pretty this time of year, especially the heavily wooded department of Yvelines just outside Paris. His personal taste was the rugged countryside of Nevada, the Australian Outback, and the deserts of the Middle East. He preferred the rain to sunshine, and today someone was smiling on him, because the heavens had opened at midday and it hadn't stopped raining since, making the humidity intense. The wipers of his car were finding it had to keep pace with the downpour, forcing Hoyle to concentrate on the road ahead – the N12 was notorious for multi car pileups given these kinds of extreme conditions.

As he passed through Versailles an idle thought struck him. It was extraordinary how many second-rate people there existed throughout the world. Supposedly competent doctors armed with all the necessary degrees and qualifications allowed patients to die on their watch on a regular basis merely because they were second-rate. Second-rate financial advisors had driven the world to financial despair. Second-rate Detectives invariably clutched at the most obvious straws, locking away the innocent while allowing the guilty to enjoy the fruits of their sins.

He chuckled, then noticed he was a few miles an hour over the speed limit and touched breaks lightly. Oops! So many criminals made the mistake of being caught and being sent to the lethal injection chamber, merely because they drew attention to themselves on the road. Second-rate criminals – yes indeed, there were plenty of those too.

It should never have been as easy as it had been for him to outwit the authorities. Thinking further back, how was it possible that the collective intelligence of the LAPD, with the noticeable exception of one very smart dick, Detective Mike Kandinski, had been so positive that Dermot had committed all the 'Worst Nightmare' murders? It was a no-brainer that Nolan had been set up, albeit in the most cunning way by a master strategist such as himself. Yet everyone but Kandinski had missed the clues.

The day Dermot was unearthed, Hoyle had immediately gone to plan B. He was the master of forward thinking. Although certain that he'd planned for every eventuality, he always known it was prudent to plan for disaster. To that end, he'd bought several passports and credit cards in false names a full year before he'd embarked on his plan to drive Dermot insane by burying him in a coffin in accordance with his worst nightmare. Money had been deposited in various numbered accounts in Switzerland, and thanks to wonderful advances in technology, these were easily accessible from anywhere in the world.

Arranging for a child in Malibu to send shivers down Dermot's spine had been easy, and so much fun. If anyone really put his mind to something, anything is possible – that had always been Nick Hoyle's mantra. Any kid on the block in South Central knew where to buy a gun, meth-amphetamines, heroin, explosives – you name it. Forged passports and credit cards? There were hundreds of criminal businessmen who made that their living from creating such counterfeit documents. There were people one could reach at any moment of the day and night who would accommodate almost any whim. For the right money, it went without saying. The 'Ginger-Fixer' was one such man. If the price suited him, he'd arrange anything. And the best part was that he insisted he never know the identity of those that needed him to arrange things for them. That single degree of separation was worth a bucket of money in itself.

Several years ago Nick had spent a bunch of evenings hanging out and making friends in the Brighton Beach area of New York; you never knew when you'd need a favor from a man who would never ask questions providing his palm was sufficiently greased, and Brighton Beach was the new stamping ground of the Russian Mafia. This was the turf of some very hard men, villains prepared to go that extra mile for that extra buck. It hadn't taken Nick long to become pals with all the right people and naturally he'd never used his real name. To these guys he was simply 'Chuck.' He'd never pretended that he was a hard man himself or a criminal – these guys thought he simply liked hanging out with them because he respected their work ethos.

It was through one of his drinking partners at the Bar 109 that he heard about the 'Ginger-Fixer'; nicknamed because of his love for spicy Thai food. Only his closest associates even knew who the 'G-Fixer' was – this was paramount since anonymity meant no one could snitch on him. But Hoyle soon came to know how the guy operated. You simply called a cell phone–one belonging to a third party with ostensibly no link to the 'Ginger Fixer'. Briefly you'd tell him what needed doing. He'd make a mental calculation and offer a price. Take it or leave it – no quibbling. As soon as the fee was deposited in a designated grocery store – his front – the 'Ginger Fixer' made sure your wishes were carried out. Simple. No feedback to the client because the 'Ginger-Fixer' would farm out the work to others for half the price he was getting, thereby keeping his own fingers clean. Even if the 'Ginger-Fixer''s immediate contact fingered him, he'd deny he paid any money to anyone, and there'd be no proof. For this was true, the money was handed over by a cousin of his – the owner of the grocery store. The 'Ginger Fixer''s track record was immaculate.

Fixing someone to find a kid to freak out Nolan was a piece of cake because no one knew the deadly inference of what the kid was going to say. The whole fee was a straight two grand. It had been fixed up while Hoyle was still in France; he'd received the confirmation on a cell phone twenty-four hours later and had immediately thrown the cell in the massive fishpond of Saint-Quentin opposite the Bois d'Arcy.

Nick wondered what the LAPD would make of the kid. Would they think Nolan had gone nuts? Or would they recognize it was *his* handiwork? Maybe they'd be telling themselves that Hoyle was back in the city. He didn't much care what the LAPD dicks thought – he felt sure he'd piqued Dermot's curiosity, and that he'd take the bait. That was the all-important thing – he felt certain he'd pushed all the right buttons.

But one question remained; had he calculated *which*

buttons to press correctly? He'd known Dermot since college and knew what made him tick; how he'd react in any given circumstance. Right now, he felt sure he'd tempted him out of his new home, where he'd been intent on laying up before garnering sufficient courage to come after him. It would be a prefect outcome if he'd succeeded in getting Dermot moving while he was still weak. Which brought him all the way back to the subject of second-rate cops. Life really was a 'wheel.'

He took a right off the D 11 past Saulx-Marchais and headed for the small village of Auteuil, wondering in what physical state he'd find his guests today. Would Cecile have calmed down and accepted that she'd have to make the best of it for a while? Why wouldn't she? He'd shown her he was the perfect gentleman, hadn't he? He hadn't lain a finger on her, and had offered her the most splendid food and wine. Her husband, Ballon? He was certainly made of stronger stuff, knowing he *had* to survive so that *she* might. He probably suspect that Hoyle would need to kill him, but it was in the nature of young people to think positively and refuse to lie down and die. He still had a shot at life, so he'd most likely take it and see where it led him.

The major stumbling block was that Hoyle was about to ask him to perform some rather grotesque surgery once again, and he had no idea where Jean Ballon would draw the ethical line in the sand and begin planning a way of overcoming his tormentor physically. Naturally, Nick would see that this moment never came to pass.

In what mental shape would he find Mademoiselle Yablonskaya? As rude, arrogant and feisty as she'd been when she regained consciousness and found herself bound and lying on her back on a camp bed in what must to her have looked like a dungeon?

"What the fuck do you think you are doing, you piece of shit!" she'd shouted at him in Russian, her language rich with expletives that were probably the legacy of a father who had worked on the docks at Volgograd. This was not the language of the next Anna Pavlova! She'd clearly inherited her parents' spunk. Nick had taken an immediate liking to this girl's feisty spirit. No need to assure her that her life was not in danger – better to make it clear that if she behaved badly she'd be in *really* bad shit. However, he initially appealed to her common sense by assuring her that she would be freed in one week."

"A week? A fucking week! What the fuck are you talking about? I have engagements! Don't you know who I *am*, you dumb fuck!" She now spoke in French..White foam at the corners of her mouth was an indication of her anger.

"You are a dancing miracle," Hoyle had replied as though oblivious to her vitriol. "An angel. I saw your Giselle at Covent Garden. I could scarcely speak for two days. You were breathtakingly graceful. You broke my heart."

That had taken the wind out of Mademoiselle Yablonskaya's sails. Hoyle was amazed at the power of vanity – the ballet dancer could forget she was tied up in some kind of cell when soothed by praise from an admirer.

"You want me to dance for you? Privately? Is that why I am here?" she'd asked, incredulously. She was now genuinely curious.

"Eventually, that would be quite wonderful. Perhaps not right now," he'd replied with a wry smile. "You will dance for me in the Champs-Élysées. But more of that later."

She had stared at him with incomprehension then. She would soon know what he meant.

As he reached the outskirts of the village of Auteuil, and had turned down a lane-way to the house he had leased, he couldn't help being amused by the irony of the words she had used. *Do you want me to dance for you?* Yes, he did. Though, strictly speaking, a *pas de deux* was a step or dance for two; she would soon be dancing a very different *pas d'un!*

He pulled up at the back of the house, well away from prying eyes. One of the principal reasons he'd leased this particular house was that it was so very private. Many years ago the building had served as a storage facility for a company that sold meat products in the department of Yvelines. Then some time ago it was converted into a cozy holiday home and sold to an English couple. When they divorced, Nick had made an offer for a lease through an online broker. He'd been looking for a property with cellar storage, and this had been ideal – one never knew how hot the spring would be in Paris and, as it turned out, this year was one of the hottest on record!

He let himself in through the back entrance and walked through the spacious kitchen, resting the two shopping bags of provisions he'd bought on the oak table. He then moved on into the hall and entered the living room where he paused to pour himself a glass of whisky. As he lifted the glass to his lips he strained to listen for any untoward noises. There were none – silence reigned supreme; just a fly banging against a windowpane in the kitchen. It was reassuring to know that should he receive any unexpected visitors, he didn't have to worry that screams might be audible from below stairs.

Having slaked his thirst, he walked back through the kitchen and opened a door that led to the basement.

His first stop would be Galina – she was not yet fully under his control. The Ballons were now manageable, so the ballerina's needs were paramount.

As he reached meat storage locker number 3, he pulled a skinny beige colored balaclava over his head, then took out a metal key. He reached inside his jacket pocket for his auto-injector – the kind doctors prescribed for anaphylaxis; he'd finally found a way to substitute Succinylcholine for the adrenaline it usually carried, a task made difficult by the pharmaceutical companies because of the safety concerns.

Hoyle's injector was filled with 'sux' – a neuromuscular blocker that induced almost immediate muscular relaxation. This wonder drug had been the Dream Healer's 'little helper' on so many occasions, and the joy of it was that those injected with it remained conscious and able to listen and reason, yet unable to move. Of course, one had to be wary of was overdosing, something that would result in heart failure. Hoyle knew he might be obliged to use it on the ballet dancer

– she clearly had violent Russian working class genes, and, unless he was mistaken, might attempt to rush him when he entered the room.

He wasn't wrong. As he gently swung the door open he noticed she was not lying on her camp bed. He immediately stabbed his right foot against the door. Sure enough, the girl launched her shoulder at it in an attempt to bang the door hard against his head. All she achieved was a bruise to her shoulder.

He heard her slump to the floor and groan.

"People can be so predictable, my little Galina," he said as he stepped inside and closed the door behind him." He held out a hand to help her up, but she spat at him and shuffled back to the camp bed.

"If you let me out right now, I promise I will forget all that has happened here."

As a ballet principal she could act well; on stage she was believable. Here in storage room 3, her acting didn't cut the mustard.

"Again, so predictable," Hoyle cooed at her.

He leant against the wall opposite Galina. "Now, we must talk briefly. You have only six days to wait. Should you not agree to my terms, you can leave today."

She looked up, surprised. "Today?"

"Yes, today. But should you choose to leave today it will be in a plastic bag. Wait another six days, and do as I say, and I can promise you will leave here alive."

Galina stared at him, totally shocked. Was this man serious? His matter-of-fact voice was deeply frightening, as was the delivery of each word. One slow word after another as though he was a mongoose mesmerizing a rabbit.

"How can I believe you?"

"In the same way one is asked to believe in God! Blind faith. What else is there? The existence of God has never been proven, yet hundreds of millions choose to believe quite blindly." Hoyle snorted with derision. "If you feel you can't believe me, you may choose the alternative option. To die."

Hoyle eased himself off the wall. "In the meantime, I shall take care of your toilet, and in an hour or so I shall bring you your dinner. You are a vegetarian, I believe? No wait, I am told you do eat chicken."

Galina was speechless. How did this man...? She rubbed her shoulder – it ached badly.

"Are you in pain? I hope you didn't damage yourself."

"No, it's bruised, nothing more."

"I'm relieved," Hoyle replied, picking up the portable toilet by the carry handle.

As he reached the door he put down the toilet and pulled the door open; his other hand was on his auto injector, just in case. But Galina decided not to chance anything.

"I think you'll enjoy the dinner. Tonight the chef recommends *Pissaladière,* Provence's famous onion tart. However, should you chose, there is a *Chèvre salade.* Do you prefer white or red?"

Hoyle could see white-hot anger in her eyes. It amused him greatly. She did not reply.

"Then I shall serve a Chablis – it goes with both dishes so perfectly. Trust me."

He closed the door behind him and turned the key. As he walked down the corridor towards the surgeon and his wife, he heard Galina shout.

"*Idi na huy huesos!*"

As Hoyle spoke no Russian he wasn't to know he'd been

called a cocksucker. It wouldn't have bothered him if he *had* known – it would simply have amused him.

Ten minutes later Galina's toilet had been emptied, cleaned and returned to an ungrateful prima ballerina, and Hoyle was at the door of storage locker number 1; the temporary guest suite of Monsieur and Madame Ballon.

Today preparations needed to be made for frsh surgery. Somehow Jean Ballon would have to be persuaded that a lack of cooperation was not an option, since Nick was beginning to suspect that he and his wife Cecile would by now have carefully considered moral an ethical criteria, and it was altogether possible that they would decide to take their chances rather than continue with what they considered sheer butchery.

They would have to be persuaded.

16.

Gassin had never seen Barbier so agitated – the French had a special name for such a frame of mind – *bouleversé*. Its dictionary definition was 'thrown into confusion.' Such a state was quite foreign to the usually placid Commissaire – he'd made his reputation as man who nothing phased. Gassin wondered whether this was because the normally unflappable man had been sent the hand personally, with the caveat that it was *he* who would be responsible if the police didn't play the game correctly? As of this morning his team had come up with little to help the Commissaire. Time was running out.

"While I appreciate you had so little time, Thierry," Barbier said, using his subordinate's Christian name as a gesture of goodwill, "but if we beleive the monster who sent the hand, we have less than twelve hours left before we're served some fresh horror."

"We all agree that the surgeon, Jean Ballon, is most likely

the key. It is too much of a coincidence that he went missing, and with his disappearance as well as that of his wife remaining unexplained, we'd be foolish not to consider that he was responsible for the amputation."

"There is no concrete evidence whatsoever to link Ballon to the hand, is there?" Barbier's words had an almost accusing tone.

Gassin continued in a deliberately soothing tone. "You gave us a box containing an unidentified hand, and a letter. Our task was to identify the host body of the hand and arrest the man or woman who had it severed from the body to which it previously belonged. You gave our team five days. As of today, we believe the hand belonged to the celebrated concert pianist Josef Kafni."

Barbier stared off. "Heaven help us..." he murmured, though Gassin had already informed him of Kafni's possible involvement.

"We also believe, though we are by no means certain, a surgeon by the name of Jean Ballon was kidnapped, along with his wife, in order to perform the surgery."

"So where is this surgeon now?"

"We are doing our utmost to find Ballon before this..." he chose his word carefully, "'situation' escalates. "However, searching Greater Paris for a man, his wife and a sociopath, all of whom may be underground in a cellar for all we know, is proving as hard as you might imagine."

Barbier flapped a hand in the air. "I hear what you saying. I appreciate I gave you a near impossible task. However, I chose you because I know such tasks are not beyond you." He drew breath. "Is there any way I can assist your team further?"

"Provide me with more personel perhaps. That would help. We have several million phone calls to make. Many more millions of locations to secure."

"You have my authority to sequester whom you wish, Thierry. Just get the job done. I don't want to be facing the media tomorrow with nothing to show them but a human hand and a recording of a man laughing at the Paris Préfécture."

Gassin looked up. "The media has not gotten wind of the hand yet, has it sir?" He was shocked.

"No, of course not. But I always fear leaks, and with a story like this, who knows who might be tempted to share such information with the newspapers? Too many people have seen the hand here at the Préfécture. And if you are correct in your assumption that this psychopath will decide to carry through his threats tomorrow – delivering to us a second hand or some other body part, regardless of whether we are right in our choice of Kafni – then there is no way we can keep a lid on this."

"There is no doubt this madman knows how to play the media at our expense, sir. To kill a man or woman is commonplace. To target a celebrity makes a better front page. To lop off the hand of a prominent figure and send it to us creates a furore."

"Before you go, Thierry, I must ask you something. The obscene rules of this game were that I identify to whom the hand belonged, or there would be some escalation. So I have to ask you – how certain are you that the hand sent to me belonged to Kafni?"

Gassin knew that the life of a second party might well depend on his answer. There was little evidence to suggest the hand was Kafni's – it was simply a theory borne of a mixture of a hunch and Kafni's sudden and unexplained disappearance.

"Commissaire, I cannot swear I am correct in my analysis, but as and when the deadline arrives you'll be obliged to respond in some way. Since you may as well make a choice based on our investigations, I would advise you to say quite categorically that we *know* for a fact the hand was Kafni's. If this is not true, we have lost nothing. If true, it might well unsettle the man and cause him to react erratically – move his hostages. In this way we might notice him, as a hunter might notice a deer that has been waiting in the undergrowth and is finally flushed out because of fear for it's safety."

"Thank you, Thierry. I feel that is sound advice," Barbier replied, then had one more thought. "This man. The one who wrote the letter. Where would you imagine he'll call me? At home or here?"

"At home, sir. If he calls here we will have it patched through to your home. The call will be naturally be traced, but I have my doubts about anything good coming of that. Even amateurs are aware of the modern powers of tracing phone calls."

Gassin stood, rather than wait to be dismissed – Barbier had that 'we are at an end' look on his face and his fingers were drumming the desk.

"I shall leave you, sir," Gassin said with a polite smiled and turned towards the door.

"Don't allow this man to make a mockery of the Sûreté, Thierry."

"I will do my utmost, Jules."

An hour later Gassin was briefing twenty-seven detectives, twenty-four of whom he had sequestered from other duties. Everyone in the conference room was standing, facing him.

"We have three questions to answer in the next few hours, and I have given a commitment, somewhat foolishly, to Commissaire Barbier that these questions will be answered by nine o'clock tomorrow morning. Question one. Where is the celebrated Josef Kafni? Question two. Where is the missing surgeon, Jean Ballon? Question three. Who is responsible for the delivery of the box containing the human hand to Commissaire Barbier?

"Every gendarme in Paris will know what Ballon and Kafni look like by now – every police station has been briefed with photos. However, unless someone witnessed the abduction of Ballon, and currently we have come up empty despite countless interviews at the hospital where he worked, as well as at his home, we have to assume he and his wife were snatched and placed in a van or some similar vehicle and transported to a venue where no one would witness their transference to their present location.

"So, current thinking? Assuming that Ballon conducted the surgical removal of the hand that was sent to Commissaire Barbier, we're looking for a locale that is both cool and most likely underground. Cool, because heat would enhance the likelihood of infection during the amputation, and bearing the current heat wave in mind we would imagine our man would have factored in a cold location. We're unsure whether the abductor intends to keep his victims alive, or even whether this is a significant issue for him. Somewhere underground would seem to be logical because it fulfills two issues, it is both cool and addresses the noise factor – noisy equipment, screams, and so on.

"So I leave you all to your work. You are the best detectives we have in France and I feel sure we will get 'a result.' Soccer terminology." A majority of the detectives in front of him smiled – he knew most of the detectives were soccer mad.

"You don't have long. I feel sure one of you will succeed. This man must be stopped before he mutilates another victim. Commissaire Barbier is expecting our man make contact with him by 9 a.m. tomorrow. If we have no fresh information by that time, he will name Josef Kafni as the owner of the hand. If this proves to be correct, we'll see if this psychopath plans to play the game by the rules he outlined in his letter and allow Kafni to go."

Gassin was not to know that another surgical operation was already scheduled for nine o'clock that night.

17.

Madame Ballon was remarkably calm, all things considered. Despite eating a decent portion of the supermarket take-out dishes that Hoyle had reheated for her, she'd lost quite a bit of weight. A 'worry-wart', that's how Hoyle viewed her. Monsieur Ballon was made of stouter stuff physically – and was both a thinker and an ethical human being by nature. Hoyle was relishing the morning's discussion – one that would inevitably lead to an ultimatum.

"One might posit the argument," Hoyle began, sitting on the stool that stood under the noose, casually addressing both Jean and Cecile, "that it is not you who maims, but I, because it is I who forces these actions upon you – you are merely the conduit. I am the *true* barbarian." Hoyle was wearing his Balaclava so that there'd be no need to hood Ballon's wife. He considered this a gesture of compassion.

"That is such a lame and hackneyed argument," Jean replied wearily. "It has been used since time immemorial. The reality is that I butchered that man because I knew that if I didn't do as I was told, Cecile might die. It was my choice, and I chose to do it."

Cecile Ballon shuddered momentarily on her cot and pulled her blankets up around her neck.

"So, considered logically," Hoyle, continued, "you performed a non-life-threatening surgical procedure to *save* a life. It seems like a good tradeoff to me."

"It was not such a great 'tradeoff' as far as Monsieur Kafni was concerned," Ballon replied acidly.

"Well, how can you be so sure? Had someone told Kafni that losing his hands would save not only his life but a stranger's, I wonder if he'd have agreed to the amputation?"

Ballon merely laughed a very hollow laugh. "Are you for real? Of course not. He's a concert pianist."

"I can see that the life of a stranger wouldn't count for much, but you consider he'd rather be dead than lose his hands? Interesting."

"It's a lot to ask of a world famous concert pianist to imagine he'd trade his hands for another person's life. You're being facile."

"Come on! People often donate organs to strangers so that others may live." Hoyle was warming to the discussion. This was entertaining.

"That's not the same thing at all. People can live without, say, a kidney or possibly a slice of liver. Even one eye."

"And Kafni can live without hands – that goes without saying. He cannot play the piano; that's all. Which is more important? His being able to tap away at the keyboards, or your darling wife dancing at the end of a rope?"

Ballon gave his captor such an immediate look of hatred and violence that Hoyle was glad he was out of Ballon's radius of violence – the chain allowed him a two feet leeway, that was all.

"You are a grown man. This simplistic conversation is the kind I might have had at school."

"Tell me, Jean," Hoyle asked, shrugging off the insult. "Would you give one of your kidneys to your wife is she'd die otherwise?"

"Of course," Ballon replied at once.

"Would you give a kidney to a perfect stranger?"

"Yes, I would," Ballon replied again after a moment.

"Did I detect some hesitation?"

"Well, of course. A stranger is not someone you love."

Hoyle tut-tutted. "There is no such thing as the Good

Samaritan, is there. We give because we feel like it; not as a gesture of humanity."

"Such is life," Ballon replied, coldly.

"Would you give your wife an arm?"

"Oh God..." Ballon sighed, the questions were becoming annoying. It was like talking to a child. But he knew he had to mollify his captor. "If I felt it would not be rejected and thus be a useless gesture, I would."

"Do you think that's normal?"

"You mean do I think others would do the same? Maybe."

"I doubt it very much."

Having allowed ten seconds to pass, aware that Cecile was now crying softly, Hoyle continued in a more soothing tone.

"You perform operations on patients every day, am I right?"

"Yes, I do. They have all signed waivers agreeing to the surgery."

Hoyle then cocked his head to the left and scrunched up his face as if to suggest that strictly speaking this was not absolutely true. "Well, not *all* of them, surely? What about babies and young children?"

"What about them?"

"Well, in the case of children, it's the parents who have given their permission. One might ask oneself, why? Because it's in the best interests of the child? In the case of, say, separating conjoined twins, parents are quite often asked which of the babies shall live and which shall die. Again, the consideration is what is best for both children. Yet, effectively, the parents have agreed for you to end the life of one of their children with your scalpel so that the other may survive."

Ballon looked down. He knew the madman had a point, ridiculous as the conversation was.

"You say nothing. I wonder why?"

Ballon looked up again. "I have lived through such a scenario, and it was the worst moment of my life. It was truly terrible for the parents too. The difference is that had I not allowed one of the children to die, both would have perished."

"The situation you find yourself in today, I'd say," Hoyle replied with a soft smile. "But let's move on."

Hoyle stood and looked up at the noose, then down at the stool, as though judging whether or not the stool was perfectly placed.

"I find all of this absolutely fascinating," he said, idly moving the stool an inch to the right.

"You find this kind of disgusting conversation... fascinating?"

"Don't be so judgmental, Jean. What appeals to me may not appeal to you and vice versa. For instance, consider this scenario. The danger to the life of Mr. A by removing an organ to allow him to donate it to Mrs. B outweighs the chances of Mrs. B accepting the organ and thereby living? What then?"

"That would not be my decision – that would be a decision made at board level."

"But you would carry out whatever decision they came to?"

"I would; most certainly."

"Similar to the actions of the guards at Auschwitz?"

Extreme anger flashed again in Ballon's eyes. "You are a madman even to suggest such a correlation."

Hoyle sniggered. "Well, I admit I was ever so slightly out of line by suggesting that, but where is one to draw the line in the sand? At what point do you question the hospital board personally? Rather than simply whipping out the 'ol' scalpel' and getting stuck in?"

"I know they would not ask me to do anything that was not in the patient's best interests."

"I see. However, I'm unsure if you're aware that in the late thirties in Germany the great bulk of the masses believed their Führer was doing what was in the best interests of their nation. Throughout the Second World War medical research was being conducted on Jews – research that German doctors knew would inevitably result in their patients' deaths."

"The German people did not know about the concentration camps."

"Good Lord. So many still believe that. Many now doubt the holocaust."

Hoyle began pacing the room, placing one foot carefully in front of the other as if balancing on a tightrope. "All right, we won't bother to go there, although historians maintain that the bulk of the German population *were* aware of the extermination camps during the final stages of the war, yet chose to look the other way. Which brings us to another point I find intriguing."

"Please! You are upsetting my wife. I don't wish to discuss this further."

Hoyle continued to pace, oblivious, as if on another planet. "Have you ever had a patient refuse treatment on religious grounds – such as a refusal to accept a transfusion of blood?"

"Yes, I have. On two occasions," Ballon replied, still anxious to placate his torturer. He realized he'd shown anger and this was not the best way to attain clemency for his wife.

"Did you ever feel that perhaps it would have been a

good idea to *force* the patient to receive the blood, because otherwise he would die?"

Ballon considered. "On one occasion the patient himself refused an operation because of the blood issue. There was nothing we could do; so I accepted the fact that it was her ethical choice."

"And she died?"

"She did. But, as I said, she had a choice in the matter."

Hoyle knew it was the Ballon's 'second occasion' that would reveal the more interesting story – it was human nature to attempt to avoid the more distressing story. "The second occasion?"

Ballon remained tightlipped, unwilling to discuss the matter further.

"The other case?"

"It concerned a child. He was twelve years old. The parents were both members of a religious sect that prohibits transfusions. It was my opinion that the child was too afraid of his parents to argue with them. It finally went to court. The child refused to dispute the issue with his parents and nodded tacit consent to their wishes. The court refused to take the child into care. He ultimately died."

Madame Ballon had stopped sniveling and was listening, wondering where all this would lead.

Hoyle nodded. "Seems like a kind of murder to me. And all in the name of God. You know something? I believe in balance. That's paramount. One should balance the patient's inherent right to his or her religious belief, against the prospect that they might die as a consequence of the exercise of such a right. It's a patient's choice to accept blood – live or die – and yet paradoxically we still consider suicide a crime. Fascinating. Quite a conundrum."

Cecile shrugged off her blankets, stood and walked over

to her husband, crouching at his feet. He wrapped an arm around her in a hug. Hoyle's hand moved instantly to his auto injector just in case this was a plan they had plotted while he was out cleaning their toilet.

Hoyle was silent for a while, staring down at the floor – it was clear to Ballon that his torturer's mind was no longer focusing on medical ethics.

"My babies were burnt to death you know," Hoyle began in a faraway voice. "Well, they died a few hours after the fire. I begged the surgeons to skin me alive so that they could graft it onto my darlings. But they told me such grafting wasn't feasible." He paused then looked up at Ballon. "I didn't believe them. I think they were simply too lazy to try untested techniques. Or else the hospital board had insurance issues with risky surgery."

"That is not the way grafting works," Ballon said in a low tone – there was something inherently tragic in this man's sadness; butcher though he was.

"You see, I would gladly have sacrificed my life for them." Hoyle looked hard at Ballon, staring deep into the surgeon's eyes. "Would you? For Cecile?"

"Of course," Ballon replied without hesitation; and with a sudden realization knew what the man before him was actually saying. He knew then that he'd die.

"I understand what you're saying. At least I think so," was all Ballon said. He cast a look at his wife; she appeared to be sleeping. "Be kind to her at least."

"I shall," Hoyle replied, and held out a hand for Ballon to shake, as though he'd made a deal. A pact. Ballon looked away. Hoyle's face clouded with a look of disappointment, then he covered his feelings with a false grin.

"Enough of this idle banter, Jean. Let's get to the point."

Ballon said nothing. He hugged Cecile ever closer.

"This evening I have to ask you to perform again as a surgeon."

"No," Ballon replied, firmly. "I will not."

"On this occasion, I will ask you to do much less than you did the last time."

"No. I will not."

"There is a 'balance' to be achieved. Remember? I just referred to such a 'balance'."

"No. Whatever it is. Cecile and I have decided. Together."

"Perhaps you are missing my point, Jean. The balance doesn't so much concern you and your wife, as the woman who is at this minute in a holding cell a few yards own the corridor."

"No. Whatever it is. No."

"Please don't annoy me, Jean. Just listen. Then by all means say no and suffer the consequences."

Ballon crushed his wife to his chest.

"If the surgery does not go ahead according to my wishes, I shall execute Mademoiselle Yablonskaya. I will place the muzzle of my gun in her mouth and blow her brains out." Hoyle had always found that to decorate his language with horrific imagery paid great dividends. "I shall then take her body out into the woods in a plastic bag and bury her."

Ballon was wide eyed, his facial expression one of fury.

"However, should you do as I say, she will live. I will set her free, in the same way as I shall set Monsieur Kafni free tomorrow morning. So the 'balance' is this – you choose whether this ballerina lives without one foot, or whether she dies with both. This choice must be made this evening."

A look of astonishment crossed Ballon's face. Even Cecile

opened her eyes and looked up from her mouse-like snuggling under his arm.

"A foot? You want me to amputate a healthy foot?"

"Correct. Just one foot. A simple amputation. Local anesthetic and narcotics will, as usual, have to be sufficient."

"It never is – the pain factor will be as appalling as it was with Kafni. The shock to her system could easily kill her."

"Kafni lived. Unless I'm unlucky, she will too. Whatever. You are skilled. So the only danger, as ever, is infection. It's up to you whether she lives or dies."

Ballon stared at his tormentor for over a minute. Finally he spoke.

"What I find amazing is that at times you appear to be an intelligent man, capable of conducting a rational, albeit at times intellectually confused, debate. So I am tempted to wonder; are even madmen imbued with moments of lucidity? Is it possible that psychopaths have moments of compassion?"

"You know, I think you may have hit on a truth there. Are you thinking of all the time and trouble I've done to bringing you delicious food? And perhaps my kindness in fetching Cecile a second blanket?" A wry grin crept across Hoyle's face. "However, I naturally maintain that I am completely sane—and lucid—*all* the time. The only difference between you and me is that we don't share the same moral and ethical values. I have come to the conclusion that life is ephemeral. We live or die by sheer chance. Serendipity. Longevity is not a human right. I see a cockroach, the cockroach does not see me, my foot stamps down, the cockroach is no more – it never saw the end of its life approaching. In this way– "

Ballon cut him short. "My wife and I have decided we would rather both die than mutilate human beings who have deserved no such fate."

Once more enjoying the banter, Hoyle responded with a

question. "What if the patient who's foot I was asking you to amputate was the architect of the ethnic cleansing in Bosnia? Would *that* alter your decision?"

"I am not the one that decides who should live or die."

"No, you are not. I am." Dermot replied, a new coldness in his voice.

Hoyle reached up and pulled down the length of rope that had the noose at the end of it and gave it a sharp tug.

Both Ballon and his wife said nothing as they watched him toss the rope to one side so that it swung in a lazy arch back and forth.

"Balance. Not only do you have to balance the ballet dancer's life with one dainty foot, or her death with both still in tact, but you must also remember that your poor wife will be obliged to literally balance on this very stool until she tires and falls. She may have to balance for an interminable time, and by then you'll be wishing you'd cut the silly girl's foot off without making such a fuss."

"No! We have decided. I will not do this thing."

Cecile began to cry again.

"Really?" Hoyle was astonished. This surgeon was willing to watch his wife hang rather than amputate a foot? It was quite unbelievable. So unbelievable, that he felt quietly confident that when push came to shove, the moral bigot would come around to his way of thinking. Almost everyone since the beginning of time had a threshold. At some point or other even the bravest gave up information before they died. And looking at the terror in the eyes of his wife, he knew Ballon would be no different.

"Surgery is scheduled for 9 p.m. this evening. I would suggest you both dine afterwards. If your darling wife is still capable of moving her jaws at that time – terror often causes rictus – she'll be feasting on *cassoulet* and a delightful Côte du Rhône. Just for a refreshing change."

He left the noose still swinging as he exited, locking the door behind him.

18.

Laurens Van de Hoot studied Dermot intently. So this was the man that Nick Hoyle had buried underground. The news story had amazed him when the details of the kidnapping were finally released to the media; who'd have thought that easy-going likable Nick Hoyle was such a monster. To have brutally murdered thirteen people in the manner of their worst nightmares and shown absolutely no remorse was astonishing. Then to bury his best friend in a coffin in the man's own backyard! Van de Hoot's wife had almost had a seizure when he'd told her of Nick's antics. '*It could so easily have been one of us,*' she'd said, shuddering at the thought. And now, sitting opposite him, was the shadow of a great author, asking him questions, clearly intent on returning to his worst nightmares at the first available moment, regardless of the consequences. Amazingly shocking.

"My advice to you," the art dealer began, "Would be to call off your quest. It can only lead to grief."

The tick over Dermot's eye twitched with annoyance – something not lost on Van de Hoot. "The fact of the matter is that I have had no contact whatsoever with him since a week before you returned to the land of the living. So I am afraid I can't help you."

Van de Hoot Fine art, just off Wilshire, had not been the first fine art dealership Dermot had visited that morning. There had been Trigg Ison at nine o'clock, Ghetto Gloss at ten, and Marc Selwyn at eleven. None had heard even a whisper of Hoyle's whereabouts for months – not since the police had put out their all points bulletin on him. Dermot wasn't in the least surprised. If it were easy to locate Hoyle, the cops would have done it by now. But there was no way he would leave for Europe until he was certain that Nick hadn't been supporting himself by dealing in America.

"Could he be dealing with you via an alias?" Dermot asked.

"It's possible, though I very much doubt it. Dealers want to see the works they're bidding on so that they can judge their importance and authenticity. The provenance. The history. You're familiar with the word provenance?"

"I am."

"Not that we're in the habit of selling any works without a solid provenance, but Nick's buyers in particular liked to feel that he too was comfortable that what they are buying was worth the money paid."

"I see," Dermot replied, standing.

"May I just say how much I admire your fortitude after such terrible adversity, Mr. Nolan. You are a hero—and not just in my book, I bet."

"I'd be a hero if I brought Nick Hoyle to justice," Dermot replied, without a smile. "To ensure no one else suffers as I did would justify almost anything."

Van de Hoot, wasn't quite sure what Nolan meant by 'almost anything' but thought better not to enquire – clearly Nolan had a score to settle.

"Would it be at all possible for your secretary to draw up a list of dealers with whom you think Hoyle might have done business in Europe? I know it's great deal to ask." He paused, then winked. "Possibly only heroes are afforded such a kindness."

Van de Hoot smiled back, holding out a hand and shaking Dermot's warmly.

"I shall email you such a list this afternoon. My pleasure, Mr. Nolan."

As Dermot opened the door, Van de Hoot added, "By the way. I am still awaiting the sequel to *Incoming Tide*. To my mind, your finest novel by far."

"You may have to wait a while. But thanks. I happen to think so too."

Neela arrived early at Dermot's favorite restaurant, the El Coyote Mexican Café on Beverly Boulevard, and had already searched out a small back room that wasn't too busy. Vig was still sound asleep in her carry cot, which Neela had placed on the floor at her side, at the same time draping a net cloth over its hood.

Now that she and Dermot lived even further away, in Point Dume rather than downtown Linley Place, she and Dermot missed the weekly intake of divine Mexican food.

By the time Dermot arrived Neela had already organized a pitcher of El C's world famous house Margaritas together with a bowl of corn chips and some spicy red salsa. There were no more than three chips left.

Dermot hugged Neela, threw Vig a silent kiss, then sat down opposite and looked at the bowl of chips.

"I was hungry – go make a federal case, mister," she said, winking.

Almost instantly Dermot's favorite waitress was standing at his elbow. "*Sr. Nolan bienvenido. Agradable verle otra vez! Usted ha sido un extranjero!*"

He laughed—it was reassuring to know that they'd missed him and now welcomed him back. Graciela was a honey – five foot two high, three foot two across and the wrong side of sixty, still wearing the wonderfully multi-colored traditional Mexican flounced dresses. Even at her age Graciela was sexier than the average thirty-something town girl.

"I go get more chips, Meester Nolan," she said in a thick accent. "En' plenty guacamole, and jalapena cheese poppers, like always."

"Perfect, Graciela."

Watching her leave, Neela took a sip of her margarita, trying to judge from Dermot's body language whether he'd had a good day or not.

"So?" she began.

"So, nothing, I'm afraid," he replied snatching the next to last chip. "I didn't really expect much. Right now it's more a question of ruling out negatives than expecting to find positives."

"No one has spoken to him?"

"He's dealt with no one. So he's not earning money from art. In America, anyway. When I gave up trying to sleep last night I made a rough assessment of much he could have squirreled away over the past five years; could be anything around a million dollars."

Neela gave him a 'wow' look.

Graciela returned with the poppers and the guacomole and chips. He thanked her with a smile.

"You hev decided, Mees Neela?"

"Yes, we have, I think," Neela replied, looking at Dermot. He simply nodded. "I'd like carnitas. And an Enchilada Howard for my husband."

Graciela laughed lightly. They had the same dishes every week.

Neela dipped her chip in the avocado pulp. "So, what now?"

"I was thinking about that for most of the night."

Neela appealed to him with her eyes. "Please, darling, there isn't anything you *have* to do. Nothing."

"But there is. Can't you see that he's challenged me? With the boy? He sent the kid to tell me this isn't over. He still intends to finish things."

"In what way?"

"I wish I knew. All I can say for certain is that thinking Nick Hoyle is going to go away is like hoping the tide won't come in. He's unbalanced and psychotic. He took pleasure in killing thirteen people. If the cops hadn't shown up when they did, he'd have killed you too. How can we pretend he's not trying to contact me again?"

"What's the alternative? Go to war with him?"

"In a sense, yes. You and Vig are my country. I will fight for my country no matter what. If this means putting my life at risk, so be it. That's how the world has gone around since time began."

"Except we are not living in the middle ages. We should know better than to simply meet force with force and sing the Star-Spangled Banner."

"A few people tried telling that to George 'Doubleyer'. Didn't help much."

"But Vig and I need you."

Graciela returned with the mains. They looked as good as ever.

"One more jug?" she asked, eyeing up the empty one on the table.

"Sure, thanks."

Graciela grinned and left them to their food.

"I can't come with you – you know that, don't you,

darling? I know I said I wasn't ever going to leave you on your own again, but I can't drag Vig around the world."

"Of course I know that. Vig is still a baby; she needs to stay at home. But I would like you to think about staying in a hotel while I'm away. The security of it is all."

"I don't think I'd be any safer in a five star hotel. I've seen enough movies to know that."

Dermot laughed. "That's Hollywood, honey! Not the real world."

They were home by two-thirty. Vig had only stirred slightly in the car on the way to Malibu, but remarkably she hadn't cried.

Scary came through the doggie flap to greet them as they entered the house. Dermot checked the alarm; everything was as he'd left it. Neela carried Vig upstairs. "I can't believe she hasn't needed changing. She's amazing."

Dermot opened the windows to let some fresh air in then wandered though to his office. The computer was in sleep mode with the white light blinking every two seconds to show it was still functioning.

Dermot sat and clicked on Entourage to access his mail. He immediately saw he'd received five new emails.

As he checked the inbox, he wondered how long it would take Van de Hoot to send the list of European dealers.

Then he froze.

The third email down under 'Today' was sent by 'The Dreamhealer.' The subject line was *'The Set-up is complete. Time to join the game. We've begun already.'*

Dermot looked at the sender's address. It was a long chain of gobbledygook letters and numbers. Just on the off chance, he hit the return key and entered some numbers at random. Within a few seconds his reply was returned to him. *Undeliverable.* He took some deep breaths, debating whether he should share the news of this email with Neela. That thought process lasted less than a few seconds. Of course he should. They were in this together – they were a team. Together they would come out the other side of their dark night. Victorious. But Nick had to be stopped. Somehow. And it seemed it would have to be with Dermot's participation – Nick was clearly insisting on that.

The 'game' was on.

19.

Hooded, Hoyle closed the door, glanced at his watch and faced Jean Ballon who was sitting on the floor with his arms wrapped protectively around his wife.

"It's time, Jean. Have you made your final decision?"

"Yes, we have," Ballon replied. "I will not help you."

At that precise moment Cecile's entire frame began to shake uncontrollably.

Hoyle walked slowly towards the couple, pulling out his auto injector.

"Then Madame Ballon. Please come to me."

She didn't move.

"Do you wish to die unconscious, or with dignity, Madame Ballon?" Hoyle knew that it was her husband, not her, that had made the decision – she was clearly panic-stricken.

"She stays with me. You will not harm her," Ballon almost shouted.

Hoyle stood over them. "This is your decision I think, Jean. Not your wife's. Am I correct?"

With the swiftest gesture he stuck Ballon with the auto injector. The surgeon's first reaction was to tense, holding yet more tightly to his wife, then his arms slackened and fell to his sides.

Hoyle held out a hand to Cecile. "Trust me, Cecile. You will be all right. Your husband will do the right thing. However, I have to show him I mean business."

Madame Ballon took his hand – she had no alternative. Every muscle in her body was pulsing.

He led her to the centre of the room where the stool stood under the noose.

"Please stand on the stool," he said, almost kindly.

She did so. What alternative did she have; her husband was unconscious and she feared the needle.

He placed the noose around her neck, pulled it tight, then turned to Ballon.

"You can hear me well. Yet you cannot move a muscle right now. In a few minutes you will regain control of your body. That is when you will have to make the choice of life or death. It will be your choice alone, not a communal one. You will be responsible. Decide now. Amputate the foot of someone you do not know? Or watch your wife dance."

As he waited for the effects of the Sux to wear off, Hoyle placed a foot against the side of the stool as if ready to kick it out from underneath her. All the while, he could see Ballon watching, powerless to do anything.

The minutes ticked by. Only the sounds of Cecile's teeth chattering broke the silence.

Then, very slowly, Ballon regained control of his muscles and began to sit up.

"So?" the Dreamhealer asked?

"So, I will do as you ask," Ballon replied, his spirit broken.

Galina Yablonskaya wasn't expecting a visit from her tormentor at this hour. She had dined, quite enjoying the food and Burgundy; served on paper plates and in a paper mug for security's sake. Her abductor normally allowed her peace and quiet until late, when he retrieved the remnants of the dinner and refreshed her toilet for the night.

"Please come with me," Hoyle requested, beckoning her with the forefinger of his right hand.

"Where am I going?"

"To another room."

"I am staying here," she replied, backing away from him, sensing danger.

"You must remember my earlier words, Mademoiselle Yablonskaya. You have no choice in the matter. You come with me and live, or argue with me and die. So do as I say. I am very serious." He took the auto injector from his pocket as an implied threat.

She looked at the needle, suddenly very scared. What could he want of her? What could be worse than death? Sexual abuse? Hardly worse than death, despite the old adage. But would he really kill her? Could she take the risk? Did she want to? She didn't even know what he had in mind?

"I will come with you," she replied in little more than a whisper.

"I'm glad. You have just saved your life. I solemnly promise – it is not my intention that you will die. Now hold out your arm. I must sedate you in case you have it in mind to become physical with me."

"I won't. That's my promise."

"A refusal to do as I wish is not an option. Hold out your arm."

There was terror in her eyes, but she eventually held it out. "You solemnly promised. God will hold you to that," she said.

Hoyle injected her. She sank to the floor of the holding cell and he crouched down and picked her up.

He carried her out, leaving the door to her room open, then walked down the corridor and opened the door to the room that had been prepared for surgery.

He entered.

The gurney, lights, and instruments were positioned as they had been before for Kafni's amputations. Ballon was standing by the side of the gurney, as before, staring up at the computer monitor above him, watching his wife trembling on the stool in another room, the noose around her neck. Despite the circumstances Ballon looked remarkably calm in his scrubs.

Hoyle laid the ballerina down and Ballon began to prepare her for surgery. He'd been told what needed to be done. Unlike Kafni, he had no idea who Galina Yablonskaya was – ballet was not Ballon's 'thing' and the ballerina was still a rising star. Had he known the magnitude of what he was about to do, he might well have baulked. As it was, he busied himself with antiseptic swabs around the ankle of her right foot.

Two hours later, all was done. Ballon was tying off the blood vessels in Galina's ankle with the most precise caution. If she was to lose a foot, at least she would suffer no undue complications. That would be his apology to this young woman.

"Make her as comfortable as you can, Jean," the Dream Healer said. I want her to feel as little pain as conceivably possible. We will continue with the pain-free regimen until the healing process kicks in."

Ballon turned to the Dream Healer. "You have absolutely no idea what you are talking about."

"Possibly not," Hoyle conceded. "The surgery, as well as all medical matters, I leave to you. We shall leave this girl here now and go visit your wife. She has been standing too long. It would be a tragedy if fatigue set in and she fell.

Ballon worked as best he could on Galina until he felt he could do no more. He was reasonably certain that she would remain unconscious for several hours, given the various narcotics Hoyle had allowed him to work with. If she awoke, the morphine drip would help dull the pain. She was strapped securely to the gurney, so there was no danger of her falling off and injuring herself further.

Locking the door to the surgery behind them, Hoyle allowed Ballon to lead the way back down the corridor to his wife's cell, placing his balaclava over his head before entering. As they came through the door, Cecile smiled through her tears and called her husband's name in a hoarse whisper.

Hoyle watched as Ballon removed the noose from his wife's neck and took her frail body in his arms.

They hugged for several minutes. He kept cooing into her ear that it was 'all right.' She continued to sob.

Hoyle held up his auto injector. "You must now return to your side of the room, Monsieur Ballon. Your wife can do as she wishes.

Ballon did as he was told, carrying Cecile with him.

Hoyle again attached Ballon to the metal ring that secured him to the wall; always ready for any sudden movement by the surgeon. There was none – Ballon was utterly exhausted.

Hoyle was content that all had gone according to plan. He knew he had more pressing matters to attend to than baby-sit the Ballons. Kafni had to be prepped for his release. Finally, he had to call Commissaire Barbier at 9 am. It was a call he was greatly looking forward to—this was proving to be an immensely satisfying 'game'.

20.

Dermot Nolan was already one hour and ten minutes into his United flight 946 198 to London via Washington D.C. and unaware of the telephone call Hoyle was about to make; one that would light the fuse of events that would to burn up the front pages the newspapers of the world. It was less than two minutes away.

In his home in Neuilly, one of the most fashionable districts of Paris, Commissaire Barbier was sweating profusely, glancing at his watch every ten seconds or so.

"What time do you make it, Gassin?" he asked, without thinking that to address a Commandant in this fashion, simply by his surname, was discourteous given the circumstances.

"Two minutes before nine, sir."

Thierry Gassin remained unfazed. He knew he had failed his boss this time. However, he was also aware that he'd been given a practically impossible task. Despite this, he'd done all that had been asked of him by this madman. He had a name. Kafni. Barbier had asked for the perpetrator's arrest, but that had been impossible given the time factor.

A further minute passed in silence, then Barbier asked again. "You are sure about the time, Thierry?"

Gassin smiled to himself but didn't allow it to show. He was not surprised to be suddenly on first name terms again with his boss—the next few minutes could be very difficult; the Commissaire clearly recognized he needed all the friends he could get.

"I would say we're seconds from our deadline."

"Good. Is every attempt being made to trace this call?"

"That goes without saying, sir."

"Are you certain we made the correct choice in awaiting the call here, as opposed to the Préfécture?"

"This is where he delivered the hand. This is where we must presume he will call."

As Barbier stared at the phone on his desk a small light on the console shone red and the phone burst into life with the volume of a fire alarm – or so it seemed to Barbier. Gassin watched him jump, equally startled, despite anticipating the call. Barbier and Gassin exchanged a glance, then Barbier's hand snaked out and grasped the receiver.

"*Oui, c'est Commissaire Barbier ici,*" the chief said.

"We shall speak in English and we shall be brief," a voice said. "Do you have a name for me?"

Again Barbier shot a glance at Gassin, who nodded back at his chief.

"Yes, I do."

"What is that name?"

"Josef Kafni."

There was an agonizingly long pause, similar to the pauses used in American game shows to make the audience sweat out whether someone has won a million dollars.

"Correct!"

Barbier's gasp of relief was almost audible – showing Gassin how much his chief had taken this case personally; he was never normally so wound up.

Barbier couldn't help himself. "So...?"

Gassin twitched imperceptibly. He hoped so much that Barbier would allow the pace to be driven by the madman, a slow one. Yet here he was endeavoring to speed up the conversation simply because he was nervous. *Damn!*

"So, you have answered my question. My congratulations. Not so much to you personally, but to the team you must have assembled."

"And...?"

Gassin winced again. *Let him speak in his own time, for Christ's sake!* Every microsecond was worth it as far as tracing the call.

"I shall keep my word and release Monsieur Kafni. After all, 'les règles de jeu'...? The rules of the game must be adhered to strictly or there is no fun to be had at all, is there Commissaire?"

Gassin made a mental note. This man was both educated and his French accent good, sounding as though he was a frequent visitor – such skills were seldom learned at school.

"You'll want to know where to pick up Kafni?"

"I do."

"Then have your people look for him at the Place des Voges in two hours."

"At eleven o'clock?"

"Correct. However, before I say goodbye today, let's discuss the second phase of my game. I need you to tell me the name of my new guest..."

Both Barbier and Gassin's stomach's tied themselves into tight knots.

"You have kidnapped someone else?" Barbier asked,

suddenly apprehensive. If this man was true to his word, they'd saved Kafni's life, yet was this psychopath simply exchanging this success for another challenge?

"Don't interrupt me, Commissaire."

"Then say what you have to say."

"I have another guest. You must tell me who he... or she... is. However, this test will be a little harder. This time you must guess which body part I shall be removing."

Barbier caught his breath – stunned. Gassin stared into space – he had never thought this case would end well. His instinct had told him that the cunning man at the end of the phone line had much more in mind than kidnapping celebrities, mutilating them and then letting them go. There would be some further terrible twist. Yet again two words flashed through his mind. Worst nightmares. *Don't let this celebrated man's worst nightmare become yours, Commissaire. Beware!* The flavor of this nightmare case was so redolent of the Nolan case. Though, as yet, he had no evidence to support his hunch, the gut feeling was there.

"I must go. I have to arrange the release of one the most celebrated pianists in the world. You have saved his life, and for that I congratulate you. Remember to play the game as well as you can. Three days this time. *Au revoir.*"

"Three days? Not a week?"

"Bite me, Commissaire! I have changed the rules to make the game even more piquant. A nice French word that; for me it sums up everything."

"Don't ring off! I have questions…"

But the line was dead. Seconds later Gassin's cell phone cheeped and he flipped it open.

"I see. Thank you."

He flipped it shut. "There was no trace, sir." How could

there have been? Barbier had blown the interview by speeding up the conversation. His chief had spoiled everything.

"Do you believe this man?"

"Do I believe he will release Kafni alive? Yes, I do. I also believe we shall soon be witnessing something quite horrific. This man was unequivocal in his words. *You must tell me which body part I shall be removing on this occasion.* There is now no escaping the likelihood that the hand was Kafni's. For a man of his stature in the world of classical music to lose a hand is most likely his..." he was tempted to say worst nightmare, but immediately decided that for now he would keep his gut feeling close to his chest. "...a death sentence in his eyes. We shall see. Meanwhile our task continues. As of this moment I would suggest we start looking for a second victim – some other celebrity who has gone missing recently."

"Have the Place des Voges flooded with personnel at once, Thierry. Meanwhile I shall assemble a team to manage the media. I anticipate the release of Kafni will be horrific."

"I imagine it will, sir," Gassin replied as he stood, though he was under no illusion that Kafni would be released anywhere near the Place des Voges. However, he now knew he had a firmer grasp of what was happening. He was psychologically closer to this man. The question was—could he catch this man within three days? Debatable. What had he said? *Les règles du jeu?* The rules of the game? Gassin knew how the line ended, and prepared himself mentally for a long campaign. *Ne sont pas juste.* They are not just. The rules of the game are not fair.

21.

By ten minutes to eleven that morning Barbier had managed to muster just under a hundred members of the elite CRS; the Gendarmes Mobiles. Their vans had been parked along the rue de Rosiers, several streets to the west of the Place des Voges –

Barbier didn't want to scare off his man by a show of force. The idea was to allow him in with his hostage, and the moment Kafni was sighted, the entire area would be locked down by the CRS. These officers knew how to keep a low profile – they were not standing at every street corner dressed in their riot gear of dark blue fatigues, padded at the shoulder, with leg guards that reached from their feet to their knees, with heads encased in helmets. No, they were out of sight and contactable only by radio. Some were in doorways, some in the back rooms of shops, some had asked permission of the proprietors of offices to temporarily station themselves on first floor landings ready at a moments notice to flood the streets.

Effectively, they could lock down the area bordered by the corner of rue des Bourgeois and rue de Serigne to the west of the Place des Voges; and the corner of the rue des Tournelles to the east at a moment's notice. A group of twenty CRS were positioned in a corner store by the rue Saint Antoine to the south.

These were hard men accustomed to expect anything. They were almost an army; their usual role to control street demonstrations.

As the riot squad awaited him with anticipation, Hoyle entered the outskirts of Paris along the Quai du Président. He had no intention of venturing anywhere near the Marais. Of course, neither Barbier nor Gassin expected him to do so – this would surely be another part of 'the game'. Cat and mouse. But what alternative did they have? If Kafni was actually released near the Place des Voges in the Marais district, and they were not ready, politicians would soon be asking for heads to fall and Barbier would shortly be out of a job.

Hoyle had sedated Kafni at half past nine, stripped him naked, and then secured him around the elbows and feet. He then carried him to the waiting Grand Espace Renault, placing him in the rear; there were no windows in this vehicle. He then drove from Auteuil to the small town of Val des Quatre Pignons, where he'd parked the van he'd stolen the previous day in the village of Les Chênes. It was a Renault holiday van somewhat similar to the Espace. Hoyle had parked it at the rear of a disused industrial estate where no prying eyes would notice the transfer of Kafni from one vehicle to the other.

Having moved the inert pianist to the newly stolen van, Hoyle was free to drive to the boulevard he'd decided was the most suitable to set Kafni free – a street where the naked, handless, pianist would attract the most attention; the rue de Rivoli, opposite the gardens of the Tuileries. This was tourist heaven! Hoyle was thrilled at the prospect of the reaction of passers by. Of course, he wouldn't have a single second to waste watching the mayhem; he had to scoot! But he felt sure that some tourist or other would capture at least part of the fun and games on a camera or cell phone.

Hoyle mentally prepared himself for the quick sequence of actions he had to perform. He'd park the van as close to the spot he'd planned to release Kafni and keep the engine running. That was step one. Step two was to crawl from the driver's seat into the back of the van and unlock the rear doors, ready to push them open. Step three was to untie the bonds securing Kafni's arms and ankles. Step four was to inject a large dose of adrenaline into the pianist. As soon as Kafni regained consciousness, it would be time for step five; kick open the rear doors of the van, and push Kafni out onto the roadway. Then he'd have to immediately jump back behind the wheel, pull into the traffic and make a right turn into the rue Cambon, where he would park and walk away from the van. There would be no trace of him anywhere – no fingerprints, no DNA. If anyone saw a man leave the van they would describe a man with long, lank, dark colored hair, a beard and mustache and baggy overalls. At the Madeleine Metro station he'd visit the toilets, stuffing the wig and overalls in a carry case. Beneath the overalls were a charcoal grey suit, white shirt and tie. Then it was simply a bus ride home to Auteuil to watch the news and enjoy the moment!

At five minutes past eleven, as the CRS were waiting for the imminent order to flood the Place des Voges, a young tourist by the name of Annalisa Bastiani was ambling down the rue de Rivoli. She was on her way to meet her fiancé at a restaurant in the Place de l'Hôtel de Ville.

She was still a good way from her destination when she noticed a white Renault van draw up at the curb. The only reason she paid attention to it was that she'd always thought it'd be cute to have one just like it in Naples, where she lived. Perfect for camping holidays.

As she walked on past the van on the other side of the street she heard a scream and her head whipped around, searching for danger. At that precise moment she noticed a man fall from the back of the van to the roadway and stumble about. Then the van accelerated away into the traffic.

At first she thought that someone might have been knocked down by the van. But wait! The figure was naked!

Jesus Christ! What the fuck's going on here!

She hardly had time to collect her thoughts when the naked man started running down the rue de Rivoli, weaving in and out of the traffic, screaming as though his lungs would burst.

Within seconds cars were swerving to avoid the naked madman, colliding with each other, slewing into the oncoming lanes. Pedestrians on either side of the street, caught up in the havoc, were running for their lives, not knowing what was happening, fearing a terrorist attack of some kind.

Annalisa froze.

Run!

As random thoughts scudded through her brain she noticed the naked man was now running in her direction; now only a matter of twenty yards away. It was only then that the full horror of what was happening became crystal clear.

The naked man had no hands. Just stumps.

"Me tuer maintenant! Toute suite. Mon, Dieu. Me tuer!!!"

Nicole's French wasn't exactly perfect, yet she knew exactly what this man was shouting. Kill me now! Oh God! Kill me!"

The naked man was running in ever-shorter circles in the middle of the road, waving his arms like windmills and screaming hysterically.

Within minutes Commissaire Barbier's wife rapped hard on the door of her husband's office and, without waiting to be asked inside, opened the door. Barbier and Gassin looked up. Her face was ashen. At precisely the same time, the phone on Barbier's desk rang.

"Forgive me, Jules," Barbier's wife said, "but you must see what's happening. It's on television. It's Kafni."

Barbier lifted the phone and listened, his expression grave.

"I see. Thank you."

That was all Commissaire Barbier said during the two minutes it took to drink in the horrific details of what had happened.

Unlike his American and the English counterparts, French Police Chiefs don't consider it *de riguer* to have a television console playing twenty-four hours a day in their office. On this day, Barbier wished he had; making a mental note to change matters in his office in the Quai des Orfèvres.

"Let's go into the drawing room," Barbier said, trying hard not to scream with anger and frustration.

Gassin attempted a calm tone. "We knew he would never release Kafni in the Place des Voges, sir. The ball was always in his court."

"I am aware of that, Thierry. It doesn't make it any easier, though. It's what people expect of us that's all-important.

Today, they witnessed something that no one should ever witness anywhere – let alone in the centre of Paris."

The television was already playing as Barbier and Gassin walked in to join Barbier's wife. She had one hand over her mouth, her face a mask of horror. There were CRS officers everywhere attempting to control the crowds, many of whom still thought they'd been caught up in a terrorist event. In the background of the shot, an ambulance had its rear doors open revealing a man lying on a stretcher, his body covered by blankets.

"Thierry. If this is some kind of a 'game', we did not 'warm up' sufficiently well. But I tell you one thing candidly; if we are obliged to play this man's game to a conclusion – we will win."

PLAY

22.

Dermot switched on his cell phone as he deplaned in Paris. There already was a text message from Neela – *Call me. Urgent. Neels. XXX.'* As he waited in the passport control line he made the call.

"Darling!"

"Is there a problem?"

"Not with me or Vig. Bad news, nevertheless. I wanted you to hear it from me before you see it on the television or read about it."

"What news?" Dermot cut in.

"Josef Kafni. The most terrible thing has happened to him."

Dermot's blood ran cold. During the interview he'd conducted with the young pianist, he'd come to like the man greatly. He was charming, eloquent and modest. He lived with his wife in Aix-en-Provence and there was not a bad bone in his body. It had been difficult not to hug the man when he bade him farewell.

"He was kidnapped," she paused. "I don't know how I can say this. Someone amputated both his hands."

Dermot let out an involuntary gasp so loud that the other people waiting in the immigration line turned sharply to look at him. Then he sank to his knees and covered his face with his hands. He couldn't speak. Tears streamed down his cheeks. The man behind him reached a supportive hand towards Dermot and touched his shoulder.

"Are you okay? Can I help you?" he asked gently.

Airport security personnel were already on their way towards him, knowing something was very amiss.

He pushed the cell phone back to his ear. "Jesus, Neels. Jesus," was all he could manage.

"Hang tough, honey! Please. This is not about you and us. It's a terrible thing, but it is not about us! It's your dear friend."

Two security guys were standing by him now, a paramedic crouching at Dermot's side, trying to hold his hand so he could check the pulse. A member of the Department of Immigration was standing to his left, solicitous.

"Yes, it is. I know it is, darling. I see the hand of that monster at work..."

"Hey!" Neela almost shouted. "There's absolutely no logical reason to jump to *any* such conclusion. Please, Dermot! Try to pull yourself together. I need you to be rational, not emotional."

"'Pinnacles'! My interview! That's why Josef was targeted!"

Dermot was aware that an Immigration officer was speaking to him, but the words were a blur of noise.

"Oh, Dermot," Neela continued. "Please try to think coherently. This isn't about *you*. This is about *Josef*. Some madman kidnapped him and did terrible things to him, yet you immediately think it's Nick Hoyle, jumping to an insane conclusion that it's some kind of a vendetta he's waging against you. You have to think logically. If someone had shot Josef in Jerusalem would you still believe it had been done to send a message to you?"

"Are you able to stand, sir?" a paramedic asked. Dermot nodded.

"I'll call you when I get to the hotel, darling."

Dermot clicked the cell phone off and waved the medic and security away. "Sorry, guys. I'm fine. I just received some very shocking news from home. You know how it is?"

"Of course, sir. I understand" the medic replied. "Are you sure you don't require any assistance?"

"Thanks so much. I'm fine."

Dermot was in a state of torment as he sat in the back of the taxi that carried him from Charles de Gaulle airport to his hotel in the rue des Beaux Arts in the Latin Quarter. Was it conceivable that he was the cause of the mutilation inflicted on that wonderful man? Much as he would have liked to go along with Neela's logic, there was a deep-seated belief that the events of that morning had their seeds in Nick's determination to drive him mad. Should he go to the police and voice his fears? Would they take him seriously? Bearing his past in mind, they most likely wouldn't, preferring to believe him to be psychologically damaged goods. He could show them the email he'd received from the Dreamhealer. But there again, that could have been anyone.

By the time he arrived at l'Hôtel he knew he would have to talk to someone at the Préfécture. The question was, with whom?

L'Hôtel had always been his favorite. Where others who could afford it went to the Crillion and the Meurice, Dermot considered l'Hôtel a no-brainer. It was the discreet yet deliciously decadent décor that appealed to him, together with the works of art by Jean Cocteau. The wonderfully lavish rich fabrics in the individually decorated double rooms, together with the original works of art in all rooms and the very indulgent bathrooms. When he'd been on his European tour promoting the book that, in many ways he wished he'd never written, *Worst Nightmares*, he'd been introduced to the hotel that had once been a home away from home to Oscar Wilde. He'd never looked back.

However, the luxury and beauty of the hotel were far from his thoughts when he arrived. He was welcomed by the same staff who had made his previous stay as wonderful as it had been, and within a few minutes, though he'd booked the smaller Mignon room, to save funds now that times had become somewhat harder. Without asking, he'd been courteously upgraded to the Penthouse suite with views over the courtyard rooftops all the way to the church of Saint Germain.

He immediately called room service for a bottle of Bourbon. Switching to CNN on the plasma screen, he debated whom he might call at the Paris police headquarters. The screen was still full of images of the morning mayhem in the rue de Rivoli. He stared in horror, watching the ambulance in the background that was taking his friend Josef to hospital.

There was a discreet knock on the door. Dermot called to the waiter to enter and he did, carrying a bottle of Kentucky Bourbon, an ice bucket and a chilled glass. He thanked the man and slipped him ten Euros.

When he'd helped himself to a generous measure of bourbon and had swallowed half of it, he lifted the receiver of the bedside phone and asked the operator downstairs to connect him with someone at the Préfécture – it didn't matter who. The operator did so without comment.

A few moments later he'd been connected. A man was identifying himself, asking how he could help the caller.

"My name is Dermot Nolan and I may have information regarding the terrible events of this morning. Would it be possible to speak to someone in charge? A detective, maybe?"

"Will you please hold one moment, Monsieur Nolan, I shall connect you with someone who will be able to help you. Please stay on the line."

Some moments passed. Then a different voice was speaking. It was Lieutenant Franc Migget. "Mr. Nolan? Good afternoon. My name is Lieutenant Migget. I am told you may have information concerning the kidnapping of Josef Kafni? Is that right?"

"Possibly. I am not sure."

"Not sure? Perhaps you can tell us then why you have called me? Any information is useful."

"I am a writer, Monsieur Migget. Several months ago I conducted an interview with Josef Kafni for a series of articles I was wrote for the New Yorker magazine, titled 'Pinnacles'. A series of articles concerning artists who had reached the pinnacle of their careers at a relatively young age."

"Yes?" Migget said encouragingly.

"I wonder if you are aware my recent history? The book, *Worst Nightmares?* My trial? I was completely exonerated."

Migget was confused about who Nolan was. "Perhaps you could give me the barest bones?"

"I was falsely accused of a series of murders. I had

written a novel, you see, based on them..."

Migget's memory banks ran hot. "Of course! Monsieur Nolan. I remember now. My apologies."

"Well, I was wondering whether there was any way..." He broke off.

"Any way that...?" Migget prompted.

"That I might come to visit you this afternoon? What I have to discuss is better said face-to-face. A senior detective in Los Angeles by the name of Hansen gave me a name to call in Paris should I need assistance. Lieutenant Santal. I believe he works out of the Paris Préfécture?"

"I am familiar with the name. I shall contact him. In the meantime perhaps you might come to see us?"

"Where shall I come?"

"Come to our office at the Quai des Orfèvres. Number 36. Give my name at the entrance. Lieutenant Franc Migget. Say that you are there to provide information. Mention the name, Commandant Gassin – he's heading up the investigation."

"I shall be with you within the hour, Franc."

"My thanks for your time, sir. I shall alert the desk to expect you."

Having booked a cab, Dermot refilled his glass and took it through to the bathroom where he had a long shower.

23.

As Dermot showered, Detective Sergeant Jim Hansen was fielding a call from Paris. At first he'd thought it was Nolan; he'd who'd informed him of his decision to visit Paris to check out art dealers who might have information concerning any sightings of Nick Hoyle. At the time, he'd cautioned Nolan to be as careful as he possibly could; to keep a low profile and to liaise with the Paris cops, offering his name as a contact at the LAPD. However, when he picked up his phone the switchboard operator at North Hollywood informed him it was a call from that legendary building he'd seen in that French crime movie '36 Quai des Orphèvres'. He'd loved the film; the depiction of French cops was of hard, clever and thoughtful police officers. He especially liked Depardieu's character – the complete antithesis of such men; mean-spirited, cruel and arrogant.

"Detective Sergeant Hansen speaking. Who's this?" Hansen asked.

"My name is Commandant Jules Gassin of the Préfécture of Police in Paris. I believe you know a man by the name of Dermot Nolan."

"That's right, sir. Did he take my advice and call you?"

"One of my detectives received a call from Mr. Nolan just now. He said you had given the name of a contact here should he need any assistance. Lieutenant Santal?"

"That's right. Nolan came to see me yesterday. Are you familiar with his notoriety? The serial murder case? The book, *Worst Nightmares*?"

"I am. It's about that I'm calling you."

Hansen was intrigued. "Go on."

"Let me be understand this clearly, Detective Hansen. Mr. Nolan traveled to Paris as a tourist? To holiday? Or do you believe his visit to France is in any way associated with the worldwide search for the man who abducted him, placing him in a coffin?"

"Yes. That's why he's with you in Paris. He decided to be a bit more pro-active."

"Was there some catalyst that prompted his trip?"

"Any what, sir?" Hansen was unfamiliar with the word.

"Some act that might have triggered something in his mind concerning Mr. Hoyle?"

"Yes, as a matter of fact, there was a…catalyst, Commandant Gassin. He told me about it yesterday. He said that he'd seen a kid near his home in Malibu, California. The kid was dressed to mimic how the bad guy in the *Worst Nightmares* book looked. You know, orange hair. He thought it was the man who'd put him in the ground had surfaced somewhere."

"I see."

"Did you read the book, Commandant? It's strong stuff. All based on the real deal."

"I did. At the time, in some ways I found it irresponsible."

"How so, sir?"

"I thought it might give some unbalanced people bad ideas. I admit it was clever, but a don't care for thrillers that show how easy it is to pick locks, make bombs, and so forth. Did this child with the orange wig *say* anything to Mr. Nolan?"

"He did."

"What exactly?"

"He called him by his name. '*Dermot*'. Then he said, '*Game on.*' Then later he said, '*Catch me if you can.*' Nolan saw it as a personal challenge."

"I see," Gassin replied. To his way of thinking that's exactly what it was. A challenge. Matched to the words of the note sent to Barbier, there was little doubt in his mind now about a correlation. However, he had no wish at this stage to feed any particular information directly to the LAPD until he had a way to filter it, as well as direct investigations his own way.

"Mr. Nolan is staying at l'Hôtel."

"Is he? He didn't tell me. I can give you his cell phone number."

"We have that already. But thank you."

"While I am speaking to you, commandant, can I ask you something? Have there been any sightings of Hoyle in France during the past few months? Interpol assures me there haven't been any, but you might know things they don't."

"None, I am afraid. However, Mr. Nolan is on his way to my office at this moment. I shall keep you advised of any developments, Detective Hansen. My thanks for your time and trouble."

"My pleasure, Commandant. If there's any way we at the LAPD can help you with your enquiries, feel free to contact me personally."

"I will, *Detectif.*"

Hansen smiled as he put down the phone. Almost immediately the door opened and de Groot entered.

"Zut! Just fielded a call from gay Paree, Chick! I am *Detectif* Hansen, no less!" he said in a thick ham French accent.

"Good grief," de Groot murmured as he sat at his desk and began flipping through some evidence sheets.

24.

Hoyle hit the Back button yet again, then the Play button. He'd been laughing so hard tears were pouring down his face.

He'd made it home without incident, picking up the Renault Espace that he'd left parked in the town of Val des Quatre Pignons. Now he was back in his big country kitchen with a *vin blanc*, watching the midday news that he'd recorded previously.

He'd caused the most amazing incident. Much bigger than he could ever have imagined. In truth he really should have expected it. After all, Kafni was world famous, as well as being French. He'd been released naked in one of the smartest and busiest streets in the world, and the pianist had done him the enormous favor of screaming his head off, begging any and everyone to put an end to his misery and kill him.

Hoyle was quietly confident that given time Kafni would change his mind and be content to live out his years in obscurity – it never ceased to surprise him how people clung to life, no matter what. It was a pity that he, Hoyle, would never be able to listen to another of Kafni's concerts, but hey, there were other pianists around – what was the name of that wonderful Greek pianist? Dino Mastryiannis! And what about that Jamaican, Orrett Rhoden? It only went to show that celebrated pianists didn't *all* come from Israel, France, England or Germany.

The real question was would Nolan take the bait? Hoyle was quietly confident that he would. It was in Dermot's nature to rise to a challenge, and there was also the element of *'if I ignore the man and don't go looking for him, it is only a matter of time before he comes looking for me, Neela or my daughter.'* That would be sound thinking, as he would most certainly come looking for the family if Dermot didn't respond to his challenge.

The next thing to consider was how much closer the French police had come to identifying him and his location. It was thinking such as this that had always kept him one step ahead of the authorities. Many serial killers imagined they were invincible, yet very few ended up that way. Why? Because they weren't prepared to 'up sticks and start afresh' when they knew the chances were that they were being directly threatened.

He idly wondered about the caliber of the man who was leading the investigation into the grievous body harm to Kafni. Was he to be reckoned with? There hadn't yet been any official media statement by the police about the incident, but there'd have to be one soon – the episode had caused a worldwide furor. He'd Googled newspapers all over the world – it had made AP, Reters, CNN, BBC World in Europe, America, Japan and Australia. The world wanted action! *Find this monster* London's ITV screamed! There would have to be a strong statement by the Préfécture by the time the evening news came around; he'd be sure to watch and judge the intellectual acumen of the French police chief heading up the team for Commissaire Barbier.

For now he felt safe in his house in Auteuil. They'd most probably guess that Ballon was involved. It stood to reason. But with the amputation of Galina's foot, he'd fulfilled his usefulness. To use him yet again would be pushing the boundaries of luck, even if the surgeon agreed to continue to chop away. It was probably a better idea to change the rules of the game – who said he had to carry on doing the same old thing? That would be so obvious. Keep 'em guessing, that was the way to go.

He looked at his watch; there was an hour to wait for the evening news. Now was the time to freshen the toilets and inform Ballon that his wife would soon be freed. It was probably a good idea to lead Jean to believe that he had changed his mind, and they would both be freed. That might keep him calmer.

Yet before he and Ballon visited Galina in her storage room to check on her recovery, it was perhaps a good time to decide on a menu for the houseguests' evening meal.

Opening the big fridge, Hoyle debated between *Navarin*, a traditional French stew made with root vegetables, or the *Coq au Vin*. The latter was always popular. Suddenly he was unsure whether or not the ballerina was a vegetarian, then he recalled she ate chicken but no red meat. Coq au Vin it was then! With a side dish of *Salade Niçoise*.

He lifted out enough for four people, deciding he also would have it for his own TV dinner.

Having organized the trays, complete with paper cups for the wine – today he was offering a delicious chilled Sancerre – he checked he had his auto injector and made his way down the steps that led from the kitchen to the corridor off which were the various storage rooms.

He knocked sharply on the door of the storage room in which the Ballons were incarcerated, calling out loudly to Cecile. "Please stand away from the door. It is for your own safety. I will not repeat myself, Madame Ballon."

He waited several seconds then placed the key in the lock and turned it, swinging he door open. Very sensibly, Madame Ballon was sitting on her camp bed, her knees up to her chin, hugging her blankets. Despite the chemicals in the portable toilet, the stench in the room was overpowering. Hoyle didn't say anything for fear of embarrassing the couple – at heart he thought himself a decent man and this was the decent thing to do. His hood helped to mask the smell.

"Tonight we dine on *Coq au Vin* and salad. I shall be serving a splendid, yet non-vintage, Sancerre.'

There was no reaction whatsoever from the Ballons. Hoyle was disappointed – such ingratitude.

"But to more important matters. I have decided on when I shall release you." He was looking at Madame Ballon at the time, so her husband could hardly quibble with him when, sometime down the line, he found he was destined to die. "You will be released in a matter of a few days. This must come as an enormous relief to you both, I feel sure. You have done well and have both been towers of strength. I congratulate you. It only goes to show that attempting something as rash as trying to attack me would have been very counter-productive."

He then walked over to Ballon. "And further good news, Jean. I shall not be asking you to conduct any further surgery. All I require is that you use your skills to ensure that Madame

Yablonskaya recovers well; well enough to be released – albeit without one foot – at the same time as you both."

There was no reaction from either of the Ballons. Hoyle spread his arms wide and smiled. "Come *on*, my friends. Are we not happy? It could all have ended so very badly. Kafni lived! The ever-so-sweet Galina will live too, and you all will be released in such a short space of time. Where is your gratitude?"

Cecile did her utmost to work a smile. Jean Ballon refused to play the game.

Hoyle clapped his hands. "So, first I shall attend to the necessary ablutions. Then I shall return, when you," he said, directing his attention to Jean, "Monsieur Ballon, will come with me and make sure that our ballerina is as comfortable as possible, and able to wine and dine. Okay?"

Neither said a word. Clearly both knew they were dealing with a lunatic.

Hoyle walked to the portable toilet and picked it up. Clearly one of the two had a tummy problem. No matter. He turned and left the room, locking the door behind him.

25.

Migget saw Dermot step out of the cab outside the entrance to number 36. Immediately a crowd of journalists crowded around him, suspecting he might be 'someone'. At first unsure who he was, they soon became almost hysterical when they recognized him as the man that had graced the front pages of almost every newspaper worldwide during the *Worst Nightmares Serial Murder Trial*. For Dermot it was like a déjà vu – those terrible weeks when he was on trial for Hoyle's murders, and the world thought *he* was the monster.

Dermot struggled to move forward, journalists holding

out microphones in his way, calling out questions, asking whether his presence in Paris had anything to do with the kidnapping and mutilation of Josef Kafni.

Migget strode forward and parted a passage for Dermot to the entrance of the building where two gendarmes were standing guard.

"Monsieur Nolan! Lieutenant Migget, from the Commissaire's office. Please come with me."

Dermot looked relieved as he shook Migget's hand and continued pressing through he media crowd.

Migget had taken the trouble to look at all available photos of Nolan taken before and during his trial so that he could recognize him easily, yet he was still shocked by the writer's current appearance. He was gaunt, if not haggard, and his hair was graying visibly.

"My name is Lieutenant Migget," the lieutenant repeated as they passed through the entrance and into the building. "We spoke on the phone."

Migget directed Nolan down a corridor towards the elevators. "Please, come with me. Excuse the crush. I am sure the press are as bad where you live."

It was silly small talk, but what else could the he say?

"They are bottom feeders the world over, Lieutenant," Dermot replied, "but they have a job to do. I'm not here to have fun, but having said that, I always love being in Paris. It's like a second home to me."

"I am glad to hear that. I would live nowhere else, myself."

There was a ping and the elevator doors opened. Stepping inside, Migget pressed a button, the doors closed, and the lift began moving upwards.

"I have taken the liberty of asking all our team to be

present this morning, so they can listen to what you have to say. Our boss will be there of course; he's a brilliant man named Gassin. Commandant Gassin. Smart as a whip. Isn't that how American might put it?"

Nolan smiled, this Lieutenant was charming and so very young.

"Our boss is head of the La Bac in the sixième, temporarily seconded to the case we are currently investigating. You will like him, I feel sure."

Nolan nodded as the elevator stopped and the doors opened.

"Please follow me, Mr. Nolan."

Migget walked down the corridor and Nolan followed. They were up at the top level of the building. Migget opened the final door on the right of the corridor and waved Dermot through.

It was a big conference room. Seated at the table were five people – four men, and a woman who had some piece of equipment in front of her which Nolan presumed to be either a recording device or a machine to take shorthand.

All but the woman rose as they entered. Migget closed the door.

"Good morning, Mr. Nolan," Commissaire Barbier said, smiling warmly, "May I introduce my team?"

Dermot glanced at them, one by one.

"Commandant Thierry Gassin is naturally on my right; he is my right hand." Barbier gave a nervous short laugh. "Lieutenants Antoine Becaux and Gideon Simon are on my left. You have already exchanged pleasantries with Lieutenant Franc Migget?"

"I have, yes."

"Let us sit and talk, then. We have much to discuss."

26.

Having checked all Galina's vital signs, Ballon inspected his handiwork at her ankle in minute detail. At any other time, he would have been justly proud of his work, but this day his stomach turned over even thinking about what he'd done to such a lovely girl. It was heart-wrenching.

When he felt there was no more he could do to make the site of the amputation any more sterile, he looked at Galina's face and studied her features. She was still unconscious.

She was very beautiful; her skin like alabaster. Not a single blemish. Her eyelids were fluttering. He judged she was still in a REM sleep, probably dreaming of something pleasurable, judging by the upturn of each side of her lips. The morphine was taking care of the pain and the narcotics were keeping her under.

He shuddered; when she awoke and saw what had been done to her, she'd freak. And all the time he'd been attending to the young girl, the monster standing at the other side of the gurney had looked totally relaxed, as though visiting a niece who was about to wake from an operation to remove her tonsils. It was deeply disturbing.

"How long can we allow her to remain unconscious?" Hoyle asked.

"My advice would be to leave her be for as long as her vital signs remain normal. You know how to read this monitor?" Ballon asked, pointing at the Holter monitor. It was an ambulatory electrocardiography device Hoyle had ordered online the moment Dermot had been discovered underground, and he'd been forced to activate Plan B. It was totally portable and the best of it's kind, short of hospital quality. It monitored the electrical activity of the heart, observing any cardiac arrhythmias. Hoyle knew the best equipment was a must – Kafni could well have had a heart attack when he'd seen his stumps for the first time.

As they returned to Ballons' storage cell, Jean couldn't help asking the questions that had bothered him for so many days.

"Why are you doing these terrible things? You must have some idea of the excruciating pain, suffering, and loss you have inflicted on both these people? There can be no justification."

"Certainly not in *your* book, Jean," Hoyle replied, as a Professor might lightly respond to a reasonable question asked by a student in college. "But you fail to see the broader picture."

"I do?"

"Yes, I am afraid you do. Consider this. You think what I have done is reprehensible, and in some respects you may be right. Of course it's a shame to amputate perfectly sound body parts. But occasionally needs must, in order to make a statement. Think of the world stage, for instance. Take the Middle East. For the greater good and safety of its citizens, the Israelis invaded Gaza last year. Why? Because the Palestinians were sending rockets willy-nilly into Israel, killing innocents there. So they Israelis felt they had to react – to make a statement, if you will. Over a thousand Palestinians were killed. War correspondents reported that around one thousand Palestinians were killed, a third of whom were children. The Israelis maintain that that Hamas was using civilians as shields. Using mosques as safe havens. Hamas denies this. Either way, it seems that both sides were prepared to take the risk of killing innocent children because they believed it was worth it, in the long run. Life is a commodity in the Middle East. Both sides knew innocents would die, yet they continued with their battle plans."

"But..."

"No! Allow me just one more example. In certain African

countries, the revolutionary militia cut the hands and feet off children who refuse to join their cause. Why? Because they are anesthetized to pain and suffering. They no longer consider mutilation a moral issue. Quite possibly they never did – such carnage is part of millions of young Africans every day life since birth.

"You think that what you are engaged in is in any way related to such international brutality?"

"I am simply demonstrating to you that people who are isolated from the moral values of the civilized world, living in a space where these count for little, are no longer disturbed nor moved by violence. I have become such a human being. I have come to terms with this. I was once different. Then I was introduced to the concept of 'the greater good.' In my case it was by Uncle Sam. To defend my country, I had to be prepared to kill at random, and that's exactly what I did. I seem to remember I initially found the killings disturbing. I don't care what people say; when you're in an intense firefight you don't have the time to check for women and children in the firing line. Eventually I had no moral qualms about pulling the trigger and watching bodies explode in front of me. It was part of day-to-day life over there. You see? Circumstance, the exigencies of my country's safety, and sheer serendipity has made me the man I am; one removed from any sense of morality.'

Ballon stared at the man with just a hint of sadness. "You are an intelligent man. Perhaps you're not a madman, after all. However, you should reflect on what you've done and consider the suffering you've caused others. Never repeat these acts, I beg you."

Nick stared off, he was in his private world of mental turmoil – he had steeled himself to live in a world without compassion or mercy, yet he was oddly moved by this surgeon. He'd become as close to considering Jean Ballon a friend as anyone since Giselle had died. A part of him was regretting the fact that he'd soon have to kill him.

He looked deep into Ballon's eyes searching for the truth.

"Have you any idea who I am?"

Ballon looked surprised. "Should I? Are you famous?"

Hoyle smiled. An interesting reply.

"Not especially, no," Hoyle replied. Was he telling the truth? Did he really not know who he was? Could he possibly allow his new friend to live? No. Despite his feelings of kinship with Jean, he knew all his plans would go up in smoke if he misjudged Ballon's response. He simply couldn't take the risk.

"Shall we go inside?" Ballon asked as he reached the door to his cell.

Nick snapped out of his reverie. "Yes, of course. Please stand to one side."

27.

"If I may, Monsieur Le Commissaire?" Gassin said, giving Barbier a deferential glance. Barbier smiled and nodded.

"*Alors*. I was greatly intrigued to hear the news from Detective Sergeant Hansen about the recent events in Malibu. It was quite a coincidence that as you were being confronted by the boy with the orange wig, I was considering the relevance of two words '*worst nightmares*'; two words included in a letter delivered just over a week ago to the home of Commissaire Barbier. Then, today, you contact us, seeking assistance."

"I suppose you could say I couldn't stand waiting around any more for the second shoe to fall."

"I can understand," Gassin continued. "You have waited so long, yet still Hoyle remains at large."

"I can never be secure in the knowledge that my family is safe while Nick Hoyle is free to roam the world."

"Of course." Barbier looked down at some notes he had made. "You are sure the boy you chanced upon was not simply a prankster?"

"I am, yes."

"May I ask your reasoning?"

"The symbolism of wig, it goes without saying. Then the words, *Catch me if you can;* they are the exact words used by the man we have come to know as 'Arnold'."

"It could be said that knowledge of the color of the wig as well as the words are common knowledge to anyone who's read your book *'Worst Nightmares.'*"

The tick over Nolan's right eye twitched in annoyance. This was exactly what Neela had thought, yet he'd hoped these French detectives would, unlike her, take him more seriously.

"The boy was one thing. The email I received was something altogether different."

"The email?" Gassin enquired.

"It was sent by a man calling himself 'The Dreamhealer.' The subject line was *'The Set-up is complete. Time to join the game. We've begun already.'*"

"The address?"

"It was a miss-mash of numbers and letters. I tried to reply but was told it was undeliverable."

"Did you make a note of the address, for what it's worth?"

"I did," Dermot replied, writing it down on a notepad and pushing it over to Gassin, who in turn pushed it to

Migget.

"Don't you ever get what Americans call a 'gut feeling' Monsieur Gassin?" Dermot asked stonily. Barbier glanced imperceptibly at Gassin – that was indeed what the Commandant was famed for.

"Yes, I do, Mr. Nolan. However, it is my duty first to think all things through logically."

"Of course," Dermot replied, attempting a smile. It ended up a twitch of the lips. "May I ask what words did the author of the note to Commissaire Barbier use?"

"Of course. The full text was *Don't let this celebrated man's worst nightmare become yours, Commissaire. Beware.*"

Dermot said nothing for a few seconds. The Frenchmen opposite all studied his reaction.

"This sentence makes my flesh crawl."

"May I ask how exactly – at the risk of seeming a fool?"

"You may, of course, Commandant. When I first read the now famous 'Diary', the words had a similar literary flavor. Call it a 'voice' if you will. As an author, I feel I can recognize such literary signatures. *My intent was to bring suffering to others, equal in measure to that which I have endured. For through suffering cometh salvation. No one can ever know true sorrow without suffering true loss.* That's an example of the words used by Hoyle. Through Arnold, of course. These new words have the same signature."

"You know the words you just quoted by heart?"

"I do. They are burned into my brain."

Migget studied Nolan more carefully. The man was extremely twitchy. The tick at his eye interested him. Was it possible that this man, who's history of mental disorders he had carefully researched earlier in the morning after he'd taken the call from Nolan, was *still* mentally unstable? Was he still in the throes of some psychosis, or was he simply desperately frightened by the possible reappearance of his tormentor?

"I believe the orange wig the boy wore went missing?" Gassin continued.

"Yes, I am afraid so. Someone on the beach must have picked it up."

Are you imagining the entire incident, Migget pondered? Hansen had told them that no one had witnessed the event, and without the wig there was no tangible proof. It was still possible that Nolan experienced what psychologists referred to as an 'episode.'

"So, Mr. Nolan, you have come to Paris to try to flush out your nemesis?" Gassin asked.

"It's a long shot, I know." It sounded so ridiculous.

"It most certainly is. Mr. Hoyle could be anywhere in Europe, if not the world. He could be in Africa for all we know. At present I have no evidence to place Hoyle even in Paris, let alone France. I simply have my deductive processes to go on, and I happen to feel that the coincidences linking the events here and in Malibu are worthy of more than general interest." He paused. "Now, I'd like to throw the debate open to anyone who has questions, Mr. Nolan. If that is agreeable to you, of course. In this way, we may be able to think laterally even further."

For the best part of an hour each of the French lieutenants grilled Dermot. They delved into the past, asking him to relate every conceivable detail of the words spoken by the man they knew as 'Arnold'; how Hoyle had reacted at the time, and how Dermot now viewed Hoyle's mental state. They asked whether or not Hoyle had ever spoken of any further retribution he might take, should Dermot survive.

"It is always possible, it goes without saying," Gassin

said, "that the kidnapping of Josef Kafni is unconnected with the reappearance of Nick Hoyle. Nevertheless, it *is* a possibility. We shall see. You are aware of the incident?"

"I heard of it only a few hours ago. My wife phoned me from California."

"It was the most inhumane act I have ever come across, or could imagine, short of ethnic cleansing," Barbier added. "Though the threads of suspicion are very slender at present, each time I consider this outrage I keep coming back to those two words *Worst Nightmares*. Everything seems to point to Mr. Hoyle. An hour ago I was appalled by the barbarity of the man who kidnapped Kafni, and those very words were on my lips yet again. For surely the loss of his hands must have been Monsieur Kafni's worst nightmare. Then one must add to this barbarous aspect the time and thought that must have gone into his release. It was as if the whole episode was simply calculated to shock in the most terrible way. Like an act of terrorism – for that is what it was. Why else release the man in the center of Paris on a busy street, naked? It's mind-blowing in its ferocity."

"How is he?" Dermot asked.

"In a hospital for now. Not so much for his physical condition but the psychological damage."

No one said anything for a few moments; all had images of the most gifted pianist of their generation waking to find his hands had been amputated.

"He's a lovely man," Dermot said eventually. "We met a couple of months ago in Los Angeles. He was playing at the Performing Arts Center of Los Angeles."

Gassin's interest was immediately piqued. "So you knew him well? It wasn't simply a stage door meeting, via friends?"

"I'd been asked to do a series of articles on celebrated artists by the New York. Called '*Pinnacles*.' The first four interviews have been published already. Josef's was the first."

"This was only months ago?" Barbier asked.

"Thereabouts, yes," Dermot replied. "That's why I feel physically ill to think of what's just occurred. Josef was so young, vibrant; the best of the best. And such a modest man. When we—"

But Gassin was firing on all cylinders now, his pupils dilated and the adrenaline pumping fast through his veins.

"Excuse me for interrupting you. Mr. Nolan. I have to ask this question. Who was the subject of your second interview?"

"A ballerina. Galina Yablonskaya. If you haven't heard of her yet, you will very shortly. She's every bit as superb as Margot Fonteyn was in her day. The critics are unanimous – she will be one of the finest prima ballerinas that ever lived. A Russian emigrée, she's now living in France."

Dermot was shocked and surprised by the expressions on all the faces opposite him. No one spoke. It was a weird moment.

"What is it?" he asked.

Gassin looked down as he searched for the right words.

"We have, of course, been investigating for many days now. Whoever sent the hand to Commissaire Barbier spoke also of 'celebrities.' It was clear he was targeting such people. So of course one of the first things we considered was whether any celebrated Parisian – it seemed logical to initially concentrate on the smaller picture – had gone missing; disappeared for no apparent reason. This man's game, you see, was to test the Préfécture. With Josef Kafni, he gave us seven days to come up with a name that matched the hand he sent us, like some kind of a trophy."

Dermot could hardly believe what he was hearing. His jaw slackened in horror.

Barbier carried on the story. "Commandant Gassin and his team reacted magnificently. At the end of the week we were able to tell this monster whom the hand belonged. Otherwise, his threat had been presumably to kill his hostage."

Gassin took over. "But the game was not over for our devious friend. We had thought he might release Kafni if we guessed correctly. We never considered the possibility that he might commit such an outrage as to amputate *both* his hands. Now, we have been told to look for another celebrity." He paused to let the words sink in.

"Jesus Christ..." Dermot stared off as the implications of what Gassin was saying sank in. "Galina...?"

"The fact is, Mr. Nolan, currently no one knows her whereabouts. She's vanished. We'll need to know the names of all those who you interviewed for your *'Pinnacles'* articles. There seems to be a pattern emerging here."

"Let's hope not. That would be incredibly savage."

"We live in a savage world, Monsieur Nolan," Gassin replied softly.

28.

Massimo Calogero was taking the mule he'd bought just two days earlier for a spin, in much the same way as affluent Americans take a new car for its first run on the highway. He'd been without an animal to draw his cart for two years, since his treasured donkey 'Anna' had died. It was a perfect day, if a little chilly. The waters of the Mediterranean lay to his right, and the road from Aspra to Ficarazzi was almost empty of vehicles. Desolate. Just the way he liked it.

He wondered how his new friend was doing. Where was he, he wondered? Most probably up to no good somewhere. He chuckled.

Massimo knew the rules; he was one of a generation of

Sicilians brought up under the comforting umbrella of the Mafia, respecting the concept of *omertà*. He was a man of his word. He thought of himself as an honorable man. A promise was a promise; a deal a deal. More importantly he knew it served his own purpose. Besides, he considered himself a good judge of character, and he guessed the man who had sought him out only three weeks ago was a man not to be crossed. Though friendly, he had made it very clear that should Massimo not keep his side of the bargain, he would return and take from him both his new mule and his life. Massimo believed him – there was something in his eyes; a quiet determination that he'd seen before as a child in the eyes of Sicilian men who were equally self-assured.

The day he'd come across this man had been a depressing one. Massimo had been seated outside his small home in Aspra Callesino, feeling a sense of despair. He was over seventy, and since Anna, his mule, had passed away he had no means of getting around. He had to rely on the kindness of strangers to buy food for him in Ficarrazi; and there weren't too many kind strangers around who liked him. Why? He had only himself to blame – he was a Mafia man through and through while all the young people nowadays were trying to build a world free from the shackles of gangsters. So there he was, dressed in his shabby black trousers and vest, sipping the last of his cheap wine, wondering what he could make of his life.

That was when the stranger called out to him.

"Ciao! Come le cose sono con lei?"

How was he feeling today? Like donkey shit, that's what he felt like!

The man didn't look at all like a tourist. More like a local, though Massimo knew everyone who lived within ten miles and this man was certainly from somewhere else. He had a dark stubbled beard and mustache, was wearing charcoal peasant clothes, carrying a rucksack, and wearing prescription glasses. Massimo's immediate reaction was to ignore the man, hoping he'd go away.

But the man did not go away. Instead he sat down in the dirt right next to Massimo, leaning his back against Massimo's house.

Still Massimo didn't react.

The stranger took off his black hat and wiped the sweat from around the rim. Massimo wondered how far this man had come? All the way from Bagheria possibly. He didn't much care. However, he was, he had to admit, a little curious.

"Today will be a lucky one for you, I feel."

This was too much for Massimo – this man was becoming annoying. The chances of it being a lucky day for him were smaller than winning the national lottery, and he didn't even have the money for a ticket. So he simply laughed derisively. "Oh yes?"

"Oh yes! Good fortune has come your way. I have been looking for a man such as you, and now I have found one."

For the first time, Massimo turned his head towards the man who spoke in bad, yet comprehensible, Italian.

"I doubt I can be of any use to you, sir. I have nothing but a small home. I have no food, and I have just this moment finished my last bottle of Donnafugato. I am in my seventies and quite useless to you."

The stranger let the old man's words hang in the air, then replied. "You can do me one favor. For this I will immediately reward you handsomely. Then later, I shall owe you a favor."

The man sounded as though he had seen too many Marlon Brando movies, but Massimo was intrigued nevertheless.

"What reward do you have in mind that would make this favor worth my while?"

"Well, let us think about what might make you happier than you are at this moment."

"Food?" Massimo began. He was about to go further when the man cut in.

"Food you shall have."

Massimo stared at the man. Was he serious? He didn't look rich.

"Wine?"

"Wine you shall have."

This was all sounding very promising, yet he wondered what he could possibly do in return for these gifts. Then a wonderful thought crossed his mind. "A donkey to replace my Anna?"

The man simply smiled. "A donkey? Easy. I shall give you money for a donkey."

Massimo stared in amazement, then came to his senses and a sneer crossed his face. "You are making a fool of an old man."

The man stuck his hand in his rucksack and withdrew a bottle of red wine. It was a Sant'Anastasia – one of Massimo's favorites. Almost at once his mouth felt dry. He licked his lips as the man pulled the cork and offered him the bottle.

"Please…"

Massimo drank, then handed the bottle back.

"What could I possibly do for you, sir?"

"You simply have to write on a calendar. On a certain day in the future I would like you to go into the local Carabinieri station in Bagheria and tell them you think you may have seen this man."

"Which man? Why?"

"Patience." The man pulled out a photograph of a

younger man; a man without facial hair. He was smartly dressed, not wearing spectacles.

"Who is this man?" Massimo asked.

The stranger could hardly keep himself from smiling, yet he did. He and the man in the photograph were one and the same, yet the old peasant could not see it.

"This man is wanted by the police in Europe and America."

Massimo mumbled something to the effect that all policemen were pigs.

"Forty days from now you will tell the Carabinieri that you have no doubt whatsoever that this man was living rough near your house for several weeks. By chance you saw this man's face on television at some bar."

"I know of such a bar," Massimo replied, almost excitedly.

"Good. That is all I request of you. In return I shall give you money for a donkey, and enough for good food and wine for a long, long time."

Massimo was still unconvinced that this man was not simply pulling his leg. "This is true?" he asked.

The man again stuck his hand in his rucksack and pulled out a calendar. "This is for you to hang on the wall of your bedroom." He then handed Massimo a pencil. "I would like you to write on the calendar all the things you do each day, under the date. But now you must listen carefully. I want you to write something on this date here," he said indicating a day forty days away. "Tell me, do you have a friend that lives close by? A casual acquaintance?"

"Enrico? He brings me food each week from Bagheria."

"Then write something under this particular day, as if reminding yourself. *'Enrico's birthday,'* perhaps?'

"Why should I do this?"

"Because it will be a reminder to visit the Carabinieri and tell them a story. Now, please listen carefully; I shall tell you a simple story, yet it is one that must be told exactly the same each time you are questioned about it."

"I understand," Massimo replied, concentrating hard.

It took the man just a few minutes to explain the story. Massimo listened to every word.

"Now, I shall ask you questions, as though I were questioning you about this story. As if I were a policeman. Please answer as you would on the day."

The stranger then asked questions for over half an hour. Massimo was spectacularly clever in his answers; the lies came easily to a man who had spent his life lying to both the Mafia *and* the police. He was relaxed and very believable.

At length the stranger was satisfied.

"Even I might believe you," the stranger said with a wry grin.

"Though I am seventy-three I still have my wits. I am not yet foolish."

"Then write the words on the calendar now."

Massimo obliged. The stranger watched as he scrawled in old people's handwriting *'Enrico's birthday?'* Then he looked up. "So... I have done this thing for you."

"Please take my hand then."

Massimo did so.

"You must promise me that you will do the things I have asked of you today. In return I shall reward you handsomely. However, I have to tell you that should you decide not to honor your promise I shall return. Do you understand me?"

Massimo sat up stiffly in his chair. "I am a man of honor. You are speaking to a Sicilian who knows the meaning of *omertà*."

"I felt sure this was the case," the man replied with a smile. "I have your reward here."

So saying he pulled an envelope from his peasant pants' pocket, extracting a bundle of notes and handing them to Massimo.

Massimo stared at the money, stunned. Five thousand Euros in small denominations!

"First of all, you should buy a donkey. Should anyone ask where the money came from you tell them you have been saving ever since Anna died."

The hairs on Massimo's neck stirred – how did this man know so much about him?

"As for the rest of the money," the stranger continued quietly, yet clearly, "keep it safely hidden and use it wisely. Do not spend it rashly, since people will wonder why you suddenly became so rich and that might point the finger at me. If you do as I say, I will find a way to reward you with an equal sum in one year's time."

"I am not a fool. I understand these things," Massimo replied.

"I feel sure you do."

The stranger rose. "This has been a lucky day after all?"

"It has indeed," Massimo replied, knowing better than to ask the stranger's name. How was he to know he had just shaken hands with the most notorious serial murderer of the past ten years?

Nick Hoyle had put in place another piece of the jigsaw.

29.

"You must sedate her! I can't have the girl screaming morning night and noon. Her system won't be able to support the effort."

"I am doing all I can," Ballon replied, calmly. "I can't do more – it might send her into a coma."

"Rubbish. Simply administer sufficient narcotics to send her into some conscious yet delirious state. She can't be tied down for another two days. Apart from anything else she'll need to go to the bathroom and, short of a colostomy bag, I see no other way than allow her some freedom of movement."

"I don't have the specialist drugs I would like."

"You'll have to make do with what I have. Just remember, everyone goes free in just over two days and nights. It'd be a shame if this girl, simply by behaving like a drama queen, spoils everything you have worked for all this time."

Five minutes later Hoyle and Ballon entered Galina's storage room. She immediately began screaming abuse. The noise didn't bother Hoyle, he knew no one above ground could hear her. He was, however, annoyed by her behavior. After all, he'd promised her life was not in danger, the operation had been concluded successfully, and she was very lucky to be alive, albeit now with only one foot. Did this young woman have no concept of others far less fortunate than her?

Her arms were strapped tight to the bed at the upper arm, and her legs at above the knee. Yet still she swore and screamed. Hoyle rather expected this prima ballerina to complain vigorously if she'd glimpsed her right foot was missing, but as with most amputations she probably could still feel it.

Hoyle placed a hand over her mouth without thinking and pressed down hard. To his surprise, she managed to bite him so hard it drew blood – quite an amount of it.

"Get a move on, Ballon, this woman is a tiger," he barked, pressing down so hard she could neither close nor open her mouth again.

Ballon tapped the needle and injected Galina with a massive yet non-life-threatening dose of Diazepam. She continued to struggle for several minutes, then the fight went out of her. As the drowsiness overtook her, Hoyle whispered in her ear. "It's far better to try to maintain your strength. You're alive, and will remain so. We're here to help you. You'll be freed in two days. But if you do not behave, I may re-think matters. No one knows you are here; so consider your situation."

Galina's eyes began rolling into her head.

"You didn't give her too much, did you, Jean?" Hoyle enquired.

"I don't think so, no," Ballon replied, repelled at being now constantly called by his Christian name by a monster such as this man. "She will need further injections later."

"Good. That's what you are here for. Tell me how often we must visit her. Meanwhile I must bring her a toilet. Somehow she must be persuaded to use it. I will give her the choice of going to the toilet and behaving, or having to excrete where she is.

Ballon looked down at Galina's face. It wasn't the first time he'd marveled at her beauty. How had have been persuaded by this butcher monster to do what he'd done? It amazed him. Was he himself completely gutless? Did *no one* else matter but his wife?

For a split second he considered jumping the butcher, then almost as though Hoyle had some sixth sense, he looked up sharply and withdrew the auto injector from his pocket.

"Let's check on your wife. What do you say, Jean?" he cooed. "How about a sandwich?"

In the corridor, on the way back to his cell, Ballon halted. Hoyle's fingers instinctively curled around the auto-injector.

"May I have a word with you?" Ballon asked, without turning around. "Privately, rather than in front of my wife?"

"Of course you can. What can I do for you?" Hoyle replied staring at Ballon's back.

"It's important to me that my wife has no idea you intend to kill me. Please grant me that."

"Don't be such a pessimist, Jean. Why would you think this way?"

"Please don't insult my intelligence. I have seen your face and you still believe I somehow know who you are. That's why you can't allow me to live."

For several seconds Hoyle was unsure how to reply. The wish to allow his new friend to live was an ever-growing phenomenon, yet a part of his psyche recognized this as a terrible weakness; one that might well bring him down. However, the nagging thought was this – was Ballon trying to fool him, or did he really have no idea who he was?

"Tell me this, Jean. You tell me bluntly that I'm a moral bankrupt because I bring suffering to others and have no concept of compassion."

"That's about the size of it, yes," Ballon conceded.

"Let me ask you about the opinion you have of yourself, then."

"If it interests you, by all means."

"You are a moral man? A principled man?"

"I like to think so."

"You would never be intentionally cruel to a human, nor an animal?"

"No, I would not."

"You have a definitive concept or right and wrong?"

"I think so," Ballon replied.

"Do you believe in a God?"

"I do. With all my heart."

"If you were to swear to something on a bible, with God as your witness, would you ever break your word?"

"No."

"So if you were to promise me, with your God as a witness, that you would never reveal who I was – assuming you *did* know my identity – would you break your word?"

"I couldn't do that. Not if I had sworn before the Lord."

"Why not? What's confession for? To apologize for failing God, surely?"

"Maybe."

"Not good enough. That's *exactly* what confession is for! Instant forgiveness. For *anything*! I could ask forgiveness for having butchered close to twenty people, and some priest would grant me absolution there and then, providing I was convincing enough. A hell of a lot of Hail Mary's I've no doubt, but I'd be absolved. Clean sheet!"

"In my case, I would honor my promise."

"You wouldn't seek to justify breaking your promise by suggesting it was made under duress?"

"No. A promise is a promise. A priest would never reveal the identity of anyone who confessed to a murder. In the same way I would never break such a promise by revealing to the police who you were. As it is, I have no idea."

"Hmmm.... how can I be sure you are not tricking me?"

"You can't. You have to trust your instincts."

Neither Ballon nor Hoyle said anything for several seconds, then Ballon broke the silence.

"I have no wish to live, having done what I have done. That is why I wanted to speak to you privately."

"Why on earth would you say that, Jean?"

"How can I rejoin civilized society as the man who has cut off the hands of Josef Kafni and the foot of that beautiful girl, simply to save his wife's life?"

"You *saved* all three lives, as it happened."

"No one will see it that way. Even me. You made me a butcher. I am no more worthy than the guards at Buchenwald."

Hoyle was thoughtful for a moment. It was true that for the rest of his life Jean would be seen as the surgeon who performed the amputations. The majority of people probably wouldn't be able to put themselves in his place and see that had he not done so, Kafni, Yablonskaya and Cecile would have died. So there was little doubt Ballon would become a social pariah, an outcast. He'd never be able to raise his head in society again. Worse still, he'd never be able to practice medicine again.

"You could dedicate yourself to saving lives in the third world, Jean. No one there would have the first idea who you were there. Think of the good you'd be doing. It wouldn't appeal to me, but you're that kind of good soul."

For a moment Hoyle wondered what on earth he'd been talking about. Who gave a damn about people in the third world? He certainly didn't. What on earth was he thinking?

"So you'll be doing me a favor by ending my life," Ballon continued, then paused, "whoever you are. You've murdered me as surely as you've murdered the pianist and this girl. I simply ask you to persuade my wife that I shall be freed too. Otherwise she might not behave, and might consequently come to some harm."

"I'll think things over, Jean. Rest assured, I shall do the right thing by Cecile – for your sake; I have come to think of you as a friend."

"God forbid," Ballon replied in a barely audible whisper.

Hoyle couldn't help but grin.

Back in storage room number two, Hoyle again chained Ballon to the ring in the wall, always showing the injector to the surgeon. Ballon didn't resist.

Upstairs in the house, a few moments later, Hoyle poured himself a wine spritzer – today he'd have to have his wits about him, so no hard liquor. The organization of Mademoiselle Yablonskaya's release had to be coordinated carefully. And it went without saying, he had to ring the changes to satisfy the media – they'd surely be expecting something equally, if not more, spectacular as the release of Kafni. Yet even Hoyle considered releasing the ballerina naked was in bad taste. Having her hopping down the Champs Elysées would probably be just as perfect – why interfere with perfection by being so politically incorrect.

Of course it was paramount that he have his exit strategy in place. Paris traffic at best was a nightmare – he chuckled, it was extraordinary how often people used that phrase when they were actually considering an annoyance rather than a real nightmare. Tomorrow he'd steal another van, of a different color, in a different village, and have it standing by for the exchange.

As he shook some cashew nuts into the palm of his hand, his thoughts drifted back to the French detectives. They'd been quite smart. Not smart enough to locate Kafni, yet smart enough to have played a decent first set, if the 'game' had been tennis. They'd fixed on Kafni. Why? The hand? Very possibly. Who else would set such store by their hands? Well, quite a few, actually. He wondered if they thought he was capable of the executing the amputations himself and were not looking for another individual, a man with surgical or medical skills. If so, they were not as smart as he thought. No, they had to suspect that he'd persuaded a surgeon to do his dirty work, so they'd be scouring France for evidence of a missing surgeon. It wouldn't be long before they stumbled across Ballon and his wife's disappearance. It was just as well that the surgeon's surgical skills wouldn't be an issue in a day or so. Cecile had never seen Hoyle's face, nor where she had been taken, so she couldn't point the finger. All she'd be able to tell the cops would be to recount the conversations they'd all had, and the timbre of his voice. Jean Ballon would be dead by then – a shame, since he liked the man. He'd become a pal.

His thoughts turned again to the ballerina. She had to be adequately sedated before she was set free, then a few seconds prior to her release be given exactly the correct dose of adrenaline so she could support herself on one leg.

As he thought logically about the girl, he couldn't help thinking he was possibly being unrealistic about hoping she would be capable of hopping along the Champs Elysées, screaming. Hopping was a difficult thing to do at the best of times—he'd never been much good with the pogo-stick as a kid, and had never been able to play a decent game of hopscotch. And one had to add a degree of difficulty to Galina's task – she'd be very disorientated and unsteady. It was such a shame! The scenario would have been so very spectacular as a follow-up to Kafni – a one-footed prima ballerina dancing down the Champs!

So, how could he make it all more 'fun'? Buy a tutu and dress her up? Nah, he might be seen and remembered when he bought such a garment. He then had a stroke of genius, jumping up to inspect what was in the tote bag Mademoiselle Yablonskaya had been carrying when he kidnapped her. He pulled out a leotard and several unopened pairs of tights. He knew that during workouts dancers wore them on the outside. Best of all, there was a pair of divine little pink Bunny Hop ballet slippers.

He placed all the stuff on the coffee table, then tossed one of the slippers back in her tote bag – she'd only need one.

30.

The sinking feeling Neela lived with in the pit of her stomach since she waved goodbye to Dermot never left her. It probably would stay there until there was some resolution of the Hoyle matter. Despite her prayers, she knew that there'd be no escaping him – it was like knowing there was a tarantula somewhere under the sheets, and waiting to be bitten by the creature. The logical answer was an exterminator. But sadly, the exterminators in America she had in mind were not criminal entrepreneurs, but the police; and neither they nor Interpol had been able to locate Dermot's nemesis and bring him to justice.

So, as the alpha male, Dermot had thought it necessary to step up to the plate to safeguard his family. And ironically, that was exactly what Hoyle had most probably had relied on. There was still unfinished business as far as Nick was concerned, and the future did not factor into his thoughts. It was the past.

Revenge.

She'd watched the Kafni footage with abject horror, hoping against hope that the incident was unconnected with any reappearance of Nick Hoyle, though her gut told her otherwise. Just now she'd seen the news footage of Dermot pressing his way through the media jackals at the Quai des Orphèfres, and it had brought back nightmares of pressing through similar media crowds during Dermot's murder trial. The Kafni story had broken with a splash across the world and the media were hungry for more, desperately hoping there would be more mayhem, and praying that somehow Dermot Nolan would be involved. Dermot was now a marked man.

She had been in two minds whether she'd feel safer

staying behind in Malibu to safeguard Virginia, or traveling to France with her husband. The latter was fraught with problems, bearing in mind the age of her child. Yet it was scary to have to wonder, twenty-four hours a day, what was happening the other side of the world, knowing that at any moment of the day and night the phone could ring and a sympathetic voice would deliver some terrible news and seek to commiserate with her.

Neela realized she'd been in the same spot, playing with toys in her playpen, for too long and looked bored and ready to cry. It was time to give Virginia some fresh air as well as walk Scary.

Plucking little Virginia from the pen, she hugged her to her chest. "Let's go and have some fun, sweetheart. What do you say?"

As she walked thought the living room to the kitchen, Scary began barking furiously. That drew her attention at once – it was unlike him. She glanced at the window and saw a shadow pass across it.

She paused and looked hard. Could it have been the shadow of a plane that had passed between her and the sun? Had she seen anything at all?

If she'd been an average individual, unscarred by former terrors, she'd have thought no more to it. As she was, she felt a surge of panic, and her guts turned to water. What the hell had caught her attention? Had someone been outside the house, looking in? Should she do what all victims do in movies and go look-see? And then be grabbed and struck down with a club?

No, not this little black duck.

She immediately pulled her cell phone out of her bag and punched number 3 – she keyed in Hansen's telephone number at North Hollywood on her speed dial several days earlier.

Hansen answered within three seconds. "Mrs. Nolan. Anything wrong? Tell me."

Just to hear a cop at the other end of the telephone line helped. She relaxed ten per cent, her eyes still glued to the windows. "I was thinking of taking my daughter for a walk and I think I saw someone or something – more like a shadow – at the window. I haven't been outside to look, I called you right away."

"That's the right thing to do. Look, stay on the line. Don't put the phone down. I'll call the guys on Malibu and ask them to send alpha-A – that's their hot car. They'll be with you in no time at all."

"It's probably nothing, Detective," Neela said beginning to wonder if she'd seen anything at all.

"Well, we'll see, won't we? Make sure all the doors are locked. And keep this line open.

Taking Hansen at his word, Neela cradled Virginia and held the receiver close to her ear. Scary was running around the room barking. Neela then walked up the stairs to the bedroom to check out the windows.

Nothing.

"There's nothing at the bedroom window, Detective. I'm going back downstairs where the dog is."

"Good. My advice is to do nothing but sit down where you are. The police will identify themselves when they arrive – make sure you see a badge."

She would have stayed where she was in the living room but for one thing, she just *had* to go pee. Sometimes people can hold it in for an eternity, right now, for Neela, that wasn't an option – the fear factor was kicking in. So she walked to the downstairs toilet. The door was open just a few inches.

As she reached out a hand, she stopped herself. *Jesus, what if someone's inside already, waiting for me in the loo?* But she was so close to relieving herself, she made herself believe she was being silly. She was a grown-up for heaven's sake. There weren't any boogiemen inside the house – all the doors and windows were locked.

Finally she couldn't wait any longer and pushed the bathroom door open.

Nothing.

She turned around and made herself comfy, keeping Vig on her lap.

That's when she heard the licking noise behind her.

Immediately she leapt up, her pants around her ankles, and turned.

There was a face pressed against the frosted glass window. The mouth was open wide, the tongue tasting the glass, an old man making orgasmic groans as he licked. And worst of all, despite the frosted glass, the orange hair was unmistakable.

She screamed, then held a hand to her mouth – realizing she'd frightened Vig, who was now staring at her, bawling her eyes out.

"What's happened?" Hansen screamed down the line. "You okay?"

Neela raced back out into the living room and checked all the doors. They were all locked. "There's someone at the bathroom window, Detective," she shouted. "An old guy. With orange hair. It's Arnold!"

Hansen realized she was becoming hysterical; he had to calm her. "Alpha-A is about one minute away. Hang in there!"

Neela stood in the center of the room trying to calm Virginia, as Hansen had tried to calm her. The next sixty seconds seemed an eternity. Then she heard a banging on the front door. One man was shouting. "It's the Malibu police, ma'am. Please open the door!"

Setting Virginia down on a sofa, Neela made her way to

the front door and looked through the peep-hole. Sure enough, there were two patrolmen there with a patrol car clearly visible in the driveway, the lights flashing red and blue. Both were holding up badges.

"Detective Hansen? The police are here. I'm going to ring off now."

"Sure thing. You're in good hands."

She immediately drew back the chain and them drew a bolt aside at the top of the door, opening the door lock.

The lead cop had a hand on his gun but it was still in its holster. His partner was standing a couple of yards back with his back to the door. He had his gun out and at his side. Scary rushed past Neela and ran into the garden, still barking his head off.

"Is there anyone in the house right now, ma'am?"

"No. I don't think so. Just my baby daughter. But a minute ago I distinctly saw a man at the bathroom window."

"Where is that exactly? This way?" The lead patrolman pointed his right.

"Yes, the back of the bathroom's that way."

At once the second patrol cop moved to the right, lifting his gun up in front of him.

Twenty seconds later he called out from the side of the house. "Jack? No one here. But there are footprints."

"What's out the back of the house, ma'am?" the lead cop asked.

"A small garden and a path leading to the reserve."

"Let's take a look, shall we? You lead the way, please ma'am."

Ten minutes later both cops had searched every possibly hiding place both inside the house and in the immediate surroundings. Nothing. No sign of an old man wearing an orange wig.

The deputies formally introduced themselves as Deputies Walsher and Steen. Then they began asking more questions.

"How old was this guy, would you say?"

"Hard to say. I could only make out a shadow, and then saw the outline of a squished face at the window."

"Then what made you think he was an *old* man?"

"It was just an impression I had. You see, we were once threatened when we lived downtown by an old guy who had orange hair. So when I saw the orange halo through the glass, I must have immediately thought it was him."

"Well, he'd have to have been darned agile to disappear that quick. You say we got hear about a minute after you saw him?"

"A minute. Maybe two."

"There's a big difference, lady. People can run a mile in four minutes."

"Old people?"

"You said he was a shadow, a squished outline? Maybe he was a young guy trying to *look* like an old guy."

Neela couldn't dispute that.

"Was he doing anything at the window? Like maybe something improper?"

"No. Well, maybe, yes. He had his lips pressed to the glass and it looked as though he was licking it."

"You mean like an ice-cone," Deputy Steen asked.

"Yeah. Like that."

"That's a weird thing to do."

"Actually not so," Neela replied.

"How so?"

Neela took a long breath. "Are you familiar with my husband?"

"Yes, ma'am. He's a famous writer."

"And you heard about the serial murder trial?"

"Of course."

"There was the old vagrant who delivered the pages of his vile diary to us. That's what started the whole terrible business. Then he committed suicide. But he had that peculiar orangey hair."

"But you just said he was dead. Suicide."

"That's right. But it turned out the old guy was simply a patsy – the bad guy was someone completely different. And when this guy – who incidentally has an arrest warrant out for him for thirteen killings – wants to scare the daylights out of my husband, he sends people around wearing orange wigs. It's like *I know where you live and I'm coming for you*. Long ago, the vagrant who killed himself pushed his face against the window of a Red Line train window, staring insanely at my husband – grinning like an idiot as he licked the glass, while he ran beside the car."

"Hey, that *is* spooky."

Deputy Walsher, put his note pad away. Steen, was still looking at the windows.

"Where is your husband right now?"

"He's in Paris."

"That's a shame. I'd prefer to think you're not alone here at night. I'll see what I can do to organize some protection for you for a few days. Can't have people scaring you and the bubba like that."

"Thanks very much for coming," Neela said – it looked as though they were anxious to leave.

"That's what you pay those big taxes for – so we'll come and rescue you when you need it," Walsher replied with an easy smile. "What we'll do is write it all this up and then have a word with Detective Sergeant Hansen at North Hollywood. He said he knew you and your husband."

Neela nodded.

"Then I'll have a word with my Captain and see what protection we can offer you in the next few days."

"That's wonderful. Means I can sleep at night."

"You may decide you want to move into a motel on a temporary basis. We can check that no one's watching you when you leave. Then people like this jerk with the orange hair won't be able to come peeking in your windows and upsetting the kid."

"That'd be wonderful, Deputy Walsher."

"My pleasure," Walsher replied.

As they drove off, Steen and Walsher put the word out on the radio to look out for anyone over the age of forty who was hanging around the area doing nothing. He mentioned the wig, but there wasn't much chance of someone wearing a fake wig keeping it on while they tried to evade the cops.

By the time the evening came and Neela drew the curtains, there was a patrol car standing in Cliff Drive.

By this time, Anakletos Greco, a forty-six year old grifter, was sitting at a table at Taverna Tony's on Civic Center Way. The Malibu Country Mart opposite the pier was his favorite dining spot – when he could afford to eat there, that was. However, today he had money in his pocket and he felt like getting drunk. His task had been easier than expected. Now it was over. All he had to be sure to do was burn the wig like he'd been told. Every once in a while it was great to help out the Ginger Fixer. He'd never gotten into any trouble in the twelve years he'd been helping him out.

31.

Dermot awoke just before three in the morning. Someone was tapping quite forcefully at his suite door and calling his name.

As he grabbed the robe that was lying at the bottom of his bed he realized he was sweating profusely, despite having set the air conditioning quite low when he'd gone to bed.

As he opened the door he saw the night manager standing there with a concerned look on his face.

"Excuse the intrusion, Monsieur Nolan. But one of the staff heard screaming coming from your room and we were worried for you. Is everything in order?"

Dermot absentmindedly ran a hand through his hair, immediately aware it was soaked with sweat and wild as a gelled-up twenty-year-old rock chick. It was then that his nightmare flooded back into his psyche. The nightmare again. The box! He'd been back in his coffin. The horror was almost too much to bear. Standing there in his robe he suddenly felt physically sick. It was all he could do not to vomit on the night manager's shoes. As it was, he managed to speak. "I must have had a nightmare. Please thank whoever it was that alerted you. Very solicitous. I'm fine. Really."

The night manager smiled and nodded. "Then I hope the rest of the night is just that, rest. No more *cauchemars*, I hope."

As the man turned to leave, Dermot quickly closed the door, raced to the loo and vomited.

Moments later, sipping a medicinal brandy, Dermot did his best to shake his brain free of the images of his nightmare. But as people who are afflicted with bad dreams will know, this is often harder than you think. The same as when jokers at college ask their buddies not to think of something gross – it's hard not to immediately do so.

Dermot knew the best thing was to concentrate hard on the day that was was about to start. What could he do this morning that might be of any help to the police? More specifically, did he know anything personal about Galina that might help them in their search for the ballerina? They'd said she was missing and that her disappearance was as yet unexplained. It certainly didn't auger well for the girl if Hoyle was involved. However, there was always the chance that Hoyle had kidnapped someone else. He hoped so much that he was right; though he recognized this was hardly the correct thing to be thinking.

He cast his mind back to his interview with Galina. She had been so happy, talking of the year ahead with such exuberance. Unlike the ballet critics, she'd reminded him of Audrey Hepburn with a few extra pounds on her, rather than Fonteyn. It was the eyes; that was it. But how to come up with anything the detectives has missed? How could he imagine he knew more about her than the detectives could glean from her family. That would be impossible. All he could do was try to analyze what Nick Hoyle might be planning; after all he knew Nick better than he knew anyone apart from Neela. And yet he always thought he'd known Nick better than anyone but had been proved so very wrong.

He glanced at his watch and made a mental calculation. It'd be just after six in the evening in Malibu. Perhaps a call home would soothe his nerves.

Neela picked up almost immediately. This was a bonus – she normally allowed at least five rings. How was Dermot to know the true reason? Panic.

"Hi, honey. It's me," he began.

"Really? I was certain it was Father Christmas," she replied in a sing-song voice. "Well I never!" She was doing her best to lighten the mood.

Dermot chuckled lightly, sending the first endorphins of the day into his system – calling Neels had definitely been a good idea. "How's things been with you guys?"

"We're fine, honey. Vig sends you big sloppy kisses and says come home soon daddy. I do the same, but my lips don't have pureed carrot and veal jus on them. How's Paris? Beautiful as ever?" There was no way in the world she was going to tell him what had happened to her. He'd freak, she knew that.

"I met with some detectives at the Préfécture, or whatever their Parker Center is called. The cops here seem pretty smart."

"Vig and I watched you arrive there on the news. What was their thinking regarding Josef?"

Dermot screwed up his face as he tried to think. "Well, they're beginning to make connections..." He debated for a few seconds, then added. "To Nick."

"Really? Already? Based on what, for God's sake?" Although Neela had suspected they might, a part of her had hoped against hope that there was no connection whatsoever, and that the kid and the old man at the window were pranksters. But in her heart she knew which was the unlikely.

"The thing is, the guy who sent the bare bones of Josef's hand to the police chief – whether he's in fact Nick or someone we don't know – called the cops when the seven day deadline ran out on Josef, and told them he'd targeted someone else, only this time they only had three days to find out who this person as. That was his disgusting 'game'. Oh, by the way, it goes without saying that anything they tell me and I pass on to you is in the strictest confidence. Okay?"

"Sure, honey. Sure." She held her breath, her sixth sense knew that he had more bad news to share. "So tell me, what else?"

"Well, the things is... Galina Yablonskaya is missing. She's disappeared."

"Oh no," Neela moaned. "The police can't think...?"

"I'm afraid they do. They're not at all sure, and they're following up a whole lot of other leads," he lied "but meanwhile they're out there on the streets trying to find her."

"Oh, dear God. He wouldn't do something terrible to her like he did with..." She was choking back tears now. It was such an obvious thought – Kafni was a pianist who had lost both hands; Yablonskaya was a dancer...

"You sure you're both okay?" Dermot asked, doing his best to steer Neela's thoughts away from amputations. As long as he felt his family was safe, he felt he had the courage to carry on. Otherwise...?

"Sure, we're dandy!" She then laughed like a kid. "Hey, never thought I'd ever say that word. What was I thinking?" She laughed again, knowing that an injection of humor always steered Dermot to an emotionally better place. "So what are your plans for today? The things you'd planned?"

"Yes. Kind of, anyway. I'm going to make a few calls. To art dealers in town. See what they might have heard on the art-world grapevine."

He was about to ask her the question he'd been asking himself since he left LAX, but stopped abruptly short. Neela picked up on his hesitation.

"What were you going to add? Come on, you have to tell me. I said it was okay to go to Paris. I didn't complain about you putting yourself in harm's way. The least you can do is tell me the way things are. All of it."

"Okay. There was something else I've been wondering

about. Nick knew where we were living. He found us in Malibu. That is, unless the kid with the wig was a prankster."

"Okay…" Neela murmured, going long with his thinking.

"So I wondered whether he knows I'm here in Paris?"

Neela thought long and hard. "Well, let's consider. If Nick is committing these crimes in Paris, then he has to be in Paris himself. Unless he's having someone else commit them for him. Which I doubt very much because from experience we know he's become a very mentally sick man who gets pleasure out of the hands-on experience."

"You're right. It's much more likely that the kid in Malibu was organized from Paris simply to draw me out."

"But how would he know you've taken the bait – it's not as if he has access to immigration records here or in France."

Dermot suddenly had a flash of realization as his eyes scanned the room. "Oh shit. Of course."

"Don't 'Oh shit' me, darling. That's scary."

"Sorry. It was just so obvious. Where do I always stay when I'm in Paris?"

"L'Hôtel?"

"Right. I'm a creature of habit. He knows that. All he has to do is check with the hotel to see if I've arrived. Or sit in a bar in the rue Bonaparte and stake out the hotel."

"Hey, what am I thinking? I watched you on the news for heaven's sake! Everyone knows you're in town."

"Right. Guess I was asking the dumbest question."

"Well, that's what happens when you don't plan things properly – you should have stayed somewhere small, private and miles away, like in Montmartre."

"Well, that's water under the bridge. I'm going to have to live with that now. If he's here and this is his handiwork, the chances are he knows I'm here. No big deal. What's he going to do? Kidnap *me* next? I'll have a word with the management and ask them to let me know if anyone calls, asking if I've checked in. Otherwise the security at night here is pretty damned good. It wouldn't be if I changed to a flea-bitten hotel in Montmartre."

"Hey, I have to go look after Vig now. She's eaten and I have to see if she's pooped and then put her down. Do what you have to do today and keep safe."

"I will, honey. I'm sending all my love down this line to you two. You're all I have, you know that."

As Dermot severed the telephone connection, Neela rang the private number that Hansen had given her. He'd offered to be available for her twenty-four seven.

"You okay?" Hansen barked quickly.

"Sure, I'm fine. I have two of Malibu's finest outside. I feel secure."

"That's good to know," Hansen replied.

"I just wanted you to know I had a telephone call from my husband just now. From Paris. I didn't tell him about my problem here. He's got enough on his plate right now without having to worry about weirdos licking bathroom windows."

"Well, that's you're decision to make. Not telling him, that is."

"I was simply hoping that should he contact you, you could keep the incident private. Is that possible?"

"That's a hard one, Mrs. Nolan. You see, if I am asked a direct question, I'm in no position to lie or prevaricate. My job would be on the line. But I can help you out in another way, perhaps. There's nothing to say that I have to share your 'secrets', shall we put it that way, with your husband. So unless he asks me flat out if there have been any incidents at your home, your secret is safe with me."

"Thanks so much, detective. You're a gem."

"Well, you know where I am if you need me."

As she put down the phone she wished that Dermot had someone at his end of the telephone available at a moments notice, or had a cop car outside with two men in it.

32.

Hoyle had one whole free day to enjoy himself as a tourist, as well as the luxury of time to put in place the last few details for the coming morning – the release details, topography etcetera. However, it had been such a nice morning that, as he sat in the back garden feasting on a *pain au chocolat* he'd bought in the local *boulangerie,* he thought it might be time to relax from the stress of dealing with difficult and depressive people such as Monsieur Ballon, his wife and the ballet dancer – a girl who never stopped complaining; she drove him nuts.

Now that he was in the fresh air, listening to the birdsong and sipping his mug of freshly brewed coffee, everything seemed all right with the world. A trip to Paris would be a pleasant way to take his mind off all the future unpleasantness associated with putting down Jean Ballon – he didn't much care for such words as murder or execution.

He'd performed all the daily tasks. The portable lavatories had been seen too and perfumed. Ballon and Cecile had grudgingly enjoyed their croissants, complete with unsalted French butter and *Bon Maman confiture.* Crushed Alsace cherries was the jam today. Cecile had shared with him his one hospitality error of the morning, French people didn't take butter with croissants; they were buttery enough. Galina had eaten very little because she was still practically in an induced coma, thanks to the huge doses of Valium she'd been fed by Ballon.

So he felt confident about leaving his home, secure in the knowledge that no one would come to the front door, no one would spy on him, and no one would hear any screaming, should there be any. In fact, today he felt in such a good mood that he thought he might shop properly for Ballon's last supper. It was only fair – no one should be asked to eat pre-heated supermarket food before going to the gallows, even if the quality of packaged food in France was a cut above what one might expect in America.

Within the hour he'd changed into dark blue pants and a shirt that would mark him as an *ouvrier*; a farm hand or factory worker. He wore a cloth cap as well, one that such workmen would wear. To all intents and purposes he was a working man out for the day.

Opening a pack of Gauloises cigarettes, he lit one and grunted with displeasure. He didn't smoke. He found the smell of French dark tobacco disgusting, but it did provide a more complete look to any cops who might be looking his way.

He turned off the D76 just after the small village of Bardelle, then hung a right on the much bigger road, the N12.

As he passed through the forest that led to the village of Maulette, he listened to the news reports. There were the usual stories of what Obama had been up to, saving the world, plus some political analysis of what had gone on the day before in the French National Assembly. Yet absolutely nothing more about Kafni. Nor were there any stories about the disappearance of Galina Yablonskaya. This was a disappointment – he'd been looking forward to these.

As he searched the sides of the road for a suitable van to steal, he pondered on what the French detectives' thinking might be.

They were half way through their three-day period. It was more than likely that their investigations had revealed the disappearance of Galina. But where on earth were they going to look? No one had witnessed her abduction, he felt sure of that. So no one would have seen the stolen van. Even if they had, it had been dumped. So what would they do?

Of course the whole point of unsettling Dermot with the kid was so that he'd react. And react he must have done. Surely it was logical to think he'd report the incident to the police. His friendly detective at North Hollywood was the most likely choice – he'd been Mike Kandinsky's former partner. Once Dermot had shared his opinion that 'Hoyle was on the move' it was probable that Hansen would share that same news with Interpol as a matter of form. That was the way that Interpol gained their information, having every iota of information about the whereabouts of criminals with a worldwide APB put out on them.

He smiled as he drove. It was all so easy to play this particular game. Interpol is told that the last victim of the serial killer, known now as the Dreamhealer, had been threatened and that maybe he'd surface soon somewhere. Where does that get them? Nowhere, because he's already in situ in Paris.

As he reached the town of Maulette he took a side street, looking for the town parking area, somewhere commuters might park before taking the train to Paris. There might be a suitable vehicle there.

Of course, if the French police were any good at all, they'd surely have picked up on the words he'd used in his first threat, his clue – *Don't let this celebrated man's worst nightmare become yours, Commissaire. Beware.* Any detective worth his salt would appreciate the significance of the words *'worst nightmare'*. The murder trial had been a cause célèbre. Added to which were the banner headlines when Dermot had been unearthed – they'd all screamed those very two words. The average kid in the streets in Los Angeles, Berlin and Paris knew more about the Dreamhealer than the name of the Secretary-General of the United Nations. So the snippet of information about the kid, that Hansen would have put on the wire, together with the two words in his message would have everyone twitchy that the Dreamhealer was planning something grizzly.

All so very easy.

There were no suitable vans in Maulette, so he headed back to the main road.

Now was the time to put his most important plan in place; the psychological torture and destabilization of Dermot. He knew how shaky Dermot's nerves had been when he'd left hospital – he'd seen him for hiumself on the news. The man couldn't even stand he was so thin and frail. Even now, he guessed that Dermot wouldn't be able to sleep properly, and that every nerve in his body would be jangling. With the appearance of the kid, he was now in the perfect state to be subjected to more scary stimuli. He wondered if Neela would by now have told him of the visit of the Arnold impersonator. Maybe. Maybe not. He knew that she might try to shield him from more worry while he was away. And joy of joys, Dermot had done exactly what Hoyle had predicted – he'd come to catch him, without having the first idea where he might be. He felt sure Dermot would start his search in France because he spoke the language. He might go to Germany after France, but the man was such a creature of habit, it was almost laughable.

As Hoyle glanced at his watch – it was ten to eleven – he saw a van parked down a side street. He he'd been drifting slowly through a village by the name of Goussainville. There wasn't a soul about. It was one of those perfectly sleepy Yvelines villages.

He drove on for about a mile, then parked quite a way down a side street close to an industrial building. Then he walked back to check out the van.

It was pretty much ideal. A Renault van reasonably similar to his own Espace. Quite a few years older. Mustard in color. Always good to change colors.

Hoyle looked around.

No one about.

Two minutes later he was in, the van was wired and he was on his way. Everything had gone very smoothly. God was with him today, he thought as he turned back onto the N12 and drove towards Paris.

33.

It was close to midday and Dermot knew he'd have to take a break from tracking down dealers; no self-respecting Parisian was going to spare him any time when it came to *le déjeurner* – lunch. Some things in Paris were sacrosanct. He already crossed four dealers off his list; Keobanith Consulting, David Levy & Associés, Cardenas Bellanger and the Gallerie Frank Elbaz.

To his immense surprise, when he returned to l'Hôtel there were only a few journalists standing outside the entrance. The concierge had taken the trouble to close the twin gates at the rue des Beaux Arts, and when Dermot's taxi arrived, the gates opened quickly and the taxi swept past them.

Now, two hours later, refreshed, he was sitting in renowned art dealer Henri Placide's huge office overlooking the Place des Voges in the Marais district.

"We used to see him maybe four five times a year. He had a superb client list, which he shared with me. In return we looked out for pieces his clients might fancy. On practically every occasion we had what he was looking for. You see, Monsieur Nick made our task so easy. For instance, he would tell us his client was looking for a Miró of a certain size – even a certain color – and we would search through our client list and see who might part with their *'petit trésor'*, their 'little treasure'. He was a very clever dealer indeed. We shall miss him."

Dermot's expression was as dark as a Sudanese fisherman. How this fat art dealer could sit opposite him, heaving a sigh of personal sadness that he would no longer be able to deal with a serial killer, in the full knowledge that Nick Hoyle had brutally murdered thirteen innocent people made him want to slap his face.

Perhaps he hadn't put Dermot together with the case and had no idea that this monster was responsible for burying him alive for several months in his own garden.

"So to your knowledge, Nick Hoyle has not dealt with anyone in Paris for some time?"

"He may have, monsieur, but not with us or anyone I have talked with over the past many months. He has seemingly vanished into thin air."

"You are aware, Monsieur Placide, that there is an arrest warrant out on him both in the Unites States and the whole of Europe for the murder of thirteen people?"

"Yes, I am aware of that. A terrible thing. And so unexpected." It was the unexpected quality of Nick's disappearance that appeared to concern him more than the killings themselves. Placide glanced at his watch, it was clearly time to add some extra weight to his already obese body.

"Yes, who would have picked it?" Dermot replied, but his sarcasm was lost on the fat man.

"I would ask you to share some late lunch with me, but I am dining with a client at his home. Nevertheless, perhaps you will allow me to make a suggestion if you still have not taken lunch. Directly below us is the delightful restaurant, Ma Bourgogne. They have a most reasonable menu at thirty-five Euros. To sit, eating such food under the seventeenth century vaults of the Place des Voges is always sublime. Their selection of wines, especially those of Burgundy, is extensive."

Dermot stood. One more minute of this gross man's chatter and he'd be forced to smack him in the mouth. One minute he was chatting about mass murder, the next he was considering food and fine wines. The man was a disgrace.

"Thank you for your time, Monsieur Placide."

"My pleasure."

Dermot headed for the door and opened it. As he passed through he heard Monsieur Placide call out to him.

"Oh, incidentally, the restaurant does not take credit cards."

Dermot pulled the door closed overly sharply.

Every available seat in every diner along the Boulevard Beaumarchais seemed packed to capacity, despite it being already two-thirty. It appeared few Parisians were feeling the pinch of recession. Besides, when you're happy the world is a wonderful place. But when the slanting shadows of tragedy envelope one's world, it's another matter entirely. Suddenly life is unbearable, wine tastes strangely sour, appetite is a thing of the past, and lovemaking becomes desperate sex.

He was still in this reverie of sadness when he crossed the street towards the Bastille Metro station. He was glancing up at the Colonne de Juillet in the centre of the Place de la Bastille when he felt eyes on him.

Human behaviorists suggest that women have this instinct in spades, whereas men are probably spending too much of their time looking at women's breasts or rear ends, thinking of sex. Either way, there was no good reason for Dermot to focus on a man standing at the corner of a café that stood close to the Metro entrance Dermot was making for. Even though he was a good seventy feet away, Dermot knew there was something oddly familiar about the way he carried himself – his gait. And though he has a stubbled face and wore a mustache of medium thickness, the bone structure screamed Hoyle!

Was it actually possible? Had Nick been stalking him all morning?

Without thinking, Dermot turned away from the Metro entrance and walked directly towards the man. He then broke into a jog; then he began to run. Every rule about waiting till one was close enough to grab one's target went out the window. He called out very loudly.

"Hey! Stop!"

The man froze for a moment, searching for the source of the shout. Then he saw Dermot, locked eyes with him, and began to run towards the Metro stairs, roughly pushing people out of the way. One woman, holding the hand of a child, fell heavily into the street and a scooter narrowly missed running her over. Passers-by, rudely thrust aside, shouted abuse. Yet the man ran full bore to the steps that led down to the Metro, taking them three at a time.

Dermot was less than five seconds behind him, continuing to call out at the top of his voice. "Stop that man! STOP HIM! He's a murderer."

By the time he was halfway down the steps to the turnstile, pedestrians were pressing themselves to the walls, standing aside; men were shielding their girlfriends, and women were clutching children to their chests.

What the fuck was happening? Was the man who was shouting a policeman? Or a madman? Did someone say the guy had a gun? '*Murderer*'? Had someone just shouted out that word? Was someone dead?

Dermot watched his quarry leap the turnstile barrier and race off in the direction of Chateau de Vincennes. There was no time to buy a ticket, so he sprinted after the man, sliding across the top of the ticket machine.

The Metro guards immediately saw him and started shouting themselves, but by then he was ten yards down the tunnel that lead to Direction Chateau de Vincennes. He knew he had a clear advantage over the running man; since the trains only ran every few minutes – the chances were guy couldn't immediately hop a train, he'd have to wait. That's when Dermot could take him down on the platform. Unless it was a two-way track with no separation. Then he might have the option of risking his life by crossing the tracks. If he did that, Dermot wasn't following – no fucking way.

A few seconds later Dermot saw the steps that lead down to the platform at the end of the connecting tunnel. It was then he felt the rush of wind and the sound of the tires of an approaching train.

Shit! No fucking luck today. It's going to be a close call.

Behind him, Dermot could hear the Metro guards calling out to him to stop. But Dermot plunged on, leaping down the twelve steps towards the platform.

At that precise moment the train entered the station.

The platform wasn't full, but it wasn't exactly empty either. He knew he'd have just a few seconds to locate Nick, who'd probably have his back against the wall trying to have other passengers shield him from Dermot.

As the train came to a halt and the passengers pressed forward, Dermot jogged lightly down the platform, weaving in and out of the throng. How on earth was he going to find Nick amongst all these people? Should he get on the train even if he hadn't seen Nick do so? It was possible Nick would play the old '*French Connection*' game; get on himself, wait to see if Dermot followed him inside, allow the doors to begin to close with Dermot inside, then jump off at the last second.

Dermot knew if he didn't get on he'd lose Nick. But unless he saw Nick still standing somewhere on the platform, it was a fifty-fifty bet he was on the train.

As the horn signaled the imminent closing of the doors, the Metro guards came flying onto the platform. Dermot picked a spot amongst the boarding passengers and made his decision – he was getting on and taking a chance. The alternative was to keep running down the platform, hoping to spot Nick; and he knew this would draw the attention of the Metro cops.

As the doors hissed closed behind him, he crouched low behind a wide French housewife and took a peek through the window. One of the Metro cops was on a cell phone; the other was running down the platform. But it appeared they weren't in a position to stop the train – arrived too late. Most likely they were alerting their counterparts at the next stop – the Gare de Lyon – one of the busiest Metro stations in Paris.

This was good news and bad. Good insofar as the platform would be really full when the train came to a halt – the Metro guards wouldn't be able to spot him easily. Bad in so far as this wouldn't help him spot Nick. And there was the added complication that the traffic cops were looking for *him*, not Nick.

He knew he didn't have much time before the train slowed down at the Gare de Lyon. While he had these few seconds, he knew it was imperative to push his way down the car and into the next. Ahead of him were three more cars – Nick could be in any of them. Alternatively, he could have lost him at Bastille if he hadn't boarded the train.

As he made his way forward, quite a few passengers swore at him or muttered invective in French – none of them enjoyed being shoved an pushed willy-nilly by a man excusing himself in English.

Half way down, he caught his sleeve in the scarf of a young woman who immediately had her head tugged hard to the right. But Dermot wasn't stopping, he leant against the obstruction and the girls scarf ripped.

"*Fils de salope! Ta mere la pute!*" she screamed at him, as she gathered her ripped scarf.

The train was still traveling at speed as Dermot reached the end of the car and looked through into the next one. It was rounding a bend. There was no sign of Nick. Maybe further on?

He opened the connecting door and stepped through, closing it behind him. Then he started again, pushing and shoving his way forward. As he did so, he pulled off his tie and pushed it deep into a pocket. He then took off his grey jacket to reveal a blue stripped shirt – the traffic cops wouldn't be looking for stripes, but a jacket.

As he passed by a seated old man, he stumbled over some groceries he had at his side. A bottle of olive oil went spinning between the seats, smashing against a stanchion, flooding the floor with oil.

"*Que la baise!*" the old man shouted, trying to get his old bones in a position to rise. "*Encul!*" he screamed at Dermot. Faggot!

Dermot was almost at the end of the second car and looking through when he felt the brakes go on. This only made him more determined that ever.

Stepping through into the third car he spotted him at once. He was crouching down by one of the exits, ready to make a quick escape at the Gare de Lyon.

Dermot ground his teeth. It had been so long. Hatred ran through his veins as the adrenaline kicked in. Now he was seconds away from finally having it out with his nemesis, hand–to-hand. Just the thought of imminent violence charged his body with a sort of electricity.

Nick hadn't seen him, that much was obvious to Dermot – he was turned away from him, crouched in a ball at the feet of several passengers.

Slowly Dermot wove his way through the crowds as the train slowed down and entered the station.

The Metro was only a few feet from a standstill when the man stood upright and braced himself to run when the doors opened. It was at this moment that Dermot launched himself into the air, crashing down on him.

As the doors opened, the two men spilled out awkwardly onto the platform, Dermot riding the man's back. Dermot began punching like a piston, first hard to the side of the guy's head, then even harder in the small of his back. The man was screaming in pain. All around them, the passengers were scattering and shouting for help. Metro cops were now running from each end of the platform towards the mêlée.

As the first cop fell on top of him, and began to wrench the two fighters apart, Dermot was finally able to turn the man onto his back.

They were then face to face.

He was a complete stranger, a much younger man than Nick. He looked scared as hell.

"*Arête! Arête!*" the man screamed. "*Je renonce! Je ne suis pas meutrier! Pickpocket, peût-etre!*"

Dermot was gasping for breath as two burly French Metro guards pulled him upright.

Jesus, what have I done Dermot thought as his blood turned to ice?

A third cop was crouched by the young man, who's face was now awash with blood pouring from a gash in his lip.

"*Que'est ce que vous faites! Fous le camp, troudoc!*" the young man screamed at Dermot.

It was only then that the young man's first few words hit home. He'd said he was no murderer – at the same time admitting he was a pickpocket! Maybe he had stolen goods on him? Maybe he could explain away his actions by telling the guards he was trying to nab the guy because he'd seen him mugging an old lady and wanted to get her stuff back? It was worth a try.

The explanation took the best part of five minutes. The guards cleared an area around Dermot and the young guy, and the trains continued to arrive and depart behind them. The guards were about to call the police when Dermot pleaded with them for the fiftieth time to search the young man's pockets. Finally, they did so, despite the pickpocket's protestations. There were three wallets inside, two clearly female.

The Metro guards then made a call to the cops and a decision was made. The young man would be taken into custody and handed over to the Paris cops. Dermot would give his ID and details of where he was staying. He was strongly cautioned that he'd done the wrong thing by attempting to take the law into his own hands, and told in no uncertain terms that he couldn't go around punching people who he suspected of some misdemeanor.

However, he was free to go.

Exhausted, Dermot walked unsteadily to one of the wooden benches on the platform and sat down, holding his head in his hands. It had been some kind of a day.

A taxi dropped him off at L'Hôtel two hours later. He felt as though he'd survived a tornado. After the incident with the pickpocket, he'd leant back against the wall of the Gare de Lyon Metro station and almost immediately had fallen asleep. An hour later a thoughtful middle-aged man had tapped his shoulder and asked if he was ill – did he need medical assistance? Dermot woke, thanked him, and mumbled that he was fine. He then walked back up to the street from the platform and caught a cab home.

At his hotel reception the concierge handed him an envelope, explaining. "Mr. Nolan, we had a call from a Commandant Gassin at the Préfécture, enquiring if you had returned. He asked me to make sure I handed you his message personally."

Dermot took the note with a smile, one that drained the last once of energy left in his body. His very bones felt bruised and his muscles were screaming at him. If it hadn't been for Neela and Virginia he'd have begged the Grim Reaper to come get him.

As the elevator rose, he caught sight of himself in the mirrored walls and was shocked. His hair was disheveled, and his right hand shirt collar was torn. Also, his left cheek wore an ugly bruise and there was a black stain of some kind on his chin, possibly grease.

In his suite he poured a drink. Number one priority. Then he headed for the bathroom, splashing cold water first, then washing his face. Priority two. Then he opened the note. *'Please call me as soon as you return from the Gare de Lyon. My thanks. Thierry Gassin. Commandant. La Bac.'*

So, word of his afternoon antics had traveled with lightning speed to the heart of the Quai des Orfèvres.

As he sipped his bourbon, Dermot wondered what their take of the incident would be. Probably they'd think he was becoming unhinged. That he was no longer in control. That he wasn't to be taken too seriously. He could understand such a reaction.

He picked up the phone and dialed the number printed under Gassin's message. The call was answered after one ring.

"Commandant Gassin's office. May I help you?"

"My name is Nolan. Dermot Nolan. I am returning Commandant Gassin's earlier call."

"Please wait," the girl said. Then Gassin was on the line.

"Monsieur Nolan. I am relieved that you called me. I have many questions to ask you."

"I am sure you do. Not least of which concerns my behavior this afternoon. Am I right?"

"Sadly so. But the good news is that in this particular matter, the buck, as they say in America, stops with me since I am the most senior officer in this area."

"I'm relieved to hear that, Commandant."

"Perhaps you can tell me what was going through your mind when you decided to create havoc on the Metro?"

"The truth? Or my excuse – the one the Metro people

found acceptable?"

"I know the latter, so perhaps the truth?"

"I thought I recognized him. I thought it was Hoyle," Dermot replied wearily.

"Where did you think you saw him for the first time?"

"Near the Bastille Metro. There was something about the structure of his face and his walk that struck a chord. I called out to him but he ran off immediately."

"Probably because he thought you had seen him robbing a woman and thought you were a plain clothes officer."

"That must have been the explanation. But if you see things from my point of view…"

"I am doing so. You thought it was a miracle, and you'd seen Nick Hoyle. So you gave chase and punched him as hard as you could."

"I'm afraid so."

"Well, the good news is that I am unwilling to proceed in any way against you. To my mind you helped apprehend a local villain."

"But you said you have bad news as well?" Dermot asked.

"I am afraid I do. The man you punched senseless had to be taken to hospital. He has assured us he plans to take civil action against you. Having reviewed all the facts of the case, I feel you might have made a very expensive mistake, Monsieur Nolan. Sure, he'll be fined for stealing, maybe even go to prison for a few months, but he will end up quite rich. His name is Yves Rikard, for future reference. May I add that everyday life may be very different in America – after all so many people end traffic disputes with a handgun – but in France we try to allow the police to settle arguments."

"I hear what you're saying, Commandant. It won't happen again. But tell me, is there any news of Galina Yablonskaya?"

"I am afraid not," Gassin replied after taking a short breath. "However, we shall be doing our utmost until the deadline expires."

The Commandant hung up, leaving Dermot to his waking nightmare thoughts. Bernard Dutont. Neurosurgeon. He was the third person he'd interviewed. An utterly selfless man who had dedicated his entire life to helping other. He was the best in Europe. Possibly the world. The most dexterous hands in the business. Just to think of Bernard's long slim fingers being chopped off by shears made Dermot shudder. Surely Nick couldn't even consider…?

Banishing any such thoughts from his mind, Dermot refreshed his glass. There was no doubt whatsoever that Bernard would be protected. He most probably had a personal detail of CRS troops outside his house right now.

34.

Gassin and his three lead investigators sat in a circle. They were so close they could almost have leant forward and banged heads. It was Gassin's favored way of intensive brainstorming; similar to an Amerian rules football huddle. All four cops were in a heightened state of '*frisson*', where they were in effect thrilled by the moment.

"We have less than twenty-four hours. So let's abandon our impossible search of Greater Paris and put ourselves into the mindset of our target.

"First, the abduction. Migget?"

"Madame Herault told us she thought she saw a man driving Yablonskaya's Mercedes in the Opera car park, but she couldn't be sure. The car has tinted windows."

"That doesn't help much," Gassin muttered, adding a rhetorical question. "The couple that stated they witnessed the transfer of Yablonskaya to the second van... Are they certain it was the ballet dancer?"

"Yes, certain. At the time they thought she had drunk too much and the man was helping her to a car. Now they know differently."

"Their description of the abductor... are they sure it was Hoyle?"

"They didn't put his face together with the face in the newspapers at the time. When they came forward, they were shown photographs of Hoyle, together with twelve look-alikes. Neither could pick Hoyle for certain. The woman picked Hoyle with four other possibles, the husband had no clue, other than he was sure the man who carried Yablonskaya to the second van was wearing army fatigues."

"If the time factor was of the essence? How would you go about the abduction?"

"Me? I'd be concerned about the noise factor," Becaux replied. "One loud scream and I'd be on the back foot. So, I'd use a fast-acting anesthetic," Becaux replied. "Or a neuromuscular blocker, such as the one Hoyle was fond of using in America."

"Succinylcholine?"

"It would be the swiftest way to subdue someone."

"Okay, moving on. The getaway vehicle? A Peugeot?"

"That's what the couple said. Black. Recent model."

"And this vehicle was located three hours ago, dumped in a car park in the village of Guyancourt, outside Versailles."

"Yes, sir. There were hair samples. The forensic

department have them now."

"So he had another car waiting?"

"Must have, sir."

"And there were no witnesses in Guyancourt?"

"No, sir. But there's a door-to-door being carried out in the area calling for witnesses."

"Good. So what kind of vehicle are we currently looking for?"

Simon answered instantly. "A vehicle with rear door access. It's not easy placing a body in a sedan. And no windows. Or maybe tinted ones. Once the subject is subdued and inside, no one can see in."

"So we are looking at vans of every size and shape?" Gassin enquired.

"Most likely not," Simon continued. "Larger is more conspicuous. Smaller, more convenient and flies under the radar more easily."

"So, a smallish van. Are we wasting our time with registration checks?" Gassin threw the question out as if to himself.

"Even if our target is *not* Hoyle, he would never use his own vehicle."

"So we are now looking for stolen vans?"

They all nodded.

"Which color would be his choice?"

"The color would not be the issue, the van would be. So which color of van is the most popular?

Becaux tapped away at his Blackberry. He had the answer

in less than five seconds. "White; as one might expect."

"So we are looking for a smallish white van that Hoyle or whoever it was that was used to transport Galina Yblonskaya from the car park in Guyancourt to wherever he took her."

All three detectives nodded.

"Becaux, please go and do a thorough search for stolen vehicles of this color and size. I want a map within the hour."

Becaux immediately left the room.

"How many CCTV cameras do we have in the rue de Rivoli. I mean, exactly."

"Twelve, sir, Migget replied. "We have footage of everything."

"Let me see it again," Gassin said, as he stood and pulled down the blinds. The team then walked over to the screen and Becaux pressed a button on the remote.

"There's the van arriving," Becaux said, pointing.

They watched as the dirty white van pulled over. Nothing initially happened. Then the rear door burst open and Kafni was seen being kicked out the back, falling heavily to the roadway.

None of the Lieutenants said anything.

"Notice the leg?" Gassin said, pressing the pause button. "Baggy overalls. He was pretending to be a workman. Franz? Put together an identikit picture – Hoyle's face with three or four day's growth. The dress the body in workmen's overalls. Then start sending it out to the press – without any mention of a name, of course."

Gassin hit the play button and they watched some more footage. The van pulled back into the traffic, the rear door still open. In the street Kafni was already going berserk.

Gassin turned off the video.

"So our man has a vehicle which he drives from wherever he keeps his victims. Then he steals another such van – one he uses for the actual abduction. The he drives this stolen vehicle back to his own van, makes the transfer, finally driving home with his victim."

He looked at his three lieutenants.

"Make sense to you all?"

They all nodded.

"So where will we find his home?" he asked them.

"Somewhere not too far from where he steals his vans?" Migget replied. "Say a perimeter of fifty kilometers from Guyancourt? Why drive further?"

"Excellent thinking. So give me a map with such a perimeter. I want the registrations of all vans that have home addresses I that area. I also want locations of all parking areas, shopping malls and railway stations within that perimeter. If Hoyle moves again, he'll need to steal another van, and we'll have him. But only if we know exactly which location to lock down."

"Moving on. We still don't have any lead concerning the surgical equipment?"

"Such articles are commonplace and freely available on the Internet."

"How about equipment such as heart monitors? We have to remember that our target would be keen to make sure his victim survived the operation."

"This is still equipment that is not so specialized as to draw attention," Migget replied. "However, the list of purchases of heart monitors here contains seventy-four names in the past month, whereas such general equipment as scalpels, forceps and suction tubes are more commonplace."

"So we take that list of seventy-four," Gassin pondered, "and cross-reference the locations of purchase with delivery in the Yvelines department. That will bring us closer".

"Now, the issue we had concerning infection…"

"Locations where the temperature could be reduced to an acceptable level?" Simon chipped in. "Here we have yet another list. Refrigeration companies that have delivered new equipment within the past six months."

"Cross-reference this list with the other two. Now, please."

Simon left the room.

"What of existing cool places – locations where food is stored and kept cold? We could even be looking at large inter-city trucks that transport meat and vegetables across Europe."

"To have one such vehicle parked for so long either in a residential area or at the side of the road would draw attention. With respect, this theory is unlikely, sir."

"True, Migget. I was just putting it out there."

A few seconds passed. "So it is more logical that we are looking at premises. Bricks and mortar?"

"Just so, Commandant."

"A shop with good air-conditioning? Or some industrial cooling systems?"

"Possibly the location we're looking for would be too small for industrial cooling systems."

"A storage facility, then – one servicing a chain of shops?"

"Much more likely."

"How would our target gain access to such a storage facility?"

"If it was currently in use, that would be hard."

"But if it was a facility that was no longer in use, Migget?"

"That would be perfect."

"Please check on all such locations. Then all the lists should be cross-referenced. When that is done, please call me."

Migget stood, reaching for his notes. "Consider it done, sir."

35.

Hoyle studied his appearance in the full-length mirror in his bedroom. This morning, he'd dressed smartly. He wore a single-breasted pale olive green summer suit, white shirt and a pale buttercup tie – no strong colors; that would draw attention to himself. He'd shaven off the beginnings of a beard he'd cultivated for several months, yet he kept a few days growth of a mustache.

In the bathroom that morning he'd dyed his short hair a very dark brown, almost black, and applied a suitably dark tanning agent to make him look almost Middle Eastern. When he was finished, he studied himself in the bathroom mirror. *Who is this man* he chuckled to himself? The addition of some pharmacy bought reading glasses was the final touch.

Mr. Nondescript.

Today was going to be the culmination of several months of intense planning. He was still a long way off from the third and final stage of his game – he'd nicknamed the first part '*Set-Up*', currently he was in '*Play*' mode. The final phase would be '*Endgame*'. Today was going to be a pivotal one in ascertaining whether he'd guessed correctly about so many things; whether he'd judged the character of so many different people correctly. It had been, and would continue to indeed be, the most delicate high wire act.

He drove the Espace to the town of Plaisir, parked it in the railway parking lot in amongst a hundred other commuter cars, then took the SNFC train from Plaisir-les-Clayes into the center of Paris. It was only just past the rush hour period, but there were still quite a few people on the train; fewer in first class where Hoyle was seated. No one paid him any attention – why should they?

He arrived in Paris just after ten in the morning, immediately taking the Metro to Saint Michel. From there it was a short stroll to the café he'd selected earlier in the month in the rue Bonaparte. Dermot was the ultimate man of habit, and a slave to nostalgia – if he rose to the bait and followed him to Europe he'd start off in France and progress from there around Europe. Paris meant l'Hôtel. Simple.

From the Café Hermes he could look directly down the rue des Beaux Arts to the entrance of l'Hôtel. He'd called Dermot's hotel the day before, pretending to be a Californian telephone operator attempting to connect a Mrs. Neela Nolan with her husband, a guest staying at the hotel.

"One moment please," the hotel operator had replied, "while I connect you." Hoyle had immediately hung up. Another correct guess. Nolan was there.

He sat far enough back inside the café so as not to reveal himself to casual passers-by in the rue Bonaparte, yet close enough to the window to have a clear view across the street into the rue des Beaux-Arts.

Hoyle ordered a pichet of house Côtes du Rhône and a Monte Christo sandwich, one of their specialties; Dijon mustard, sliced ham, sliced turkey, Swiss cheese and mayo. Toasted. A cholesterol time bomb.

The waiter returned a few moments later with the wine and poured a splash into his glass.

How was it possible, Hoyle wondered, that it never have

occurred to Dermot that he was giving himself away by staying in the same hotel he had visited for over ten years? Hoyle's old one-time friend wasn't stupid, so it couldn't be as simple as that. It was most likely an ingrained mindset. Dermot saw himself as the chaser, so it never crossed his mind that he should think to cover his own tracks in case he in turn was being *chased*. But this simplistic analysis raised a whole raft of other issues.

It had never been in Dermot's nature to distrust anyone, until they gave him cause. That was immensely naïve. Dermot was not the kind of man who would ever look at people in the street and wonder what they might look like naked; which of the strangers who passed him was a pedophile, who could conceivably have killed a human being, who might be an armed robber, who was on their way home from a mistress to a wife, which of the people crushed against one in a Metro might suddenly go crazy with a knife.

Nick knew that such thoughts occurred to him personally on a minute-by-minute, day-by-day basis, simply out of idle curiosity.

The toasted sandwich arrived. The bread was a rich deep brown as well as crisp, the smell incredibly pervasive. Idly, Hoyle wondered whether a Monte Christo sandwich might have enticed Galina out of her pouty mood. The sullen girl hadn't eaten for twenty-four hours, despite having been offered three varied delicious dishes. It was high time, Hoyle mused, that she got over the loss of her foot and looked forward to a life without dancing.

As Hoyle waited for Dermot to show, he played a game that lonely people often do. They ask themselves questions, based on a topic they pluck out of the air. So, what would be it be today?

Contrasting mindsets! It was an interesting way to wile away the time until Dermot surfaced. His and Dermot's mindsets being the antithesis of each other, it would make the time pass swiftly. Why exactly were they so different? Most likely because Dermot was essentially a good man, despite temporarily acceding to his own best interests over those of the victim's families. He, by contrast, was 'bad to the bone'. He smiled, as the George Thorogood song began to play automatically in his head.

It didn't bother Hoyle in the least to recognize that he' become inherently evil, where once he had been as exemplary as Dermot. That had been long ago; a time when he'd usually seen the best in people, tried to make the world a better place, cared for the down at heel, aided the outcasts of the world, fed the hungry and helped the needy. Now he despised such people because they offered up a mirror to his dark soul – whenever he saw innocence, he saw his own personal turpitude. When he saw happiness, he was reminded of the despair he'd felt when Giselle and the twins were wrenched away from him.

It always seemed to come back to one single issue. If there was a God, why did he strike down those who believed in him? Once, he'd believed. Once, a long time ago, he and Giselle had gone to mass and prayed; not for themselves, but for the well being of the world at large as well as ones they loved. He and Giselle had led a godly life with seldom the smallest sin to confess on Sunday. So why had Giselle and the children been struck down so cruelly? It made no sense. It was an outrage. And the priest's words at the funerals had been so trite and predictable. *It is not for us to know God's will.* That was the gist of the homily at Giselle's funeral. *God is testing you* was the second, when the twins were buried together in one tiny casket.

Why would God the father test one of his flock by burning his children alive? It was an absurd premise. The truth was so much simpler. There *was* no God. Tragedy was meted out in a haphazard fashion, striking when one least expected. Leading a life in the moral sunshine was no safeguard, because if there *was* a God in heaven, he was not in the habit of handing out brownie points.

As Hoyle held up a hand to the waiter for a second pichet, his heart missed a beat and the broadest grin crossed his face. There he was! It was Dermot, walking down the street. He waved the waiter away. "Later," he told him pleasantly.

Hoyle was now totally focused. This was the moment he'd anticipated for so long – he would savor it and take his time. He had everything planned to the smallest detail. Even if Dermot should fail to act predictably and not visit his favorite lunch spot, Hoyle was the epitome of adaptability – another restaurant would do equally well.

The previous night, for the first time in months Dermot had slept soundly. Today he felt physically refreshed, yet thoughts of the adorably innocent Galina were an ever-present knot in the pit of his stomach. He knew the police had less than twenty-four hours to find her. If they failed, there was only the barest chance that she'd be released unharmed. In reality, there was no chance whatsoever – it was simply not in Nick's nature to be merciful; his life was now dictated by a taste for a morbid succession of horrors.

Although Dermot did his best not to dwell on any particular detail of what Hoyle might do to Galina, the most likely scenario based on what Hoyle had done to Josef was too horrific to contemplate. Of course, there was always the possibility that some other innocent would die in a matter of hours. But only if Gassin and his team picked the wrong subject. Hardly likely. Of course in his heart of hearts, Dermot knew the game they were all playing was Hoyle's own deadly game, and the next progression would be for Hoyle to butcher Galina as he had done Kafni. The kid with the wig, the email he'd sent, the words in the note to the Commissaire, the words spoken by Arnold, the fact that Kafni was the first victim, that it was his worst nightmare to lose his hands, and finally the fact that Kafni had been the subject of Dermot's first interview...

It had to be Nick Hoyle.

Two hours before leaving the hotel he'd called Neela. There had been a note at reception that she'd tried to getting through to him during the day but had been cut off.

"Honey? Hope I didn't call too late?"

"Never. How are you? Don't let things get you down, whatever happens."

"I won't. I'm hanging tough, believe me. What's new with you?"

It wasn't in her nature to lie, but since Neela felt secure in the knowledge she was being looked after for the time being by Malibu's finest she thought she'd still keep the news of the Arnold look-alike to herself.

There was an odd hiatus – both of them were holding truths from each other, for the best of all possible reasons of course, but it made conversation difficult.

"Are the French police confident that they can find Galina before…"

"I don't feel that, no. They're confident she was the 'celebrity' Hoyle chose as his second victim."

"They are agreed Hoyle is the perpetrator of this new nightmare?"

"That's debatable. Were I in their shoes I would think differently to what I do now. I might think someone is copying Hoyle's modus operandi. Only you and I can know it's him for sure, because we've both suffered at his hands." He paused. "God, I miss you so much."

"Me too. Remember, if you need me I'll come to you. I'm sure I can leave Vig with my mother."

"No, I'd feel safer knowing she's with you."

"What's today got in store for you?"

"No idea right now. I have to wait till tomorrow morning to see what the outcome of the second kidnapping is."

"It must be terrible for you to be so alone."

"I'm coping."

"So, what's next?"

"No idea. Depends on events. Give Vig a big cuddle from me."

"Will do. Take care, Mister Man."

Now, sometime later, Dermot's mind was full of visions of Neela asleep in her bed, her beautiful face at rest, Virginia asleep in her cot beside her.

As the mental photos flipped like a slideshow, he turned right into the rue Bonaparte, towards the quai Malaquais. He had no inkling that he'd passed no more than fifty feet from the man he was searching for.

Dermot knew he had to wait out the events of the next crucial few hours out, while at the same time desperately trying to figure out any way he could help Gassin track down Nick. Walking was probably the best way to calm his nerves, though today was even hotter than the previous five; scorching heat, blue skies, no breeze, high humidity.

The Seine sparkled, lovers walked arm in arm, laughing at private jokes, dogs scampered about looking for water. The world around him was filled with happy young men and women, amorous tourists enjoying life. Life's tragedies only had meaning when they assaulted personally. Otherwise, life was good.

Dermot continued up to where the road became the quai Voltaire, staring at the cool almost inky serenity of the Seine, a stark contrast to his mood. He eventually stopped at the corner of the rue de Bac for yet another coffee. Paris was a city of coffee houses almost rivalling Milan and Rome. When at a loose end, have an espresso and a Pastis.

Dermot sat at a table inside – the heat was becoming intolerable. Having ordered, he glanced up at the television above the bar. It was tuned to France 24, a news media channel. A young girl was talking – presumably about politics because the photo behind her was of the Palais Bourbon. Since he couldn't hear the sound properly, he contented himself with looking at the pictures. It was then that a photo of Josef Kafni replaced that of the national assembly. Dermot could tell by the suddenly serious expression of the newsreader that she was informing France of some bad news.

He immediately rose from his chair and called to the barman. "Please! I know this man. Can you turn up the volume? Please!"

The barman did as he was asked. Dermot stood beneath the small old-fashioned television.

The newsreader continued her report. Now Dermot could hear.

"The world famous concert pianist had been in hospital for several days suffering deep depression following his abduction and mutilation, resulting in the loss of both hands. His body had been in the water for several hours. The police are viewing Josef Kafni's death as a suicide. He is survived by a wife. She was abducted at the same time as her husband and is still missing."

"You knew this man?" the old patron asked, curious, as the following report began. But Dermot was in another world where he could hear nothing but the echoes of her words. *The police are viewing Josef Kafni's death as a suicide.*

"*Monsieur? Ça va?*

Dermot snapped back mentally into the real world, nodding to the patron. Yes, he was all right.

He took a sip of his coffee but it tasted very bitter, as did life. Kafni couldn't bear life without his hands, so he had committed suicide. Dermot could understand his rationale. He wondered if it was selfish to consider taking his own life – would it ever improve? Would he, Neela and Vig ever lead a normal life again? Not while Hoyle was alive, that was for sure.

He walked to the zinc-covered bar and placed more than enough money in a saucer, then exited the café, to continue his mindless promenade.

Fifty yards down the road Hoyle folded his copy of L'Equipe – he'd been reading of yet more drug scandals involving international cycling teams. As he saw Dermot exit the café, he eased himself off a wall he'd been leaning against.

Hoyle hadn't heard of Kafni's suicide yet, so he had no reason to know what thoughts were uppermost in Dermot's mind. Glancing at his watch he saw it was now close to midday. It was looking less and less likely that Dermot was heading for his favorite restaurant, *Au Chien qui Fume*, in the rue de Pont-Neuf – that was in the opposite direction. So where was he heading? What was wrong with him, anyway? Any normal human being thought of food at midday. Dermot? No, he was probably thinking of churches or libraries!

He saw Dermot turn into the rue de l'Université. Hoyle quickened his pace just in case Dermot disappeared into a building – it was always possible he was calling on a friend of which Hoyle was unaware.

But as Hoyle turned in the rue de l'Université, he was relieved to see Dermot still ambling aimlessly along the street.

Half way down Dermot stopped by a small restaurant, looking through the window, cupping a hand against the sun so he could see inside. He then studied the menu framed by the door.

Hoyle smiled. Bingo! He was about to stop for food! Not one of the restaurants Hoyle had had in mind, but *tant pis*— never mind. He'd have to think quickly. He'd never visited this particular restaurant; *L'Oie sans Jambes*, but it would probably suit his purposes. If not, all bets would be off. But there'd always be another day. A nuisance, no more. The name of the bistro was ironical. *The Goose without Legs*? It was actually quite funny, bearing in mind his latest victim's current physical shape.

So, it was time for Plan B. This involved all the key elements of Plan A. First, wait for twenty minutes, allowing Dermot to find a table, order, and have his first course served to him at his table for one.

In many respects this was an ideal location for what he had in mind; it was an older style restaurant—one probably not very full; one where he could execute his plan away from too many close prying eyes.

Twenty minutes later, as Hoyle entered the restaurant, he was thrilled to see the restaurant was practically empty. He'd been fully expecting the worst possible scenario – that the first person he'd be looking at would be Dermot. Then he'd see exactly how good his disguise was. However, it was quickly apparent that the place was a labyrinth of small rooms and anterooms.

There was a central eating area, which had several tables in the middle and several banquet seats set against the walls, each of which was upholstered in red plush. Only two banquets and one table were occupied. Off to the left and right were two further, more intimate areas.

Without entering these smaller rooms, Hoyle had no way of knowing in which Dermot was sitting. As the overly tall, emaciated maitre d' appeared from the back of the restaurant Hoyle noticed there was also an eating nook at the back to the right.

The interior was very fifties; smoke-stained walls with old fashioned Paris furniture. The diners seated in the main room, were all in their sixties. All in all, it was an ideal restaurant for his purposes.

The maitre d' approached him without a smile. He looked tired, anorexic and depressed. If he'd entered the Nosferatu look-alike competition he'd have won hands down.

"A table, Monsieur?" he asked.

"Yes, please. May I look and see where I'd like to sit," Hoyle replied in perfect French.

"Of course, sir."

Hoyle smiled, his fingers curling over the auto injector in his pocket. It was filled with Succinylcholine.

Quickly, Hoyle mentally prepared himself for the next vital few minutes as an Olympic gymnast might visualize their routine, microsecond by microsecond. Seconds later he was fired up and ready.

He walked towards the first room on the right.

As he entered, he saw two middle-aged women in one of the booths, and an elderly man with a much younger androgynous looking youth seated on the other banquet. There were two other seats available.

Dermot was not there.

He turned and made his way back to the central room and across to the second room.

He immediately saw Dermot. He was seated in a booth with his back to the door. Hoyle blessed his luck, hoping that it held firm. The second banquet was empty. Hoyle could hardly believe his good fortune!

The small anteroom was quiet as the grave; all Hoyle could hear was the faint sound of knives scraping against plates behind him in the central room. The moment had come.

He walked into the room as silently as he could. Dermot was on his left. As he passed the booth, he pretended to stumble, falling to his knees with a grunt of feigned surprise and annoyance. As he'd predicted, Dermot rose to see if he could help in any way – he was basically a good man at heart.

"Are you all right?" Dermot asked the swarthy man with the glasses and pale olive suit.

"Thank you, Monsieur," Hoyle replied, amazed that Dermot had no idea who he was, even at a few feet. Of course, Hoyle was shielding most of his face, pretending he'd hit his forehead, but he congratulated himself nevertheless on his disguise.

As Hoyle rose, Dermot began to sit down again. Hoyle turned to face him, but still Dermot failed to recognize him.

"May I buy you an aperitif, by way of thanks, sir?" Hoyle asked in a Mediterranean accent, one he felt suited his dark Algerian appearance.

Dermot simply smiled briefly and looked away. His mind was still a million miles away, on another planet. "Thank you, that won't be necessary, I've already ordered some burgundy," he replied.

That's when he was surprised to see that the swarthy man was wearing latex gloves.

But by this time it was too late.

Hoyle leant forward and stuck Dermot's upper arm with the needle, forcing him backwards into the red banquet seat, pressing his left hand hard over Dermot's mouth to stifle the shout of surprise.

The struggle lasted just a few seconds. Then the neuromuscular blocker kicked in and Dermot sank back into his seat, limp as a rag doll. Dermot's eyes stared blankly at his attacker, as they had all those months ago when Nick had hammered down the top of his coffin.

Hoyle was very aware that Dermot could see and hear everything. He'd know exactly what was happening to him. Of course, any movement was out of the question.

As Hoyle relaxed his grip and sat down opposite Dermot, the Maitre d' appeared at the door. He'd probably heard something and come to see if everything was in order. He looked inquiringly at Hoyle, who simply stared into space.

"I am ready to order now," Hoyle said, to gain the waiter's attention. "I will have the same as my friend here. We will share the wine for now and order more as and when we need more."

"Of course, Monsieur," the spidery waiter replied, leaving Hoyle and Dermot alone in the room.

Hoyle looked deep into Dermot's eyes then down at the plate of deep-fried brie and raspberry sauce, studying it as might a food critic.

"Hmmm. A little sugary to my taste. I'll leave you the sweetness," he said, taking a piece of the cheese with his fingers and popping it in his mouth. "Actually,"he added, with an appreciative shrug, "it's not at all bad. Hope you don't mind my snitching some of your wine too."

He knew Dermot could not speak, so he poured some of Dermot's white wine into a second glass and chugalugged the contents.

"I don't have much time today. I just thought…well, you've gone to so much trouble to find me, I thought I'd make your life just that much easier and come and find *you*."

Hoyle could see Dermot vainly struggling to move his lips even half an inch. It was an impossibility.

"I hope you are enjoying my 'game'. You should, because were it not for you, Kafni would still have both his divine hands, and Madamoiselle Yablonskaya would still have both her dancing feet."

He stared at Dermot, looking for and spotting the smallest of reactions. The pupils dilated – clearly the news of Galina's amputation had hit home hard. Hoyle chuckled.

"Had you remained in your…" he paused to give emphasis to the word, "…wooden box, all would have been well. But sadly you survived, and now I'm obliged to continue your nightmare, taking it to new heights."

Hoyle popped another morsel of cheese in his mouth and refreshed his glass.

"I shall be leaving Paris shortly. A lovely place for a holiday, but to live here? Nah. I'm one of those Americans who think the French are arrogant.

"So when you recover, I'd be grateful if you'd remember me to the Paris police and tell them to..." he positively beamed at Dermot, "...*catch me if they can*. This really applies to you more than the local boys in blue."

Finishing his second glass of wine, Hoyle rose.

"I shall eventually summon you to a meeting, so we can end this game – fun though it has been up until now. This won't be that long in the future. I would advise you to do two things. One: tell no one I have made contact when I finally do so. Two: come alone. Should you decide to do otherwise, you will never see me again."

He leant across the table and reached inside Dermot's jacket pocket, withdrawing his wallet. "I am afraid I have to do this, otherwise people will dispute my purpose here today."

Hoyle pocketed the wallet, then his wine glass on which just might be some DNA where he'd sipped. Then he walked to the doorway and turned. "Oh yes, I forgot to finish what I was saying. If you don't agree to my terms and keep this matter between us, and should you not come alone, *you* will never see me, but your wife and child will.

"*Bon appétit*," Hoyle said in a dreary monotone, then left Dermot alone.

Feeling did not return to Dermot's limbs for eight minutes. During that time the Maitre d' returned with the second plate of Brie, together with more raspberry sauce.

Placing it opposite Dermot, he again briefly glanced at

him. The diner appeared to be dozing. Yet there was a strange look in his eyes; or so the gaunt Maitre d' thought.

Ten minutes later as the head waiter was serving customers in the central room, he heard someone calling from the room where he had served the two cheese appetizers. Turning his head towards the sound, he was shocked to see Dermot crawling like a semi-anesthetized cockroach from the smaller room into the central area. It was the man who he'd thought was dozing!

"*Mon dieu!*" he said, striding towards Dermot and crouching down. "Monsieur! Are you ill?"

Dermot managed a few weak words. "Please call the police. I've ... been... attacked."

36.

Gassin, Becaux, Migget and Simon had been working without a break for ten hours. Sandwiches and Perrier water had been sent in on a regular basis, but only the water was taken.

Gassin looked a good five years older than when he'd showered that morning.

"The lists! Show me the lists," he called to his team.

Each hour, on the hour, he'd called for the lists. Each time he looked at them, the number of possibilities were fewer. But they were still a long way from tracking Galina. The list of stolen vehicles had been reduced from one hundred and twenty to sixty. The list of car parks where cars might be easily stolen in the Yvelines department was huge – over three hundred. Gassin was doing his best to organize a police surveillance of as many locations on that list as possible, but it was a question of manpower, plain and simple. The list of operating cold storage facilities had been reduced from ninety-three to twelve. None looked likely candidates. Simon was compiling a list of cold store facilities that were no longer operating. Currently there were over two hundred in the Greater Paris and Yvelines area. The list of people who had bought heart monitors in the past six months was over two hundred, and it was quite possible that this equipment could be bought on the Internet and shipped to France from overseas.

Gassin and his lieutenants again sat down in their circle of chairs, handing their chief the lists they had made.

As Gassin read the final list and prepared to talk, there was a knock at the door. A police woman entered.

"I asked not to be disturbed?" Gassin said, not too sternly.

"I apologize, sir. I was instructed by Commissaire Barbier to tell you that Mr. Nolan has just been taken to the Assistance Publique-Hospitaux de Paris in the Avenue Victoria."

The policewoman left, leaving all four men looking stunned. Gassin reached for a phone and hit a speed dial button.

"Gassin here, sir. What happened?"

He listened for a couple of minutes.

Gassin replaced the receiver then addressed his team. "It would appear that Dermot Nolan was mugged in a restaurant in the sixième during lunch. He was robbed. But here's the thing. Listen to this. Nolan maintains his attacker was none other than Nick Hoyle – the so-called Dreamhealer.

"He's said as much?" Becaux asked. The detective was veering towards the belief that Nolan was still mentally unbalanced enough to see Nick Hoyle at every corner of the street – like a mirage in the desert. Yet, if he indeed *had* been injected with Sux, then there would be some difficulty in disbelieving him.

"The problem with Succinylcholine is that it remains in

the body for such a short time. It breaks down so easily," Gassin muttered to himself.

"There must have been witnesses?" Migget asked.

"One old man. A waiter. The initial report states he saw an Algerian enter the restaurant and sit down opposite Nolan. They chatted for some time, then the Algerian left."

"Despite my reservations," Becaux said, "concerning Nolan's mental health–reservations I know you're familiar with, sir – if he has Sux in his system it has to be Hoyle. Yes?"

No one appeared to dispute this. Becaux continued. "But you said he was mugged. Was he robbed?"

"He was," Gassin replied. "His wallet was taken."

"The perpetrator was ID'd by the maitre d' as Algerian looking. And this waiter maintained Nolan was chatting to him before the attack – they were sharing lunch?"

"That's not very clear at this moment," Gain replied.

"It's all very odd," Becaux continued. "Nolan would hardly spend time chatting to Hoyle, unless he stuck him with Sux. It's more probable he struck up a conversation with a stranger he thought was a decent man yet turned out to be a thief."

Becaux looked at his colleagues. All were deep in thought.

"There are too many unexplained pieces of this puzzle right now," Gassin offered. "And nothing is what it seems to be. Add to the mix that Nolan has only recently recovered from psychiatric treatment and we have a very emotionally disturbed man on our hands."

Gassin stood. "I'll go and speak to him. Meanwhile send out the CRS if you think there's *any* solid lead. And see how many of the car park locations we can secure in the next few hours. That's paramount. It's all we can do at the moment."

On the journey to the Publique-Hospitaux, Gassin switched on his cell phone and was updated on the tragic death of Josef Kafni. The pianist had discharged himself from hospital and appeared to the medical team to be compos mentis. Though naturally concerned about Kafni's state of mind, the staff had no power to keep him under supervision against his will, so he left, alone. Two hours later several emergency calls were received stating that a man had been seen throwing himself off the Pont Neuf. It was Kafni. Apparently the fall killed him instantly.

Arriving at the hospital, Gassin was directed to a private room on the fifth floor. Dermot was sitting up in bed, watching the television monitor.

"Thank you for coming, Commandant. Despite rumors to the contrary I am sane and in good health. I shall be discharging myself as soon as you leave – I only stayed here to wait for you, and talk."

"No. I thank *you* Mr. Nolan," Gassin replied holding out a hand.

Dermot took it and smiled warmly. "I think we're on first name terms now, what do you say?"

"Fine. Dermot," Gassin smiled back.

"It was Nick Hoyle," Dermot continued after a few moments of silence.

Gassin was at a loss how to begin.

"It was?" the Commandant replied.

Dermot picked up on Gassin's tone; it had a dubious lilt.

"You weren't there," Dermot said, a trifle harshly. "I was. I have known the man intimately for many, many years. Once we were like brothers. I can see through a disguise. At the time not instantly, my mind was elsewhere."

"Let me ask you a question, and please don't take any

offense."

"Of course I won't, Commandant."

"Thierry."

"Thierry."

"You were sitting in…shall we call it a 'private' room?"

"No, it was simply a room that was empty, set apart from the central room."

"You preferred this room because…?"

"Because I had just seen the television reports of Josef's suicide and I was deeply depressed, I wanted to be alone."

"I see. Yes, it was a very terrible tragedy."

Gassin clawed for suitable words. "So, while you were sitting there a man entered the room?"

"Correct."

"Did you recognize him as Nick Hoyle right away?"

"No, I didn't. I was miles away, as I said just now. Not concentrating. Then the man appeared to slip and fall. A ruse, of course. I rose to extend a hand to help him up. That's when he stabbed me with the syringe. I didn't stand a chance. I was incredibly stupid."

"So, let me get this straight; you didn't recognize him as Hoyle until you were immobile and staring at him?"

"Correct."

"Then you recognized him immediately?"

From Dermot's reaction Gassin could see this was not the case.

"Well… no. Not for some seconds. His face was so deeply

tanned with make-up, and he had a mustache. But it was what he said."

Dermot repeated every word of the conversation barring the last two sentences. There was no way in the world he was going to tell Gassin that Hoyle had threatened Neela and Vig again – he simply couldn't put his faith in the police any more. Who knew, he might have to take Hoyle up on his personal challenge, and then the last thing he wanted was the police dogging his steps, getting in the way. He might even be forced to kill Hoyle, who knew what the endgame might be?

Gassin listened intently to Dermot's detailed yet incomplete report, especially the part when he stated why he was taking the wallet.

"He took the wallet so that we might think he tried to rob you, when in reality he was there to torment you?"

"I don't really need to reinforce that theory – I was there and that was exactly what he told me."

Dermot was becoming irritable; Gassin could see that.

"And his voice?"

"It was Nick's. I could never forget it."

Gassin looked away as though deep in thought.

"You don't for one second think I'm loony, do you?"

Gassin smiled. "Loony? A quaint word. No, of course not."

"Then why all these questions? I'm telling you, it was Hoyle. He stuck me with the neuromuscular blocker as he did before. Then told me he was the author of these crimes. What more do you need? Fingerprints?"

"The restaurant was dusted, Dermot. There were no prints."

"He was wearing gloves!"

"Of course he was," Gassin replied, in the knowledge that the old maitre d' had no recollection of the Algerian having worn any gloves.

"Please don't make fun of me, Commandant."

"Forgive me, I do not wish to give that impression."

That seemed to placate Dermot – he was silent for a while.

"How far forward are you in the Yablonskaya investigation, Thierry?"

"We are, as you Americans say, *'getting there.'* But we have not so many hours left and we have, as yet, not *'gotten there'*."

"Will you? Get there, I mean?"

"I hope so," Gassin replied, rising. "I must leave you now, Dermot. Keep yourself safe and get some serious rest. I shall keep you up to date with everything as it happens."

Gassin opened the door then turned. "Dermot, may I give you some advice? As a friend?"

"Of course. I would be glad of any advice."

"Then, with the utmost respect, may I suggest you go home to America to put yourself out of the reach of this man. If he is in Paris–"

"If?" Dermot almost shouted. "Are you doubting me?"

"A trip of the tongue. Forgive me."

Dermot didn't feel like telling him it didn't matter.

"You must not only consider your personal safety, but that of your wife and daughter…"

Dermot immediately looked alarmed. "Has something happened to my wife?"

"Not as far as I am aware," Gassin replied, making a mental note to call Hansen to see if there had been any problems his end. "However, I can't see you're helping matters too much simply by being here."

"I have been successful enough to bring Hoyle out in the open after months of his lying low. Surely that is help enough," Dermot replied somewhat coldly.

There was nothing Gassin could say that wouldn't yet again cast doubt on Hoyle's appearance, so he left matters at that.

"*Au revoir*, Dermot. Take care. If you should need anything, please call me on my cell phone. Normally you get through at once."

As Gassin left, Dermot was swinging his legs out of bed and reaching for his clothes.

Down the corridor, Gassin found the doctor who had attended Dermot and asked him if he could have a few moments of his time.

In a small consulting room, the doctor sat opposite Gassin.

"There was no evidence of any drug?"

"No, there was not. However, as you know, Succinylcholine..."

"Doctor, did you find any evidence of Monsieur Nolan having been stuck by a needle?"

"Yes, we did. At least, it seems more likely than not. You see there is no way of telling exactly when the mark we believe to be the needle stick was caused. For instance, he could have stuck himself in the arm an hour previously."

"With an empty syringe? To reinforce his story?"

"Exactly."

"I am curious. Why would you think of this as a possibility, Doctor?"

"I am simply being thorough. There were no traces of any narcotic or anesthetic in his system when he was brought in. Added to this, his body was functioning normally."

"You thought the needle stick could have been self-inflicted?"

"At first, no. But it was Mr. Nolan's demeanor that disturbed me."

"In what way, Doctor?"

"His manner was erratic and exaggerated. He was speaking very fast; about being a victim. He scared my staff. Told them he had been assaulted by a serial killer who, for all he knew, might be here in the hospital."

"You thought he was crazy?"

"Initially, we *all* did. Then a supervisor recognized him and they talked about his past; the book and so one."

"And this changed your opinion? About whether he was behaving in a psychotic manner?"

"It made me wonder whether Mr. Nolan had recovered adequately from his terrible ordeal."

"Or whether he should still be undergoing psychiatric counseling?"

"Exactly, Commandant. Exactly."

Fifteen minutes later Gassin was knocking at the apartment

door of the Maitre d' of the *Oie sand Jambes* restaurant. The apartment was situated on the fifteenth floor of a depressingly gray block of 1950's housing developments on the Quai de Bercy. The man's name was Benjamin Toupis. He had gone home immediately after being questioned by the gendarmes who'd been called to the restaurant. Police notes suggested the elderly man was deeply upset, and not a little frightened by what had happened.

The moment Toupis opened the door to him, Gassin knew the man had had a few drinks too many.

"Monsieur Toupis? I am Commandant Gassin. May I step inside and ask you a few questions? It will not take very long."

"I answered all the police questions, already," Toupis answered sullenly.

"You did, and we are most grateful. However, if you could spare me say ten more minutes?"

Wearily, Toupis waved the Commandant into his apartment.

It was a small squalid set of rooms. Dirty dishes and empty glasses were everywhere. Toupis made an effort to clear the coffee table of dirty glasses, ashtrays, plates with encrusted food scraps, finally gesturing Gassin to sit. He did so.

"Can I get you a drink, sir," Toupis asked. "As you see, I have one already."

"My thanks but no thanks. Not this moment."

Toupis drank half of what he had in his glass – it looked like a spirit rather than wine – and waited for the questions. Gassin took a photo from his pocket.

"Have you ever seen this man before, Monsieur Toupis?" Gassin asked, handing the photo to Toupis.

Toupis squinted at the photo, then took out his reading

glasses from an inside pocket to study it harder. Eventually, he handed it back to Gassin. "No. Never. I would remember. This man looks like an American. The man who came into the restaurant was an Algerian. Could have been Lebanese, I suppose."

"You are sure of this?"

"I served once for the Foreign Legion..." He paused then smiled wryly as he saw Gassin's reaction. "You find this hard to believe? Because I drink a lot? Because my body is shot to hell?"

"Not at all," Gassin replied, though it was surprising information.

"I served with many North African men. I can tell the difference between a white man and a North African."

"You told the police that they were talking at the table."

"Yes, the Algerian was already seated at the table when he ordered his appetizer. The other man said nothing."

"Did the other man, Monsieur Nolan, look ill?"

"No. He just sat there, saying nothing."

"Did you see the Algerian man leave?"

"No. It was only when I saw the other man...Monsieur Nolan? That's his name?"

Gassin nodded.

"When I saw him on the floor I knew something was very wrong and I called the police."

There wasn't much else Gassin could ask. It was indeed a puzzle. How could he disbelieve Nolan when he maintained he'd been confronted by Hoyle, face to face? Why would Nolan choose to lie? Perhaps Nolan was seeing ghosts and phantoms – if he was indeed, as Antoine Becaux was suggesting, still emotionally and psychologically unstable enough to see visions and misinterpret faces and facts. Could Nolan have been in some kind of delirium? Had he made up the conversation? It certainly made sense that he had been subdued with *some* kind of an anesthetic, otherwise what the hell was he doing when the Algerian – or whoever he was – was frisking him and relieving him of his wallet. But why was Dermot chatting to the man? Was it simply that the maitre d' *assumed* they were chatting, when in fact Dermot was already under the influence of some drug such as Succinylcholine, and it was Hoyle who was doing all the talking.

As he drove back to his office he continued to ponder on what exactly had happened in the restaurant; because this fundamentally either gave credence to Hoyle's involvement in Kafni's death, or did the opposite. Was Nolan still in the possession of all his marbles, or was he seeing things?

The kid in Malibu. No one but Nolan saw him, and there was no evidence found; no wig, no kid. Toupis' version of what went down was in stark contrast to Nolan's. Was he simply mugged for his money? If so, Nolan was in the grip of some psychotic episode? Or was he deliberately lying? If he was completely sane yet lying, why? Could he find any possible reason for Nolan to have self-injected?

As he crossed the Pont de Sully a thought came to him. Was it conceivable that the whole idea of Dermot Nolan's visit was to smoke out Nick Hoyle?

Gassin immediately tried to interpret everything that Dermot had done that would fit in with this possibility. He'd had spent many months obsessed by Hoyle but unable to gain any closure because his nemesis had gone to ground. This made Nolan so agitated that he hatched a plan to utilize the worldwide media to again draw attention to Hoyle's disappearance. While the story had been huge when Hoyle initially disappeared, along the line it had lost momentum. Was he now trying to refocus the attention of the world press on the location of the serial killer?

It was a theory that deserved merit.

Of course it was close to impossible to entertain the theory that Nolan was involved in Kafni's death. But he had to remember that the use made of the two words that had initially sparked Gassin's interest, *Worst Nightmares*, could as easily have been a deliberate ploy by person or persons unknown to point the finger at Hoyle. After all, as the world media had so many times pointed out, those words were on the lips of the men and women in the streets on a daily basis.

So could Dermot have lied about the kid with the orange hair? Had it been a hallucinogenic episode? Maybe. If he'd deliberately lied, then why? To stir LAPD into reinvigorating their investigation. Maybe Nolan thought the Immigration guys had let Hoyle slip through their net through sheer incompetence – somehow managed to leave the country? If so, his anger would be directed at the authorities and he'd be doing all he could to stir up Interpol too. That would mean traveling to Europe, and staging a show that would make the front pages of every newspaper in Europe.

The one thing Dermot couldn't have foreseen was that someone would commit the horrific crime of cutting the hands off world famous pianist Josef Kafni at exactly same time! That crime had stolen the limelight. So when he was mugged in the restaurant, it was like a gift from heaven – he could say it was Hoyle! *'Serial killer, responsible for thirteen horrific deaths in America, alive and roaming the streets of Paris!'* What an incredible headline that would have been. But once again there had been an even greater story unfolding – Josef Kafni, the maestro without hands, had thrown himself off the Pont Neuf! That was the headline *de jour*.

It would be interesting to see whether the news media got wind of the incident in the *l'Oie sans Jambes*. Toupis might try to interest the media in the story and make a few Euros, but Gassin wasn't at all sure the man knew how important that story might be. Notwithstanding Toupis, it surely would make the papers, albeit on an inside page. But the front page would be reserved for Kafni.

Gassin was so wired by his train of thought that when a visual image of Yablonskaya entered his head – standing on the stumps of her ankles, the feet missing – that his foot instinctively jerked onto the brakes, and the car stopped suddenly. There was a harsh smack as the vehicle behind collided with the rear of Gassin's car.

Gassin opened his driver's door as he reached for his badge. This wasn't going to be a good day for the guy behind.

37.

Hoyle alighted from the train at Plaisir-les-Clayes and walked towards his Espace. Everything had gone wonderfully well. Much better than he could have ever iagined. It was sheer luck that Nolan had been dining alone. Such incredible privacy. There was no doubt that by now Dermot would be in a state of exaggerated panic – screaming to the police that he had been attacked by Nick Hoyle! What were they going to do about it! The cops would be wondering, *what the hell's all this about? Is this guy for real? Has he lost it completely?* Because what evidence would Nolan have? Nothing. No prints, no DNA – Hoyle had taken his wine glass with him. The waiter could only attest that a swarthy looking man had entered the restaurant and sat down with Nolan. So the reappearance of Hoyle? *I don't think so.*

It was all such fun. Once again he was making Dermot look like such an ass, turning his allies against him and driving him nuts. *Some good things,* Hoyle thought with a smile.

As Hoyle drove his Espace out of the parking lot in Plaisir, Commandant Gassin was opening the door to his office. At that precise moment his cell phone cheeped.

Inside, the three musketeers were still working hard. Migget held up a hand, but Gassin motioned him to wait until he'd listened to the call.

As Gassin listened his stomach heaved. Was there no end to the twists and sudden turns of this case?

He flipped the phone shut. Becaux, Simon and Migget looked at him, fully aware that something bad must have occured. What could it be? They were still hours from the deadline. Had the kidnapper changed the rules again?

"Information please, gentlemen," Gassin said after a beat or two, trying to unscramble his brain.

"We instigated five CRS raids since you left. Two cold store units with white vans outside. One a semi-trailer, one together with a cream van. Two shops with refrigeration facilities, the owners of which had form and vans."

"And?"

"Nothing sir. However, the lists are becoming much shorter."

"He may not *be* on the list!" Gassin barked, then immediately regretted his tone; after all they were doing their best. "I'm sorry, gentlemen. I have just received some news which puts a huge spanner in the works."

They all looked at Gassin, waiting for him to enlarge.

"Interpol has just been in touch with Commissaire Barbier. It seems that Mr. Hoyle cannot be responsible for the present abductions."

"How so, sir?" Migget asked.

"He is dead," Gassin replied flatly.

"Do we have a body, sir?" This time it was Simon.

"No, not as yet. No body."

"Then he is not dead. Not definitively. He *may* be dead," Simon added.

"I'm glad you see it that way. I agree. I always see dead ends as a place that have escape routes. You have lifted my depression," Gassin replied with a smile.

"What was the information, sir?" Becaux asked.

"The Sicilian police have informed Interpol that an informant has come forward. The man positively identified the photograph Interpol published as that of Nick Hoyle. The man maintains Hoyle had been living rough on the informant's land for several months. Of course, at that time he had no idea that the man he was sharing food with was a serial killer. When by chance he saw Hoyle's photograph on the television he recognized him."

"You said he was dead, sir," Migget said.

"The informant watched him walk out into the sea at a place called Aspra in northern Sicily. Hoyle was apparently depressed and drunk. Our informant watched him until his head went under. He called out to him, but there was no response."

"The informant called the police immediately?"

"No. Two days later. Initially he did nothing – he's an old man; he didn't initially want any involvement with the authorities. Then he felt bad about things, thinking the man might have had a wife and family. It was then he chanced upon the picture on the television."

"Chanced?" Migget said with a sarcastic tone in his voice.

Gassin locked eyes with him, asking a question.

Migget answered quickly. "Everything about the Kafni death and the arrival of Nolan has been awash with coincidence. I just don't buy this."

"Interesting," Gassin replied. "Are you suggesting that Hoyle somehow engineered his own death?"

"It happens all the time, sir. I would be happier if I was

looking down at him on a tray in the morgue. Then, and only then, I might believe Hoyle was dead – but only when I had DNA proof."

"Whether Hoyle is dead is not our most pressing problem. We shall address that tomorrow morning. We have much to do."

As Gassin and his team got back to work, Hoyle was fixing himself a long gin and tonic and relaxing in his living room. He'd stopped at the Champion supermarket and spent considerable time selecting the food for dinner – after all, it was to be Jean Ballon's last supper; it had to be special. He'd chosen lobster bisque for a starter, his own favorite soup, followed by Chateaubriand with a cognac sauce – the sauce was in a separate container – with a parmesan flan with tomatoes and basil as an alternative to meat. To finish he would offer *choux a la crème* – delicious choux pastry cream puffs filled with cream. What more could a condemned man wish for? The wine? What else but champagne! The others would think it was to celebrate their release. So which to serve? No question here. Krug! Hoyle didn't want to appear cheap. Only he would know it would be the last liquid to slip down the surgeon's throat.

38.

Dermot knew there'd be no question of keeping any more secrets from Neela. If she saw what had happened to him in Paris on the news, she'd never forgive him for not sharing it with her.

So the first thing he did when he returned to l'Hôtel was to call her.

"Hi, honey. How's things?" he asked when he was connected.

"Fine. Just fine." The lies never came easy to Neela, not as easy as Dermot's had during the murder trial.

"Just called to say I'm fine too. I mean, really."

"What do you mean but that; the 'really' bit?" she asked, in doubt as to whether he was about to tell her something bad had happened.

"There was an incident. That's all. I'm fine."

Neela's stomach turned to water. "An incident? What incident?"

"He came for me."

There was a stunned silence the other end of the line as Neela took in the full impact of his words.

"He came? Who came? Nick? Oh, Jesus…"

"Hey, take it easy, Neels. I told you I'm fine. I'm talking to you from my suite in l'Hôtel. I'm sitting on my hotel bed."

"Then just tell me what the heck happened with you; I'm dying here."

"What?" Dermot was immediately panicked.

"Dying with anticipation and dread, for Christ's sake! Tell me what happened."

"I didn't recognize him. He was in some kind of disguise. Looked dark, like some Lebanese guy. I was in a restaurant and he came in and stuck me with that Sux stuff. Then he calmly told me he was having fun playing his disgusting game, that he was about to disappear someplace else. He said he'd be in touch sometime soon, and we'd have it out between us. Just him and me."

Dermot listened, waiting for a response, but there wasn't one. All he could hear was Neela weeping softly.

"Neels? Don't cry. Everything'll be okay. I promise you."

"How can you say that, when the truth is it's never worked out that way before? Nothing has *ever* been fine. The police have never been able to stop him. And now he brazenly walks up to you, in the center of Paris, sticks you with a needle and says he's going to come after you yet again!"

"Hey, steady, Neels. At least he's out in the open, no? That means he can be recognized and possibly found. It's not like before, when we didn't know whether he was alive or dead; whether he was about to appear and terrorize us. Now it's different. We know he was in Paris today. That means you and Vig are safe for now. By the time I've finished with the authorities, the borders will be locked down so tight that there'll be no way he can get back to the U.S. to haunt you, Vig, *or* me!"

"Really...?" Neela replied. She didn't believe it – in her opinion Nick was the Scarlet Pimpernel, *we seek him here, we seek him there, those Frenchies seek him everywhere.*

"Yes, really. You have to believe it!"

Neela continued to cry for a few moments, then pulled herself together sufficiently to ask him to come home. "We need you home with us, honey. I can't face every day, not knowing what's happening to you in Europe, waiting for just such a call as this. It's driving me crazy and that's exactly what Hoyle wants."

"Nick *wants* me to come home! That's his angle! If I come home, he'll have won!"

"If you come home, you'll be able to look after our child, for heaven's sake! And me! Doesn't that count any more? Or is tracking down your demon now the paramount factor? For Christ's' sake, prioritize!"

Dermot was temporarily shocked. "Did something happen?"

Neela couldn't keep it in any more. "*Sure,* something

happened," Neela cried out through her tears.

"Why didn't you tell me, honey?" Dermot replied in a more soothing tone, yet terrified about what she might say. "Tell me."

"Someone came to the house. He was dressed like Arnold. He pressed his face to the bathroom window, just like you told me Arnold did in the train that time. It was disgusting. I was sitting on the loo with Vig in my lap waiting for the police to arrive – I'd called Hansen, when I saw a shadow outside. The man scared me to death – all I could think of was tiny Vig."

"Calm down, Neels. When did this happen?"

"Couple of days ago."

"Why didn't you tell me, for heaven's sake?"

"Because I didn't want to worry you – you had enough to worry about. Besides, Hansen called the Malibu police and they came out."

"They found the guy?"

"No, he'd gone by then."

"He was just there to scare you. Like me and the kid."

"Well, he succeeded. Anyway, I told Hansen what happened. He got the Malibu Sheriff's office to put a patrol car outside for two days."

"It's still there? The patrol car?"

"No, not any more – that's why I need you home. I can look after you, and you can look after us; for Christ's sake I simply can't cope any more."

Dermot could tell she wasn't in control. He had no choice. "Honey, I'm coming home today. Okay? I'm coming. Right now I want you to take Vig and move into the Bel Air Hotel.

They have the best security. Call Hansen and tell him you're moving there till I get back, and tell him what happened to me. Ask him to contact whoever he thinks are the right people to get the borders locked down somehow. Tell him we're certain Hoyle's coming home; to have it out with me."

"Okay," Neela breathed in a whisper. "Okay..."

"You pick up Vig's things and go. Got that? Now."

"Okay..." Neela replied. Dermot could imagine her entire body shaking.

"I love you," Dermot said, then put down the phone and looked at his watch. Could he, in good faith, really leave before the 9 a.m. deadline tomorrow? If he did, he'd be in the air when Galina was either released or killed. And Gassin and his men were hopefully close to tightening the net around Hoyle. How could he leave when he was so close to witnessing Hoyle being taken down at last?

He picked up the phone.

"Mr. Nolan. Can I help you?" It was the concierge downstairs, ever attentive.

"Yes, I am afraid I have to get back to America urgently. Something has come up. Can you possibly make a reservation for me for tomorrow. A flight around midday?"

"Of course, Monsieur Nolan. Leave it with me. I have all your details with me here downstairs, it should be no problem."

Gassin and his team worked throughout the night. Teams of CRS police were sent out every half hour to locations Gassin thought worthy of merit. One hundred and thirteen car parks were now under surveillance in the Yvelines department. Seventy-three still remained unguarded. All they could do was continue to play hunches and blunder about in the dark, ever pairing down the numbers on the lists. Gassin was at least assured now that he had the correct name – Yablonskaya. Yet the horror of thinking she might be mutilated in the same way as Kafni dogged his thoughts. It was unthinkable, yet... thinkable.

At midnight Gassin received a call from Barbier.

"How's it going, Thierry? There was a deal of CRS action last night, I hear."

"Yes, sir. It was the only hand we had to play – to take our chances."

"Still no ballet dancer?"

"No, sir."

"Well, keep busy. You're doing all you can, I know. Be at my home by 8 a.m. please. Try not to draw any media attention. I will be giving a press conference at the Préfécture at 10 am."

Gassin knew it would most probably be the most anticipated press conference the media had attended for years – France had already been rocked by Kafni's horrific amputations. Then the suicide. Unless they somehow managed to free Galina Yablonskaya before she was mutilated by the butcher, the entire world press would be crowding them. Heads would fall; though that was of little significance to Gassin personally. However, he knew it would be an issue to Barbier.

It was going to be a long night.

39.

Hoyle looked at the clock face atop the church. At any second the large hand would reach the top of the hour and it would be time to make the call. He was in the outskirts of Versailles, and had parked his Espace a mile away from the public phone booth in which he was standing.

As the bells began to chime he dialed.

The pickup was practically instantaneous. Hoyle was pleased; these people were now taking him seriously.

"Good morning girls and boys! This is our master of ceremonies," Hoyle said like a ringmaster in a circus.

"Good morning. This is Commissaire Barbier speaking," Barbier replied quietly yet firmly.

"Dang! I was expecting Hilary Clinton," Hoyle replied, then laughed. "Do you have a name for me? A life hangs in the balance."

"I do. Galina Yablonskaya."

"You are…" he paused as game show hosts do just before they reveal an answer, "you are………CORRECT! Another triumph for your team, Commissaire!"

"Then fulfill your part of the bargain and release her."

"I will, never fear. However, since you know I lied on the last occasion, because I knew you would try to send the cavalry to catch me, I'll make up for it now by giving you a clue as to where to find her. Listen up! The dancer will be released close to home."

"When will—"

Hoyle talked over Barbier. "You'll hear from me again. Three more days. Who is my target this time? Some initials as a clue? No, just one. 'D.' So 'Game on!' as they say!"

Hoyle cut the connection. No traces today.

Back at his temporary home in Auteil, Hoyle served breakfast to the Ballons. Cecile was surprisingly chirpy – possibly because she hoped she'd be released today. By contrast, Jean was quiet; he felt certain he'd not be set free, yet hoped his wife wasn't thinking along those lines.

Having as usual armed himself with his auto injector, Hoyle took Ballon to check on Galina.

She was extremely quiet, her eyes fixed on the syringe in Hoyle's hand. Ballon wished her a good morning and asked if he could check her condition.

"Today I shall set you free," Hoyle told her.

"*Va d'empaler encoule, batard,*" she muttered. *Go fuck yourself, bastard.* "You have crippled me, I have no life left."

"Hey, that's not the right attitude at *all*. Imagine if you had survived a plane crash?"

"If I had no leg I would run back into the wreckage," she replied.

"Well, why don't you review the situation in five years? You'll most likely be a happy housewife by then. You're a good looking woman; you'll find a good man."

Ballon handed her some painkillers. "Take these as you need them. I must go now. There are no words…" he began, but she cut him off hard, staring into the surgeon's face.

"No, you are right. There are none, you butcher! How will you ever live with yourself?"

Hoyle couldn't help but smile – the girl's invective was directed at Ballon rather than himself because it was Ballon who had cut her foot from her leg!

A few minutes later the surgeon was back in his storage room, chained to the wall. Hoyle had refreshed all the toilets and taken all the breakfast trays upstairs to the kitchen. Soon everything was tidy again.

Back in Ballon's storage room, Hoyle addressed the surgeon and his wife, making sure he was looking at Cecile as he spoke – he didn't care to lie to the condemned man. "Today you shall go free. It has been an interesting time, I feel sure you will agree with me. Enough is enough, and you will wish to be reunited with your loved ones."

Cecile said nothing. Neither did Jean. They just stared.

"First things first. I must release our ballerina. Her case is more urgent. So please come with me, Jean, and we will attempt to make her as comfortable as possible – given the lack of a foot – for the journey to Paris."

Jean Ballon stood.

"Just bear this in mind, Jean. You must behave yourself. If you do, all will be well; Galina will go home and you will have saved your wife's life. Any other hero scenario at the eleventh hour would be unthinkable. Am I right?"

"You are right," Ballon replied with undisguised hatred in his eyes.

Sedating Galina was surprisingly difficult. She was a feisty girl and resolutely refused to allow anyone near her. She struggled like a lioness when she saw Ballon approaching with the syringe. Had Hoyle not tied her hands behind her back and secured her one good leg to a ring in the wall, she would have led them a merry dance. As it was, it took Hoyle some moments to get his arms around her and stop her thrashing. That gave Ballon the chance to inject her with Sux. She soon slackened in Hoyle's arms.

"Give her a sedative when she's in the van – I need her to be..." he paused to give Ballon the precise word he had in mind. "Limp... that's the word. I need her to be limp until I give her the adrenaline.

Hoyle unzipped the small medical bag he had brought with him and withdrew two syringes and two ampules of adrenaline.

Ballon watched as Hoyle filled both syringes. "One is more than enough. Two is a dangerous dose."

"We shall see, Jean. We shall see."

"You told me you weren't going to kill the girl. She has suffered enough. I ask you not to jeopardize her life."

"That is the last thing I want, Jean. You see, when I release her, I want to watch her dance!"

Jean Ballon studied Hoyle – the man was clearly mad. There was no reasoning with madmen.

By 6 a.m., squads of special riot police, the CRS, were out in force all over Paris. Realistically Gassin knew he couldn't cover the entire city. If it had been possible to lock down the city, Barbier would have done so, since Gassin had told him he was sure Galina Yablonskaya would be *brought* into the center of Paris rather than already *being* there. It was a hunch – it was easier to remain anonymous in the suburbs than in the heart of the city. So there was a watch on all arterial roads leading into Paris, the cops asked to look out for any vehicle they could not see directly into as it passed. This had been a massive operation that had stretched the CRS to the limit.

The first location to be secured was naturally Galina's home and those of her immediate family. *Close to home,* that's what the kidnapper had said, but it was hardly likely that he was being forthright. It was a 'game', after all, as far as Hoyle was concerned. So what, or whose, 'home' was he referring to?

To the police watching the N12 entry to the Paris ring road the chauffeur driven Mercedes they saw approaching the checkpoint didn't raise any flags. However, since the young CRS officer, named Fichet, was a thorough and ambitious young man, he flagged the car down – it had tinted windows and his orders were to flag down any vehicle he couldn't see inside.

The driver pulled over immediately, reaching for his license.

"Can I help you?" Hoyle asked with a friendly smile, as the window purred its way down.

Fichet looked past the chauffeur into the back. No one.

"I hope this won't take too long, officer. I need to be at the Père Lachaise cemetery ASAP."

"May I see your driving license, sir?" Fichet asked.

"Of course, officer," Hoyle replied handing the cop one of his forged licenses. It had cost him a lot, but the best always did. So he imagined it would be good enough to fool this young turk.

Fichet handed it back and waved him on without another word. Hoyle was on his way.

Gassin thought he'd covered all the most likely bases, but he failed to think of the Russian Embassy in the Boulevard Lannes, just off the Périférique; the road that circled Paris. There were no CRS riot police within a mile of the Embassy, just one or two gendarmes on routine security-watch outside a few of the various Embassies and consulates.

Both sides of the Boulevard Lannes had attractive wrought iron barriers separating the roadway and the footpath. This day there was little or no traffic, and the young security cop on duty outside the Russian Embassy, Marc Gideon, was bored.

He had no reason to concern himself with the chauffeur driven Mercedes that had pulled in a few yards up the road. Luxury cars were two a penny in this street. Probably picking up some diplomat. But since he was bored, he watched the car just out of idle curiosity. The chauffeur, wearing a smart cap, opened the driver's door and walked to the rear of the Mercedes, opening the trunk. That's when the screaming started. It came as a very rude shock. Gideon jumped he was so surprised.

Then everything happened so quickly that Gideon didn't have the time to react at all for several seconds. The last thing he'd been expecting was an incident in this quiet street. Now the noise was like Bedlam.

His first reaction was to reach for his side arm. By the time he had it out of his holster, he saw the chauffeur had already lifted a body out of the trunk of the car and let it drop to the roadway. It was a young woman!

Gideon raced forward, calling to the chauffeur to stop where he was, but the man paid no attention, leaping back into the driver's seat and slamming the door shut. A second later the gears were engaged and the rear tires were smoking. Then the car powered off up the street.

Gideon looked in horror at the woman who had fallen. She had somehow managed to get up off the ground and was stumbling about like a drunk. Dressed in what looked like ballet clothes – tights, leg warmers and a T-shirt – she was screaming like a banshee, hopping on one foot down the street. It was only then Gideon saw that she had a bright red ballet shoe on one foot, but he couldn't see the second shoe – possibly she'd lost it; maybe that's why she was hopping?

The screaming became a high-pitched wail. Windows along the street were opening and people were beginning to look out of windows. It was horrific, yet mesmerizing. Gideon didn't know whether use his police radio to call for assistance or assist the girl at once and then call. He opted to race towards the young woman.

It was only as he reached her and she flung her arms around hi neck that he realized why she'd been hopping. Her right foot was missing!

He scooped up Galina and ran to the sidewalk, lowering

her as gently as he could. All the while Gideon spoke to her very calmly, trying to soothe her, though he'd never been less calm in his life.

As the girl lay beside him sobbing, Gideon called in to base.

A black van of CRS troops were with him within two minutes. One minute later Galina was in an ambulance speeding to hospital.

The CRS found the abandoned Mercedes just five blocks away in the rue Montevideo. The chauffeurs cap had been left on the driver's seat. The lining hard been torn out, presumably because of the DNA. Passers-by told the CRS lieutenants that they seen a man dressed in a black suit running towards the Metro station at the Port Dauphine.

Word reached Gassin moments after Gideon had called in the incident. He immediately ordered the area around the embassy flooded with every available CRS officer. The Porte Dauphine Metro station was awash with police within six or so minutes. It was too late; they found no one. Because the man they were chasing had entered and exited the station in one swift move, having thrown his jacket and tie in a dumpster.

40.

Commissaire Barbier held a press conference two hours after Galina Yablonskaya was admitted to hospital. He knew he had no alternative but to read out an official statement as soon as he possibly could, because some very lucky young kid living in an apartment on the boulevard Lannes, a boy who'd taken the day off school pretending he was sick, had heard the screams and recorded the entire horrific episode on his cell phone. He'd immediately called *CANAL +*, the kid's favorite TV channel, and had sold the footage for a thousand Euros. So, before Barbier had time to try calling in favors from the TV chiefs, the news was out there. Little did the kid know how much CANAL + had charged Fox News for the American rights! Programs were being interrupted all over Europe as the second Paris horror video was beamed to the world. The heading was "*Barbarity!*"

As soon as the press had been fed, Barbier strode out of the conference room to confer with Gassin—he knew it would very probably be the end of the line for him. The questions the press fired at him had been very hard to parry. '*When did you know that Mademoiselle Yablonskaya had been kidnapped?*' the Figaro had asked. '*Is the perpetrator the same person who mutilated Josef Kafni?*' was the International Herald Tribune's question. The Parisien Libéré asked, '*Are we dealing with a new Jeckyl and Hyde?*' The final question had been '*How is it possible for this to happen twice in our beautiful city? What have the police been doing?*' '*As much as we can,*' Barbier had replied, realizing just after he'd said it that it was the most piss weak statement he'd ever made in his entire life.

Now he was sipping a coffee with Gassin – the Commissaire wondering how on earth he could extract himself from the *tas de merde* he was knee deep in, while Gassin was wondering how on earth they could avert any further butchery. Both knew they had to find the man who was doing these terrible things, yet still they had precious few clues.

"Again we were too late, Thierry."

Gassin knew there was no answer to that blunt statement.

"*Close to home.* She was born in Russia. The Embassy. Your team misinterpreted the clue."

"With respect, sir, I think we all did," Gassin replied quietly.

"He will do it again. I am certain of that. He clearly enjoys this madness."

"He cannot touch Monsieur Dutont. He is the third celebrity that Nolan interviewed. He is without doubt the 'D'."

"You still cling to your theory that these abominations were carried out by the American serial killer, Nick Hoyle? Despite the Sicilian revelations?"

Gassin shrugged. He did; yet he knew he had no evidence of any kind to back up his hunch. Just the two words that he'd picked from the note initially sent by the kidnapper to Barbier – *worst nightmares.*

But then, there was the Sicilian…

"So, where do we go from here, Thierry? We can't afford to wait for another limbless body to show up on our doorstep." He fixed Gassin with a seaching look. "Do you wish to be relieved of this case?"

"We are narrowing the parameters every hour, sir. Allow me and my men to continue our investigations. I am sure I will achieve a result."

"Please do, Commandant."

Gassin walked to the door, then turned. "One thing, sir. Here I need your clearance."

"Simply ask me, Thierry."

"I would like to fly to Sicily as soon as I can."

"Of course," Barbier replied.

"I would like to interview our Sicilian. I think he is wrong."

"I can hardly believe it. You are the dog with the bone. No evidence of Hoyle's involvement, and now that someone tells you he saw him die, you disbelieve him."

"I do, Jules. You used to have faith in my instincts. I can't give you a reason today but—"

"Then you must follow your instincts, Thierry, and go."

Gassin smiled warmly – his old friend still had faith in him.

As Gassin helped himself to a coffee in the Alitalia business class lounge prior to his flight from Charles de Gaulle to Punta Raisi in Palermo, he happened to look up at one of the television monitors hanging from the ceiling. The backdrop behind the newsreader was the Arc de Triomphe. Immediately, Gassin rose and walked close to the screen so that he could hear the sound. The newsreader was explaining what had happened while the video feed cut to and from some footage recorded earlier by a witness with a cell phone.

"There is still no information about the whereabouts of Josef Kafni's wife, who was abducted at the same time as the pianist."

No one else in the lounge seemed at all interested in the carnage that was being referred to – all were busy hunched over computers, or eating snacks and drinking free beverages.

"One source is suggesting that Monsieur Ballon may have been associated with the celebrity amputations, now being referred to as the *'Dr. Hyde Case'*."

Gassin swore under his breath – things were getting completely out of hand, the case was becoming a cause celèbre.

More amateur footage of Cecile's release started playing. It was totally shocking. This time it was a blindfolded Madame Ballon that was running in amongst the rush hour traffic circling the Arc. Cars, trucks and buses were swerving violently as Cecile ran blindly forward. Despite the poor sound quality of the cell phone, it was still possible to hear her screaming as she clutched at the duct tape, trying to tear it away from her eyes.

"Jesus..." Gassin murmured, and then reached for his cell.

"Commissaire? It's Gassin. I am watching the footage on the television news. However, my flight will be called in a few minutes. I still feel it is imperative I interview this Sicilian. I will be back by late afternoon."

"Commandant Gassin..." Barbier replied, now formal and down to business. Gassin wondered who was in the room with him? The Ministre d'Intérieur perhaps? This was getting bigger by the second. "Are you certain you are making the correct decision? Our problem now is that although Madame Ballon has been released unharmed, there is no sign of her husband. It is very possible that he has been harmed. He could even be our man!"

"I have left Lieutenant Becaux in charge in my absence. My entire team have been briefed about what to do, and they are very capable. I shall be at the end of my cell phone for all but the time it takes me to get to Sicily."

"As you wish, Commandant. I leave this decision to you."

Was Barbier subtly trying to pass the buck if things went awry? Frankly, Gassin didn't give a damn; his priority was to stop Hoyle at all costs. With every second he was more certain the man wasn't dead at all; he was still in Paris and the Sicilian was a ruse. The probability was that the media and Barbier would ignore him and start going after the wrong man.

He looked up as his flight was called.

'Alitalia announce the departure of flight ACZ 0316 to Palermo. Boarding at gate 32.'

As he walked to the gate, Gassin called Becaux on his dedicated personal number. Becaux answered at once.

"Madame Ballon is well and safe, sir. She's being sedated. I am outside her hospital bedroom now, attempting to get the doctor to hold off too much medication until I've had a chance to get a detailed statement."

"Good. What about Ballon?"

"No sign, sir. Madame Ballon keeps telling us their kidnapper promised to release them both, but she hasn't seen her husband since this morning."

"What's your thinking, Antoine?"

"It's not favorable, sir."

"Come on, what's your thinking Antoine?" Gassin repeated; he didn't have time for niceties.

"I'd say the kidnapper killed him, sir. Ballon most probably saw the face of the kidnapper while performing the surgery. Before Madame Ballon was loaded into the back of the ambulance she told us that she had been hooded each time the man was in her presence. When she was not hooded, Hoyle was hooded. It seems Ballon was not hooded when he was in his cell with her, and the butcher was with them."

"Did she give a description of the man, based on what her husband told her?"

"Yes, but it's not too helpful."

Gassin sighed wearily. "I shall be out of range for just two hours, Antoine; there's no Skyphone on this flight. I want even the smallest detail from Madame Ballon. Location, sounds, voices, food, everything. I shall be back this evening. You'd better get the team set up for a long night."

"Yes sir."

Gassin arrived at the gate and pulled out his boarding card. "One more thing, Antoine. Monsieur Bernard Dutont..."

"He is on his way to a safe house in Amboise, with his wife and two children. There is a four-man team. No one will get even close."

"Good work, Antoine. I will be in touch in two hours and five minutes, depending on the wind."

Gassin then boarded the aircraft.

41.

Hoyle felt strangely lonely when he returned to his house in Auteuil. All his guests had left. He had no one to cook and clean for, no one to talk to. He was alone again, as he'd been since Giselle and his babies were taken from him and he'd entered his world of emptiness. Jean Ballon had shown courage. He'd demonstrated he'd give up his life for his wife, whom he clearly adored. Not only was he a brave man but also a talented surgeon. For the first time in many years, Nick had had someone to chat to – to interact with. What had Jean once told him? That he was not inherently a bad man but needed treatment? Nick thought about that. Why did he care? He was happy being bad, wasn't he? He was content to be devoid of human compassion, no? Yet a tiny voice was calling to him from what was now perhaps just one single synapse sparking in his brain cortex. It was Giselle; he knew the voice. *Darling, don't do this thing. You were a kind and loving man once. What has happened? Seek help.*

As he became aware of a tear welling in his eye, Hoyle recovered, slapped his face hard with the palm of his hand and forced a grim smile. What the fuck was he thinking? Was he dreaming? Get away!

He directed his attention to Massimo, the Sicilian who he also remembered fondly; knowing the old man would not let him down. Then he cleared his mind of all idle thoughts and did his best to focus.

Today was packing-up day; he had to leave very soon. He knew of serial killers who seemed to have literally begged to be caught. Despite trying to think otherwise, ever-asserting their superior intelligence, taunting the police, profilers and psychologists, they subconsciously enjoyed the frisson of knowing the authorities were closing in – it was such an extreme thrill that they didn't allow for anything *but* capture. It was only then that they fully understood what life in prison – albeit often a psychiatric hospital – would be like. No, Hoyle enjoyed life too much. It was so sweet. The sun and fresh breezes in north Sicily, the fine wines and food of France, movies, books – in fact, everything but romantic companionship; for one could never buy romance, and that was his dream oyster, rather than any tawdry 'coupling'.

However, he had been in this house now for three months; first preparing, then buying the equipment he needed – always in very small amounts to avoid any awkward questions such as *can you remember anyone in the past few months buying a substantial quantity of surgical equipment?* This particular holiday had now to come to an end, because even if the cops were dumb, they'd be narrowing the parameters of their search and soon would be getting close. So today was a time to pack, finish all the delightful snacks that were still left in the fridge, and move on.

He'd been sorry to be forced by necessity to put Jean Ballon down – he preferred the less violent euphemism reserved for animals. The incident had been more of a struggle than he'd expected. The Sux had, for the first time, not kicked in immediately and he'd been forced to use a rope around Ballon's neck. He'd kicked for quite some time. Regrettable, and oddly upsetting. Maybe there was something to the Stockholm syndrome? But the saving grace of having a house that would most likely not be raided for many days, if not weeks, was that Jean could be laid out in a dignified way rather than being simply dumped in a river or buried in a shallow grave – Hoyle had had enough of that sort of thing.

He'd lain Jean down next to Madame Kafni, covering them both with a scented sheet.

Everything was ready for the next move, the next pretty house had been leased; a small holiday cottage on the D3 just south of the small village of Tronc two miles north east of Poitiers. Everything had been paid for in advance on the Internet, so there was no need to touch base with anyone on arrival. He'd emailed, through the usual string of dead end addresses, that the key to the cottage should be left to the left hand side of the door.

There really wasn't much else to do. He'd worn gloves for the entire duration of his stay in the house. All he had to concern himself with now was DNA; hence the very thorough cleaning job he'd have to conduct. He groaned at the thought – but that went with the territory of being a serial killer.

By mid afternoon he'd cleaned the entire upper house, had a delightful lunch of duck liver paté and veal stew, and was now preparing to clean downstairs.

Wearing his iPod containing his favorite Jaques Brel songs, he collected a bucket filled with warm soapy water, with a decent splash of ammonia, a strong bristled brush and several cloths.

The portable toilets had to be emptied into the lavatories upstairs and thoroughly cleaned. That only took half an hour. Then the floors, then the beds and stools and finally the surgical equipment and the gurney.

By 5 p.m. the house was spotless. He knew he'd have to clean the upstairs lavatory just moments before leaving, as it would of course have DNA samples. That was no problem.

As for a car, he would steal one half way to his destination, most probably in or near Orléans. His current car would remain where it was, hidden in the garage behind the house.

Cleaning the Ballon's storage room had been depressing because he again felt a nagging sensation that he might miss his friend, Ballon. Yet he couldn't allow affection to cloud his judgment – the surgeon had had to die; he'd seen too much, and was an intelligent man who could most likely be able to help the police in their quest to track him down. It was better to play safe.

Jean looked very much at peace where Hoyle had laid him out on the trestle bed, next to Kafni's wife. Madame Kafni still looked oddly serene; now smelling slightly, but not offensively. Of course Cecile had had no idea whatsoever that her husband was to die after she had been released. At first she'd refused to leave, but Jean had begged her to do as she was told. Hoyle had wondered if Ballon knew of his fate then, and had steeled himself to it, afraid that if there were any problems, Hoyle would have to kill Cecile too.

As it was she'd behaved admirably, lying on the floor behind the front seats, wearing a hood and covered by a rug. Her wrists and ankles had been bound.

Since it was his last trip into Paris he'd decided to take his Espace all the way and not bother about stealing another car. He wouldn't be needing the Renault again.

"I'll cut you free in Paris. In the center. All right? Trust me, Cecile. Please don't make any trouble for yourself, not at this late stage."

She hadn't – there hadn't been so much as a peep out of her the entire trip. When Hoyle was a hundred meters from the Place Charles de Gaulle, he'd slowed and put on his hazard lights, as though his car had a mechanical problem. Then he opened the hood and walked to the rear of the car and sat in. Seconds later he was talking to Cecile Ballon, soothing her nerves as he cut her free.

"Now close your eyes. Do not open them or I shall have to kill you."

She did as she was told.

He then lifted off her hood and wrapped duct tape around her head to cover her eyes.

"You may now sit up in the seat. When I tell you to go, open the door and step out. Slam the door as you leave. Understood?"

"Understood," she replied, sitting up and placing her hand on the door handle.

Hoyle climbed into the driver's seat and filtered back into the stream of traffic. As they entered the hurly-burly of the Place Charles de Gaulle, Hoyle wove his way to a spot as close as possible to the Arc de Triomphe. At one stage, a group of young people in a Mini pointed at Cecile in the back seat with the duct tape around her head and laughed – they must have thought it was some kind of prank. The driver even honked his horn. No one else even bothered to look at Madame Ballon.

Hoyle then slowed down to almost a stop.

"Get out now! You are free."

Cecile didn't need asking twice, she threw open the door, tripped as she exited, and fell into the roadway, tugging at the duct tape as she did so.

Hoyle immediately started weaving through the traffic towards the Avenue Hoche.

Two minutes later he parked the car in the rue Balzac, off the rue de Fauburg St. Honoré. He exited the car, melting into the crowd and was gone.

Hoyle knew he'd never see Cecile again. In different circumstances he felt they might have been friends. Maybe she was boring? Who knew? He did know he'd miss Jean Ballon hugely; he hadn't shared a discussion with another human being for over a year.

Now he would soon say goodbye to his temporary home in Yvelines and, as ever, move on.

The Gypsy life for him!

42.

Massimo felt he was up for the challenge. This was far from being his first brush with the law, he'd been grilled many times by the carabinieri, and it amused him to think that he was being treated like a hero! He'd been picked up by a chauffeur-driven limousine and driven the fifty miles to Palermo, then housed in the most luxurious hotel. He eaten a spectacular dinner in his room; the cop had asked if he wouldn't mind staying there, presumably because the other guests would be horrified to see a dirty old peasant like him sitting in their fine dining room. It didn't bother him, he was used to people looking askance at him; it happened each time he and Brando, the donkey he had bought with the stranger's money, went to town.

Today, he'd been told he was to meet a Frenchman who had flown all the way from Paris to talk to him about his curious meeting with the American who he'd seen die. *Ha-ha!* He was going to have fun – he'd give the performance of his life! It didn't concern him what his benefactor had done; by bringing Brando into his life the man had changed it utterly. Now he had to fulfill his side of the bargain.

The door to the meeting room in the Palermo central police station opened and a uniformed carabinieri entered, carrying a cup of coffee and a pastry in a paper napkin. He didn't make eye contact with Massimo, or smile; he just did as he'd been told then made for the door. *I smell bad, that's what it is; this boy is unused to the peasant smell,* thought Massimo.

As the cop exited, a man Massimo judged to be about sixty appeared at the door. He was carrying a plastic bag. With him was the detective he'd spoken to the previous morning.

"Signor Calogero, I have someone to see you," the Sicilian cop said as he gestured to Gassin to enter the room.

"*Buon giorno,*" Massimo greeted the Frenchman.

The Policeman sat down at one of the stark wooden chairs that were set opposite Massimo. He held out a friendly hand. Massimo took it, surprised at the good manners of the Frenchman – the Sicilian detectives had all treated him with contempt, presumably because he was both dirty, and a peasant.

"I have just read the statement you made, Massimo. Very interesting. You know why I am here?"

"Not exactly, no, sir," Massimo replied; he knew it would be a smart move to seem obliging and good mannered – who knew, he might get another fine meal at the Hilton.

"Well, let us start at the beginning. I have brought with me a gift for you from Paris. So saying he reached inside the plastic bag and withdrew a bottle of brandy, passing it across the table to Massimo.

Massimo smiled broadly, this was getting better by the minute. Then a darker thought occurred to him. This American stranger who'd given him all the money... was he more important than he'd at first thought? Was Massimo involving himself in matters far more serious than he had initially anticipated? Could he cope? Yes, of course he could – he was just as smart as the man opposite him now. As a young man the questions asked by the cops were usually coupled with blows to parts of the body that did not show the bruising. He had survived those brutal investigations and remained true to his vow of *omertà*; he would remain true to his vow today.

The Frenchman reached into his inside jacket pocket and pulled out several postcard-sized photographs. There were two of Hoyle; one a close-up head shot, another of Hoyle at some beach, looking over his shoulder. He neatly laid them out on the interview table facing Massimo.

"Have you seen this man before?"

Massimo gave the photos a cursory glance and looked back up at the Frenchman. Was this a test?

"*Si, certo!*" he relied pointing to the one snap of Hoyle. "Of course, that is why I am here, heh?"

"Yes, it is," the Frenchman replied. "By the way, how rude of me. My name is Thierry Gassin. Feel free to call me Thierry. May I call you Massimo?"

"*Si! Certo, ancora!*" Massimo replied cheerily. This was going to be easier than he thought."

"There is no doubt in your mind that this was the man you met?"

"None! He was living on the scrub land behind the house where I live."

"The land belongs to you?"

Massimo laughed. As if he was a landowner! "No. Is public land! Olive trees that give no olives. This man had set up a camp. You follow? I used to see the fires he lit to cook."

"Did you eventually go meet this man?"

"*Si*! He was my neighbor! He never wore fancy clothes. Had no fancy car. Same as me. A fellow traveler, they say. A *paysan*," he added proudly.

"How long did he stay living in this scrub land?"

Massimo looked upward, as though trying to calculate the time span. "Say, about three weeks."

"During that time, did you become friends?"

"Maybe." Massimo was being cagey. If he told this man they had become buddies he would know an awful amount about him. This would be hard to fabricate. Better say they met every once in a while, but the stranger kept himself to himself.

"What did you talk about?"

"Usual things. The weather. Where to find free food."

"Did he tell you where he was from?"

"No need. His accent. American. I am thinking he was from there."

"Weren't you curious why an American was living rough on the scrub land behind your home?"

"*Si! Certo*! But it would have been rude to ask. I see the sadness in his eyes." Massimo was now waxing lyrical – *the sadness in his eyes, oh so very lyrical!* He wanted to laugh, but kept himself in check.

"Did he tell you his name?"

Massimo chuckled. "I ask him this many times, but he never straight with me. It was like a game."

"A game?"

"*Si.* He had a name for himself, a nickname I think. He call himself '*Il medico di sogno.*'

Gassin, nodded. He spoke good Italian. *The Dream Doctor*? "Did you ask him why he called himself this strange nickname?"

"No, I just laughed. He was not too serious. I think it was the only time he laughed too." Massimo liked this touch – the sadness in his eyes, the only time he laughed. Such lyricism from a simple man. Of course he knew well that to share this name, the 'Dreamhealer', was paramount; it was the most important thing he had to pass on to the police on... 'Enrico's Birthday.'

"Let us talk about the day this *Medico di Sogno* went swimming, never to return."

Massimo simply nodded. This was easier than he thought. Now he had a wonderful friend he could live out his remaining years with; Brando.

"Tell me about this day, Massimo. Take your time."

Massimo again looked around him as if to recall that day, when in fact he was doing his best to recall the fantasy day he'd prepared.

"I went to town with Brando, my donkey, to buy things. Wine and some rabbit for my stew. Then I fed my donkey and prepared my stew, which I placed on a very slow flame in my kitchen – rabbit stew is best left for many hours, sir."

"Thierry, please."

"*Si! Certo!* Thierry. Then I sat in my chair outside my house from about five o'clock in the afternoon onwards. I must have fallen asleep because he touched my arm and I awoke."

"It was the Dream Doctor?"

"Yes, it was him. He asked me if I would spend the evening with him. He was lonely and needed some human company."

"Those were his words?"

"Not exactly, *Signor* Thierry. I am trying to remember the words, but it was long time ago."

"I understand. Please continue."

"There was fear in his eyes, and I asked him if everything was all right. I felt sorry for him."

"Why sorry?"

"Because I could see by his clothes that he unused to the life he now was leading. He came from a different world. They were not cheap clothes, but good clothes; now soiled and broken. For some reason he had fallen on hard times, was alone and had no friends."

"So did you agree to spend the evening with this man?"

"I did. I asked him if he wanted to share my stew. I told him we could take it to the beach and look out into the ocean – I live the other side of the road from the beach. I suggested we could make a night of it. I had some wine and am always happy to share."

"And that evening he returned?"

"No, he never went away. Remember, it was already evening."

"What time did you take the stew to the beach."

"We never took stew to the beach. We ate in my kitchen. He also brought some wine; a flagon. Two liters. So we ate and drink – the rabbit was very tasty; I cook well. Just some wild tarragon – there is a great deal growing behind my house. If you add some vinegar and salt..."

Gassin cut him short with a smile. "Why did you go to the beach?"

"It was his idea. He wanted to swim. I told him it not such a good idea because we had drunk so such wine, and I could see he is becoming sad again. He was not a happy drunk."

"You thought he was drunk?"

"Well...yes, I did."

"How long were you on the beach before your friend decided to go swimming?"

Massimo pretended to ponder. "Ten minutes, maybe. He started taking off clothes. Strange! He folded them so neatly, as if packing a suitcase to go away. He said nothing."

Massimo paused, wondering if he could decorate the scene even more with some lyrical sense of sadness. He decided against it.

"Then?"

"After he had taken all clothing off he stood and looked up at the stars." That was it! He'd found his personal touch of sadness. The stars! That was wonderful! He reminded himself that he must write a book. "There was no problem with his nakedness, not there at night in the darkness. No one would be walking our way on such a night – the wind had risen and the water was angry." Massimo was on a roll!

"Not the perfect night for a swim?"

"Indeed not, *Signor* Thierry. I told him so, but he simply held out his hand and thanked me for my kindness. Oh, and he complimented me on the rabbit stew!"

"And then?"

"Then he walked into the water. I watched him until he was swimming. He swam straight out to sea. I was concerned when I saw him so far out because there exist many bad currents off the beach."

"How long did you stay on the beach, waiting for the *Medico di Sogno* to return?"

"After twenty minutes or so I walked to the water's edge and called his name."

"His name?"

A brief flash of confusion passed across Massimo's face. "I called out *Signor Medico*! Many times."

Gassin studied Massimo. The man was very convincing, yet this slight hesitation was a worry. It was as though he'd gotten carried away with his story and then, quite suddenly, had forgotten he didn't know Nick Hoyle's name. But his recovery had been excellent."

"When did you go home?"

"I waited for several hours, thinking that possibly my friend had been caught in a rip tide and been taken further down the beach. I hoped he would suddenly appear out of the shadows and return to his clothes."

"But he never did?"

"No. Never."

"Where are the clothes now? Did you take them back to your home?"

Massimo looked blankly at the Frenchman. The clothes. What did he do with the clothes? If he said he took them, they would want to see what he had done with them. And there *were* no clothes.

"I left them where he place them; I still think he might return during the night."

Gassin drilled him with a stare. Sure enough, the Sicilian looked away. To the left. A classic lie. But why would this man lie? Because he had been asked to? For money? It was as simple as that. It all made sense. He'd talked to the Italian Inspector for half an hour before his meeting with Massimo. The Inspector had told him that during his investigations many people had been interviewed. Massimo Calogero was a well-known character in Aspra. He kept to himself and had no friends barring a man by the name of Enrico who sometimes brought him his groceries. The one thing that struck the Inspector as odd was that some weeks ago, Massimo had bought a new donkey – the one he owned for so many years had died three years ago. So how had he managed to buy a new one? Massimo had answered that he had been saving for three years doing odd jobs for people in the area. When pressed about who he had worked for, he replied he had helped out tourists, people the inspector knew could never be asked awkward questions because they had gone home.

"Did you report your friend as missing?"

"No. I keep myself to myself. I like not to interfere."

"But you must have concluded that your friend had drowned?"

"I thought, yes. A release. He was filled with such sadness. I could see it in his eyes."

"Did you return to the beach the following morning?"

"Yes, I did."

"Were the clothes still there?"

This was a hard one. Say yes, and he'd be asked where they were now. Say no and it was possible that the stranger was still alive, having returned to retrieve them during the night. "Yes, they were still there. Later that day from my home I see someone walking down the beach. He stopped by the clothes – he must have taken them for himself.

Gassin smiled his most reassuring smile. "Well, I would

like to thank you very much, Massimo, for clearing up this man's disappearance. His wife will be relieved to have some sort of closure to her husband's disappearance."

"I am happy to be able to help. *Signor* Thierry."

Gassin stood, gathering the photos he'd laid on the table. As he did so, he stared at one of them. "That's a very special tattoo isn't it?" he said smiling at the snap of Hoyle at the beach. Massimo looked at him blankly, so Gassin turned the photograph around so that Massimo could see. A huge eagle tattoo filled most of Hoyle's back."

Massimo grinned. "Si! *Bellissima*! A work of art! I ask him where it had been done. He told me California."

That was all Gassin needed to know. The tattoo had been superimposed on the photo of a lookalike's body via Photoshop. Hoyle had no such tattoo. But how was this gun for hire to know that? He couldn't.

Gassin could have dumped Massimo in the shit, but he chose not to – what was there to be gained? This was a poor old beach bum, strapped for money. Why put him in prison? Gassin had come to find answers and he'd found them.

So Hoyle was alive. Gassin's gut told him he was in Paris.

43.

Becaux used his considerable charm to persuade the middle-aged doctor attending Cecile Ballon to allow him into her private room to conduct a short interview. He explained to the attractive young doctor how vital it was to gain some knowledge about where she'd been imprisoned – her husband was still missing, and his life could perhaps be saved if the police were to find him. Only Cecile had knowledge of where they had been kept.

When Becaux entered Cecile's room, she turned her head towards the door to see who had entered.

"Madame Ballon, my name is Lieutenant Becaux. Antoine Becaux. I am a detective at the Préfécture. I know how you must be feeling, but we have to find your husband right away, and that means—"

"You have no idea how I might be feeling," Cecile replied. It wasn't so much an accusing tone as a statement of fact. "I have been waiting to speak to you for hours but the doctors wouldn't let you in."

Becaux drew up a chair close to Cecile's bed, noticing that her face was unmarked, though there was some evidence of rope marks around her slim neck.

"We must determine immediately where you were held prisoner, Madame Ballon. Begin with your abduction, then we can move forward. Do you mind if I record this interview?" he said placing a tape recorder on the table next to her.

"Of course not."

He turned it on.

"I was adducted separately from Jean – my husband. When I arrived at the house, I had no idea the man had taken Jean as well. I thought initially he meant to rape me."

"Do you remember your abduction? Were you conscious?"

"I was. The man must have approached me from behind because at first I felt as if I had been stung by a bee. Within a few seconds I found I couldn't move and I began to fall down. That's when I became aware that I was in the arms of a man, being lifted into the trunk of a car. It happened in the late evening outside my home, it's a very quiet neighborhood.

"You remember the make of car?"

"It was a Mercedes. A big one. Black."

"Did you see your attacker?"

"No, I didn't. I was facing away from him. Then he laid me in the trunk of the car and placed a hood over my head. He told me that if I took it off he would have to kill me."

"How long did the drive take?"

"You mean before I arrived at the house?"

"Yes."

"Just over an hour."

Becaux was silent for some seconds – she could have been driven in any direction in an hour's driving radius.

"I know what you are thinking. However, I think I can help you significantly. You see I have a gift. I have perfect pitch."

"That's the musical term?"

"I trained at the Conservatoire when I was younger. To be an opera singer. But I wasn't as good as I thought. Eventually I became a jazz singer. My point is this – I can describe quite clearly what I heard while I was in that car and it may help determine in which direction I was taken."

Becaux was definitely interested now. "What exactly is perfect pitch?"

"In essence, it's the ability to name tones by ear. One can learn the art; I was simply born with it. I'll give you an example of perfect pitch. One of my idols was a famous jazz singer called Cleo Lane. She was married to Johnny Dankworth, the wonderful saxophone player. He was caught speeding in his car in England many years ago. In court he maintained he couldn't have been traveling over the speed limit because he knew the pitch of his car when it was doing over 80 m.p.h."

"Did he win his case?"

"Sadly, he did not. The magistrate thought he was having him on. Doubting minds, you see. But Johnny wasn't joking, he was serious. Possibly lying, but serious. Anyway, that's not the point."

This woman is fascinating, Becaux thought – he'd heard of people remembering sounds before. Could she direct him to where she'd been kept hostage?

"You were kidnapped in the fifteenth arrondissement?"

"Correct. The first bells I heard were heavy bells. I would say it was a big church. An A flat. Deep. Then we traveled about fifteen minutes when I heard the sirens. At the time I thought they must be for me, then I realized they were the Pompiers. There must have been a fire, a big one."

Becaux made a mental note – where had there been a big fire at that time on that day? That would show which direction the kidnapper had taken.

"Then there was an F sharp bell. A smaller one. And ten minutes later an A. Finally there was a C sharp. Almost immediately the car turned right and within five minutes we stopped. When the engine was turned off I could hear nothing. Just the birds. Then the man opened the trunk and told me to get out. It was a struggle, but I managed it. I still couldn't hear anything that might tell me where I was. He told me to hold his arm as he was taking me somewhere. We walked forward and into a house. An older style house I'd say, judging by the sound of the creaky door. Then we walked across a big room and he opened a door that lead down to a cellar."

"How big was the cellar?"

"Very big. There was a corridor. Quite long. As we walked, I ran my hand along the walls of the corridor. We passed two other rooms before we reached ours. The door was heavy and reinforced. Metal of some kind."

"What was inside?"

"The man directed me to one corner and told me there

271

was a camp bed there and I should sit. For the second time I thought he would rape me. But he didn't. He told me to wait there while he fetched my husband. I was overjoyed and dismayed at the same time. To have Jean with me was wonderful, but to know he'd been kidnapped too..."

"I understand. What happened when he brought your husband to you?"

"The man shouted from outside the door, saying I must have my hood on or he would have to kill me."

"You'd taken it off?"

"Well, of course. When the man was gone I wanted to see where I was. I was terrified.

"Then when Jean came into the room, the man said he would leave us for a while."

Cecile Ballon explained how they had fallen into each other's arms. Jean told her how the man apparently wanted him to perform some operation, the details of which he was at that time uncertain. A primitive operating room existed at the end of the corridor.

"Was Jean wearing a hood when he came into the room?"

"When the man left, I took off my hood again. No, Jean was not wearing a hood. This frightened me because of what the man had said. I think Jean was scared too but we didn't talk about it."

"Did you husband describe the man?"

"Yes. He described him in great detail. He wanted me to be able to tell you what he looked like if anything happened to him.

She then described Hoyle's appearance. Without the immediate aid of a sketch artist there was little doubt that it matched Hoyle, even with the beard and mustache. Becaux took a photo from his pocket and showed it to her.

"Given your husband's description, would you say this man fits the bill?"

She studied Hoyle's features. "Yes, I would. Though, never having seen him..."

During the following twenty-five minutes Becaux went into the detail of everything Cecile could remember about the time she and her husband had spent underground. Finally, she recounted her release day.

"As we drove back into Paris I tried to see if I had been right about the bells – I went through them again in my mind, but in reverse order. I was right about them all!"

Becaux stood. He knew time was of the essence. He still feared that Jean Ballon was now dead, but it was imperative to locate where the Ballons had been kept hostage.

"You have been very brave, Madame Ballon. And such a great help. I shall do some investigative work on the bells, and if I have difficulty, perhaps you might find it possible to come with us in a car and listen again?"

"Of course! You must find Jean. Please."

"I am sure we shall—with your help."

44.

Hoyle had the house locked up tight by eight in the evening. He'd covered Jean Ballon's body with a sheet soaked in ammonia, in the same manner he'd covered Madame Kafni; it helped slow the effects of decomposition. Not that it mattered too much, a body locked in a cellar would hardly leech too much odor into the air around the house since the storage room had no windows.

The cleaning was complete and he had packed

everything. Just one medium sized tote bag; that was all. He left whatever food there was left in the freezer, just in case whoever next visited the house – the cops – might get peckish as they waited for the morticians to arrive to collect Ballon's body.

Walking towards the main road, he felt another pang of sadness – this had been a home for a while, and he'd had some good times here. Now he was to embark on the next stage of his adventure. Bernard Dutont.

He knew where the man lived and it might take a few days to scout him out – it was paramount he knew Dutont's daily schedule, since it was fundamentally important that he know when Dutont would be alone.

Hoyle waited at the bus stop near his house for fifteen minutes. When the bus arrived he climbed on board. He was wearing a shabby coat, the collar turned up high, a sun hat, and prescription glasses so strong that Hoyle found it quite difficult to see the steps of the bus. The mustache had gone but the stubble around his chin and cheeks had been allowed to grow back. Overall, he looked unremarkable, which was perfect.

The ride to Versailles didn't take too long. Soon he was on a train to Poitiers.

As Hoyle tucked into a railway sandwich and a cold beer, Gassin was already back in Paris and on his way to the Quai des Orfèvres. It had been a long yet reasonably satisfactory day; his only problem still being that he had no positive evidence to prove his 'Hoyle' theory. There was no doubt in Gassin's mind that Hoyle was the brutal architect of the abductions of Kafni and Yablonskaya; there were simply too many unexplained questions to believe otherwise. The sheer savagery of the mutilations fitted Hoyle's profile – there was no compassion, the scenarios were almost comic in their disgustingly cruel conception and realization. And despite what Becaux and many others had suggested, he believed Nolan when he said he was positive he'd come face to face with Hoyle in the restaurant. In Gassin's mind Nolan was being set up to be disbelieved. Hoyle was conducting a campaign to drive the author nuts, while at the same time laying the foundations for investigators such as himself to conclude that Nolan had a screw loose. After all, with a Sicilian witness coming forward to state positively that he'd witnessed Hoyle walk into the sea and drown some three weeks ago, how could one believe Nolan when he said he'd been attacked by Hoyle in a Paris restaurant only one day previously? Of course the correct 'play' might be to convince Hoyle – who would most certainly be taking a great interest in all press future statements released by the Préfécture de Police – that the police now thought he was dead and that Nolan was suffering mental problems.

However, to release such a statement would be tantamount to saying they'd thought all along that the prime suspect was a world famous serial murderer, yet they'd failed to tell the public. This would outrage many. So another way of achieving the same purpose was necessary; possibly one involving the help of both Nolan, his wife, and the Los Angeles Police Department.

Migget was awaiting Gassin's arrival, opening the passenger door of the police car as the vehicle stopped.

"Commissaire Barbier is in our meeting room, sir. He's very anxious indeed," Migget said, hinting it was more than anxiety; it was close to hysteria.

Gassin smiled. He liked Migget's oblique yet frank way of speaking. They strode into the building.

"I'm not surprised," Gassin replied as they walked. "This case is gaining notoriety every damned second."

"What did we learn, sir?"

Gassin liked the fact that he used the plural rather than the singular – they were all in the same boat and sank or swam together.

"Hoyle is not dead. The man was paid. Keep this to yourself for the time being; we have much to do. First things first; we'll do our best to get Commissaire Barbier up to speed, then I want to go through everything Madame Ballon told Becaux with you and the team."

Barbier was standing when Gassin opened the door. Becaux and Simon were at their phones as ever, chasing down leads.

"Thierry! Good to have you back in town. The media is going ballistic. Yet no one has even been murdered! *That's* the most surprising thing."

Gassin was for a moment speechless. His boss was surprised that the media were making such a stir when no one had actually died? A world famous concert pianist had been butchered and driven to commit suicide, a prima ballerina had been violently brutalized, a surgeon was missing *presumed* dead, as was the pianist's wife, and Barbier didn't think these acts qualified as big time news?

"I am convinced Hoyle is still alive, sir. The man I went to see was lying. I eventually caught him in a lie."

"You are sure he was lying?"

"I am sure."

"Alright. So Nick Hoyle is alive. Does this bring us any further forward?"

"In some respects, yes it does."

"What respects."

"We are finally one hundred per cent certain who we are looking for."

"We are?" Barbier looked dubious, yet he could not ignore the Lachaise case. Gassin had closed that case based on his gut feelings, and here were these feelings at work again. The question was, did he feel confident enough in Gassin's gut to put his entire career at risk? A problem.

"So how do you intend to proceed, Commandant?"

"Our first priority is to locate the house where the Ballons were held captive. Lieutenant Becaux interviewed Madame Ballon while I was away. She is a very smart woman, who I believe gave us a great deal of valuable information. First thing tomorrow morning we intend taking her on a trip from her home to where she was taken."

"How can you do that, Thierry?"

"Madame Ballon remembers hearing various church bells. We are hoping to find a course that matches these sounds. She mentioned hearing the sound of fire engines. We have checked and it appears that there was a major fire just outside Versailles on the Avenue Clémont Ader."

"Why wait till morning?"

"Because Madame Ballon has been sedated, Commissionaire. The doctor's decision, not ours."

"I see," Barbier responded truculently – in his view there was no time for these niceties.

Gassin continued. "I would like your permission – just between us here in this room – to approach the friendly faction of the media; people who I trust. I will ask them to give as much coverage as possible to reports now emanating out of Sicily that the world famous serial killer Nick Hoyle is dead. Drowned."

Barbier looked totally shocked. "You wish to release false information? That Hoyle is dead? And by doing so, take all the pressure off him, since people will no longer be looking out for him? That is madness."

"Not so, sir. It will lull him into a false sense of security."

Barbier did not reply.

"We have to do exactly the opposite to what Hoyle expects. Otherwise we risk playing along with the game he has mapped out and planned to the last detail. He's a smart sonofabitch. Hopefully we can be smarter. So we make him think he has fooled us, and then we do the complete opposite to what we might have done had we believed he was dead."

Barbier looked as though he were mulling over this plan favorably, so Gassin ploughed on. "I am still debating whether I can do this without letting Dermot Nolan into our little secret; it would not be fair to allow him to think Hoyle was dead, and that he and his family were out of danger, when in fact that was far from being the case."

"Nolan is unstable, Gassin. Are you sure this is wise? To involve him in this scheme?"

"Yes. I believe so. My reasoning is this. Nolan thinks that everyone, including us at the Préfécture, believe he is acting hysterically. He thinks I don't believe him when he says Hoyle was in that restaurant, when in fact I am quite *certain* he was there. So to bring Nolan into our confidence will be a gesture of good faith. He will feel that he is being actively involved in finding Hoyle – because we believe Hoyle is the perpetrator of these acts of savagery."

"How will these media stories generated by you, stating Hoyle is dead, help us?"

"They will aid us greatly because they will forge a two-edged sword. Hoyle will relax his guard, and at the same time his photograph will once more be plastered on the front pages of all newspapers throughout France; and with any luck throughout Europe. As well as on television. So if Hoyle plans to poke his nose out of his warren, someone will surely spot him."

Barbier pondered on what had just been suggested. The alternative to allowing Gassin to run with the ball was to replace his friend and all his team with others. This entailed going back to square one. He didn't want that. Besides, Gassin was an old friend and the Commandant had always been a results man, so despite his having still little else to go on but hunches, he determined to allow Gassin to carry on his investigations as he chose fit.

"Do whatever you think appropriate, Commandant. You can count on my full support."

45.

Dermot was waiting for Gassin in the art deco bar at the Hotel Buci in the Latin Quarter. The Commandant had just caught him in time at L'Hôtel – Dermot's taxi had been due twenty minutes later to take him to the airport for his flight home to Los Angeles. On the phone, Gassin had impressed on Dermot the gravity of the news he had for him; details he didn't feel happy relaying over an open telephone line. His curiosity seriously piqued, Dermot had agreed to meet the Commandant in the bar at the Buci – it was both close to where he was staying and it was rumoured to serve the best cocktails in Paris. Well, that was what Gassin had told him; it was one shared by all the Commandant's friends.

Gassin arrived only a few moments after Dermot. They sat in the supremely lush and comfortable brown leather armchairs in the bar.

"You have had time to view the art work?" Gassin asked, trying to begin with a little small talk.

"My mind was elsewhere, Commandant. You'll have to forgive me."

"Of course. But along the way it's a shame not to smell the roses. Isn't that an English phrase?"

"I believe so," Dermot replied.

"You have not ordered?"

"I was waiting for you."

As a young man appeared, a delightful miniature Schnauzer appeared out of nowhere and snuffled at Dermot's feet. Dermot looked down and ruffled it's coat; the animal immediately putting him in a more relaxed space, reminding him of Scary.

"Two martinis please, Emmanuel," Gassin said – it was clear he and the waiter knew each other well.

Dermot continued playing with the dog. "What's his name?"

"Hers," Emmanuel replied. "And it's Lilly."

"How delightful. You can leave her with us if you like. She's a soothing influence."

Emmanuel smiled – Lilly had this effect on everyone.

"You always stay at l'Hôtel?" Gassin enquired. It was an observation rather than a question.

"Yes. Why do you ask?"

"It's a fine hotel. One of the best."

"But...?"

"*Quant a moi*... as for me, the Buci is the most delightful hotel in Paris. Small, '*intime*', everything one could wish for – and so close to the market across the way."

Dermot was dumbfounded. What on earth was this man talking about? Hotels? Cheese markets?

"Excuse me for rambling on, Monsieur Nolan, but I simply love this place. But let's press on."

"I wish you would, Commandant. I have a plane to catch."

"Please call me Thierry."

"Of course. Tell me, why did you wish to see me so urgently? My flight leaves in two and a half hours."

"I have some news to share with you. Important news concerning Nick Hoyle."

Dermot immediately stopped stroking the dog and looked up.

"Before I share the information with you, I would like to assure you that I never disbelieved a single word you told me the other day at the hospital."

"I'm relieved," Dermot replied somewhat coldly.

"Well, you must see things from our standpoint. You must understand that we have to check out all the circumstances before we can call a statement the truth."

Dermot said nothing.

"Please bear with me, Dermot."

"Of course."

"Almost simultaneously to your interaction with Hoyle, Interpol received news that a man in Sicily had come forward to inform the police in Palermo that he had seen Hoyle. More accurately, he told the carabinieri that Hoyle had been living rough in an area behind where he lived – on the north coast of Sicily. However, it was one final statement that aroused the most interest."

"And that was?"

"That he had watched Hoyle walk into the Mediterranean, never to return. In effect, he had watched him commit suicide. Several weeks ago."

"Then the man was lying."

"You know that because you met up with Hoyle just recently. But I had to be sure, just in case you had not sufficiently recovered emotionally from your ordeal underground…"

"You thought I might have been imagining things?"

"It was a possibility that it was my duty to investigate. Though I have to tell you now that it was not a thought I entertained, despite the Commissaire's opinion."

"The man in Sicily. Why was he lying?"

"For money. I flew out to Palermo to meet him face to face. He was an old man and very credible. I had to keep my wits about me. I caught him in a lie and that is why I am here—to tell you that as team leader of this investigation, I have placed Nick Hoyle at the top of our suspect list."

"You agree with me, then?"

"I do."

"So what now?"

"Well, this is where you can help us."

"Nothing could please me more. You want me to stay in Paris?"

"No. Quite the opposite. You see," Gassin paused as the martinis arrived in the most magnificent Baccarat crystal glasses. "You see," he began again, "Hoyle is playing a game with you as well as the Préfecture. It is my opinion that to find him and put him behind bars, we must play our own game."

"How do you propose we do this?"

"To begin with I have contacted several journalists who I've had dealings with in the past. I have asked them to run stories about 'The Dreamhealer.' These stories will also run with the Sicilian's account of how the Dreamhealer, or the *Dotore di Medico* as Hoyle supposedly referred to himself, committed suicide."

"How will this help us? People will stop looking for him. It will take the pressure off him, rather than put pressure *on* him."

"That was my superior, Commissaire Barbier's, thinking. I disagree. My point is this; given these revelations, newspapers will place Hoyle's photograph on their front pages yet again. And remember, it's been some time since they were there. People need reminding. So while initially Hoyle will be delighted to think that his ruse worked – for he undoubtedly paid this Sicilian to lie so that we would think he was dead and that someone else was responsible for Kafni and Yablonskaya – everyone who reads a newspaper in France or watches the evening news, will soon have a mental picture of his face yet again."

"I see. So if anyone sees him they'll want to alert the press to tell them they got it wrong?"

"Precisely. Now remember, when we release the news that the suicide story was a fake, it'll hit the front pages even harder. So, initially we throw Hoyle a bone, he catches it and thinks he can get around more freely, then we toss another bone to the hungry press and he realizes that the whole world is looking for him again. That brings me to my second point."

"Which is?"

"You must return to Los Angeles."

"Why?"

"Because Hoyle is at this moment preparing to kidnap his third subject."

A wave of anxiety coursed through Dermot's veins. "Another person associated with me?"

"We think so. Definitely. That's his game, to make you suffer by inflicting people's worst nightmares on them, while you watch and can do nothing about it."

"Dutont? How can he possibly reach—?"

Gassin held up a hand. "He can't. But he may not know that. We have Dutont in a safe house outside Paris. Only our team knows where he and his family are."

"So what is your point, Thierry? Why do I leave?"

"Since Hoyle is doing everything because of you, how is he going to feel if you simply pack up and go home? He will be furious. You agree?"

"Quite possibly."

"It would be like cooking a birthday cake and the birthday boy leaving the party before blowing out the candles."

"You think it might stop him mutilating someone else?"

"It might. It might also make him do something else."

"What would that be?"

"Follow you back to America."

"But that would be out of your jurisdiction?"

"For anything he might do in the future in America, true. But we would seek extradition if and when he is found for the crimes he has committed here in France. If he makes any move to return to America we would be watching like hawks – at every border."

"Hoyle know's I know he's alive."

"Of course. But he thinks that we now view you as a mentally disturbed man with no credibility. That will delight him, and actually encourage him to follow you."

Dermot lifted his glass for the first time and sipped. It was the best martini he'd ever tasted. Gassin noted Dermot twotch with pleasure. He knew his friend would react in this way as the Buci used Jean-Marc XO vodka from the Cognac region of France for their martinis and, short of the Russian necter, Kauffmann Imperial Vintage Vodka, there was surely no better vodka in the world.

"You're really asking me to draw Hoyle back to America and put my family at risk?"

"In a way I am afraid this is true. However, we'll make absolutely sure that you have sufficient protection. I shall make certain the police in Los Angeles are *au fait* with everything we know. All our secrets. If Hoyle returns to Los Angeles, there will be a welcoming party. In the meantime, Hoyle may decide to refrain from any further mayhem in France."

Dermot was in two minds as to whether Gassin's plan was simply to get rid of 'Hoyle the serial killer' from French soil. It was possible; the media was currently behaving like ravening beasts, calling for the blood of the Commissaire. Yet after further thought, he had to agree that somehow it was imperative to obstruct Hoyle's plans if they could. And save a life, if not many lives.

"Let's shake his tree," Gassin said deliberately. "Isn't that an American phrase meaning to surprise and upset? Mess with his head? Another such phrase. You see, my instinct tells me he is trying to drive you mad, so why don't we hit back and drive *him* crazy?" Gassin smiled a wicked smile.

For the first time in a very long time Dermot thought he had an ally – someone who could really help him. "I like the way you think, Thierry. Can I share all of this with my wife?"

"When you arrive home, of course. I'd rather you didn't telephone her right now."

"I understand, Thierry. I'm very grateful you haven't passed me off as mentally challenged."

"Nothing could be further from my thoughts. I understand the pressures you've been under for a long time." He paused to finish his martini. "May I now ask for a big favor? Could you possibly change your flight? If you can spare me an hour, I can arrange for you to fly out two hours later than you had planned."

"What do you have in mind, Thierry?"

"I want you to talk to the media at the airport. It shouldn't take long."

"What do I say?"

"You will look thoroughly dejected, arguing very forcibly that there is no way in the world that the Dreamhealer is dead, but you have finally decided not to 'play his game.' I want you look right down the barrel of the camera when you say this. Then you tell Hoyle, via the television camera, that you have decided to take your ball and go home. You tell him to go to hell."

Dermot looked quite excited by this scenario.

"After all, if it's a 'game' Monsieur Hoyle wants to play," Gassin ended, "why don't we change the rules, so as to give us the advantage?"

"I like it. Let's do it, Commandant."

"I have a car waiting outside."

46.

At 5 a.m. Gassin and Becaux were back at the hospital. Cecile had been alerted to the fact they were coming to collect her and was waiting for them in the reception area.

"Madame Ballon, good morning. Thank you so much for this help," Gassin started.

"I want to find my husband. Today. I want him home. I want an end to this nightmare," she said; her face a white mask of fear.

"Then let us waste no time," Gassin replied, walking her outside, opening the passenger door of the big Renault. "During the night we conducted some very detailed research on church bells. I have a list of them with me, together with their individual tones. I would prefer you to tell me which ones you recognize before I confirm them. This may be imperative as far as evidence is concerned when this man is brought to trial."

"I understand," Cecile replied as the car moved off.

"We will begin at your home, although we have already ascertained where the fire was on that night. Very close to the N12. However, we have to drive the entire journey, rather than take shortcuts."

When they reached the Ballon's apartment Gassin reached for the airline slumber shades. "I hope you will bear with me, but we must conduct this trip as an evidentiary ride. This means you cannot see where you are being driven, as before with your abductor. So while I hesitate to ask, could you please wear these shades?"

"Of course," Cecile replied.

They set off towards Versailles, though Cecile had no idea in which direction she was being taken. They'd chosen Versailles because of the direction of the fire. Also because St. Marks Church was there, and the lead bell had an A flat tone.

"That's the A flat tone," Cecile stated with certainly as the church bell struck a quarter past six. Gassin checked it off the route he intended taking, based upon Becaux's previous research on bells.

They stopped at the village of Bois-d'Arcy and waited for the seven o'clock chime.

"That's it! F sharp."

"Good, let's move on, Antoine."

They continued on to Mareil-Le-Guyon, then stopped

again. The clock there refused to chime the quarter and Gassin knew he might have to wait a long time. So he asked Antoine to go fetch some coffees for them all.

Sure enough, at 8 a.m. the bells began to peel. He looked at Cecile, she was smiling.

"C sharp!"

"Bingo," Gassin replied as Becaux collected the paper coffee mugs. "Now please put on your slumber shades again and we'll move on."

She did so.

"Now you must now judge how long you were driving before the car turned to the right."

"I will. Just drive and I'll tell you."

They'd only been traveling for some minutes when Cecile spoke. "It was about now. It felt as though we were at some large junction. We filtered off the big road onto a much smaller one."

Becaux nodded at Gassin. The big N12 intersection with the smaller Avenue Léon Crété was almost upon them. Becaux was hard pressed not to fly past it. As it was, he took the right curve and were soon on their way north.

"We passed through one small village. I know this because we reduced speed to let people cross the street – I heard all the chatter and sounds of children too. I thought we were in the middle of a village."

Becaux pointed to the village of Bardelle on the map.

"We are now less than a mile from the house where we stopped."

Gassin was already searching through his notes and files. "Antoine, please pull over. Excuse us, Cecile, we have to check on a few things."

Gassin drew a circle around the location in the folder marked *'Storage facilities – non-current.'* The address was in the village that they would come to next – Auteuil. He flipped his cell phone open and dialed; now he needed backup. He felt he was close to Hoyle's lair; he could smell it.

"Why are we waiting, Commandant?"

"There is a car and a van following us. I have asked them to go ahead to an address we have identified as once being a storage facility for this area. They are CRS. They will search this house while you are kept at a safe distance."

For the first time during the trip Cecile Ballon began to cry. Gassin wondered if she feared she would soon have the murder of her husband confirmed to her, and she was terrified.

Half a minute later a van loaded with CRS personnel drove past them and up the D 76 towards Auteuil. They were followed by a squad car, also containing four police officers.

Gassin waited ten minutes. They were agony for Cecile Ballon.

"Okay, let's go," he said to Becaux, who fired up the car and drove north.

When they arrived at Hoyle's house, the whole area had been secured by armed policemen in full riot gear. They were all wearing their face shields up, which told Gassin that either they had Hoyle in custody or he'd flown the coop.

"Please stay here, Madame Ballon. You may take off your eye shades." So saying, Gassin stepped out of the car and approached a CRS lieutenant who was already on his way over to Gassin's car.

"Monsieur Ballon is dead, sir. In the basement. There is a woman lying next to him. She is dead too. Her description fits that of Madame Kafni. She has been dead many days."

"Any signs of Hoyle?"

"No sir. It looks as though he cleaned the house very thoroughly and left. Recently. Within twelve hours would be my guess."

Gassin wondered whether Hoyle had known they were this close. Possibly he was worried that Cecile Ballon could somehow lead the police to his hideout. It was a miracle he hadn't executed her. If Cecile Ballon hadn't been sedated the previous night...

"An ambulance is on its way. Is that Madame Ballon in your car, Commandant?"

"Yes, it is. I shall have to send her home once I have broken the news to her. There is no question it's Ballon?"

"None sir. We are currently confirming the identity of the second body."

"What a damned shame."

Cecile initially reacted to the news quietly, as though she'd expected the worst. As the ambulance came into view she broke down and sobbed like a child. Gassin thought it the saddest thing he had witnessed in many years.

"Antoine will take you home, Cecile," he said at last. "Is there someone who can be with you when you get there? Your sister possibly?"

"Yes, please call Audrey. I couldn't bear to be alone. Not now."

Gassin nodded at Becaux who made the call to Audrey Fontaineau, Cecile's sister. He'd contacted her the night before and suggested she might like to care for her sister if things went awry. She'd agreed.

As Becaux left, Gassin joined the CRS lead lieutenant he'd

been talking to earlier, asking to be shown downstairs.

Jean Ballon and Madame Kafni had been removed and driven back to Paris in the ambulance, but their primitive twin catafalques, the beds on which they'd been laid out were still there, as were the sheets. The room stank of ammonia and death.

From this room they made their way to the surgery. The gurney was spotless, positioned in the corner of the room, together with all the other surgical equipment. Despite having done his best to clean this room, the Luma Light still picked up evidence of bloodstains on the floor.

Gassin found the whole experience acutely disturbing, despite all his years in the force. He wondered what on earth could make any human being behave in such a savage way. What had happened to Hoyle to make him this way? He'd heard of soldiers returning from war zones changed men, but this was way different. Possibly it was the amalgam of Hoyle's moral anesthesia during his tour of duty in Iraq, coupled with the rage he felt when his wife died so tragically due to such a combination of haphazard circumstances. Immediately followed by the even more horrifying deaths of his twins in the hospital inferno. Could all of this have driven him so crazy that he was reborn as a man who enjoyed *'bringing suffering to others'*?

Fifteen minutes later, Gassin left the crime scene to the forensics boys – he had more important things to concentrate on, not the last of which was to inform Barbier that their worst nightmares had been realized. They now had two dead bodies to add to two mutilated ones.

And Hoyle had once again vanished.

47.

Hoyle cruised into the outskirts of the town of Poitiers on the rue de la Vincennes past the suburb of Buxerolles. He knew where Dutont lived; half way down the rue Camille Girault. He also knew the man worked from home, so was available to him twenty-four seven. He was an artisan; a glassblower, who's pieces were revered by the cognoscenti. Even Hoyle had heard of him before in the art world, before his life had changed.

His name and that of the neurosurgeon Dermot had interviewed were the same. That was the delicious twist in Hoyle's new game. The name was everything – not the man. The Paris cops would be guarding the neurosurgeon, positive there was no way 'The Butcher' could access the man. And while they were guarding the neurosurgeon's home, or perhaps staking out some secret safe house, he, Hoyle, would in turn be staking out a man of the same name, hundreds of miles away. What a game! Who said he had to target the exact same man? No one. *He* set the rules. And in this particular game, it was a man by the *name* of Bernard Dutont who was about to have a very bad day at the office.

But first things first. Sleep. To cover his tracks he'd decided to pass himself off as a homeless person. Such people had no ID cards nor driving licenses. They were sad people who had nowhere to go. Hoyle knew there were almost ninety thousand of such people throughout France. Many charitable organizations cared for them; the Abbé Pierre Foundation, Secours Catholique, Emmaüs, Red Cross, Restos du Coeur, Samu Social, DAL. Tonight he would become a drifter. Tomorrow he would find Monsieur Dutont.

While Hoyle morphed into a bum, Dermot was already well into his flight to Los Angeles, attempting to make sense of everything Gassin had told him. He wondered how he could tell Neela the truth. Would she freak out? Had he been fair to agree to Gassin's plans? Was it the correct thing to do, to use Neela and Vig as pawns in this terrible game? He'd practically made them his Judas goats. It was a frightening thing to consider. Yet Hoyle somehow had to be found and stopped.

As he watched the stewardess refill his champagne glass, he couldn't rid himself of the nagging feeling – the realization – that he was in fact in the tight grip of a compulsion. Revenge. Was *this* the man he'd become? Would he really put his family at risk just to bring Hoyle down? What would he do if he finally came face to face with his nemesis? He knew the answer; it was deeply embedded in his heart. He would kill him. Yet, how could he do so; take justice in his own hands and leave Neela without a husband and Vig without a father? Wouldn't such an action place him in a similar pitch black place to Hoyle – make him a murderer? He'd been accused of murders, and had at the time been revolted and angered to be thought one. So what was different now? His mindset? Had he been reduced to the depraved mentality of a man who thought revenge was okay? Someone who thought that to kill a man who had himself killed so many, and would surely do so again, required summary justice?

As those around him in the cabin began to turn off their reading lights and tried to sleep, Dermot began to fantasize.

He was face-to-face with Nick. They were staring at each other. Nick wore an evil smile. Both had identical handguns pointed at each other.

"You'll never pull the trigger. It's not in your nature, Dermot."

"No?"

"No. You are flawed, but basically a decent man. By contrast, I am not. I am emotionally dead. Who made me this way? *You* did, of course. You violated my trust, you stole my wife, and you fathered children I thought were my own."

"Giselle and ¹ had one moment of passion, Nick. It was not an evil thing. It was a breach of trust; that goes without saying. But neither of us envisioned what it might lead to."

Dermot could see Hoyle's jaw working hard. He directed his gun to Dermot's crotch. It was clear to Dermot that Nick didn't want him to die easily.

"Nothing in this life justifies the terrible things you've done, Nick. You should be locked away in a hospital. You should be on medication. You have no place in the real world."

"I enjoy the real world, Dermot. *For I shall bring suffering...* Remember those words? Of course you do, they are the words of Albert K. Arnold. *My* words."

Dermot did not reply. He knew what he had to do. He couldn't wait for Nick to maim him, then finish him off. Now was his one moment – while Nick was relaxed in the belief that Dermot would never turn killer.

He squeezed the trigger.

The explosion rang in his ears, much more loudly than he could ever have imagined. In movies Hoyle would have stared at him in utter disbelief, then sunk to his knees. In reality Nick was punched backwards by the force of the 9.5 gram parabellum hollow point slug as it made contact. He lay crumpled about three feet back, the blood pooling around a gaping exit wound in his back.

Dermot jerked violently in his chair. The steward who was taking his empty glass away turned to see all was well, then asked Dermot if he needed any help reconfiguring his seat into a bed.

While Dermot slipped into his dream world, Nick Hoyle entered a building in the suburb of Saint-Cyprien, run by the Poitiers Municipality of the Sisters of Charity. He'd left his holdall in a car he'd just stolen – it was never a good idea to show up at such places with any belongings at all.

Inside the building, a nun was sitting behind a desk, doing paperwork. In the lobby around her were several men, some sitting with their hands clasped in their laps, others reading old magazines. Hoyle could scarcely hide his revulsion. What was wrong with these useless people; did they have nothing else to do but sponge off those with backbone?

He walked to the nun, who immediately stopped her clerical work and looked up with a friendly smile.

"Can I help you?" she asked.

Hoyle smiled a sad smile. "I met a fellow traveler today who told me I might find a bed here for one night. I am so very tired."

"I am sure this can be arranged. What is your name?" she asked.

"Bill."

"Well, Bill, we have a dormitory here with a comfortable bed. We have just finished serving supper, but if you are hungry, I can ask Lisle if she can find something for you to eat."

"Thank you. I haven't eaten for two days, Mademoiselle."

"Sister."

"Of course. Sister. Excuse me."

"The dining room is through that door," the woman said pointing to her right.

The last thing Hoyle wanted was to have to eat the warm slop that homeless people seemed to relish. Just the thought of it made his stomach turn over. However, it was important to seem 'needy,' so he thanked the nun and walked to the dining room.

The big room was filled with long trestle tables and benches. It would have seated a hundred, but right then only about ten men were still eating. They were all staring at a television on a table.

As he sat a door opened at the rear of the room a middle-aged woman appeared, carrying a plate of food. She smiled broadly at Hoyle as she placed it in front of him. Hoyle beamed a cringing smile of gratitude at her.

"*Bon appétit, monsieur!*" she said, then left.

It was then that he saw his face on the television and his blood ran cold.

Hoyle was sitting too far away from the screen to hear the sound clearly, but he could hardly move seats, so he leant forward to listen to what the newsreader was saying.

It was a story concerning his own death! It took all of Hoyle's control not to leap up and cheer! After all, it wasn't every day that one read reports of one's own death, yet was still alive. He was reminded of Mark Twain's famous remark after his obituary was published in error in the New York Journal – *the report of my death was an exaggeration.* Well, well, Hoyle thought to himself, every day a new thrill.

The photograph beside the newsreader on the screen was about three years old. He looked ten years younger and was smartly dressed. Hoyle marveled at the stupidity of the cops – they'd bought Massimo's story! The man had done well, no need to return there and beat him and his donkey to death.

A shot of a stretch of beach was the next photo to pop up next to the newsreader on the screen. The man talked of Sicily, and Hoyle distinctly heard the words '*notorious Dream Healer*' twinned with '*serial killer*' and finally the words '*worst nightmares*'.

Without thinking he ran a hand over his face and felt the stubble around his chin and upper lip. How could anyone recognize him from that photograph? Then he laughed at the thought; they would not be looking for him because he was dead!

As he saw the photo of the book *Worst Nightmares* appear on the screen, he felt a hand on his shoulder and he jumped – it was like being touched by an electric cattle prod.

"I am so sorry, Bill. I startled you?" It was the nun from

the reception.

Hoyle felt like sticking her with a syringe full of Sux and then crucifying her, by nailing her to a door. Instead he tried to gather his thoughts.

"I'm sorry," he replied. "I am unused to being touched by strangers."

She looked at him closely. "That is such a shame. Everyone should receive some love and physical affection every now and then, such as a hug." She looked at his uneaten plate of food. "You have no appetite, Bill?"

"I am almost too tired to eat," he replied forking some warm mashed potato into his mouth and almost gagging.

"Well, try to eat something. You need energy for tomorrow."

Hoyle didn't think too much eye-to-eye contact was a good thing right then, so he looked down, privately smirking at the relevance of what she had just said. Tomorrow he would kill a man, and this nun had no idea she was feeding him so he could do such devilish things. How delicious was that?

The nun walked away with a cheery wave and Hoyle continued to pretend to eat.

Shortly afterwards, a very old man wearing a black shiny suit – one he'd probably worn for ten years – rose from a table close to the television and walked towards the door. As he passed Hoyle, the old man glanced at him and their eyes met. He immediately stopped dead in his tracks.

"Excuse me…" The old man said in a faltering tone. "Aren't you…?"

This would be interesting, Hoyle thought. He smiled warmly. "Sit down a moment, and let me tell you if I am."

The man sat.

"Now, tell me. Exactly who do you think I am?"

The old man's expression turned from curiosity to realization. "You look like that actor! That's it! *La Famille Plouffe!* But you look older, I'm afraid. No hard feelings intended."

"None taken," Hoyle replied. He'd always been told that he looked like an American soap star, but no one could ever remember which one. Now he looked like a French soapy actor. Great!

As the old guy shuffled off, Hoyle chuckled. Here was a man who had just been staring at a photograph of him on the television, and one minute later had been looking him in the eye. Yet still he couldn't put both faces together. It was so funny Hoyle wanted to share the moment with someone else – but there was no one he could share this serendipity with. He thought of his dead friend, Jean. Such a shame. He missed him so much. There was no one he could share anything with any more.

A twinge of sadness invaded his psyche as he toyed with his soft warm pap. He had to admit that life had been very lonely since Dermot had been discovered in his tomb and he'd been forced out on the road. He missed the warmth of Neela's friendship. But, he mused, there were many people far worse off than himself. Dutont for one. He was alive at this moment, possibly drinking in some bar, thinking of getting laid that night. He had no idea what was going to happen to him in the morning.

Hoyle pushed his food around the plate, stood and walked towards the dormitory to sleep.

48.

Neela was shocked by Dermot's appearance as he came through the customs area. He looked ten years older than when he'd left for Paris; disheveled, yet she copuld see he didn't care about his appearance. Never a good sign.

Dermot wrapped Neela in his arms and hugged her, then lifted Vig out of her stroller. As he cuddled his daughter, tears welled up in Dermot's eyes – tears he tried to choke back because he didn't want Neela to realize how emotional he was right then. Then he gently handed her back to Neela.

"Let's get out of here, honey. Let's go home," he said.

On the drive back to Malibu, Dermot told her about everything that had happened while he'd been in Paris. Now that she was at his side, he felt he could tell her stuff he'd been reticent to share on the telephone when he couldn't gauge her reaction. She was shocked to the core when Dermot detailed the meeting with Hoyle in *L'Oie sans Jambes* restaurant.

"I would've died of heart failure there and then."

"I think I got close."

"How come he got so close before you recognized him?"

"I just wasn't prepared. You know? My mind was on so many other things. The last thing I was expecting was him to appear in some disguise and stick me with that...stuff."

"That's it, isn't it?"

"What is?"

"That's what he relies on. That no one sees him coming. Then he sticks them, and they've got a matter of seconds to react before they're putty in his hands. What did he look like?"

"Even across the table I had trouble putting his face together with the last time I saw him. It's more drawn. He's dyed his hair almost black. He's really tanned. I'd say he's also applied a lot of make-up to make him look North African – a pretty clever disguise considering how many there are in Paris."

"But why?"

"Why is he still dogging me? I suppose because when I was discovered and brought back to the living world, he suddenly no longer had any closure to his own personal journey of vengeance. It's ironic isn't it, that he never gave a thought to bringing closure to his victims families, and yet he's consumed by it."

As soon as the words escaped his lips Dermot knew that he'd also been responsible from keeping certain facts from the police, thereby preventing closure. He'd been abjectly remorseful later, whereas Hoyle had not.

"What do we do now? Just wait for him to come at us? I couldn't bear that. We have to think of Vig – keep her safe. He's never going to stop till he feels you've suffered enough."

"I *haven't*?"

"Did he give you any idea what he wants from you?"

"He wants to toy with me like a cat with a mouse, that's my guess. I think he won't stop what he refers to as his 'game' until I'm dead. He's in the grip of a psychotic episode. He can still function as a normal human being – and function very cleverly – but what he does is inhuman."

There was no way he was going to tell her of Hoyle's final threat—that if he didn't agree to show up for 'the final meeting' he would come after the family; he wasn't about to put Neela through that terror. And since Hoyle had suggested that if he came alone to the final meeting, his family might be safe, he was fine with keeping the final threat to himself.

Since Neela felt now was the appropriate time to be completely forthright with Dermot, she told him about the man licking the glass in the bathroom. Dermot paled as he listened.

"It was good of Hansen to get the Malibu deputies to house-sit. Are they still there?"

"Not like at first. They come around every four hours or so to check the house out. I've got them on the speed dial as well as Hansen."

"Did Hansen ever call back? To tell you if he tracked the guy down?"

"He called back, sure. Calls every morning. They never found the guy. The only description I had of him was based on a blur at the frosted glass bathroom window. The guy was a tongue with orange hair.

"So what's this Frenchie detective going to do now? What's his name again?"

"Gassin. Thierry Gassin. He's hoping that my sudden departure will destabilize Nick – that he won't carry through the next step of his 'game.'"

"What step is that? Or should I say who's that going to be? You thinking the same as me? Dutont?"

"Of course; but Hoyle's not that stupid. It's obvious to us, and it's obvious to the French police. They'll have Bernard cotton-wooled for sure. So what he's up to, no one knows. But whatever it is, Gassin's pretty sure that my leaving will take the fun out of everything he's got planned. It's like he's only doing it all to drive me crazy. He told me that if I'd never been found, Josef and Galina would never have been butchered – that it's my fault."

They sat in silence for a while till they started up PCH towards Malibu. Each was trying to wrap their heads around what was happening, what sense to make of it, and what the authorities were doing to protect them.

"Hansen wants you to call him soonest – I think he wants to talk to you."

"I'd say that Gassin's been in touch and they've worked out how they plan to play 'the game,'" Dermot replied.

"The man at the bathroom window…?" Neela began.

"He was sent to scare you. That'd be my thinking. Hoyle isn't going to harm you unless I don't play the game properly – that's according to his new set of rules. He's not going to have anyone other than himself laying on fingers. He initially set up the kid just to show us he was back. Then, when you were at your most vulnerable, he organized someone to give you another big scare, hoping you'd immediately tell me, and that would in turn scare the living daylights out of *me*."

Dermot reached for his cell phone and dialed.

"Detective Hansen? It's Dermot Nolan. I just got in from Paris. Neela told me you'd been kind enough to look after them while I was away."

"My pleasure, Mr. Nolan," Dermot heard Hansen say the other end of the line. "What do you think about us having a private chat?"

"Sure, any time."

"Well, let's get a shift on, and get the train rolling. What do you say? In cases like this time's always a major factor. We're not exactly sure how Hoyle will react when he finds out you've left France. But really, that's the whole idea – to make him stop what he's doing, butchering people, and crawl out of the woodwork so we can get a handle on where he is."

"When's good for you?"

"Did you fly business class? In those bed things?"

"Yes, as a matter of fact I did."

"Well, I guess you're rested. So how about we say I'll be at your house in an hour or so?"

"Sure," Dermot replied. He too wanted to get the ball rolling. More importantly, if this was a game at all similar to tennis, he wanted to serve first.

49.

Gassin and his three musketeers had the blinds drawn down, watching a series of photographs on a giant plasma screen. They were CCTV images of cars.

"There it is again, outside Versailles," Gassin said as they looked at a picture of the car they'd found in a garage behind Hoyle's rental. "One more victim and we'd have had him. But he moved on. And judging by the care he's taken to sanitize the house, I'd say he's starting afresh. He could be anywhere; we may have to rely on someone recognizing him."

"Maybe he's thinking of doing the last thing we expect; coming after Dutont when we're convinced it'd be the most stupid thing he could do?"

"We've got six people staking out the house."

"You think he watched us take the family to Amboise?"

"Maybe. But if he did, he'd know we have the family locked down like Fort Knox."

"He's very smart," Migget said. "With a tour of duty in Iraq behind him, who knows what he may have up his sleeve. A rocket launcher? Rocket propelled grenades could do some serious damage."

"How would he get hold of that kind of weapon at short notice?" Gassin replied. "He'd have to have accessed them in France – borders would have been a massive problem."

"Why short notice, boss?" This time it was Simon. "It took him the best part of a year to come out of the woodwork and start playing his game. I'd say he's been planning everything in great detail, paying particular attention to how we might react. He'd have to have a whole set of plan B's to switch to."

"That's true, Gideon," Gassin replied. "His attention to detail is a hallmark of the man. "However, my take on the man is that he gets his kicks out of the personal touch. Firing a grenade into a house hoping it'd find its mark and take out Dutont is not his style."

The others nodded, clearly they agreed.

"Now that the surgeon is dead, we have to wonder what he has in mind to perpetrate next. Removing more body parts is no longer an option unless he snatches another medico, or he plans a more brutal approach – the abattoir as opposed to the ER."

It was a sobering thought.

"The news articles will be in all the papers tomorrow. Hoyle is sure to read them – he misses nothing."

Gassin had called in a lot of favors from his press buddies. Of course the story was front page anyway. But Gassin had been sure to advise the journalists to red flag the fact that notorious novelist Dermot Nolan had just left France for California, since the writer was convinced that the appalling injuries inflicted on Kafni and Yablonskaya were committed by the serial killer known as the Dreamhealer, yet no one would believe him. Gassin was hoping this would upset Hoyle's applecart. Hoyle's thinking might be *does he really believe he can just walk away and think I'll not follow? What's with this guy? He must know I'll keep coming after him as long as I can still draw breath?* Wherever Hoyle was in the morning, he'd be sure to read the papers and watch TV. Hoyle's face would again be on front pages as well as on the television, but this time it would be a photoshopped picture of him looking more like he'd looked in the restaurant – very dark-skinned with a hint of stubble. Then, hopefully, the shit would hit the fan.

Hoyle was up early. The dormitory had been full of smelly old men and the stench of so many dirty street people had been appalling. Hoyle had tried opening a window at around four in the morning, but it had been painted shut. So he'd had to put up with the sound of men farting in their sleep till nearly 6 a.m. when he'd heard movement in the kitchens.

He hadn't taken any of his clothes off for fear he might be feasted on by fleas and bed bugs, though in truth the bunks looked very neat and clean. So he simply rolled out of his bed and made his way to the dining room, hoping he could grab a quick cup of coffee before he set off for a more substantial breakfast in town.

He found a kettle, a mug and a huge tin of Nescafé on the serving table. As he waited for the water to boil he turned on the television. A newsreader was detailing how a Cessna had flown into the side of an Apartment in Nantes killing all on board as well as twelve people in the apartment. Hoyle sat and stirred his coffee, looking up at the screen. Next up was the ugly face of Zimbabwe's President Mugabe shouting invective at journalists. *The usual political shit,* he thought, idly wondering why the U.N. didn't take out this dictator with a smart bomb.

As he took his first sip of coffee, a photo of Dermot popped up on the right hand side of the screen next to the newsreader. Hoyle leant closer. The newsreader and the photo were replaced by a video of Dermot at the airport, surrounded by TV journalists. *What the fuck?* What was Dermot doing at Charles de Gaulle Airport? This wasn't part of the script! He was supposed to stay in France for fuck's sake!

"I don't believe one word of what this man in Sicily has told the media. Nick Hoyle is alive. He's out there right now, somewhere in Paris!" Hoyle heard Dermot say as he shifted his gaze from the journalists and stared into the camera. "The most brutal serial killer of this decade is playing with the police and the media. Yet it is I who people refuse to listen to. They believe this peasant in Palermo, choosing to call *me* insane! Well, let me be very plain; I saw the serial; killer Nick Hoyle two days ago. He threatened to kill me and my family."

Hoyle was now seething with anger. Dermot was spoiling everything!

"I've had enough," Dermot continued. "Let him do his worst. I'm not going to spend one more moment of my life pandering to an insane man. I am going home to safeguard my family."

Hoyle's blood was boiling. He'd gone to a hell of a lot of trouble organizing the cruel death of Dutont and now the bastard Nolan had decided to leave town! This was unforgivable!

Without realizing the extent of his anger, Hoyle brought the palm of his hand down hard on the table. The sound rang around the room, shaking every single piece of furniture. Within seconds a nun and a male caretaker ran into the dining room, concerned about what they were going to find.

Hoyle stood. "I'm sorry about the noise, I'm afraid I stumbled."

The nun looked relieved. "You're not hurt then?"

"No, I'm fine, thank you," Hoyle replied quietly, glancing up obliquely at the television – it was now the sports news, and a Paris Saint Germain footballer was chatting about his retirement.

An hour later, Hoyle had eaten a full American breakfast at a local truck stop, and was making his way to Dutont's home in the suburb of Buxerolles.

There, he'd watched Dutont leave his house half way down the rue Camille Girault, climb into his C4 Picasso and drive to his factory, which Hoyle knew was situated in a nearby industrial neighborhood – he'd scouted out the building for a full week to make sure Dutont worked alone. He knew there was a fair chance Dutont never shut off the furnaces – it was often more cost effective to keep them fired up, even if it meant one day a week wasted. Apparently some glass blowers rented out the free day to other professionals.

However, there was always a chance that Dutont might have to fire up the furnace this particular morning, so Hoyle bided his time, determining to go meet him at around eleven.

Hoyle checked his watch as he sat in his stolen car – he'd read every word of the Figaro and had been delighted at the interest that had been paid to his recent exploits. Interestingly enough, there seemed to be some difference of editorial opinion as to whether or not he was dead. The front page screamed that the *Worst Nightmares serial killer is dead! Sicilian tells all!* But inside there was a whole sub-editorial about Hoyle. Here the journalist made a case for Nolan being not much more than a whacko, yet should he be taken seriously? This journalist asked whether Nolan or the Sicilian were to be believed. Why would the Sicilian lie, he asked? For money! Was it really plausible that Hoyle would have gone all that way, interviewed some Italian rustic and asked him to spin some fancy tale? No! But he refused to rule out that The Dreamhealer was still alive

Hoyle found it all very amusing. He even held up the various snaps of himself in the newspaper and looked in the rear view mirror to see what the actual likeness was like. Even photoshopped, it wasn't even close.

Yet one thing preyed on his mind, and it burned as angrily as any glass-blowing furnace; it was Dermot's casual behavior, leaving Paris when he, Hoyle, had made so many plans well into the next month. Now everything would have to be changed and a great deal of deposits foregone. His anger threatened to burn a hole in his soul. There was only one release valve – take it out on Dutont; he'd be the catharsis.

Originally Dutont was to have survived. Badly scalded of course, but Hoyle was thinking of sparing his life. Now the rules of the game dictated he should die. It would be Dermot's fault entirely. He would take pleasure in telling Dermot that had he played the game properly, Dutont would have lived.

Eleven o'clock – time to go visit Monsieur Dutont.

Hoyle checked in his rear view mirror – there was no one in the street. He opened the driver's door and stepped onto the sidewalk.

Dutont's premises were quite large. The buildings on either side of his were unoccupied; it wasn't an attractive part of town and the area had in former times been busier. There was an audible rumble from deep within the building, low and whirring, as the gases burned hot. Hoyle had never visited a glass blowing factory before and was looking forward to the experience. It was going to be fun.

There were several doors open, allowing entry to the large central space; maybe to allow the breezes in, Hoyle mused. As he approached the central door, his fingers closed over the syringe in his pocket – his little ubiquitous miracle helper.

Looking in from the doorway, Hoyle was amazed by the huge space. Standing with his back to him, facing the opening of a two-foot square open furnace that looked like the doorway to hell, was a man. Dutont was wearing a brimless cap, gloves and protective glasses. In front of him there were three separate, almost white hot, furnaces.

Hoyle had researched the process and knew that the first of the three furnaces, one that contained the crucible of molten glass was usually referred to as *'the furnace.'* The second was called the *'glory hole,'* and was used to reheat a piece of glass in between the steps of working with it. The third furnace was called the *'lehr'* or *'annealer,'* and was used to slowly cool the glass over a period of a few hours to a few days, depending on the size of the pieces.

Hoyle found it all fascinating. Now he was about to see if it really was so difficult to hold a blow iron. Would the heat outside the furnace be as intense as he had imagined?

Dutont was standing by a flat, level, non-combustible bench top about five feet long and two and a half feet deep. This, Hoyle knew, was his work area. There was a back shield for safety and for practical reasons, it was made of similar non-combustible material providing a good deal of fire protection; glass was easier to see if the background had a flat, smooth non-textured surface. The bench top was black to make the glass more visible when held against it.

Dutont had not heard him enter; the roaring of the furnaces was too great.

Hoyle stared at the half open furnace and marveled at the heat, the color was a creamy yellow, and over two thousand three hundred degrees. How anyone could stand so close and not be burned amazed him.

Dutont was now tinkering with a selection of iron and steel tools he had set out on his bench – he'd arrived at the most optimum time, just when the glass blower was about to start creating something wonderful. Once again the gods were smiling on him! He was alone. That was perfect; it was always difficult to subdue more than one person at the same time. If there were two subjects he'd have to be within striking distance of both parties and be very discreet with the first jab. Just in case he was carrying a Kel-Tec P-32 ACP semi automatic in his left pocket. It was always handy to carry such a small gun, often referred to as a Mouse-gun, for emergencies, though he'd never been forced to resort to firing it. The pistol had been very easy to source in Paris.

Hoyle walked very slowly forward, the roar of the jets in his ears. He found the noise both heady and exhilarating; so much so that initially he wasn't so much focusing on the killing as on the glass blowing.

When he was two feet from Dutont, Hoyle spoke, making sure his tone was casual and smooth.

"Monsieur Dutont?" he asked.

Dutont turned suddenly, surprised that someone should be so close to him, instinctively bringing up an arm up as if to ward off a blow.

"I'm sorry! It's okay," Hoyle said, smiling. "I didn't mean to surprise you."

Dutont took a deep breath as he studied Hoyle. "Well, you did surprise me. Walking up so silently. I work alone, so I don't expect company. Can I ask what you want here?"

"I am a member of the AGA. The Association. I found your name on the Internet?"

Dutont relaxed a little – not much, but enough. "Oh, yes? You are a glass blower yourself?"

"No, I am learning though. One day…"

"I wish you'd called me on the telephone. You almost stopped my heart just then," Dutont said with a smile.

Some kind of irony, Hoyle thought. Dutont was standing toe to toe with the most celebrated serial killer of the new millennium, and his heart was settling from panic to relaxation.

"So, you would like to see what I do?"

"Very much indeed."

"All right. But I have work to do, so this must be brief."

"It will be, Monsieur Dutont. It will be," Hoyle replied.

Dutont caught a curious edge in Hoyle's voice; not enough to scare him, but sufficient to raise the hairs on the back of his neck.

Dutont explained about there being three furnaces in one, then continued. "Inside the main furnace is around four hundred pounds of molten glass."

"That much?" Hoyle was impressed.

"Usually it's five hundred, but today I don't need so much."

Hoyle had a mental image blip where he saw Dutont encased in five hundred pounds of clear glass; like a trophy spider encased in silicone. Of course he knew that to achieve this would be impossible; human flesh would practically evaporate at over two thousand degrees. It was an amusing image, nevertheless.

"Hey, how about this – suppose I show you how I make something?"

"That'd be great," Hoyle replied, almost like a kid.

"What you want me to make? Think of something."

"How about a mouse," Hoyle replied without really thinking about it, his left hand closing on the small gun in his pocket.

"A mouse. Okay, it's a mouse! I tell you what; let's make it a fat rat, they're bigger."

"Okay...a rat," Hoyle replied. Very suitable, after all he *was* a rat; a pretty deadly one at that.

Dutont lifted the blowhose and pushed it into the furnace towards the molten glass. A few seconds later he was pulling it out – it had a white mass on the end about the size of a Coke bottle, but rounder.

"The blowhose here is what you blow air through to shape the glass. Right now I won't be blowing because I'm making a mouse and that's solid."

Hoyle nodded, fascinated that he could be so close to boiling glass and not get burned by the heat.

"We've got the mouthpiece at my end and a swivel at the other so I can rotate the glass. The swivel is connected to the glass by a latex tubing assembly."

"Fascinating..."

"Isn't it, though," Dutont agreed as he put the blowhose on a rest, all the while rotating the rod.

Then he sat and reached behind him, selecting some tweezers and calipers from his bench.

"Now look here. I can pull the glass and tweak it to make a snout, ears and stuff like that. It's easy when you know how."

"Sure looks it," Hoyle replied as he saw the rat come to

life. It already had a long nose and two rounded ears.

"Then, when we have the body the way we like it, we use a cutting tool. Once we have laid the glass animal down on the bench, that is."

One snip and the rat was lying on the bench. Then Dutont used the calipers to pull at the rear end of the piece of glass to make the long tail."

"How hot is it now?" Hoyle asked.

"It is so hot it would burn a hole clean through you," Dutont replied with a grin. "It doesn't look so hot now, but I promise you it is. Whatever you do, don't touch it for a long time."

He used the tweezers to separate the rat's front and rear legs a bit more then stood it upright – the whole thing had taken less than two minutes.

"That is for you. A present." He then held out a hand to Hoyle. "But forgive me, I have not yet introduced myself. My name is Bernard Dutont."

"I know," Hoyle replied. The name was about to be his death sentence. "I'm Tom."

"Good to meet you, Tom," Dutont said as he warmly shook Hoyle's hand. The moment they broke contact, Hoyle looked over Dutont's shoulder, pretending to see something. "What is that over there?" he asked.

As Dutont turned away from him, the needle was out of Hoyle's pocket and in the glass blower's arm.

The glass blower briefly winced at the pain.

"What was that?" Dutont said almost to himself, wondering if he had been touched by a spot of hot glass. Within seconds the Succinylcholine was doing it's job and Dutont's knees were beginning to wobble.

"What the..." Dutont barely managed as Hoyle stepped forward and held Dutont so he could set the glass blower down on a seat by his bench.

Knowing he had at least eight minutes before the neuromuscular blocker wore off, Hoyle crouched close to his rat, admiring Dutont's artistry.

"You are a very clever man, monsieur. In a way I am sorry that you just happened to share the same name as someone else. This could so easily have been a lesson rather than an execution.

Dutont's pupils dilated. He could hear Hoyle's words yet could not move a muscle. This was his most intimate horror, to have some madman on the loose near his precious furnace, able to access his precious glass.

"Now I appreciate that I know diddly-squat about hot glass, but I think I'll give it a go. Why don't you sit and watch me, then maybe give me marks out of ten later?"

Dutont just stared.

"So...we take this rod here," Hoyle said calmly, picking up the blowhose, "And stick it in here," he continued, poking it in to the furnace, "and dip it in the...goo?"

Very carefully Hoyle withdrew the rod. There was far more white-hot glass on it than before. "Uh-oh! Got a bit too much, eh? Never mind," he said, rotating the molten glass so it didn't drip. "It looks a bit like a football, wouldn't you say? Do you play?"

Hoyle laid the rod down briefly, so that it was supported by an upright.

"Let's see if I can make a rat too. See how easy it is. What do you say?"

He picked up a tweezer and pulled at the end of the glass; it was like pulling at warm candy.

"There you go! An ear. Let's try another. Got to have two ears."

But as he pulled, the glass seemed to go out of shape; the second ear was twice the size of the first ear. Hoyle gave a short snort of annoyance. "Damn, this isn't as easy as I thought."

He pulled at the first ear to attempt matching it to the second, but no matter how hard he tried, the glass looked like a blob with two bits sticking out of it.

"Guess it's harder than I thought," he muttered, then lost interest. "Let's call my attempt a four out of ten, eh? Now for something else. I want you to help me out here. I feel like conducting an experiment."

Hoyle studied Dutont's face closely. It was a blank mask, except... except for the smallest twitch – a tick – beneath his right eye.

"I'd like you to hold out your hands, palms up and place them on the table." He tut-tutted to himself. "Silly old me. You're pretty much immobile, aren't you? I'll help you out."

Hoyle then took Dutont's hands and placed them palms up on the workbench, almost like a religious tableau. The tick below the glass blower's eye spasmed at more frequent intervals.

"You see, my original thought was to encase your hands completely in glass. Like an exhibit. That'd be just amazing! Don't you think? But I can't have been thinking things through properly because what I forgot about was the heat. It'd burn right though the hands, wouldn't it? Might Perspex be a better choice?"

Hoyle lifted the rod with the big gobbet of glass on the end and positioned it above Dutont's hand. "For what we are about to receive," Hoyle chanted, as if saying grace, "Let us be truly thankful."

As he began to lower the rod, he heard a child's call to his right.

"Papa!"

Hoyle's head snapped around.

Who the hell...?

It was a young boy, dressed in a T-shirt and shorts. He was standing stock-still, in a state of shock, staring at the glass blower. Almost immediately, the child was joined by an identical boy – it had to be a twin. Both were dressed alike.

The seconds passed. Hoyle had no idea what to do. Had the interlopers been adults he'd have instantly shot them in the head with his Mouse gun. But these were children, no more than four years old. If his own twins had lived, they'd have been exactly the same age, and look exactly like these beautiful children with their curly black hair and rosy cheeks.

"Papa! Are you all right?" the first boy called out, but Dutont could not move.

"Is my Papa all right?" the boy asked Hoyle. The second boy whispered something into his brother's ear; Hoyle couldn't distinguish what it was.

"Your papa will be fine, boys."

Hoyle was in two minds about what action to take. Kill them all? That made solid sense. He could throw the boys into the furnace.

His left hand closed over the butt of his gun, withdrawing half of it.

He then changed his mind. Could he really shoot both children in the head and burn them? No. He might miss one and the other would run screaming from the building. Besides they were twins! They could have been *his* twins!

Despair lanced through his heart as his brain startled to boil as hot as the furnace itself.

His babies! His own two innocent babies had been so cruelly taken from him. He knew what torment the glass blower would be suffering that very second. How could he take his sons from him? Yet what alternative did he have? Dutont and both children had seen him. He *had* to kill them!

As the first boy began to walk towards his father, Hoyle rested the blowhose down on the upright, and took one pace forward so that he was now between the boy and his father. "Go home, now. Both of you. Your father will be all right. He will join you shortly. Now run!"

The boy was hesitant.

"Do as I say. Run!"

The boys turned and ran out the side entrance.

Hoyle crouched down next to the glass blower. "Your children saved your life. May they grow up to be fathers too. Keep them safe. I should have kept mine safe. But I failed. I will never forgive myself for that."

Hoyle turned and walked out of the building.

He looked back one last time; Dutont was still sitting there, immobile; his palms facing upwards on the bench. Had he been praying? No. God didn't answer such prayers. He had prayed once himself, yet no one had been listening. It was he, Hoyle, not this man's God, that had spared him.

50.

Gassin was in Barbier's lavish Neuilly living room. The Commissaire was pacing up and down, wringing his hands. He was clearly in a major funk.

"It keeps getting worse, Thierry."

"The man's an accomplished serial killer – he's been on the run for months, having killed thirteen people in America. How can we realistically expect to put hands on his collar so soon?"

"Because we have to, that's why! We must show the Americans a lesson. That means being one step ahead, not one step behind."

Gassin wondered exactly what Barbier thought his personal input had been up till now, other than passing the buck, giving impressive press conferences where he promised a quick resolution of the mutilations, and then asking his team to take the blame.

Barbier looked at his watch. It was only minutes from the time the man would call. "Should I take him by surprise and refer to him by his name? Hoyle?"

Gassin was horrified by the naïveté of his boss. "No, Jules. Please do not. Just keep him talking as long as you can; not that we'll be able to track him, simply because the more he says, the more clues we have."

The door opened and Barbier's slender wife entered with a tray of coffee. Barbier shot her a look of exasperation. "For God's sake, Mireille, we are not thinking of coffee at a time like this."

Gassin didn't know where to look; clearly Madame Barbier was embarrassed by her husband's tone.

As Mireille Barbier backed out of the living room the phone rang and Barbier snatched up the receiver. "Commissaire Barbier."

"Yes, you are, aren't you," a voice replied.

Barbier was annoyed by the teasing tone, his nerves already in shreds. "Please continue," he said, rather shortly.

Gassin wished he'd insisted on taking the call; Barbier was no diplomat, even when lives were in the balance.

"You have a name for me this morning, Commissaire?"

"I do. Bernard Dutont. The neurosurgeon."

There was a slight hiatus. Then Hoyle spoke again. "Well, *almost* right."

Barbier was momentarily confused. "Almost? What do you mean?"

"I had hoped your team would have been smarter."

"How smarter?"

"Let me put it this way. It was surely obvious that you would protect your neurosurgeon. That was to be expected. How could I possibly *interfere*, for want of a better word, with *your* Bernard Dutont?" Hoyle accentuated the word 'your.'

Gassin's stomach turned over. Of course! How could he have been so dimwitted.

"However, as it turned out, I decided to spare *my* Bernard Dutont. You are very lucky in this regard. But enough of that. I am here to tell you that I am extremely angry."

"How so?" Barbier asked.

"Mr. Nolan was supposed to play my game as were you. Now he has decided to take his ball and go home."

"So...?"

"I have gone to a great deal of trouble to organize the logistics of my game, and he has spoiled everything. So we must go back to the blocks, as they say in athletics circles. This has been a false start; now we must begin again."

"What are you after, Monsieur Hoyle?" Barbier blurted out.

Gassin raised his hands to his face in anguish. *Oh, no!*

"Who?" There was a chuckle the other end of the line. "Hoyle, the *Dotore di Medico*, is dead. I read that only yesterday in *Le Figaro*. However, please tell Mr. Nolan that this matter is not over. It is now more personal than ever. We will start the game again. At a time of my choosing, not his. And at that time he will do as I say and go where I ask. Gotta run! *Hasta la vista!*"

The line went dead.

51.

Hoyle knew it was time to cut and run. As far as the 'game' was concerned, Dermot had played foul. Hoyle had invested a great deal of his money preparing for the coming two months in France, but all of this had to be cancelled. It was heartbreaking so see almost half of his savings go up in smoke in this fashion. *Les regles de jeu ne sont pas juste* – how true! The rules of the game were *never* just!

So they knew who he was. The Massimo ruse had been unsuccessful. He'd hoped the police would think Dermot had lost his mind. However, the Commissaire had called him by name. Was it possible they were simply trying it on? Were they still unsure whether or not to believe the Sicilian? Had he not been thorough enough discrediting Nolan; picturing him as a complete flake? Clearly the way to go was to continue to reinforce the belief that he was dead. And the best way to do that was to demonstrate that someone else was out there mutilating people. That was it! The idea came to him in a rush. Discredit the French! Make life hell for them! Call a national newspaper, pretend to be some American homicidal maniac and inform the crime desk journalist that he would this time kill, rather than simply maim. And for what reason? Because the Préfécture were giving credit to someone who was dead – Nick Hoyle – for the masterly mutilations of which he was so proud! That would sound insane enough to be believable. The beauty of making this single phone call would be because it gave an exclusive to a newspaper who would be sure to run it on the front page, berating the Préfécture for being so dumb as to anger the serial 'Butcher' sufficiently to goad him to fresh heights.

There was only one problem with this plan; it was a time factor. He needed to lie low, rather than take his time targeting someone. It was likely the police planned to release the news that they were now certain Nick Hoyle was still alive, last seen somewhere near Poitiers. Everyone and their dog would be on the lookout for him. That was why it was so important to convince a journalist that the Dreamhealer was dead. So that everyone was looking for the wrong man?

Now was the right time to become a fat man. It was simply a matter of wearing all the clothes he had in his hold all. That would put on a couple of stone. Then add a shuffling walk, a hunching of the shoulders, a stoop. The prescription glasses would add a nice touch. He'd look like a feeble old man.

An hour later Hoyle was making a telephone call.

Claude Vagnier was researching a break-and-enter case that had occurred overnight when the call came through.

He'd worked the crime desk at Le Monde for seven years and had always done his best to mix serious reporting with flashy crime stories. His ambition was ultimately to write *roman policiers*; crime stories. The break-and-enter case had intrigued him because the target house belonged to a prominent French movie star, whose wife had been badly beaten. It was the kind of copy that always drew readers.

The caller sounded like an angry American with a deep southern accent.

"Le Monde? Are you Le Monde? The newspaper? Who's this? What's your name?"

Vagnier politely identified himself.

"Vagnier? Right. I want you to put things straight. Today!"

"Put what straight, sir? What is your name?"

"Like I'm gonna tell you that!" Hoyle replied, laughing. "You can call me *Monsieur le Chirurgien.* That's French for surgeon, ain't it?"

"Sure, but why are you calling me?"

"I'll make this short and sweet. The cops are telling the world that a guy named Hoyle – you know, the serial killer from way back – that Worst Nightmares guy...?" He paused to let the words sink in, then continued. "They're saying that *he* did the things that *I* just did. That ain't right. The guy's dead! Everyone knows that!"

Vagnier tried to gather his thoughts.

"You mean the Dreamhealer?"

"Yeah, *that* guy."

"So what's he got to do with you?"

"Nothing! Sweet nothing! That's my whole point. It's me that did Kafni and the ballet dancer. It's me that visited the glass guy in Poitiers. So you go tell those stupid police assholes that you spoke to me and I'm real mad about it. So freakin' mad I'm gonna do someone today and tag him with my name so you'll all *know* who the fuck I am!"

Vagnier was now completely spooked by this talk of murder. "How can I reach you again?" he asked.

"You can't, you dipshit! I'm gonna go tag some poor bastard, so go tell Inspector Clouseau, or whatever his damned name is, that it's me doing it, not Hoyle. Okay?"

Vagnier could scarcely speak; it was a first for him to be lost for words, and it deeply disturbed him to hear a man talk in this way.

"By the way, this is an exclusive, so enjoy it, bud! I ain't rung no one else. Looks like you got yourself a scoop!"

The line went dead.

Across town Gassin was again trying to pacify Barbier on the telephone. The Commissaire had been fielding calls from editors all morning, as well as the Minister. Everyone was asking hard questions; how close were they to closing down 'The Butcher', as they now tagged him. Was the Dreamhealer dead, or wasn't he? Could people sleep securely at night while some brutal killer was still loose; about to break into houses to cut off body parts?

Commissaire Barbier wanted answers from Gassin.

"We missed him by just a matter of hours, sir."

"Might as well have been one minute," Barbier replied stonily. "Where are we now? Nowhere. What about this glass blower, Dutont? *Merde de cochon!* That's really stirred up the media again. Unbelievably, he spared the man's life for some reason. No one's told me why yet. You care to tell me? Just so I know what to tell the Minister!"

"Again sir, it sits very well with my assumption that it is definitely Hoyle that's behind all these games."

"Really? Why?"

"Hoyle was about to drop a few pounds of molten glass onto Dutont's hands when his children came in and spoiled everything."

"Are you saying he didn't go through with it because the man's kids were watching? He's done the most obscene things in the past, why on earth would an audience of two *children* stop him?"

"Because it's his Achilles heel. You see, he was married once, and his wife died giving birth to twins. Then the two boys died as a result of burns in a fire at the post-natal hospital. That's one of the main reasons Hoyle went completely nuts."

"He saw Dutont's kids, and thought of them as his own? Is that what you're suggesting?"

"Exactly, sir. He told Dutont that his children had saved his life. It's not hard to see the correlation to Hoyle's history."

Gassin heard a telephone ring the other end of the line.

"Don't hang up. I have to take this call," Barbier said stiffly.

Gassin waited. He could just make out Barbier's voice on the other line, but couldn't make out the conversation. His tone was angry. Then he came back on the line.

"You'll be receiving a call any second. André Kalid just called me as a matter of courtesy. You know who he is, I imagine?"

"A deputy editor at Le Monde? Yes, I know him well."

"Well, you're going to know him a whole lot better in a few minutes. It seems one of his crime desk people just received a telephone call from someone calling himself 'The Surgeon'. An American who's spitting chips right now because Nolan's been saying it was Hoyle who butchered Kafni and Yablonskaya. The Yank says *he* did it."

Gassin was silent. He knew this was exactly what Hoyle would do – stir the pot, inflame the public, put the press offside.

"You're not saying anything, Gassin." It wasn't Christian names today.

"I'm thinking, sir. This is Hoyle's work."

"Yes, you keep saying this. But what if you're wrong? What if Hoyle is dead and we're spending all our time looking for a dead man? And meanwhile this other person, 'The Surgeon,' gets so upset he kills someone else? Because that's exactly what he told the crime reporter at Le Monde; someone called Vagnier. He said he'd tag the guy with his name!"

"I have to make some calls right away, Commissaire. I'll get back to you as soon as we have made significant progress."

"Meanwhile, what am I supposed to tell the media this morning? That we're sure it's Hoyle? Christ! One minute we're saying Hoyle drowned, the next we're saying he didn't."

"Tell them we *know* it's Hoyle. Tell them the Sicilian was mistaken."

"Well, I tell you something, Gassin. You don't make my life any easier by changing tack every few hours."

He paused. There was silence. Gassin let it ride.

It was Barbier who broke the hiatus. "So we ignore the threat to kill and tag?"

"Correct. It's Hoyle. He'll do whatever he has in mind regardless of media stories. He's trying to make us look bad and turn the public against us. The best thing we can do is to out-think him. He playing us off against each other at a time when he have to have solidarity."

Barbier said nothing. Gassin paused for breath.

"Do I still have your confidence, Jules?" Gassin asked. "This is a moment that will define the case down the line. We can't let Hoyle manipulate us in this way."

"Look, Thierry," Barbier replied in a more affable tone. "You are the smartest detective I've ever come across. I'd be crazy not to place my confidence in you. But playing the media today? It's going to be hard."

"Tell them 'The Surgeon' does not exist. Tell them it is Hoyle up to his tricks. Make it that simple. Tell them we're confident we'll find Hoyle soon and put him away. I truly believe I have a handle on this man. It's a matter of time before he slips up and I have him. Then I'll hand him to you, and you'll come out of this smelling of roses."

Barbier snorted. "You think? What if this 'Surgeon' guy kills someone later today like he says he will? And then tags him? Sure, *we'll* know it's Hoyle, but the media will scream it's someone else. They'll say we were too pigheaded to change our tune and *we're* responsible for the fallout."

"You tell the media we know Hoyle is trying to put us off the scent. There's no way we can prevent every murder in the Greater Paris – no one would believe that was possible."

"Okay, Thierry, I'll play along. Just don't let me down. You'd better be right."

Barbier ended the call his end. Almost immediately Simon called him from Poitiers – he'd flown down in a chopper as soon as the news of Dutont's assault had been received at the Préfécture.

52.

Dermot was now sure that Hansen was avoiding his calls. It had been two days since Hansen had driven up to Malibu. They'd discussed Gassin's take on how to proceed, and Hansen had been at pains to assure Dermot that he personally was doing everything humanly possible to make certain Hoyle couldn't slip into the country unnoticed. Since that meeting Dermot had done little else than sit around his Point Dume home wondering what was going to happen next.

It was all very well, Dermot pondered, for the French police and the LAPD to combine their resources and work on ways of trapping Hoyle when the man came after him, but they weren't very understanding about how the Judas goats were feeling. It was his family he'd put at risk, and now, more than ever, he needed to be kept in the picture twenty-four seven.

He dialed Hansen's number again. To his surprise Hansen picked up.

"Mr. Nolan. Dermot. How are you today?"

"Well, I can tell you one thing, Detective, I'd be a deal happier if you kept me in the loop about what's going down in France. I left there two days ago and right then all we knew was that Hoyle had a third victim in mind. Can you begin to think what it must be like to know there's someone in another country thinking about chopping people up just to annoy you? And feeling that it's *your* fault?"

"Well, we all know it's not."

"What?"

"Your fault. We know Hoyle's flipped completely, and it's just a matter of time before we catch him. Meantime, we're doing everything we can this end, and the French are doing the same their end. The bottom line is that we're making damned sure you and your family are safe and have nothing to worry about."

"Nothing to worry about?" Dermot almost shouted. "What about Dutont? Is he okay?"

"The neurosurgeon you ran in your story is fine."

Dermot could feel Hansen hadn't told the whole story, so he nudged him. "Someone else *isn't* so fine? Is that what you're going to tell me now?"

"You see," Hansen began in a tone that Dermot knew smelled of prevarication. "The thing is, much as I'd like to call you every few hours and fill you in on what's been happening in France, I work almost sixteen hours a day. Of those sixteen hours I have to spend maybe fourteen on cases that come up every day; murders, rapes, assaults, and stuff like that. You see, the world continues to turn, and we have to deal with cases, like a triage nurse handling people in a hospital."

"Tell me what's happened. I can tell there's something."

"Okay. It seems that your surgeon pal wasn't the target at all. Hoyle was being sneaky. He knew they'd keep the guy safe, so he went after someone else named Bernard Dutont. Seems none of the French cops thought of that one."

"Would you have?" Dermot cut in, then immediately regretted his attitude; Hansen was doing all he could to help and didn't need that type of snide remark.

"Well, I'd like to think I would have, yes."

"I apologize, Jim. I know it's easy to think of things—"

"After the event? Yes, it is. Anyway, the guy wasn't injured. Hoyle backed off at the last minute 'cos this guy Dutont, down in a town called Poitiers, had two kids. They bust into the scene just as Hoyle was about to do some serious damage to Dutont. Seems he couldn't bring himself to kill the kids."

"Were they twins?" Dermot asked.

"You guessed. Yes, they were. So now everyone except some of the media are convinced it's Hoyle we're looking for; for Kafni and his wife, Yablonskaya, the surgeon, and Dutont. So, I can tell you one thing. Right now he's going find it real hard to get about without someone picking him out. His face has been plastered on every French national newspaper for two days and he's been on TV too."

Dermot was silent for a moment.

"I just don't get it," he said finally. "I don't care how fucking smart Nick Hoyle is, he's *still* managing to avoid the police while everyone in France is out looking for him. How is this possible?"

"Wish I could tell you that, Dermot. It amazes me too. Fact is, it amazed me that he somehow managed to get himself to France on forged documents with every immigration officer in the country looking out for him."

"What'd be your guess?"

"North would mean Canada. But he'd still have to avoid the Canadian immigration guys, who I reckon are as hot as our guys here. Me? I'd say the Mexican border. Once he's there he could sneak about till he got to some place like Cancun and then hop a fishing boat to Havana – those guys don't pay too much attention to our Ten Most Wanted photos. And from there, well, he could go anywhere and no one would give a shit. Then he just waits till the heat's off, and slips into Europe via the back door."

"Where?"

"North Africa. Algeria, maybe. You can buy almost anything there; so to buy a working holiday on a boat that services Marseille every week wouldn't be too hard. And remember, the French weren't expecting him."

"He was on the Interpol hot list, for God's sake!"

"It's a mighty long list. Just think about it; you're a customs and immigration guy at Marseille and you've got a hundred vessels coming in a day. You've also got a list of guys that are 'most wanted.' But what are you going to do; carry the pictures around with you? Or carry them in your head? Nah, it'd be easy for Hoyle to have bought a good passport and made himself look dark and kind of Algerian."

"Is that how he's going to get back *into* America?"

"No way. America's a different story. He tries that; we'll catch him. That I'll promise you right now."

Dermot wished he was as certain of that as Hansen. Hansen *had* to believe American borders were secure. Dermot knew they leaked like sieves. Sometime soon, he knew he'd feel a hand on his shoulder again.

"Can you promise me something?"

"Do my best, Mr. Nolan," Hansen replied.

"Don't make me have to call you every day. Just let me know whatever it is you know. Does Gassin fill you in on a regular basis?"

"Yes and no. If I can help him, yes. If it's something he has to deal with? No, maybe not."

When he was through with Hansen Dermot called Gassin but it was Simon who answered. Apparently Gassin was still interviewing the glass blower and his kids. Simon assured him he'd call back asap. He didn't mention Hoyle's threat to tag and kill someone in the wrong place at the wrong time by the end of the day. How could he tell Nolan that it'd be because Hoyle was angry with Nolan for leaving the country before he'd finished playing out his sick 'game'.

53.

Despite his photo being carried on both television and newspapers, no one noticed a middle-aged to elderly fat man in a dark coat, prescription glasses and a fedora with a gaily colored feather stuck in the band, board the TGV high speed train from Poitiers station, bound for Paris.

Hoyle was carrying a cane. It reminded him of the good old days when he used to pretend to Dermot and Neela that he'd been crippled in Iraq. Now, again, the device was proving useful.

As he shuffled along the platform towards a first class carriage, his shoulders hunched forward, a young man actually stepped forward to help him up into the train. Hoyle thanked him in French, then chuckled.

It was the 3.40 p.m. afternoon service to Paris and there weren't many people on the train. Hoyle found himself a quiet spot and pretended to sleep, covering his face. In his hand he held his ticket between thumb and forefinger, knowing the conductor would most likely clip the ticket without bothering to wake a tired old guy with a walking stick.

Oddly enough, he did drop off during the trip. When he awoke the train was slowing down in the outskirts of Paris. He glanced at his ticket. It had been clipped.

He smiled.

Again, he was helped off the train, this time by a minister of the church. Hoyle mumbled a barely perceptible '*Merci, Monsieur*,' as he stepped down onto the platform. Within five minutes he was in the Metro on his way to his preferred killing ground.

As Hoyle prepared to kill; Gassin, Migget, Becaux and Simon worked like beavers in the small office that was their control room.

"He could be anywhere. How can we predict what he'll do, sir?" Migget said, almost to himself.

"We can't. All we can do is predict what he *might* do, given his modus operandi. We must ask ourselves where he might do it."

"Surely, movement will be a problem for him. Practically everyone in France has seen his image over the past week."

"If it were you, Franc, where would you prefer to strike – somewhere busy or somewhere remote?"

"That would depend, sir."

"On what?"

"The fewer people around, the less chance of being recognized. But we have to remember that his disguises have been outstanding in the past. The Lebanese man? That's how the Maitre d' described him. So in some respects I might prefer to be one of a crowd. A crowd walking through a busy street has little time to look around, notice things. But a few people standing on a street corner, they have plenty of time."

"You think he might already have left Poitiers?"

"That would be my guess, sir. A guess, nonetheless."

"By car?"

"I'd say not," Becaux said. "Road blocks. He must know we would have random road-blocks on all roads leading out of central Poitiers. Even with a miraculous disguise, if the car were stopped, there's a fair chance he'd be recognized."

"So we're left with trains. That's what I was thinking, Antoine. That's why there are fifty people watching the Gare de Lyon at this very moment. But let's move forward. If you were he, would you be concerned about the mutilation factor – that would make his task hard."

"He could simply chop off a finger to make a point. A pen knife would do the job."

"True, Antoine. Yet not very dramatic. I feel our man Hoyle has an affinity for high drama. I think a single finger will, this time, not be enough for him."

As Gassin pondered on the degree of mutilation Hoyle had in mind, the Dream Healer was already at Châtelet Les Halles, one of the busiest Metro stations in Paris.

The platform on which he was standing was packed with commuters. It was a quarter to six in the evening with everyone in a rush to get home. Hoyle had already scrawled the note he would use; it was neatly folded in his pocket. His right hand fingers were holding it tight. The paper bore the signature – 'The Surgeon.'

He had three distinct things to do. Select someone close enough to him on the platform who was standing near to the edge. It had to be where the train entered the station. Here it would still be running at speed.

An older person would be ideal. He or she would also have to be presenting a handy coat pocket in which to insert the note. And finally, and much more importantly, Hoyle would have to be able to position himself behind the target, allowing one person in between the two of them. He could hardly be standing directly behind his victim, as it would be obvious to everyone who had done the pushing. Better to let someone else take the blame by allowing his cane to do the final subtle push.

It took him some time to work his way to the correct end of the platform, where the train would enter at speed. While he'd been doing this, two trains had entered and left. Having rehearsed sufficiently, he looked around so he could decide who was going to die today.

This was fun, he thought, idly. Life and death on a whim. Delicious!

It took him only a minute or so to spot the perfect victim. She was a woman of around sixty, wearing a big brown coat that almost reached her ankles. She was shuffling about, constantly looking at her watch, as if late for an appointment. This was a woman in a hurry; someone who was doing a stirling job of selfishly shuffling through the crowds at other people's expense to get to the platform's edge.

Hoyle shuffled ever close to her. To anyone around he could easily have been her husband – both wore coats, his black, hers brown. Both looked around sixty and a bit frail.

When he was standing directly behind her, he noticed with joy that she was also carrying a stout stick. Ideal!

As he heard the train approaching, he slipped the note in her pocket, pretending as he did so to stumble slightly. Then he shifted back just enough to allow a young North African to take his place directly behind the woman.

As the wind rushed into the station, the crowd made their last-second moves, to be ready to step on board as soon as the doors opened. That's when Hoyle slowly raised his cane to waist height and threaded it very gently between the African and a young man standing to his left.

The rest was a piece of cake. The train roared in, Hoyle stabbed the cane forward and in a flash the woman was gone. Simple as that, thought Hoyle as the crowd started screaming.

Time to leave.

Two minutes later the fat man in the black coat and fedora was on a train traveling in the opposite direction to Marne-La-Vallée, wondering how many of the old bag's limbs had been sliced through. An arm? Both? Both legs, maybe? Possibly a head? That would have been ideal!

END GAME

54.

It would have been an exaggeration to suggest that France was gripped by fear of 'The Surgeon' in the months that followed the murder of Madame Rechy in the Metro at Châtellet-Les-Halles; but it was a fact that a current of unease ran through France; Paris in particular. Despite the panic of the moment at Châtelet-Les-Halles, as the crowd screamed and raced for the exits, several commuters who were later interviewed were adamant that the woman hadn't stumbled and fallen, as originally thought, but had been propelled forward. However, there were so many disparate descriptions of those who had been seen close to Madame Rechy that the detectives came away with little more than a vague list of over thirty people; some old, some young, some men, some women.

The moment she was examined at the morgue, the note

was found in her brown coat pocket and the shit really hit the fan. *'Dead! 'Cos you made me mad. Your fault! The Surgeon.'*

The media howled that yet again someone had fooled the incompetent Paris police. Again the authorities were humming and haaring about who was the culprit – was it 'The Surgeon' or was it Hoyle? Was Hoyle the 'Surgeon'? The press shouted that the Préfécture had made a massive mistake by suggesting that it was Nick Hoyle, formerly known as the 'Dream Healer' before his suicide, who had been responsible for the mutilations of Kafni and Yablonskaya. If they hadn't inflamed the American who'd called Le Monde, it was highly likely that the Rechy woman would still be alive today.

Journalists across Europe argued their cases. Most were of the opinion that Rechy's death was the work of the new figure, 'The Surgeon', the man who had already struck five times; Kafni and his wife, Ballon and his wife, and Yablonskaya. Why would the police, they argued, have thought to link Nick Hoyle to these killings when it did not fit his modus operandi in the slightest degree? Hoyle had murdered thirteen people in America according to their worst nightmares. He had not simply mutilated them and allowed them to live. What made the authorities so certain Hoyle had been in France at all? Just the word of Dermot Nolan, a man recovering from severe depression. They even strongly suggested Nolan was mentally unbalanced and possibly suffering hallucinations.

Questions were asked in the Parliament of France. The Prime Minister himself was accused of running a lax government, staffed by indecisive ministers. The Ministre d'Intérieur was told to fix things, and naturally the first two heads to fall were Barbier and Gassin. The Minister saw fit not to resign. Gassin returned to his former post as Commissariat Principal of the sixth arrondissement of Paris, and head of La BAC; Barbier was posted overseas to New Caledonia.

Commandant Henri Veron, the man seconded from the Marseille district to take over as Commissaire from Barbier, made sure that Gassin and his team worked unofficially beside the new investigative boss.

The rolling of heads seemed to satisfy the media; once the Minister had admitted to the shortcomings of the Préfécture, and distanced himself from the debacle, there was little else they could ask of the Minister.

But as poor Madame Rechy was being buried, every journalist in Paris waited with baited breath for 'The Surgeon' to strike again.

They were to be hugely disappointed. For though the murder count in Paris in particular, and France remained a healthy steady number – it being proudly pointed out by *France Soir* that France stood at number forty in terms of murders per thousand population, while America was at twenty-four – not a single murder committed after the death of Madame Rechy could be attributed to either 'The Surgeon' or 'The Dream Healer'.

It was a disappointment to everyone but the rather smug new Commissaire, who, by effectively doing nothing but sit and twiddle his thumbs at the Préfécture, was smelling like roses merely because Hoyle had gone to ground. It was clear to the new boss that either or both of the serial killers had gone elsewhere or died; but he was happy as a clam nevertheless. The *Ministre d'Intérieur*, of course, took full credit for everything; for scaring off the killer. So while the media prayed for more butchery to sell more copies of their newspapers, the serial killer felt unwilling to oblige.

During the weeks that followed the Paris Metro killing, Gassin kept in touch with Dermot on a daily basis. As did Hansen from North Hollywood. But the truth of the matter was that neither cop had any idea where Hoyle had disappeared to, nor how he'd managed to slip through their net. Dermot and Neela were of the opinion that Hoyle had gone to ground because his 'game' had not worked out the way he'd planned, and he was now biding his time until he felt he could organize his entry back into America to continue to torture Dermot.

Given this state of affairs, life was practically impossible for Neela and Dermot – they felt as if they had been staked out in a clearing in the African veldt, and at any moment a lion would crash through trees and devour them.

Days became months. Dermot's general health declined, more particularly his mental health. He lost weight, became obsessed with anything around him that could be interpreted as a sign of the 'second coming' of Nick Hoyle. Each time he left the house with Neela and Virginia he looked like a spooked CIA Presidential security guy, eyes twitching from side to side. He carried a cell phone in his hand at all times, ready to answer the call he feared would eventually come from Hoyle, ready to hit the panic button to Hansen.

The call never came.

The calls Dermot made to Gassin fell from one a day to one a week; Gassin had no information to offer him. Aside from a few crank calls that were investigated and proved to be unproductive, the Paris police were no further forward in their search for Hoyle. He had, again, vanished into the mist like a wraith.

When the fifth month of pseudo-tranquility passed – one very similar to the 'Phoney War,'; the period of time during World War Two from September 1939 to April 1940 when, after the blitzkrieg attack on Poland in September 1939, seemingly nothing happened – Dermot snapped emotionally.

He could no longer live in the isolation of Point Dume. He felt that he was out of the loop there, and that his family was vulnerable in such a lonely area. And since the Nolans' financial situation had improved dramatically due to the royalties of the biographical Worst Nightmares book, *'Diary of an American Madman,'* Dermot and Neela decided to make the move back to town.

The idea was to find a house as close as possible to the North Hollywood Precinct in Burbank Boulevard. If Hoyle dared to come within a hundred yards of their new home, the LAPD could be there within minutes. As well as this security, Dermot was adamant that he needed quarters to house a permanent security guy who'd live on the premises, armed and ready to defend the family.

They found a cute house almost immediately, in Cumpston Street, a few blocks from the North Hollywood Precinct house. It came at a good price, since the Nolans were one of the very few cashed up people around. The house had four bedrooms and a small garden. At the back there was a self-contained unit, complete with an intercom system that connected to the main house. It was ideal.

The first thing Dermot did was contact a guy who'd been recommended to him by Jim Hansen; Bud Aprile, a retired cop who worked for one of the best security companies in California, Boyd & Associates. *'Means Total Security,'* was their catch phrase. Dermot liked the sound of that, and Aprile looked the part – fifty-six, built like a stonewall, intelligent. Furthermore, he had a license to carry, which Dermot found assuring.

So, five months after Madame Rechy had perished and the phoney war had begun, both Neela and Dermot felt secure for the first time in a very long time. But though Neela continued to reassure Dermot that a new phase of their lives had begun, he waited for the second shoe to fall – he was the realist of the two. He knew better.

Almost immediately after the move, Dermot was commissioned by *Vanity Fair* to submit several short stories. This was almost immediately followed by similar offers by other prestigious magazines in London and Paris.

But though Dermot managed to fool Neela into believing that he felt they'd put Nick Hoyle behind them, he had a very different mindset.

He was now a man on a mission.

55.

Hoyle had always known that the best things in life took time. His favorite mottos were 'never rush,' and the English Boy

Scout's motto, 'be prepared'. The Paris fiasco had taken him over a year to prepare and, thanks to Dermot's aberrant behavior, almost two-thirds of his plans had to be ditched. All that money gone! Just because Dermot had decided to leave town. However, those weeks in Paris had sown the seeds; that was the main thing. He now had Dermot exactly where he needed him; on edge, waiting.

Hoyle's thinking was this. During the months between the delivery of the original Worst Nightmares' manuscript to Dermot's house in Linley Place, Hoyle had managed very effectively to tap into Dermot's desperation to succeed again as a writer; more precisely his abject fear of failure. Step by laborious step, he'd managed to mess with Dermot's head to such an extent that he'd turned a basically good man into a moral degenerate. It had been necessary to do it in very gradual steps because he knew Dermot wouldn't easily do anything that was ethically reprehensible. That was why he'd dangled the carrot of literary success, suggesting just the smallest deviation from the straight and narrow was necessary. Nick had been the perfect Shakespearean character, Iago. Very slowly he'd whispered suggestions into Dermot ear so that step-by-step Dermot eventually reached the point of no return without even realizing he was there. All he'd done was to involve himself in many almost imperceptible steps down Dermot's primrose path – none of which on their own were that blameworthy; yet put together were very damning.

Eventually, Dermot ended up a broken man, looking at life in prison. It had all been so easy – Dermot had acted so predictably.

Hoyle was quite certain that once he'd changed so radically, he'd never be the same again; like when a guy cheats on his wife and the wife finds out. That was Hoyle's analogy. Nothing's ever the same – the trust's gone. And if a husband gets away with it once? He'll do it again! Why? Because his mindset is changed. He's done something he thought was bad and he's gotten away with it, so why not do it again? The second time's a pice of cake!

Seen through Dermot's eyes, he no longer felt he had his

previous high moral standards, that was a gimme. He'd know he was less than perfect. There'd be things he might contemplate now that he wouldn't have dreamt of doing before his metamorphosis. Once, Dermot was the definitive good guy. Now he was flawed.

It amused Hoyle every time he compared the old Dermot; the man who had been his closest friend for all those years, the man that had eventually betrayed him, with the new Dermot, the broken reed who would do anything to save his family. Anything! Possibly even kill?

This was what so intrigued Hoyle. How far would Dermot go if he pushed the right buttons?

In the aftermath of the Rechy Metro killing, Hoyle stayed for three days in a homeless shelter on the outskirts of Paris. The residents were so self-absorbed with their own misery they paid no attention to yet another hopeless fat guy who slept in his clothes and kept himself to himself.

Three days and nights later, Hoyle reckoned it was safe to break cover and make for the south coast. It went without saying that he had to avoid railway stations and airports. Even stealing a car was fraught with danger – one could never be sure how long it'd be before the owner reported the car missing and roadblocks all over the country were a genuine concern.

So he decided to hitchhike, targeting the big rigs rather than cars – truckies often enjoyed the company of strangers who might keep them amused and awake; cars never rewarded the hitchhiker with more than a hundred or so miles. More people in different cars meant more people who might identify him.

It took Hoyle, the fat old guy with the fedora and prescription glasses, just one hour to pick up a ride on the Périphérique, Paris' ring road, to the Bouches du Rhône on the south coast. The truck was a giant refrigerated eighteen wheeler on it's way back to Marseille – Hoyle had been looking out for such trucks for this very reason, the ones with pictures of fish products on their sides. They were most likely doing the Marseille to Paris fish run and heading home.

The driver had been a jolly guy; a big eater, fond of stopping every three hours or so at some Routier or other, eating monstrous amounts of food. He chatted a lot, which made the ride far easier for Hoyle since the guy was more interested in his own voice than asking Hoyle questions.

Soon he was in Marseille looking for another homeless shelter. This wasn't hard to find. The next step was to source a ticket to North Africa. Here he'd have to use the utmost caution.

The idea was to sign on as a deck hand on a small vessel that was on its way to either Algiers or Tunis. However, no one was going to employ an old fat man, so he'd have to risk showing himself as the age and weight he was, which was dangerous, as people might now recognize him. Wearing working men's clothes with his dark swarthy make-up and several days growth did a lot to help to make him blend in with most of the other casual laborers in the docks area of Marseilles – there were thousands of sailors such as himself, as well as many hundreds seeking a job. He was to become one of them. The identification papers weren't a problem; he had plenty of those. He selected the Moroccan passport he'd bought in America before he left – it was professional quality and he knew the customs and immigration guys in a busy port had their work cut out for them anyhow; they'd only give it a cursory glance. How the cops ever nailed anyone they were looking for amazed him. Probably they only nabbed dumb-ass criminals.

It took him three days working the waterfront bars to make friends with a few sailors. Over countless drinks, he told them he was looking for a passage back to Morocco and was prepared to work his passage the hard way. Since they had no reason to think he had any devious motives, they told him they'd keep an ear open for anything that might come up.

Within a week he was put in touch with the skipper of a

Tunisian freighter that was on it's way back to Tunis via Cagliari in Corsica. That same evening his pal, Zini, set Hoyle up with the mate of the freighter, a Tunisian by the name of Tarafah. A couple of hours drinking later Tarafah and Hoyle were good pals.

Hoyle's name was now Arslane Meti, the name in his forged passport. He admitted to Tarafah that strictly speaking he wasn't a sailor by trade and had no ticket, but was not only prepared to do his fair share of hard work but would also contribute significantly to the booze bill, at the same time handing Tarafah a fold of Euros to show good faith.

Two days later the Califa sailed for Cagliari. The dockside paperwork was a breeze; Tarafah was a regular in Marseilles and clearly well known and respected. If Tarafah said he was okay, then the skipper knew he was okay.

A few days later Hoyle disembarked in Tunis. The trip had been fun. Hoyle had missed the companionship of other men; he liked the crew, and they'd drunk one hell of a lot of booze, booze Hoyle had bought and paid for. It was easy to make shallow friends.

The customs guys did no more than glance at his passport, he looked so much like on of them; he'd kept his hair very black and made sure that his complexion was dark as night.

The money he had stashed in European accounts was easy to access in Tunis. And not only was it a good place to lie low, it was also a fun city and the cost of living was minimal. Added to which, he liked the food.

So while Gassin and his people were scouring France for evidence of Hoyle, and Hansen and the Department of Immigration were on high alert for him at all entry points into the United States, Hoyle was holidaying in a delightful seven bedroomed listed mansion in Sidi Bou Said, ten miles from the center of Tunis. At forty Euros a night he had cable TV, Internet connection, ocean views, a pool – everything a serial killer on the lam could ask for.

While holidaying in the sunshine, Hoyle made plans. That's where the Internet was such a an incredible tool – everything imaginable was possible with the click of a mouse; funds transfers, purchasing equipment in foreign countries, rentals in spurious names – everything!

Hoyle thought a six month period of inactivity would be prudent, so he marked a date in his diary and got down to the serious business of relaxing by the pool during the day as he made his evil plans, and partying each evening in the hot spots of Sidi Bou Said and Tunis. He hadn't had so much fun in years.

Six months after his arrival in Tunis, Hoyle was rested and as fit as he'd ever been. All his plans were in place and he was positively aching for some action. Good as relaxing in the sun was, he needed something to set the adrenaline rushing – that was the legacy of one tour in Iraq; action meant danger, intrigue, putting his own life on the line, and physical violence. He couldn't wait to get stuck in again – the endgame was about to unfold.

56.

While Nick Hoyle tanned himself to an even darker color in Tunisia, Dermot was making his own very private plans to counter whatever his nemesis might have in mind for him and his family when he finally surfaced stateside.

Dermot knew he couldn't share his plans with Neela – that was out of the question. The last thing he'd contemplate was putting his family in harm's way, or involving them in any way with the course of action he had in mind; his plans involved ending the game in whatever manner he thought was appropriate, and if that meant crossing the line of decent moral behavior, so be it.

Employing Bud the security guy had been to ensure the safety of Neela and Vig. Bud had come well recommended, and as far as Dermot could judge he was meticulous in his work. You could ask him at any moment of the day and night where Neela and the baby were, and he'd know exactly in which room they were. Bud had also installed infra-red optical devices around the home which were connected to a console which he carried with him 24/7; it was half a laptop in size. In his self-contained unit there was a big computer screen, which was divided into six sections, each showing a picture of some part of the house and grounds. Bud had also installed panic buttons in every room of the house, including the bathrooms. Wherever Neela could be, all she had to do was press and button and Bud would know where she was instantly.

Neela didn't realize that in Dermot's mind this security was designed for her and the child, not so much for himself. If he carried out what he had determined to do, he'd have to be a free agent, unfettered by anyone knowing where he might be. Of course, once he was in the house, he show up on every computer screen; but once he left the grounds he could be anywhere, doing anything – and this was the way he wanted things. He knew that it was only a matter of time before Hoyle called him. He'd given Dermot that promise in Paris at the *L'Oie sans Jambes*. He knew Hoyle's threat wasn't an idle one.

There was no doubt in Dermot's mind that Hoyle was keeping his head down until the police and customs surveillance had been downgraded; then he'd come. And what notice would Dermot have? Probably none. The call would be made, he'd answer, and he'd have to be ready to do what he had to do.

Initially he'd done his best to try to factor Hansen into his plans, but as the months passed he began to lose faith in the LAPD – sure, they'd be a help if Hoyle intended busting into the house and setting it on fire, because the precinct house was so close, but Hoyle was hardly likely to do that. But locating Hoyle? Finding a man who resolutely refused to be pinned down? The LAPD would be hopeless. A man of Hoyle's cunning? Nah. Give them a sniff of Hoyle and he'd simply slip away. Then Dermot would have to wait in fear another six months to a year. That was not going to happen. Besides, even if the cops did manage to arrest Hoyle, how long before he managed to confound them again? A great lawyer, and he'd somehow manipulate the judicial system. Besides, their lives would be turned upside down by the lengthy trial process.

No, Dermot had had enough of trials. If he found a way to get close to Hoyle, only one of them would walk away. That's why he couldn't tell Neela.

Dermot realized that when the telephone call came, he'd have to be ready to leave the house instantly. He wouldn't have time to organize anything; everything would have to be prepared beforehand.

To that end he'd bought himself a gun. This hadn't been easy because, unlike Hoyle, Dermot was unfamiliar with places where you could simply say the word, hand over a bundle of cash, and get a well-oiled gun in return. A few scary trips into Watts had set him straight about how things were done. In the predominantly African American neighborhoods he visited, he realized no one cared about the identity of those who wanted guns, nor their reason for buying them. It was like selling candy to kids – you want a gun, you got a gun, end of story.

The choice of weapon hadn't been very easy, thanks to many helpful Internet sites. Ultimately Dermot had found the Kentucky Coalition to Carry Concealed Weapons people knew more than most, so he took their advice; his most important criteria was concealment over blasting power. The site had also been helpful enough to caution him to learn how to operate the chosen weapon and have the level of skill necessary to use it safely and effectively. The explained the gun had to fit snugly into his hand because he'd be spending a lot of time with it. It had to be comfortable to shoot, and hopefully to carry, although master trainer Clint Smith was quoted online as saying a gun should be *comforting*, rather than *comfortable*. *'Your pistol should be powerful enough to do the job, and accurate enough to hit the target. It should be completely reliable, and its operation should be as familiar to you as riding a bicycle or brushing your teeth.'*

He took the advice not to go with what they called a

'pocket gun' because such guns usually lacked stopping power and were known for their inaccuracy. He finally settled on a choice between the Kimber Pro-Carry and the Sig 22X – he'd go with whichever automatic was available to buy on the day. It turned out, surprisingly since it was the rarer gun, to be the Kimber Pro-Carry. The Kentucky guys had advised on a belt holster, thin yet strong. The Haitian gun dealer he dealt with was happy to oblige; he had quite a selection strapped to his body.

Since Dermot's experience with handguns was nil, he joined a club in Long Beach and took some lessons on a range. Soon he could do almost everything – most importantly, hit a saucer at ten yards.

When he felt happy with the 'carry,' he took it with him everywhere. This took care, as he had to make certain Neela never saw the gun, and that meant stashing it carefully in a secret place when he went to bed – he'd have to rely on Bud's firepower when he turned in – then pick it up again in the morning. Neela asked a few times earlier on why he'd recently taken to wearing jackets, but she soon lost interest.

Dermot suspected he wouldn't fool Bud, and he didn't. Only two days into the gun carry, Bud drew him aside and asked him whether he really it a good idea to carry a concealed weapon. Dermot explained that he'd done some training and was comfortable with the Kimber. Bud advised him not to use it unless he could see a gun pointed at either his family or himself.

"I've heard of people shooting intruders simply because they broke into a house, Bud. And getting away with it."

"Sure. Matter of fact, I'd do the same. But if it turns out the guy or gal you shoot didn't have a weapon, the ADA isn't going to like you much, 'specially if you pump more than one or two rounds into the perp."

"Can we please keep this between us, Bud? About my gun? I don't want to scare Neela, and you know what women are when it comes to weaponry."

"Sure. It's registered?" Bud asked, then continued without giving Dermot the chance to tell him otherwise. "Sure it is."

57.

Hoyle hitched his way down to Monrovia in Liberia in petrol tankers. Took time, but it was worth the effort – it was always a good idea to avoid airport security, and the journey was by road so no one gave a damn at border crossings; bored guards simply glancing at passports and paperwork. The one time he'd been forced to take a small plane journey, it had been to cross the Western Sahara. He'd hitched a ride on a charter cargo flight from Tan Tan in Morocco to Dakar in Senegal and from there a ride on a Medicins Sans Frontiers plane from there to Monrovia, posing as an aid worker.

In Dakar, using the connections Tarafah had supplied him with, he worked the docks until he made contact with the skipper of a Liberian oil tanker that was due to sail to Caracas in Venezuela. A bunch of dollar bills later, Hoyle was on his way across the Atlantic.

From Caracas it was a piece of cake to head west on a stolen motorbike through Panama and then up towards the Mexican border. This was to prove the most delicate border to breach unnoticed.

Hoyle knew that to cross with a number of other Mexican nationals was probably the best way to go. If they were spotted, the fact was that the border control agents rarely caught everyone in the party, so provided he was either in the rear or to one side of the bunch of illegals, he had a much better chance of getting through. The cold fact was that well over a million illegals crossed from Mexico to America every year. So, how hard could it be?

Where to cross? Hoyle gave that serious consideration. Border enforcement had been strengthened in urban areas, and immigrants were increasingly attempting to cross over the more remote and dangerous desert areas along the Arizona border. But if Mexican women and children could do it, so could he. He'd done a tour of duty in Iraq – he enjoyed the arid desert. He'd run twenty miles in the sand with a full pack – this'd be a cakewalk.

However, his first attempt at crossing proved to be a disaster. Finally God hadn't been on Hoyle's side. Maybe some border guard had been praying harder than he had that day? It looked as though someone had ratted the party out because the border guys were waiting for them. As the guards shouted at them to stop, some raised their hands immediately, others, such as Hoyle, ran back into Mexico. Because Hoyle was way back on the left flank, he ran solidly till the pursuit stopped. Then it was back to the town of Noageles to recover and try again.

Two weeks later he attached himself to another group, a smaller one of fifteen men. This time they had no difficulty cutting their way through the wires and walking into Arizona.

He spent two nights in Sierra Vista, then moved on to Tombstone. Tombstone because of all the movies he'd seen as a kid; he'd always wanted to be a gunslinger as a five year old. Then he moved on to Tucson. Two days of R & R later, Hoyle hitched a lift towards San Diego, stopping off at Chula Vista, a few miles south, to meet the man he'd made arrangements with earlier for the supply of materials he needed.

Hoyle's skin was nut brown, his hair raven black, his body honed and lean. He felt in perfect condition.

He was ready.

"See you later, honey," Dermot called up the stairs to Neela. It was eleven in the morning and he was off for his morning run. He'd been running for several weeks now to establish to Neela and Bud that this was part of his usual regimen. It was also vital to get in prime shape for any confrontation with Nick. He needed to be physically as tough, if not tougher, than him. He stayed out on the road for about an hour and a half. This meant that if Hoyle should ever contact him and ask for a meet, he could simply put on his jogging clothes, leave the house, and do whatever needed to be done. He'd then return, and as far as anyone was concerned, he'd been exercising.

"Have fun!" Neela called down from the bedroom. "If you're carrying the iPod, for heaven's sake watch for traffic!"

The Kimber Pro-Carry felt snug on his hip, covered by his Nike zip-up jacket.

On his way out the front gate he noticed Bud standing by the garage. He smiled and nodded at his protector.

While Dermot jogged, his mind was elsewhere.

How long was this going to go on? Months? A year? Would he *ever* be free of Hoyle? The man had scarred him permanently. He knew he'd never been the same man he was. And Hoyle would never be the same man he'd once known at college.

Things had been so different then. Life was wonderful, they'd both had high ideals, they'd both wanted to change the world, to do their bit to elect the right people, politicians such as Obama, who would do the right thing and provide an equal education for everyone, and a health system for the poor as well as the rich.

That was then. Hoyle had changed all that. Hoyle had searched for and found a darker side to Dermot's nature; one he never suspected existed. Dermot wondered whether everyone had a scary side? It was a piece of cake to be Mr. Nice-Guy when things were going well – but people changed very radically when the bad times came rolling by. That's when their true nature emerged. Hoyle had most certainly discovered his black soul when Giselle died and the twins were burnt to death. And when he discovered his best friend had fathered the kids he'd thought were his own, he'd snapped. That's when Hoyle stopped being Mr. Nice Guy.

So what kind of a man had Dermot become? Did he really want to know? Was he a hypocrite to judge Hoyle? No, that wasn't possible – the man had no compassion, he was a killer, nothing ever touched his heart. He'd torn teeth from the Mouth Maiden's jaws with pliers and been oblivious to her pitiful screams. He'd placed a plastic bag over an asthmatic's head and watched his eyeballs bulge and his skin turn blue. He'd watched Laura Nash fry in the boiling sun and then cut out her tongue simply because her screaming annoyed him. No, he couldn't think of himself as being in the same bracket as Hoyle.

Yet he *was* thinking seriously of killing a human being – taking vengeance on Hoyle; prepared to do whatever it took. What if someone got in the way? What if Dermot had a shot and someone got in the way? Would he hesitate? No way. So, he'd become a monster too. He couldn't really distinguish good from bad anymore himself – he was a shadow of his former self; driven into the netherworld by circumstance.

Was his first priority safeguarding Vig and Neela? He liked to think so, but in his heart he knew it was something far less altruistic – killing Hoyle. After that he could die happy.

As Dermot switched off the light at day's end, he could only think of the following twenty-four hours. Maybe tomorrow would be the day. It didn't matter really. The day after would be fine too.

As Dermot drifted off to his usual nightmare world, Hoyle opened the fridge door, reaching inside for a four-inch square cellophaned package. His hand took on a bluish hue; it was the light of the fridge. The thermostat had been turned down low; Hoyle knew the explosive had to remain malleable.

His fingers closed round the yellow parcel. Lifting it out, he pushed the fridge door shut and crossed to the nightstand in his hotel bedroom.

He crossed to the pantry and opened the cupboard, concentrating on the steady rhythm of his breathing. Slowly in, hold, then slowly out.

The airless motel room was cheap and cheerless, smelling

of cleaning fragrances, humidity and urine. Hoyle had drawn the curtain across the single small window – the one that looked down onto the pool. A bare bulb of the bedside lamp provided the only light source – he'd taken the shade off to provide more light.

He spread the money belt lengthways from left to right across the table.

He placed the essential ingredients carefully next to the belt – the length of coiled wire, the nine volt battery, the simple light switch, the small light bulb, and the three-inch silver cylinder, the thickness of half a pencil, from which two wires protruded. His provider had been very thorough – everything he'd asked for had been supplied. But Hoyle always worked with the best, and he'd known his provider since Iraq; they'd served together, after which his buddy had turned to a life of crime.

Hoyle laid the components carefully on the table, just below the money belt; the loop of wire to the left, the switch and the tiny light bulb in the center, the cylinder to the right.

The various small components seemed to have a life of their own. Sufficient explosive to reduce a human being to the smallest of tissue fragments. Enough to reduce a life to body vapor.

Unfolding the coiled wire, he laid it flat the full length of the vinyl belt, threading the wire through the customized eyeholes. The main bulk of the waistband contained three compartments, two the same size as the squares of explosive, designed to hold the Metabel snugly, a smaller one to accommodate the nine-volt battery. A hole in the belt to the left held the switching mechanism.

His fingers worked surely and efficiently. The wires were attached to the battery, the light bulb and the firing switch. In under a minute the circuit was complete, and ready to be tested.

He flicked the switch, enjoying the familiar pressure of the hard plastic lever on the thumb of his left hand. The light shone brightly. All set and ready to arm.

Disconnecting the wires from the light, he placed the bulb to one side, and reached for the three-inch army issue detonator, the white lead wires distinguishing it from commercial issue. Inside was the central core bridge wire – the heat sensitive element that would set off the charge of PETN as the electricity coursed through it.

He gently lifted two slices of the yellow Metabel from the first compartment, placed the detonator between them, then pressed the sandwich together. Then he disconnected one wire from the small battery, and connected the twin white wires to the circuit. Finally he opened the flap of the first compartment and slipped the yellow material inside, then patted the Velcro shut.

Its twin, the second stack, was loaded into the compartment directly adjacent, and the second flap closed.

Then he attached the colored wires that had no function other to confuse Dermot. Blue, green, white, purple, red. An orange wire made the connection. This only this one needed to be pulled free to deactivate the I.E.D.

Finally he checked the firing switch. It was in the 'off' position.

He looked away for a second, clearing his mind of all thoughts, then looked back at the switch. It was as he had thought, clearly marked 'off.' Now was the time for the greatest care.

A twist, and the last wire – a flouro violet one – was secured to the battery.

It was all ready. Everything worked perfectly. Now to find the perfect victim.

This was going to be…a blast!

58.

The day began like any other day during the previous few months in Cumpston Street. Neela and Dermot awoke, Vig was changed and fed her breakfast, Dermot and Neela drank their coffee and ate pancakes and maple syrup. At precisely 7.30 a.m. Bud called Dermot to check in. It looked to be shaping up as another day waiting for the call.

As he strapped his holster to his belt – Neela was showering – Dermot had no way of knowing that the life of some young girl he'd never set eyes on before was going to depend on how fast he could get to her apartment that morning.

As he laced up the second running shoes his cell phone rang and something in the deepest recesses of Dermot's brain told him the time had come.

Stepping deep into his walk-in wardrobe so that Neela couldn't hear him speaking, Dermot flipped his cell open and looked at the read out – the number meant nothing to him, yet he committed it to memory at once. Then he clicked the receive button to take the call.

"Game's back on, buddy," the voice said.

There was no mistaking Hoyle's voice.

"You going to do as I tell you? Or are you going to make me come for your child?"

"Say it. Whatever it is. Say it," Dermot replied, cold as ice. He'd been expecting his heart to race, but he'd been waiting so long for this inevitable moment that his pulse didn't quicken at all, neither did any sweat break out in the center of his back – he was sublimely still and confident. He knew everything he'd planned for was about to be brought to fruition. This day it would be him or Hoyle. Only one of them would be alive as the sun set; perhaps both of them would lie dead, that didn't matter. As long as there was a conclusion to Neela and Vig's reign of terror. Then he would have succeeded.

"Game on?"

"Whatever," Dermot replied. "Just tell me what you want!"

"You have thirty minutes to save a life. Time starts from when this connection ends. You see, I have a young girl with me here. She looks *very* scared. She can't move. The sux, you see. Remember?" He chuckled. "The thing is this. She's got a belt of explosives around her slim little waist and I'm about to give you a full half hour to find her and disarm the device."

Dermot knew there'd be some sick twist to whatever Hoyle came up with, he'd expected that – explosives strapped around the waist of some poor innocent young girl didn't surprise him. However, this scenario didn't look like shaping up as the endplay he'd hoped for. There wasn't any one-on-one; it was him saving a third party's life.

"Where is she?"

"Well, that's the most intriguing part of the game."

"How so?"

"It's a riddle. A conundrum. A puzzle." It sounded as though Hoyle was having fun.

"If you don't give me an address, how can I save her?"

"I'm going to give you one big clue. Then it's up to you to figure out where she is." Nick paused, but Dermot said nothing.

"Remember the top ten list we had at college?"

"You mean novels? Of course I do. Top ten best ever?"

"That's the one. Well, you just call the list to mind and work it out. The address is all there. Go figure."

"Will I see you?"

"I'd be thinking about that list, if I were you."

"Will I see *you*?" Dermot repeated harshly, aware that he was more concerned with revenge than on saving the girl's life.

"Wouldn't think so, Nightmare Man. Who knows? Maybe. Maybe next time? I'd just focus on keeping this cutie alive, rather than on what you'd like to do to me. Oh, one last thing – you call the cops and she'd dead."

Dermot heard a click.

"That's right. I hit the timer switch. You have thirty minutes and counting."

The line went dead and Dermot made for the bedroom door.

"Shit...." Dermot murmured to himself, his mind whirling. The fucking novel list! The one they'd each came up with at college every term. Was it Nick's list or his own list. Fuck, he should have asked; now he had to think of both! The question was could he remember all the titles after all these years? Maybe; not many new titles had made the top fifty since then, let alone the top ten. But this was an impossible task, finding a Los Angeles street address using nothing but a list of the ten best novels in the world – well, what he and Nick had thought were the best, and they almost matched the Modern Day library list.

No time for complaints now. A life hangs in the balance. Get the hell on with it, for Christ's sake!

He grabbed a pen and paper and began to scribble.

Numbers, I need numbers.

There's had to be numbers there somewhere. Books with numbers... *Fahrenheir 451*! Had that been in the top ten? No! In the top fifty, not the top ten.

Shit!

Catch-22! That was *definitely* there – one of Nick's favorites.

Yes!

He scrawled down the numbers. 22. A house number? An apartment?

Orwell's 1984!

Of course! It had been on both their lists as well as the Board List at Modern Library! Four figures! Much more useful. A street address in Burbank was hardly going to be a double-digit number; it had to be longer!

Yes! Got to be it!

But what other novels were there with numbers in them? Was he missing any?

His mind was blank for several seconds, and a knot began to tie tight in his gut – every second was precious. *The Fountainhead*! Top ten but no numbers... *Lolita*... *The Sound and the Fury*...

Write down as many as possible! Write, for fuck's sake. Then make sense of them.

Ulysses... *The Great Gatsby*... *To the Lighthouse*... Hey! Was there a clue there? Was there some lighthouse close by? No.

Keep writing!

Catcher in the Rye... *Clockwork Orange*... *Animal Farm*... *Portrait of the Artist as a Young Man*... *Darkness at Noon?*

He wanted to pound a wall in frustration but knew he had to keep silent.

Where the hell is this getting me?

He swore under his breath.

Start again! There were only three possible numbers. Orwell's *1984* was logically the first choice as it could be a street address. So could one of the others be an apartment number? Possibly. It could hardly be the other way around.

So, number 1984 on some street. Apartment 22 or apartment 451. 22 was much more likely.

He knew he'd have to make a quick decision and move on; he'd already used several minutes.

The computer! Go to Google Earth!

Wherever she was, she had to be reasonably close to where he was now. Thirty minutes? Meant maybe a ten minute max radius.

Dermot powered up the computer and typed in '*map of Cumpston Street, Los Angeles*'. Immediately he was given various choices, the top hit being a map of where he lived. He flicked the zoom slide up until he could make out all the names of the street.

Shit! Where to fucking begin? She could be anywhere!

The only saving grace of this puzzle was that most street names around him sounded Spanish. There weren't too many novels called Cahuenga, Lankershim or Oxnard.

He glanced down the list. *The Sound and the Fury*? Nah! *Ulysses?* Maybe. He typed in the word.

Nothing! Shit!

Then he typed in *Gatsby*? Nothing. *Lighthouse*. No! Then he got to *Animal Farm* and something there seemed to fit. Wasn't there a Farm Street? No! Farmdale street – that was it!

Well, maybe.

He typed it in. Yes! There was a Farmdale Street off

Oxnard just past Lankershim!

Dermot took a very deep breath. Did he have time to debate the address and search for other possible addresses? He glanced at his watch. No! It had to be Farmdale or the girl was history!

Dermot leaped down the stairs, taking them three at a time. It was hard not making a racket, the noise of Neela in the shower helped.

In a few seconds he was at the front door. He closed the door behind him and began walking to the car. It was agony to walk, rather than run, but he knew Bud would be watching from somewhere; he couldn't give him any heads-up about what was happening.

The moment he was behind the wheel of his Beemer all the rules changed. He knew Hoyle was right, there was nothing to be gained by calling the cops to explain what was going down and expecting them to be there within twenty or so minutes. It was possible Hoyle had been lying about the whole scenario, including the girl and the bomb, and was planning to hijack him on the way. Dermot couldn't take the chance on the girl – maybe her life *did* depend on him.

Farmdale – isn't there a Kinkos someplace really close to Farmdale?

It wasn't too far. He didn't need any map, or the SatNav in the car.

He took a right onto Burbank and floored the accelerator, hoping there'd be no cops around. By the time he was crossing Woodman he was doing seventy. The lights were with him – lucky! He knew his fortune couldn't last, there were around fifteen sets of lights to go.

He flew across Fulton heading east, his speed now around seventy-five. Still no cops – someone was smiling on him today; maybe they were smiling on the girl, who knew? Cars around him were pulling over to avoid him; clearly they thought the Beemer meant trouble.

He flew past Los Angeles Valley Junior College to his left and passed under Coldwater. He had now hit around eighty. He sped across Bellaire Ave on a red light, weaving between a Caddy and a Lexus. The Lexus put on the anchors and drifted sideways, sideswiping and taking out a mailbox as it mounted the sidewalk.

Dermot glanced at his watch, then cursed silently – what the fuck was the point of *knowing* how much time he had; he was either going to make it or not.

The clock was ticking.

Nevertheless, as he shot under the Hollywood Freeway like a bullet fired from an automatic he mentally calculated how many minutes he had left.

Three minutes? Maybe less. Shit! Shit!

Was he was going to die today too with Hoyle the winner? No fucking way.

Fifty yards from Farmdale he had to make a split second decision – he wanted to take a right, but a huge semi-trailer was racing towards him in the opposite lane. Could he make it across the face of the huge Mack truck? Maybe. If not, he was history; but he was traveling too fast to stop and turn around in time to save the kid.

Wrenching the wheel right, he stamped hard on the accelerator. The engine screamed a welcome response and the Beemer bucked forwards. The truck driver braked hard, and his rig began to slew to the right.

Fuuuuuck!

Dermot managed to control a four-wheel drift as his Beemer passed right in front of the cattle bars. Then the truck corrected and he was past.

Dermot made it by an inch.

Where was the fucking apartment building?

1984. Look at the building numbers!

It had to be the standout building in the street, all the others were detached suburban houses. He stared with disbelief at the number. 1984! It was there!

Hitting the brakes, the car shuddered to a halt, rubbing black tire skids along twenty feet of roadway. Dermot pushed open the driver's door and started running. He could hear someone behind him shouting at him "Hey, what the fuck, mister?" Dermot paid no attention, leaping over the grass verge as he raced inside the building and up the stairs – number twelve had to be on the second floor; couldn't be apartment 451, the building didn't have four floors!

On the second floor he saw there were only five apartments. So it had to be floor 2, apartment 2.

He kicked his foot hard against the lock and the doorframe splintered into fragments, the door fallings inwards.

There she was, facing him!

The young girl was duct-tapped to a kitchen chair. She was wearing a black hood that had been taped around her neck. He couldn't hear screams or sobs, so he assumed she'd been gagged as well.

No time to take off the hood; he had to concentrate of the I.E.D. Around her waist Hoyle had strapped some kind of a waistband. At the front was a mechanism with a digital watch, the read out flicking over every second. This was attached to some a stack of yellowish stuff. Plastic explosive? Had to be.

Dermot crouched down quickly in front of her. Her body was shaking like there was an earthquake happening.

"Hey! You're going to be okay, all right?" he told her in as casual a tone as he could manage. "I'm here to help you! Quit shaking!"

It made no difference, she shook like a reed in a typhoon.

She was making low guttural sounds.

The read-out was still flashing, counting down the seconds.

How to disarm the damned thing? Fuck! He wasn't some bomb disposal guy! The seconds were ticking by, the readout was flashing.

Concentrate! Or we're both vapor.

His heart was pounding like a hammer drill; the girl shaking like she'd been wired to the mains. There were about seven small colored wires leading in and out of the improvised explosive device.

Shit! Another test! What fucking color! It has to be one of the novels!

He looked at the digital read-out on the clock. One minute forty-four seconds!

Fuuuuuuuuuuuuck... Clockwork Orange! Orange! Has to be!

He pulled hard on the wire and it disengaged from the mechanism. Immediately the clock stopped.

The pain in his chest was so intense he wondered for a moment if he was having a coronary. Then he realized it was more likely to be contractions of his chest muscles, rather than his heart.

He was about to pull off the girl's hood when instinct kicked in and he thought better of it. What was he going to do; stick around now the girl was safe and tell the cops all about it? No way. He'd just played the first round of the game and he'd won! He was going to win all of Hoyle's freaking games until he got his chance to kill him! No way was he going to involve the cops – this was something very personal and it could only end one way. The cops would fuck things up the way they had before.

He'd hardly had time to breathe before he heard the

shouting in the corridor behind him. There was a window behind the girl. Outside was a fire escape.

As he reached the window, he heard shouting in the corridor leading to the apartment. Several people were screaming at each other, their feet pounding towards the open door of the girl's apartment.

Dermot pulled hard at the window latches but realized in an instant that the damned window was painted over!

What the fuck now? Jesus Christ, I'm trapped!

He smashed at the base of the window with his fist and the whole glass plane exploded outwards. He then smashed at the frame with his fist and after three blows that gave too and the entire window fell outwards and down to the street. Dermot swung one leg onto the sill. As he did so a young guy appeared at the door. He'd been running and was out of breath.

The sight of the hooded girl with what couldn't be anything other than an explosive device strapped to her waist immediately freaked him out and he screamed.

"BOMB!"

As Dermot swung his other leg through the broken window frame, the young man eyeballed him.

The kid said nothing, the shock of the I.E.D, then a terrorist, was too much for him. Dermot rolled onto the fire escape outside.

Within seconds several other people arrived at the open doorway behind the first kid. They all gaped at the hooded girl and the bomb. One woman screamed and ran back down the hallway screaming.

"It's gonna explode!"

It took Dermot less than seven seconds to make it down the fire stairs and back to his Beemer. The street was a mass of people running everywhere; into the building, away from the building. The young guy who'd seen him first was now at the window, looking down at the Beemer and pointing down at the driver.

"Stop him! He's fucking *Al Qaeda!*" he yelled, but no one way paying him any attention – probably because he was shouting so loudly no one could make out what he was saying.

The third time someone yelled the word 'bomb', everyone seemed to understand and the scene went berserk.

"BOMB! There's a fucking BOMB up here! Call the cops, for fuck's sake!" the young man screamed. That's when the crowd started running away from the building in sheer panic.

People were now running in all directions down the street, some sliding over the hood of Dermot's Beemer in a panic to get away from the apartment block. A heavily pregnant woman tripped as she stepped off the sidewalk and fell, but no one stopped to help her; she got trampled by three kids who'd come to gawp and now were running for their lives.

No one even looked at Dermot – they were too busy running for their lives. A few seconds later he'd made a U-turn and was on his way back to Burbank Boulevard.

As he cruised back down Farmdale to Burbank a patrol car came screaming around the corner towards him, passing at speed.

Dermot drove for ten minutes then turned off the main drag and into a side street. He pulled over and killed the engine. He was in a state of extreme emotional trauma; his arms and legs had been shaking so much he'd found it difficult to keep the car traveling in a straight line.

A million violent images were crowding his brain – an explosion, the girl's stomach ripping open and coating him with guts and shredded tissue, blood spraying the walls. He had no way of focusing on any one of them in particular; it was as if his brain was having a meltdown – and it was terrifying. Was this what true madness was like – a blur of brilliant white flashes coupled with a rushing howling noise at both temples?

He wanted to get out of the car and scream, but he knew he couldn't give in! He couldn't go mad! No way. He'd won the first round, for fuck's sake! He'd fucking won, and he knew the rounds to come would be harder. He'd win those too! And when it all ended, he'd feed the barrel of his Kimber to the madman and pull the trigger. How incredibly satisfying that would be!

First he had to stop shaking and pull himself together. That was paramount.

He started breathing in and out very deeply, his eyes shut; holding in the air for three seconds at a time, then allowing it to escape slowly. He stretched his legs and shook his arms gently at his sides.

It took a full fifteen minutes for the shaking to subside. Then he opened his eyes and looked out at the street. No one. Thank God. All he needed was someone looking in and thinking he'd had a fit or, worse still, was dead.

The flashing images had stopped whirring, replaced by a single image of the girl who's life he had just saved. He remembered her trembling violently, her hooded and duct-taped head jerking back and forth, side to side.

He tried to clear his head and focus on the street. No more images, please! No more nightmares.

Focus on something real!

He'd saved a life! It was such a wonderful feeling. She was about to be reduced to vapor and he'd saved her. He'd done it!

His nerves were so wired that he gave an involuntary half

shout of glee.

I'm a fucking hero!

He felt suddenly so empowered that his next thought came as a rude shock. What had he just been thinking? That he was going to enjoy sticking a gun in the mouth of a fellow human being and watching the brains fly out the back of his head? And the thought had actually *thrilled* him?

Dermot checked both hands; they were hardly still but he could certainly drive. No, he'd wait until he'd calmed completely; he'd tell Neela he sat in North Hollywood Park to think about story-lines.

Very suddenly, raw emotion took over and he burst into tears. His shoulders heaved, his body shook. What kind of person had Hoyle turned him into? He remembered how bad he'd felt keeping the details of Hoyle's murders under wraps just so he could get the damned Worst Nightmares book published. That had been disgusting. He'd known families and loved ones were hurting and needed closure. And what did he do? Nothing at all! Such an incredibly selfish act. After the trial he'd promised himself he'd become a better man. He'd make up for his brutal behavior. Yet now, six months down the track, he was in an even darker space mentally than before.

The girl this morning – why had he not called the cops? Was it really because he thought there wouldn't be sufficient time for the police to get there? Or was it because he wanted to be the hero? So he could continue to play some savage game – one he hoped would end with him murdering Hoyle? Yes, was the answer. He knew that. He knew he'd morphed into a modern day Dorian Gray, and it came as a shock.

A terrible shock. So frightening he froze for several minutes.

Was there a way back? Yes, of course there was. He knew what he should do – it suddenly became very clear; he should immediately go to the cops and tell them what was going on. They would protect Neela and Vig. Bud was there too, didn't he? There was no way Hoyle could get anywhere close to him. Now he could tell everyone – Hoyle was back! He was in Los Angeles!

What the hell had he been thinking just now? He and Gassin had achieved everything they'd set out to achieve; to lure Hoyle back to America, to a city that had an outstanding police department, capable – with the help of the FBI and Homeland Security – of locking down entire neighborhoods, if not the whole city. Hoyle was trapped! Why put anyone else at risk by tacitly agreeing to play on? If he did agree, then Hoyle would have to start tracking down another victim, and who knew, this time Dermot might slip up.

The scales had fallen from Dermot's eyes, and it was a wonderful revelation. He'd do the right thing for once in his life, and stop dwelling on his own sick sense of retribution.

He reached for his cell phone and began to dial. Then he hesitated. Better drive round to Hansen right away – no need for any call. Not right away…

Yet even then a small voice in the back of Dermot's head was asking the question—*why aren't you calling Hansen now? Are you putting off the moment to give you time to change your mind? Are you absolutely sure you want to do this thing? Come on, you saved the girl; you can do it again. The cops'll fuck up for sure. Hoyle told you, if you involved the cops in this you'd never see him again.*

Dermot shuddered. What exactly had he threatened? '*You will never see me, but your wife and child will.*'

Dermot started up the car, banishing the invidious thoughts that were invading his psyche like some sick virus. I *will* do the right thing, he told himself as he pulled out and headed back to Burbank Boulevard.

I'm going to go straight to North Hollywood to get things moving. I will not become a monster! Hoyle's never going to drag me down into his pit of degradation. No fucking way.

As he crossed over Mulholland on Laurel Canyon, the

hideous voices in his head were getting more assertive.

What the hell are you thinking, Dermot? You're going to tell that fat body builder with no brains Hansen what just happened and expect him to be able to do something about it? You must be crazy. It's you and Hoyle – that's what it is, plain and simple. You go to the cops, you lose him. Then he comes back sometime – maybe not this month, maybe not even this year, but sometime. And Neels is going to die. Maybe even little Vig. Can you live with that thought, mister? I don't think so. You did good today. Real good. You can do the same thing tomorrow. And the next day – no one has to die because of any decision you make now. No one! Just keep your powder dry, Dermot. You can do this thing. Rid the world of this devil forever. Don't even think of going to the cops.

"No! Shut the fuck up!" he screamed aloud as he threaded his way through the traffic towards North Hollywood. I'm going to do the right thing. I am not so brutalized that I can no longer distinguish between right and wrong!"

Minutes later he drew up outside the North Hollywood Precinct and parked in a visitor spot, killing the engine.

He'd made up his mind. It had been a violent battle with his 'voices', but the inner man had won out over the demon, and he felt a cathartic wave of relief surge through him as he opened the car door.

That's when the cell phone he'd dropped on the passenger seat started ringing.

He hesitated. Answer? No. Could be him! Better hold off and answer with Hansen and de Groot listening in.

Then the 'voices' started to coo at him again.

Answer the cell, Dermot. See what he says. Another two minutes and you've crossed your Rubicon and all bets will be off. The moment you tell the cops you'll never be able to set things straight by yourself. You'll have to sit on your hands like you did before and watch the cops fuck up.

Dermot stared at the cell phone. It kept ringing.

Remember what it felt like in Paris? When you couldn't do a fucking thing? And people were having limbs hacked off by that butcher? Well, don't even think about going back there. Pick up the damned phone!!!

Dermot sat in and snatched up the phone.

"Yes?"

"Fucking A, man! Hey, you were *whiz*! I knew you could do it. Maybe next time we have to increase the skill factor."

"You're one disgusting fuck, Nick. You know that?"

"Guess I do, Dermot. Guess I do. But, hey, that's me!"

Dermot remained silent, waiting for the next move from Hoyle.

"Right now you are so incredibly close to screwing up the game, Dermot. So very close. So take my advice. Don't fuck with me; play the game and see where it leads you. You can *do* this, Dermot. You're smart. You don't need any help. You can outsmart me! Whatderyasay? No need to go inside and ask daddy for help."

"Shit... Are you're watching me?" The thought chilled him to the bone, despite the hot day. A trickle of sweat ran down the center of his back. He glanced in every direction but couldn't see anyone who could have possibly been Hoyle.

"Sure *am*!" Hoyle laughed delightedly. "You look, how should I say, a bit shaken? Yeah. Well, that's to be expected. You're allowed after that stunt with the Metabel – I expect you've never seen the power of that stuff? Well, I have. I've seen it open an armored vehicle at twenty paces. Some kind of kick, that yellow plastic!"

"Where the fuck are you?"

"Well, here's the thing," Hoyle replied with a chuckle.

"I'm not about to tell you that, am I? You see, I'm hiding. That was my first game of choice, Hide and Seek."

"You can see me from where you are?"

"Sure can. I can read you mind from where I am. Fact is, I can read your very soul."

Dermot looked around him. Nick could be anywhere, in a window looking down, in a parked car, in a doorway. Anywhere.

"You thinking of ratting me out to Hansen, aren't you?"

"No, I'm not," Dermot replied.

Hoyle simply laughed. "I can read you like a book. That's a lie."

Dermot didn't reply, he just continued to scan the street and buildings.

"You want to play my game of one-on-one in a civilized fashion? See if you can outwit me? I know what I'd prefer to do."

"Cut the crap, Nick! Show yourself and you got me," he shouted into the cell.

"That's the way, Tiger."

Dermot looked upwards at the windows, staring at each, one by one. Still nothing! It was insane that Nick could see him, watch him, judge his reactions, and he was so powerless to stop him! But somehow he just couldn't bring himself to break the connection. It was the voices that drove him now!

"Go home, Dermot. Don't even think of telling Hansen. You've saved a life so you should be proud. Same time tomorrow? Game on?"

Dermot's index finger continued to hover over the keys.

"I can seeeeeee you!" The teasing tone was chilling. "Don't *doooooooo* it!"

The phone clicked. Dial tone.

Dermot closed his eyes.

When he finally opened his eyes, Dermot scanned the street for fifteen minutes for any sign of Hoyle. Finally he drove home. On his way he bought a wrist watch with a digital readout. He knew he'd need it soon. There'd be seconds between life and death tomorrow.

Seconds were vital.

59.

On his computer split screen Bud watched Dermot open the gate of the house and walk in, closing it behind him. A lifetime of experience in body language told him his employer was not the same man who had left the house just over an hour ago. A jog in the park? He didn't think so. So what had changed? He rose from his computer.

"Hi there, Mr. Nolan," Bud called out as Dermot was about to enter the house through the kitchen door. "You look like you might have overdone the exercise, huh?" Bud was simply fishing; it wasn't that Dermot looked as if he'd run five miles, but rather that he'd seen a ghost or watched someone die.

"Oh….hi, Bud. Everything locked down?"

"Everything's fine here. No worries. Your wife's reading in the study and Virginia's with her."

Bud studied Dermot like a true pro – he took in every

detail of his face, hands and clothing, without having to look directly at them. The key was to lock on to a central spot and then let peripheral vision kick in; looking directly at torn clothing or scuff marks was far too obvious and led inevitably to a *So, what are you staring at?* comment. The fact was there was a tear of about six inches in the ankle of Dermot's joggers and what looked like a grease smudge right down the left side. So jogging in the park? No way. Something had happened. But Nolan wasn't about to share it. This guy was going to be hard to keep secure, that was for sure.

"See anyone out there? Like, see anything unusual?" Bud asked.

"No. Same old, same old," Dermot replied with a terrible fake smile. "I'll touch base later, okay Bud?"

"Sure, Mr. Nolan. Anytime," Bud replied, then walked back to his office. If something like this happened again, he'd have to tell someone – to hell with confidentiality. He noticed Dermot's new digital watch. "Hey, nice watch!"

Neela was reading one of Dermot's roughs for a short story for Esquire. She looked up as he entered.

"How was the run, honey? You look like you overdid it."

"That's what Bud just said. I must look like shit."

"Not at all. You just look like you ran five miles, is all. Have a shower and I'll fix you something to eat."

Dermot crouched down beside Vig. She was trying to stand, staring up at him with the most adorable expression of happiness.

"And how's my sweetheart today?" he burbled to Vig.

"Hey! *I'm* your sweetheart, *she's* your little pumpkin. Okay?"

"Sure you are. You're both sweethearts. Without the two of you, you could take me out and shoot me."

Neela frowned. "Hey, that's never going to happen. I hate it when you say things like that."

"I know honey," Dermot replied, doing his very best to lighten up, "Just know I love you both stupendously! That's all."

Upstairs under the shower he had another spontaneous crying episode. It had to be the aftershock of what had happened that day. He was surprised at the autonomic reaction – his shoulders started to shake, he began to convulse, then the sobbing began.

He tried to keep the noise down as much as he could; he couldn't have Neela hearing. Fortunately the shower recess was the one place Bud didn't have a camera.

As he toweled off, he made a quick mental assessment of what had happened and how it might impact on the future.

He'd made the most important decision of his life; one he wasn't at all sure had been the correct one. He'd acceded to Hoyle's threats, because he'd been seriously scared for Neela and Vig. He knew it had been an insane decision – but Hoyle at been right there somewhere and he still couldn't see him!

Why hadn't he walked straight in and told Hansen? That was the question? Did he want revenge, pure and simple, and he'd do anything necessary in order to mete out justice to this monster himself, without police interference?

He knew the answer.

So what was going to happen now? He had to be prepared. Hoyle would have planned every single minute of the next game. How could he prepare?

What would the fallout be of the girl with the bomb? He'd been seen very clearly by the young kid who'd burst into the room as he was on his way out the window. Would he have recognized him as Dermot Nolan? He'd been the focus of the media for a long time during the trial, his photograph on the front pages almost every day only a year ago. Would the kid have retained the image? If not, he could have been anyone. Besides, he'd been the Good Samaritan for God's sake! He'd pulled the wire that saved the girl's life! Why would the cops be looking for him? It was a lame thought – sure, they'd be looking for him; how did he know there was a girl there in the first place, with a bomb strapped around her waist? How was he able to disarm the I.E.D. so fast? What did he know?

Neela called out from below. She's fixed some eggs. He called back that he'd be down in two minutes. He knew he'd have to pull himself together and try to be as relaxed as possible for the next few hours.

The television news would soon be full of the story, and what a story it was going to be. A young hooded girl with plastic explosive around her waist rescued by a mystery man? One hell of a good story. It was amazing how Hoyle could come up with these horrifically graphic scenarios, seemingly at will – pianists with their hands amputated, ballerinas hobbling down the Champs Elysées with one foot missing…

Neela called again – the eggs were getting cold. He'd have to go down and seem sufficiently shocked by the news story on TV, whatever it was – shocked enough to convince Neela and Bud, anyway.

Downstairs Neela had already started in on her eggs. She didn't look up as he entered; she was watching the small plasma screen at the end of the bench-top. Dermot caught sight of it. Shit, the Bomb Girl story was half way through.

"Can you believe this, honey? Happened just a few blocks down the road. It's getting to be like Iraq here. Un-fuckin-believable! Someone strapped high explosives to a girl's chest and left her to explode."

Dermot grunted a tone of surprise and watched the vision of the exterior of the building, an ambulance, a big crowd of rubberneckers, and at least five patrol cars.

"She die?" Dermot asked as if he was hearing this for the first time.

"No, it didn't go off. She was lucky. The cops deactivated it in time."

The cops did, Dermot thought? Well, that suited him, if they were taking the credit. That made him invisible. He wasn't there. That was fine with him.

"How was the run?"

"Fine. But you're right. I need to take it easier. I'm not as young as I think any more."

"Last thing we need is a heart attack, honey," Neela said, leaning close to him and stroking his forehead. Meanwhile the newsreader was replaced by a sports reporter and the pictures were of slam dunks and Tiger Woods accepting his millionth trophy.

Dermot started in on his eggs – it was the first time that day that his heart rate had fallen below 'extreme.' What else could he do now but wait for the game to continue tomorrow.

What did Hoyle have up his sleeve?

60.

After a long lazy lunch at a Denny's food outlet, Hoyle returned to his apartment. It might have been better described as a single room in a prefabricated building with a communal toilet and shower. The building stank, and the parched garden was like a Chenobyl wasteland. But Hoyle wasn't thinking luxury when he moved in; he was thinking 'anonymous'. No one in the seventies cement block building took the slightest interest in other residents, preferring to avoid eye-contact at all costs. This was perfect for Hoyle.

The first thing he did as he sat down on the bed was to laugh aloud. Dermot had reacted exactly as he'd assumed. There was always the risk when dealing with a basically good man that he'd do the right thing and spill everything to the cops.

Not today!

Hoyle poured a generous measure of vodka into a tooth mug from a bottle he'd bought at Ralphs yesterday. Time to make those last minute preparations for the next play. Boy, was this one going to be fun.

He'd already identified and selected the couple. They lived in Camelia Avenue in Sherman Oaks. Not too far from Cumpston Street, but far enough to make the ride interesting.

Mr. and Mrs. Geery were a retired couple living in a very modest home. Hoyle had visited several people at different locations before he'd come down in favor of the Geerys. They were perfect because Mrs. Geery was a semi cripple, and this meant her husband would probably spend more time with her in the house and thus be more likely to be at home when Hoyle came calling. When he'd knocked on their front door for the first time, George Geery had taken some time to come the door. So it followed that he was either a little deaf, which was good, or unsteady on his legs too, even better. Hoyle had pretended he was a market researcher, and Mr. Geery had taken pity on him – everyone knew it was a hard job researching because no one wanted to take time out to help those people. George was kind enough to listen to him long enough for Hoyle to look over the old guy's shoulder into the house and see the general topography. The garage was to one side and Hoyle could see a door that connected the side of the house to it.

"So you own one car, Mr. Geery?" Hoyle asked, pen poised over a sheet of printed paper.

"That's right. Pretty old, but it still goes mighty good."

"You use it every day?" Hoyle wanted to make sure there was gas in the car when he came to visit the following day.

"Oh, yeah. I always have it gassed up for emergencies," Geery had said smiling.

"TV?"

"Yeah. Got one."

"Cell phone?"

"Nah. Got a land line."

Hoyle made up some more stuff until he made a show of finishing up the Q & A. He then shook Geery's hand and thanked him for his time.

This was the '*couple perfecto*!' They lived in a quiet street, had a car that was gassed up and ready to go, answered the door to everyone, and were feeble enough to be overpowered with no trouble. Tomorrow it would be up to Dermot whether they lived or died.

That evening Neela and Dermot watched *Desperate Housewives* and ate Mexican take-out. Bud kept an eye on them both in the privacy of his own apartment, as well as the sleeping form of Virginia upstairs in her nursery bedroom. Bud was watching a re-run of *Cops*.

Neela laughed a lot during the show while Dermot stared at the set trying to appear normal and make all the right noises. But he was focusing on the morning. What time would the call come? What would Hoyle have in mind? Would he make it this time? Would he spot Hoyle and have just one moment to have a crack at him with his Kimber? Just to squeeze off one shot would be such an exquisite pleasure.

Without realizing what he was doing he caressed the butt of the gun with his fingers.

61.

Hoyle had to wait for over twenty minutes for the shower to be free. At least there were three toilets; that was a mercy. Some old guy was in shower singing badly. Hoyle had an almost irresistible impulse to yank open the door and head-butt the old fool until his skull broke open, but he knew he shouldn't crap on his own doorstep, so to speak. So he waited patiently until the clocked ticked over to 8 a.m.

By 9 a.m. he was in the nearest breakfast joint, The Golden Cup, a local favored by the gay community. He had a big serve of pancakes with crispy bacon on the side, washed down with three mugs of watery coffee. All the while he meticulously went through his plans – the entry, who to target first, how to maintain total control, the noise factor, how long it'd take to carry them to the garage. Lastly, yet most importantly, how long the Geery's would survive before their knight in shining armor showed up? If he used towels and bedspreads to block the doors, maybe thirty minutes. Without them, maybe more.

As the waitress gave him another refill, he settled on towels, as well as tape around the windows. Half an hour would be the limit. They were old and frail for heaven's sake, they wouldn't last as long as young people.

Back in his room, Hoyle looped the tubing he'd bought at the hardware store into a roll and stuffed it in his hold all. Then he watched the local news, then *Jeopardy* and finally *How the Earth was Made: Deepest Place on Earth*. Then he left the building, walked to a Seven Eleven, bought a cheap phone and set it up.

By eleven o'clock he was outside the Geery house. He made one approach, but as he reached the gate someone was passing by on the other side of the road. Better to be cautious. He passed by and walked back five minutes later when the coast was clear.

He knocked on the door.

As before, it took George Geery some time to open the door. Could have been his bones, could have been his bowels. Either way, Hoyle stood as still as possible by the side of the door trying to be inconspicuous – as far as the neighbors were concerned.

The door opened and Geery was there – all smiles.

"Hey, it's you again, young feller. Richards wasn't it?"

"That's right. Tim Richards. American Home Surveys. Look, I'm sure you're busy and that, but may I come in for a moment. Looks like being your lucky day; I got a gift for you."

George Gerry's expression changed to one of expectancy. "You don't say."

"But I do. I'd like to show you a brochure and you can decide which prize you and your wife might care to choose."

"Well, sure thing. Come on in," Geery replied. Hoyle walked through.

Mrs. Geery was where she'd been the last time, sitting in a comfy armchair, doing a crossword puzzle. She looked up briefly and mouthed a word of greeting that was barely audible. Hoyle smiled back as he fingered the syringe in his pocket – one full shot would be enough for both these old farts.

Ten minutes later the couple were sitting in the front seats of their old Chevy. Everything had gone like clockwork – it usually did. Mrs. Geery didn't even notice Hoyle stick her husband; she was far too busy looking at the pictures of lovely prizes. When he slumped back on the sofa, she realized something was wrong.

"Oh my lord! George!" she cried at George then looked at the stranger. "Mister, what have you done?"

Old Mrs Geery suddenly looked very scared and tried to rise up out of her deep armchair, but she was no match for Hoyle, who stuck her in the chest with the second half of the syringe of Succinylcholine.

Hoyle carried them one by one through the door from the lounge room to their Chevy and positioned George in the driver's seat and his wife in the passenger seat. Then he took out the duct tape and wound it around their mouths, leaving their noses free. Then he wound the tape around their bodies with the arms inside. There was no way now that this old couple could move more than an inch.

Finally he attached the hose that he'd brought with him and stuffed one end in the exhaust of the Chevy and the other end through the rear window of the car, making sure to cram a towel he'd found in the Geery bathroom around the opening.

Then he made the call.

That day, Dermot rose at six in the morning. He'd woken on the hour, every hour since midnight. At six o'clock he gave up trying to sleep, and slipped out of bed to the bathroom, trying not to wake either Vig or Neela. Unfortunately, he managed to wake both – Vig started to cry, and Neela heard her, immediately getting out of bed to tend to her.

"Couldn't sleep. I had this idea for a story. Think I'll go sketch it out in the office," Dermot whispered to her.

He showered and dressed, then went to sit in his office.

The hours dragged by. Bud dropped by at eight to say hello and ask after Neela and the baby. Every hour or so Neela popped her head inside the office door to see if Dermot needed anything. Each time he had to concentrate on actually writing some words down on the page.

At twenty minutes past eleven that morning his cell phone rang. Dermot immediately stood and closed the office door.

"Hello…"

"Hi there, buddy."

It was Hoyle.

"Okay. Shoot," Dermot said after a few seconds of agonizing silence. "What have you got for me today?"

"Well, here's the thing. Yesterday was a bit too easy. You were good, don't worry. But today? Something more complicated."

Dermot's guts coiled like a spring, but he knew he'd have to keep his fury in check. There were things he'd like to say, but now wasn't the time. He had to think clearly.

"How was it easy? A lot of people nearly died."

"Sure, it could have gone wrong. But that's life! You saved her – doesn't that give you a warm fuzzy feeling?"

"Am I going to get another fuzzy feeling today? You going to have the balls to face me?"

"Maybe," Hoyle replied, then paused. "Maybe not. You'll have to see. I'll be there *somewhere*, that's for sure. Up to you to spot me! Then catch me if you can. That's the game, isn't it? Always has been. Nothing's changed."

"Okay. Bring it on, Nick," Dermot said coldly.

"Today I have the cutest contestants. An elderly couple needing your help. Again it's a race against time. That's the fun of the game, don't you think? The not knowing if you're going to make it – whether they're going to live or die?"

Dermot said nothing.

Give me the details you shit!

"Like I said, yesterday was too easy. I virtually *gave* you the name and address with the book list. Too simple. Today, I'm giving you extra time, but..." he paused deliberately. "Today it's a musical puzzle. Okay?"

Silence. Hoyle was waiting for a reaction.

"Just get on with it, Nick," Dermot replied eventually.

"George Geery. He's a Russian. Family emigrated from Russia in 1916. He was born 1937. But those numbers aren't the clues. George lives Sherman Oaks. It's not so far to go."

"So what *is* the fucking clue?"

"Shostakovich's Eleventh Symphony."

"That's it?" Dermot was incredulous.

"Why not? It was always your favorite? That and the cello concerto. Remember?"

"Sure. I remember."

"Well, that's it. Get started."

"How long have I got this time?"

"Well, that's the thing. I'm not exactly sure. It's not like they're going to explode – this time they're going to need a little fresh air."

"What are you talking about?"

"They're suckin' in carbon monoxide in a big way. Go and open the doors. Let them breathe, why don't you? I'd reckon you've got twenty-five minutes. Could be less. They're old, see. Lungs probably not what they used to be."

"Give me a fucking address, you madman! An address!"

"Won't!" Hoyle replied putting on the voice a five-year-old schoolgirl. "Figure it out! You can do it. Their lives are in your hands. I never said this was going to be easy. The Eleventh!"

"If I see you, I'm going to kill you. Okay?"

"Hey! Wasting *time*, Dermot," Hoyle replied in a high sing-song girly voice. "They're suckin' it in, like I said. Now you just lost another minute..."

The line went dead.

Dermot's brain suddenly became scrambled eggs. What the hell? Shostakovich's Eleventh Symphony?

Quit complaining. Get on with it!

A number. He'd started with a street number before, so he'd do it again. What number was hidden there? Eleventh? That had to be an apartment number of a room. But wait! He said they were being gassed in a car? So short of gassing them in the street where anyone could see them, they'd have to live in a house. So house number 11? Too simple. And too small. Possible, but unlikely.

What the hell else do I know about the Eleventh? Was it called something, like the Beethoven Symphonies; Eroica, Pastoral, Choral...

The Eleventh was written in the late fifties... Earned Shostakovich the Lenin Prize... Maybe there was a Lenin Street?...The symphony referred to the events of the Russian Revolution of....That was it! 1905! Had to be. The address....1905.

You sure about that? Maybe not. Maybe I haven't thought for long enough? Think again! Do it! Okay... What was the Eleventh symphony always referred to as? 'The Year 1905.'

Bingo!

That was the confirmation! That was the address!

Now, what's the street name?

His fingers stabbed at the computer keys. Google Earth. Maps. Addresses. Anything reasonably close that sounded Russian. Lenin? No, nothing. Stalin? No. St. Petersburg? Nix. Dimitri? Nah. Russia? No. Revolution? Symphony? No.

He looked at his digital watch. He'd taken only a few minutes but he would almost smell the carbon monoxide. He had to think faster!

Was there something about the Eleventh Symphony that marked it? It was about the revolution...

Tchaikovsky's 1812 leapt to mind. Those pounding cannons. Cannons! Maybe that was sit? The constant background of the cannons in the Eleventh; he'd always loved that low rumble. In fact he'd mentioned it more than once to Nick when they were at college.

Got to be the cannons!

He typed in the word Cannon.

There it was! Cannon Street. Just off Hatteras Street, past Oxnard!

Am I sure? Fuck, no.

He had two choices. Sit around and debate other possibilities or make a choice. The Geery's were being gassed. He'd tried all relevant names, and Cannon was the only one that figured.

Go!

The seconds blipped by in dark blue on his digital watch.

Blip, blip, blip.

Go! Move!!!

Trying to make as little sound as humanly possible strode out of the office, through the living room to the front door, checking the Kimber was secure in its holster as he went.

"I'll be back in an hour, honey," he called out loudly to Neela but didn't stay long enough to hear if she heard him.

He pulled the garage door open and was about to unlock

the car when he saw Bud standing in the street – it was as if he'd appeared out of nowhere, like a genie out of a bottle.

"Hey, Dermot. Anything wrong?" he asked casually.

"Nah, nothing, Bud. Just thought I'd take a drive."

"Seem to be in one heck of a hurry. Not that it's any of my business."

Dermot didn't have time to argue the toss with Bud, he fired up the car.

"Gotta go, Bud," he replied with a stupid smile. "Sun'll be setting soon."

Four thirty-five seconds gone.

Bud knew there was something wrong here, but what the hell could he do if his employer wouldn't share things with him? He stepped to one side as Dermot eased the car over the sidewalk and into the street.

"Any problems, call me," he shouted loudly as the Beemer screamed off up the street.

Bud walked back into the garden to check out Neela and the kid. Then he made a call to an old buddy – Nolan was in big trouble and there wasn't a damned thing he could do right now to help him.

He was going to change all that, not just for Dermot, but for the wife and kid.

Dermot mentally factored in how long it was going to take him to get there. How far down Lankershim was Cannon Avenue? Fifteen minutes? Yes, if he was really lucky. A lot depended on how long it took to get on the Hollywood Freeway. If there ever was a good time of day to get along the Freeway, this might be it.

The readout on his watch was five minutes and thirty-six seconds as he took the on ramp at Oxnard. He'd refrained from speeding simply because he knew that if the cops stopped him the Geery couple would be dead meat. He looked around. No cop cars. He pushed down on the accelerator and his speed shot up to eighty.

Seven minutes sixteen seconds.

What was he going to do when he got to the Geery's? It was vital to have a plan.

Switch off the engine. Open all doors and windows, if there were any. Drag the couple out into the street? No, better to carry them into the house and open all the windows—if he dragged them onto the sidewalk he'd have a crowd around him in minutes, all asking what the hell had happened and calling the cops at the same time. If they were still breathing, what then? CPR. He immediately ground his teeth in anguish. How many times had he meant to take that fucking course so he'd know exactly how many compressions and at what intervals?

Eleven minutes and fifty-seven minutes.

By the time he got to Sherman way and peeled off to the right, he was doing over ninety, and scared to death that he might be stopped. But time was vital, he couldn't help himself.

He looked at the digital readout – twelve minutes and fifteen seconds. He knew he'd have to add at least four minutes to that figure to allow for his conversation with Hoyle and then with Bud.

Shit, this was going to be a close call.

He managed to control himself as he drove down Sherman way; he was doing just over sixty when he crossed Laurel Canyon – mercifully the lights were with him.

The readout had hit fourteen minutes as he stood hard on the brakes at a red light on Lankershim. Fuck! He was so close! To be stopped here was agony. Just a few blocks to go and he couldn't move. The seconds ticked by.

Fifteen minutes and two seconds.

The lights changed and Dermot stamped on the accelerator, narrowly avoiding some idiot driver who'd thought he could make the crossing on the last micro second of the orange and had misjudged it.

Dermot slowed right down as he reached the turn-off left into Cannon – the last thing he wanted was to draw the attention of the neighbors by screaming to a halt and busting into the Geery's house.

The street was quiet. The only person he could see was some teenage kid throwing hoops. He stopped outside 1905. A lot depended on his guess!

As Dermot approached the front door, the kid looked in his direction briefly then continued to play.

Sixteen minutes and some – maybe he'd made it in time.

He looked around debating on how hard he'd have to slam into the doorjamb with his shoulder. Pretty hard. Kicking wasn't an option – if some neighbor saw him kick the door down they'd call the cops.

The door gave easier than he'd though. He exploded through and immediately smelled the exhaust fumes, then saw the connecting door to the garage was standing open.

Immediately, Dermot threw open all the windows, propped open the door and dived for the connecting door.

The engine was still burbling away. The old couple looked unconscious but this could easily have been caused by the neuromuscular blocker that Hoyle always used on his victims. Thank God it's not a new car, he thought, the engine would be idling far faster and pushing out more deadly fumes.

First up, Dermot threw open all the doors of the old Chevy, and killed the engine. Then he raced to the garage door and cranked it open. Thankfully there was a light breeze outside – he could feel it swirl around him. He prayed that no one would walk past the garage door while he was pulling the Geerys out of the car. He also prayed harder that they weren't dead.

Dermot pulled out the old girl first. Using a fireman's lift he slung her over his shoulder and carried her into the house, placing her on the floor by the window. She didn't look like she was breathing. He didn't have time to use CPR until he'd gone back for old man Geery. George was only a few pounds heavier than his wife, but unlike her, he was breathing when Dermot grabbed him. He started spluttering the moment Dermot hoisted him over his shoulder.

He lay George Geery down next to his wife and started in on Mrs. Geery – she looked to be in far worse shape than her husband.

He tilted her head back to see if she was breathing. She wasn't, so he pinched her nose and covered her mouth with his and blew until he saw her chest rise. That was a relief, but he knew he wasn't out of the woods yet. He gave her two separate breaths, each taking one second.

She still wasn't responding well, neither coughing nor moving so he began the chest compressions, pushing down on her chest between her breasts, pumping at around one hundred times a minute. He knew he'd have to be gentle, she was old and he didn't want to break her ribs.

Behind him, Mr. Geery was beginning to realize something really bad had happened. Why was he lying in the living room feeling like death? Who was this stranger and what the hell was he doing kissing his wife?

"Whoa! What the hell?" Geery spluttered, but Dermot remained focused on his wife. He continued with two breaths and thirty pump intervals until he could see that she was beginning to breathe on her own.

"Hey, mister! What the heck's going on here? Omygod, Greta! Is she gonna be okay?"

"Call 9-1-1. Now! Tell them you've been inhaling carbon

monoxide. Tell them to get the hell over here right now. Okay George?"

George stared at him, incredulous. "You know my name?"

Dermot placed both hands on George's shoulders as he rose to a kneeling position and spoke as calmly as he could. "Do it now, George. Make the call. Okay? Now!"

So saying, he handed George the receiver of the land line, punching in the emergency number. "Your wife's going to be fine. So are you. Just make the call."

George simply stared at the phone, he was still in shock. Dermot then took the receiver from his trembling hand—the old guy was a basket case.

"There's an emergency. 1905 Canon Avenue, Sherman Oaks. A couple in a car. Looks like they swallowed a heap of carbon monoxide. They're still breathing but they need help. Now."

Dermot clicked off and ran to the front door, pausing for a split second to look at Mrs. Geery – she was now sitting up and rubbing her eyes, groaning.

"What's your name, stranger?" George managed just as Dermot turned to leave.

Dermot didn't reply. He made for the Beemer and pulled open the driver's door, switching on the ignition. Seconds later he'd made a U-turn and was driving agonizingly slowly down the street.

Then he stopped abruptly and pulled out his Kimber. Hoyle! Where was that sick fuck now? Was he watching like he had been before? Was he in some car, parked out in the street? Did he have enough time to check out the street before the ambulance and the cops got there?

Maybe.

He drove slowly up the nearest cross street, Valerio Street, looking into each car and van that he passed. No one was sitting in. Then he turned back and did the same the opposite side.

No one.

As he reached Sherman Way he knew he'd have to scoot – he could hear the Ambulance siren.

Hoyle was in fact standing at the rear of a food truck at the corner of Sherman way and Carmellia. He was chowing down his third chile rellenos tartlet. It tasted damned good. There were about a dozen or so Mexican workers standing around and he blended in well. He watched Dermot turn into Sherman way just as the ambulance turned into Cannon. He smiled wryly – Dermot was getting good at this shit.

Tomorrow he'd up the ante.

Why not?

62.

Dermot didn't feel as rattled as he had during the first game. Maybe because his own life hadn't been at stake this time – there had been no explosives at the Geery house, just gasses. This observation caused him to suddenly think seriously about his actions and motives. Did he really give a damn about saving lives? Was that what was so very important? Was saving other people just a way to get to Hoyle? If he'd thought the cops would have had a better chance getting of getting to the Geerys in time, would he have called them and screwed up all his own plans to take down Hoyle. He hoped so. But deep down inside he feared this wasn't the case. It was like a rerun to the past when he'd had to decide whether the safety of strangers and the feelings of the families of the recently bereaved mattered more than his and his own family's financial future. As well as his reputation. He'd opted to be selfish then, later telling the world he was deeply sorry for his actions, pleading with them to forgive him. Now he was in the same situation, and he was doing the same thing, putting innocent people at risk just for the chance of gunning down his enemy.

On his way home he stopped off at a Vons supermarket and bought a bottle of vodka. He'd drunk nearly a third of it in the parking lot before his nerves settled and he felt he could return home and face both Neela and Bud. He had to appear normal. Then he'd prepare for tomorrow. Another game.

There was a Chevy four-door standing outside his house when he nudged the Beemer into the garage. Bud was standing by the garage door when he stepped out.

Was Bud like one of those dogs that has a sense when its master's going to come home, he thought, as he gave his security man a warm smile.

"Hi Dermot. How was the day?"

"Day? Only been out for an hour or so."

"Just a figure of speech," Bud replied easily, adding. "You have a visitor."

"You know who?" Dermot asked, there was no reason why Bud should know.

"As a matter of fact I *do* know. It's Jim Hansen. We worked in the same division way back. Not partners or anything like that, just the same building. He's one of the good guys, is Jim."

Dermot did his best to sound unconcerned. "Yeah, I know him well. He helped us out in a big way when we had our troubles with stalkers in Malibu. Wonder what he's got to tell me? How long's he been here?"

"Just five minutes. Asked where you'd gotten to. I told

him you were taking a ride. That right?"

Dermot eyeballed Bud. What was he really saying? "That's right. Just a ride."

There was a very short awkward moment, then Dermot turned, walked to the living room door and entered the house.

Hansen was sitting on the sofa sipping what in a movie theatre they call a family drink. It resembled a pitcher. Neela was sitting opposite him; Vig was in a carry-cot at her side, Arnie standing obediently by her side like a dutiful guard dog. 'Big' Jim took up more than two-thirds of the seating space of the three seater sofa. He stood as Dermot entered.

"Mr. Nolan. I mean, Dermot. Good to see you. How's things?"

"Not so bad, Detective. Still waiting for the combined police forces of the world to find a man that every human on earth has seen a snapshot of; barring those primitive tribes in the Amazon Basin."

Hansen didn't take offense, he was used to complaints from people who's cases hadn't been cleared within a week, let alone over a year. "Yeah, well I know how you feel. The real world's a different place from CSI Miami and NCIS. They clear every case in a week 'cos they're Hollywood heroes. Geniuses! Me and Chick, we're just ordinary cops grinding away."

"How is your partner? De Groot? That his name?"

"Sure is. Chick de Groot. You've got a good memory. He's out looking into a case. Something really weird that went down near here. An old couple were attacked in their own home by some madman who tried to gas them to death in their own car. Faked suicide."

"They're dead?" Dermot asked with a straight face, his heart hammering in his chest.

"No. Seems they're both gonna make it. The old guy had a heart attack on his way to hospital, but he's still going to make it. Anyway, as I was so close, I thought I'd drop by and see you guys."

"But why a North Hollywood detective in this neck of the woods? I would've thought the Van Nuys cops would be handling the case."

Hansen did his best to look confused.

Dermot immediately knew he'd fucked up. Hansen hadn't told him it hadn't happened on his own turf. "Well, I was just guessing that it happened near here – you said close – as opposed to over the hill. So I figured they'd send people out from Burbank or Van Nuys. Mind you, I don't know much about the organization of the LAPD."

Neela shot Dermot a look, confused. He was babbling. Why? Like most wives, she could spot moments when her husband was saying one thing and meaning another.

"Well, you're right," Hansen continued. "Did happen close to here. Only reason we checked on the case was 'cos Chick knows the lead detective and the same thing happened off Sunset only a week ago. He organized himself a ride back, separate to me – when he's done, that is."

Hansen let a second or two pass. Was Nolan buying his story? Maybe. Probably not.

Dermot changed the subject to give him some space. "Any word from the French? Gassin?"

"Yeah, he keeps in touch. Keeps me posted. He thinks there's a chance Hoyle could be in Panama. His guys have been hard at it. Done one hell of a job – it's the most painstaking investigative work imaginable. But here's the thing; Interpol took down a drug shipment a couple of weeks back in Corsica – technically that's part of France; a big island – and this guy who was working on the freighter used to bring in the blow, offered to roll over and tell the police a bunch of stuff if they went easy on him." He screwed up his face, trying to recall the name. "Talafah! That's the sailor's name. Anyways, that started Gassin going, and his team just wouldn't let up after that. Said they put themselves in Hoyle's place and figured out what he'd do next that way. Seems he took some R & R in a place north of Tunis called Sidi Bou Said. On top of that, the pilot of a small plane recognized him – he took a ride from Tan Tan to Dakar. Dakar's in Africa – Senegal. Never knew that before. Then he hitched some Liberian oil tanker and someone recognized him and called it in."

"And now?" Dermot's heart rate was still at a dangerous level. "They think he might be here?" He pretended to look shocked and walked over to Neela, taking her hand. "Jesus…"

"Well, they think he may have made his way up north to Mexico. We checked with the Mexican Immigration people and there's been no sighting of him – and let me tell you, there are more photos of Hoyle in Mexican border posts now than Butch and Sundance back in the late eighteen eighties."

Hansen attempted a laugh but it was hollow. Neela tried to smile but Hansen could see she was now clearly spooked.

"So we still haven't the first idea where Hoyle might be at this particular moment?" Neela asked.

"If anyone knew, we'd pick him up in no time."

Hansen glanced back to Dermot from Neela. It was the look in Hansen's eyes that did it – why was he putting the pressure on? Had he left some kind of personal fingerprint at the Geery's? Had the young guy who saw him leave the bomb girl picked out his picture? If so, surely Hansen wouldn't be hedging in this way, he'd come right out and ask him what the fuck he thought he was doing holding back information from the LAPD.

"Look, I'd better go." He stood, looking back at Neela. "Nice to see you again, Mrs. Nolan."

"Neela, please."

"Sure, Neela. I'm just glad you took my advice about the extra security. Bud's a good guy." He turned his gaze on Dermot. "He doesn't miss much. He'll keep the family safe.

Only time you need to worry about, is any time you spend outside the house without Bud close by. So my advice to you is to stick together – and that includes Bud Aprile."

Dermot walked to the door and opened it for Hansen.

"Thanks for dropping by, Jim," Neela said with a smile.

"My pleasure," he replied, then faced Dermot. "Just remember, this isn't a cold case by a long shot, Dermot. If Hoyle's here we'll know about it and we'll be watching."

Dermot watched him climb into his Chevy. As he closed the door, Bud walked over to him and they exchanged a few words through the driver's window. Then Bud stood and the Chevy moved off into the traffic.

Neela knew she'd have to tread very carefully, but she was certain something was up, and she needed to get to the bottom of it. So when Dermot returned from seeing Hansen out she gave him a long hug. "Honey? What do you think that was all about? Hansen was acting strangely, don't you think?"

Dermot wasn't going where she was asking him to go. "What do you mean?" he replied, all innocent, "He was just being thorough if you ask me."

"You think? It seemed to me he was wanting to say something else, but didn't know how to say it."

"Like what, honey?"

"Like he thought you knew something and weren't telling him?"

"Look, if I knew something was going down, *you'd* be the first to know, then I'd tell the LAPD – from Bud, we rely on them for our safety."

"So what's this about those old people being gassed?"

"I heard it on channel five. Another of those weird stories. Someone tried to kill them and pretend it was a double suicide."

"Where?"

"Can't remember. Somewhere close, I think."

"That's awful," she replied, then had a thought. "It's kind of weird that Hansen shows up here and acts peculiar. I don't know what your take was on what he said, I thought he was suggesting you were keeping something from him."

Dermot shrugged. She'd said it twice now. "Really? You think so? I'd say he just came to fill us in about the progress Commandant Gassin's made. Which brings me to another point."

"Which is?"

Dermot pretended to look worried. "Seems they all think Hoyle could have got back into America. LA for all we know. Now *that's* a real worry. We have to think about what we do."

"Do? What do you mean? What can we do? We sit tight and let the cops do what *they* do." She stared at Dermot for a few seconds, concerned. "Why? Do you have something else in mind? Tell me it isn't true."

Dermot knew at that moment that he was on his own – she'd never countenance any peremptory illegal step. But there was no way in the world he was going to share his homicidal instincts with her; she was one of the vast majority for whom killing was anathema, unless forced under extreme stress.

"I think I'll go write some pages, if that's okay with you," Dermot said rising; he needed to sign off on this line of conversation.

"Sure, go write," Neela replied.

As Dermot reached the door he thought he heard Neela

crying so he turned. She was covering her face with her hands.

"Hey, what's all this, Neels?" he said kneeling down in front of her and taking her hands.

Tears were streaming down her cheeks, her face smudged with black make-up. There was a desperation in her eyes he'd never seen before.

"Dermot. Please. Whatever you're doing, please, *please* don't."

"What do you mean, darling?" Dermot asked in a soft whisper.

"It's happening again and I simply can't bear it." She could no longer look him in the eyes because there she only saw lies.

"What's happening? Why are you crying? Tell me."

"Oh God, don't make me have to say it. I don't want to go there and re-live it all – sometimes it's simply too much," she replied in a whisper.

"Honey, I'm not with you."

Neela looked up. "Before the book was published…" She broke off.

"Yes…?"

"You lied to me," she replied in a firmer, slightly shrill tone. "You'd never lied to me before. Never. But you did then. You told me that you were sure the book was fiction and there were no dead bodies out there. You said there was no need to worry about the families of these people because they didn't exist; when in reality you knew there were bodies everywhere!"

"Hey, calm down, Neels," Dermot said softly, brushing away some hair that had fallen over her forehead.

"You promised faithfully you'd never lie to me again. You begged me to forgive you for lying the first time, and I did."

"So...?"

"I know you're keeping something from me and it scares me to death."

Dermot's blood turned to ice. What could he say? The nightmare was back – he could tell her the truth now and risk everything, or lie to her again and risk losing her for the second time. He settled on a compromise.

Hugging her closely to his body he whispered. "Neels, there's something I can't tell you right now. I'm never going to lie to you again. That's a promise. You have to trust me now; this is a bad time for us, and there's something I have to see through. I know I can handle things, so you simply have to believe in me."

Neela looked into his eyes and she finally knew she wasn't being lied to.

"Is it him?" she asked.

"Yes. I'm afraid so."

"He's back?"

Dermot nodded.

Neela was so terrified she was almost breathless. "Why can't you tell Hansen? Please, my darling. Why can't you let him help us?"

"Because Nick will know and he'll disappear again."

"Dear God, Dermot, don't do this to me. Whatever you have planned, don't do it. I beg you."

"Trust me, Neels. Please trust me. I can bring him down. Then we'll be free of him forever."

Neels stared at Dermot in total shock, her mouth open wide.

"You're going to kill him..." It was a statement, not a question.

"No. Not unless he threatens you, Vig or myself directly. That's a promise," Dermot replied. He'd make damned sure Hoyle did threaten him. "Just have faith in me for a few more days. I can do this."

"Days? I have to live this nightmare for days? Please God..."

"One more day. Two at most. Then we'll tell Hansen. Okay?"

Neela buried her head in his chest and didn't reply.

63.

De Groot was grilling the young guy who'd seen the 'Bomb Samaritan,' as the tabloid press had nicknamed him, while Hansen was at the hospital trying to get a description of their savior from the Geerys.

The young guy was looking around him, taking everything in. He'd never been inside a cop shop before and it was clearly fascinating. Across from the De Groot's desk was a very tired-looking pouty black hooker – her breasts were bursting through her T; the worst kind of surgical implants. Her skirt measured maybe two and a half inches. She was not wearing anything underwear – that much was abundantly clear to the casual observer. And the young kid was definitely 'observing'.

De Groot smiled, then leant over his desk, his eyes flicking from the hooker to the horny young guy. "Hot looking chick, huh? Seen that kind before?"

The young guy never took his eyes off the black girl. "Guess not…"

"That's why you still have an immune system, kid."

The young man's eyes refocused – this time, on De Groot.

"So… forget the trash over there. Focus. Huh? You looked through the photo sheets and you're telling me you can't pick him? That about right?" de Groot asked.

"Well…" the young guy began, unsure of himself, "there's a few faces here that kinda fit. But to say for *sure*? That's somethin' else. Wouldn't wanna shit on some innocent dude." He looked up. "Know what I mean?"

"Sure do," de Groot replied. Best way to gain trust and illicit one hundred per cent help was to be a pal. "So we're left with these three guys? The others are too old, or just plain don't look right. That the way it is?"

"I guess."

De Groot spread three headshots on the table. Two were of nobodies, one was of Dermot. They all looked roughly similar – same age, same hair, same facial structure.

"Have another look. Humor me, okay?"

"Okay," the young guy replied, looking down.

"I dunno," he said after a full minute. "Tie me down an' make me pick? I'd say…him," he said, pushing the photo of Dermot forward. "But I'd have to be tied down."

This was plenty enough for De Groot, but way not enough for anyone else in the world. In terms of evidence? Useless. But right now he wasn't thinking evidence, he was thinking *what the fuck's Nolan holding out on us for?*"

"Well, thanks Brad for taking the time. It really helps, you know."

"I hope so, sir," Brad replied. De Groot smiled.

Sir.

Kids.

When the young guy was gone, de Groot picked up the phone and called Hansen.

"Jim? You finished there?"

"Just left the Geery woman. She's in pretty bad shape; what with the heart failure and all. Her husband's fine – a tough old guy. Real nice. Feisty as hell."

"What was the reaction to the mug shots?"

"No clean decisions. Picked out two possibles. Nolan was one of them."

"Same with me. One of three."

"Good enough for me, Chick."

"Ditto. But what's the sonofabitch up to this time? You tell me?"

"There's something happening we don't know."

"Like?"

"Like Hoyle's got the drop on him... somehow. Like Nolan's shit scared to tell us what's happening 'cos he knows that if he does, his family's dead?"

"Gimme a break, Jim, he's got Bud watching the house, just aching to pull the trigger and take Hoyle out; and he's got the LAPD one block away on Burbank. What kind of leverage can Hoyle have, for Christ's sake?"

There was silence on the line as both detectives mulled over this problem. It was de Groot who spoke first. "How about this one, Jim? Nolan's taking this real personal?"

Hansen thought about this for a moment or two then asked, "Tell me more."

"What about if he thinks he can take out Hoyle without us? Think about it, Jim. His life has been turned upside down. His career was totally bombed, his marriage was shot to hell, he was accused of being a serial killer and then stuck in a coffin underground by his former best pal and left to die." He paused for effect. "Don't you think he might want to handle the retribution in a personal way?"

Hansen said nothing.

"Come on, Jim. Wouldn't you?"

The logic was inescapable.

"Okay. I hear you. So what happens next?"

"Seems to me we have to close down Nolan without him knowing. Right now. My guess is that, as that French guy Gassin suggested, Hoyle has made contact. He's making Nolan do stuff. It's his sick game."

"We wait till the next call tomorrow?"

"I'd say so. Look at the timeline – one vic a day. Let's see what's happens tomorrow. Let's just see how things pan out. But this time we're right behind Nolan. He saves someone? We're right there, up his ass, asking questions. And the best part is there's fair chance Hoyle's going to be in the area, watching."

Hansen paused, wondering how much manpower his Captain would give him – de Groot was dead right, it was unlikely Hoyle could resist watching. If they could just manage to lock down a few city blocks, that'd be great.

"You still there, Jim?"

"Sure. Just wondering what Garcia's going to say. If he gives us enough guys, we could make things happen tomorrow."

"Go ask him, Muscleman," de Groot replied, a smile in his voice.

Hansen replaced the receiver and stood. He never like asking favors of his Captain – he was a real hard-nose – but today he had to.

64.

Neela didn't let Dermot out of her sight all day. She was panicked, but did her best to keep her feelings to herself; she knew Dermot was most likely as terrified as she was and was secretly planning what moves to make the following day. At one point during the afternoon she very nearly broke down and called Hansen. But she didn't – Dermot had taken her into his confidence and begged her to trust him. But she'd already made her decision.

In the evening she asked Bud to join them for dinner and he gratefully accepted; he knew what a great cook she was and rustling up food was the least of his talents. But the conversation flowed like soft putty, making the evening awkward. Nevertheless, Neela liked having an armed and able ex-cop at the table.

She had no way of knowing that both the men at the dinner table were armed.

At nine o'clock she and Dermot watched Will Smith in 'Hitch' and then went to bed. Neither of them felt like making love, so they just curled up like forks and spoons and tried to drift off into sleep. Neela made it to Neverland around midnight, having unconsciously moved over to her side of the bed.

Dermot 's head was too full of horrific images and thoughts to sleep. He'd promised Neels that if he couldn't find a way of finishing things within two days he'd tell the cops what was happening. But how the hell was he going to do that? He was no closer to Hoyle than he'd been before disarming the bomb on the hooded girl – what made him think tomorrow would be any different? He'd just be given an even more impossible task and be too flat out saving a life to have any chance of coming face to face with Hoyle. So what use was it not telling the cops?

Finally sleep overtook him.

When Dermot awoke, he was immediately alert.

It was just after six in the morning. He remembered this feeling as a child – knowing something was very wrong. In one case his father had left a gas jet on in the kitchen; the entire family would have been dead had his instinct not kicked in. On another occasion he knew there was a stranger in the house. This time it had been a young drug addict who had broken in. The addict had made no sound at all, but Dermot had known he was there, had woken his father, and the kid had been subdued while Dermot's mother called the police. Dermot put it down to an instinct similar to that which women have when they're being watched.

Somehow they know.

So, that morning Dermot knew he had to get up and check the house.

Three minutes later he had his Nike jogging suit on, his Kimber holstered at his hip, and he was wearing running shoes.

A search of every room proved fruitless. The doors and windows were armed; if anyone had broken the alarms would be screaming in Bud's unit.

The house was dead quiet.

Then the cell phone in his pajama pocket cheeped and he knew why he'd known something bad was about to happen.

"Morning, sunshine," Hoyle's voice was the barest whisper. "I'd keep your voice down, buddy – don't want to wake the wife and kiddy, do we? Not to mention the, er, '*help*'."

Hoyle's reference to Bud didn't surprise Dermot in the least, he figured Hoyle knew of the new security arrangements.

"You know something, Nick?" Dermot began.

Hoyle chuckled. "No. Why don't you tell me something I don't know."

"You're scared of me."

There was a second's silence. "Me? Scared of *you*? You have to be kidding."

"You think because you killed people in Iraq you don't get scared?"

"Well, I guess. Yes."

"Well, it's not that kind of scared."

Hoyle said nothing – he was figuring out what Dermot was on about.

"That's why you hide behind your 'game.' You make the rules, always skewed in your favor, so you can't lose. The only people who lose are the poor bastards you maim or kill. That's what makes you so gutless. Deep down it's because you're scared of me. You think I'm a better man than you are. That's what it is. I make you feel inferior."

"I don't think so," Hoyle replied. But now there was an edge to his voice; it wasn't so singsong and amused.

"Because you can't face me. That's the reason, isn't it Nick? So you hide behind threats of killing innocent people or coming after my family. It's all because you're too scared to come after *me* any more."

"Seems to me I did a pretty good job on you the last time, buddy," Hoyle replied, his tone suggesting he'd emotionally recovered slightly, and getting a second wind of bravura.

"Only cowards king hit people – smack 'em while they're looking away. Only the spineless resort to injecting drugs into people when they're not looking, because they haven't got the spunk to take people on face-to-face." Dermot knew it was a ploy that Hoyle would most likely see through, but it was worth a try.

"Tell you what, tough guy. Why don't we meet soon? Then it's you and me. Just us. Then we'll see who's the real tough guy. You lose? Your kid loses too. You'll die knowing Virginia's going to lose too."

It took all of Dermot's composure not to scream invective at Hoyle right then, but somehow he contained himself.

"But let's think of today," Hoyle continued. "You perform today, and you're on a promise tomorrow. How does that sound?"

"We'll have it out personally tomorrow?"

"Why not?"

"Okay."

"Good."

"Well, this morning I've been kind of busy already. Early bird and the worm? You know what I mean?"

Dermot didn't reply.

"Today you're on foot. There's a kid lives on Klump Avenue. Number 1193. You know the street?"

"No."

"You'd better look it up, 'cos this kid's underwater. In a pool. You'll find him wearing a bunch of scuba gear. But here's the thing. He's unconscious and weighted down. And the tank's got..." Hoyle paused for thought, debating exactly how long the kid had. "Seventeen minutes? Twenty max. Depends how scared he is. Scared people suck in a lot of oxygen. Got get him, Tiger. Be a man."

Hoyle clicked off and Dermot was left in stunned silence. No puzzle? Why? Why had he changed the rules? This was too simple?

Quit debating this one. Move!

He made for the office at once, booting up the computer. A few seconds later he'd Google-Earthed Klump Avenue. It wasn't far – he reckoned he could run there in maybe seven minutes. So why had Hoyle given him more time than was necessary? Had he booby-trapped the kid in the pool? More interestingly, why was he on foot this time? The answer wasn't so hard to figure. He'd given Dermot enough time to shake off Bud. He realized Dermot desperately wanted to do this on his own, without his paid security dogging him.

How to leave the house? Was Bud already awake, watching the computer screens? If so, the only exit from the house was out the rear toilet window, one from which he could drop down behind the house and then climb the fence and be on Cumpston Street.

The house was as quiet as his own grave had been all those months back. He shuddered at the thought, then listened again just in case Vig had woken and started to cry.

She hadn't, so he entered the bathroom toilet and locked the door behind him. Then he turned the key in the window lock and swung it open. A few moments later he was through and lowing himself onto the soft earth behind the house.

Standing on the grassy verge of Cumpston Street he paused and looked up and down the street.

No one. Just some parked cars.

He started jogging up the street towards Tujunga; it was

about four hundred meters to the intersection of Tujunga and Lankershim. He made it in just under three minutes. He could have run faster, but if the neighbors were watching from their breakfast rooms they'd be watching a man out for a jog, rather than someone running from the scene of a crime.

Burbank Boulevard was surprising free of traffic – it had to be the time, it was early. He jogged on down the road – Klump was the third intersection.

This is too fucking easy. What's the catch?

Standing at the corner, he registered that the number would be off to the left. He made for it.

The house was an ordinary bungalow. Quite wide at the front.

Even though he knew he had no time to waste, he stood on the grass verge in front of the house, debating on what action to take.

What the fuck do I do now? Knock on the door? Jesus.

He took a deep breath and made for the door, banging very hard on it with one hand, at the same time pressing the doorbell with the other.

The seconds passed.

Ten. Twenty. Thirty. Nothing!

Out of time! Don't just stand there. Kick the fucker in or something!

Leaning back a foot or so to gain momentum, he threw his shoulder against the door and the frame groaned but held. He repeated the action until the only thing that held the door to the frame was the slim golden security chain. Losing all patience he raised a foot and kicked hard against it and it flew off inside the house.

That's when everything happened at once.

As Dermot stormed inside, he heard a woman somewhere at the back of the house screaming her head off. Dermot could hear someone else, a man, yell out "What the fuck! Get out of my house! I'm calling the cops! I got a gun here!"

The pool! Got to get to the pool! Sort everything else later! A kid's life's in the balance!

He ran through the house, throwing open the door that lead to the garden. Sure enough, there was a pool!

He was about to leap into the water when the old man behind him loosed off the first blast of his shotgun. The sound was deafening. Dermot flattened himself near the pool coping.

"Get the hell down, mister!" the old man yelled at him from behind. "Face down. Next shot's gonna cream your ass!"

"The kid! He's in the pool, for Christ's sake! Help him!"

"What the hell are you talkin' about, boy? Ain't got no damned son. And I'm sure as hell there's no kid in my pool."

Dermot edged just three inches forward so he could see into the water.

The pool was dry. No water. Just some leaves.

"Marie!" The old guy shouted over his shoulder. "Where're the freakin' cops?"

"They're right here, sir," Hansen replied.

Even though Dermot was prostrate and couldn't see him, there was no question about the voice.

"So what have we got up to today, Mr. Nolan? You care to tell me?" Hansen asked matter-of-factly.

The old guy stared at Detective Hansen as he showed him the gold badge. He didn't have his gun out, but two uniformed cops behind him did. "You know this piece of shit,

Detective?" the old guy asked, confused.

"Guess I do, sir. Please put down your weapon, sir. We'll take this from here."

65.

Hansen had to arrest Dermot for Break and Enter – he had no choice in the matter because the feisty old man with the shotgun insisted.

"I'm gonna crucify you, you dumb-ass sonofabitch" the old guy yelled right into Dermot's ear as he was cuffed and led to the patrol car. The fact that Dermot had been carrying a weapon when searched didn't make things any easier for Hansen, trying to give Nolan a break.

As they drove off, Dermot became aware of the major police activity in the area. It stunned him. There were cops at every intersection, cops checking out cars, cops knocking on doors of houses. There were tactical response cops everywhere.

It didn't take him long to realize he'd been had. Hansen had been watching him. But he couldn't have been following him for long because he hadn't been at the Bomb girl's place. Nor at the Geery home. Nevertheless, he'd been I.D.'d and Hansen had read him as easily as a comic book. One night's surveillance and he'd struck pay dirt.

Dermot asked for legal representation on the way to North Hollywood and was allowed to make a call. Once again his old friend Harold Fountain, lawyer to the rich and famous, came to his assistance – he didn't complain about the time of morning, this was why he was paid handsomely.

Fountain was in his early fifties, craggy features, silver hair, his looks and charismatic demeanor making him the first choice lawyer to the Rodeo blue rinse brigade. He'd stuck by

Dermot the first time, despite the lies and prevarications, and had defended him in court with the help of celebrated trial attorney Tim Leadbeater. There was a part of him that wasn't looking forward to the reunion with Dermot.

When Fountain arrived at North Hollywood, he and Dermot had a short discussion in private.

"I'm really hoping that this time you can be frank with me, Mr. Nolan." He was still wedded to formality. "I still have my own personal nightmares about the facts you withheld from me during our discussions with Tim Leadbeater."

Dermot knew he'd have to lie to his attorney again, and felt sorry about it, but he hadn't come this far to throw everything away; Nick had told him he was twenty-four hours away from a face-to-face meeting; that was his single priority. So if he had to lie, he would. It wasn't as if it was a trial situation. It was an initial statement. Even if the court decided to go hard on him, what was he looking at – a rap over the knuckles by the judge and a fine? He'd offered to fix the door; any way the old guy wanted it.

"Why there? Who told you a kid was drowning?"

"Harold, this has all got way out of hand. In my defense let me state that I've only recently stopped seeing a psychiatrist. You have to remember how long I was trapped underground…"

"Believe me, Dermot, I do understand the devastating effect it must have had on you. But what exactly are you suggesting?"

"I woke up early this morning. I was very disoriented. I'd been taking sleeping pills – Amitriptyline, I think, but don't quote me – and I didn't know where I was. I must have been dreaming, because I got out of bed right away and knew I had to save the boy! I can only think I was still in some dreamlike trance. Side effects such as sleep eating and sleep driving are not uncommon. Well, that's what it says on the Internet."

"I'm told you didn't just walk out the door," Fountain

continued. "That would have been the normal course of action. Instead you sneaked out the window? Can you think why?"

So Bud had ratted him out. He should have guessed. He knew tomorrow he'd have to be extremely careful.

"You're suggesting you were sleep walking? Really?" Fountain was used to Dermot's excuses and vagaries, but this was almost as incredible as when Dermot had suggested Scary the dog had brought home all the grizzly forensic evidence found during the Worst Nightmares trial.

"What more can I tell you? I was obsessed. I had an address in my head and I knew I had to do something to help the kid."

"But there *was* no kid."

"Exactly! It was a dream. Don't you see? If there had been a kid in danger, then how would I have known? I'd have had to be the best clairvoyant in La La Land. The whole thing was a figment of my imagination!"

Fountain stared off for a second or two. "I shall certainly maintain that argument, if you wish me to. However, I don't see many people buying the story." His gaze returned to Dermot. "For instance, when did you wake up – by that I mean, when did you realize you were sleep-walking?"

Dermot thought quickly. "When the gun went off. That shook me to the core. I flattened myself on the pool surround and wondered what the hell was I doing there!"

"Well, basically I don't think you have any case to answer, insofar as you clearly lacked any intent to steal. The owner of the house may come after you for a sizable restitution, and he may get some smart lawyer to hit you for pain and suffering caused. What is more important is what the judge may think of your mental state."

Dermot knew this would be an issue. Had Hoyle orchestrated this whole scenario so he'd lose all credibility – so that the cops, and more particularly a judge, would order him to undergo treatment in some mental facility? That was a terrifying thought; to be locked up again, albeit in a hospital as opposed to a coffin. Had this been the endgame Hoyle had been after all along? If he couldn't drive him mad, then how about showing him as a madman so that others would lock him away?

"Do you think I'm crazy, Harold?"

The microsecond pause was a giveaway. "Of course not, Mr. Nolan. You've been under a great deal of understandable distress since you were, how shall I say, entombed. I shall point this out to the judge. Meanwhile Mrs. Nolan is on her way to post bail if they do decide to press charges, which I am certain they won't. However, I would suggest you try to behave in the most calm and balanced manner until this case proceeds so that I can point to you as having had only one – one – such incident."

"It's never happened before, and I don't see it happening again, Harold. I shall stop taking the sleeping tablets as a precaution."

"Just one last thing. You were carrying a loaded weapon when you were arrested."

"Wouldn't *you* if you were me? With a serial killer out there threatening your wife and children?"

"The difference would be that I would apply for a license. Also a license to carry."

"I'd never get a license to carry."

"You have a point, I suppose."

It turned out the whole incident didn't even go as far as a charge. It was Hansen's Captain who conducted the interview, and his judgment was that he was dealing with a crackpot, rather than a criminal. It was better not to clog up the justice system, so the charge was dropped. Captain Higueras made it clear, however, that he hoped Dermot would keep a low profile in the coming months.

Just as Dermot was about to leave the building, Hansen tapped him on the shoulder. "Hey, Dermot? You got a second?"

Neela had already returned home to relieve her hastily enlisted babysitter, and although the last thing Dermot wanted was more questions from Hansen, he acceded in a friendly fashion. "Sure. Where? Here?"

"Nah, let's go grab a coffee, what do you say?"

They walked outside and Hansen made for his favorite coffee haunt, one the other cops didn't frequent; in Hansen's opinion a coffee break should be just that, a break, not an excuse to sit around chewing the fat with other detectives.

"I have to tell you I never heard of this kind of sleepwalking before."

"Well, I've heard of it but never experienced it – it was so weird. One minute I'm in some trancelike state, then some old man is firing a shotgun over my head and the next thing I know the place is flooded with cops and you're standing above me asking the guy with the shotgun not to shoot me."

Hansen chuckled. "Sounds kind of funny when you put it that way." He drank his black coffee never taking his eyes off Dermot.

After a few seconds the silence was too much for an already jittery Dermot. "So, what *was* all that activity this morning? You know, all those cops everywhere? What was all that about?"

"A baby was taken from her bed at midnight. By four we had word on where the kid might be, so we locked down the area. Then you show up in the middle of everything and there's gunshots. I get a call, so I came to see what was going down."

Dermot studied Hansen. If he was telling the truth that was wonderful news. Maybe Hansen hadn't been tailing him at all? Maybe he'd just showed up in the wrong place at the wrong time, like Hansen said? It was possible. Not likely, but possible. But how did the cops know he'd climbed out the bathroom window? Because Bud had seen him and called Hansen? Maybe. The only alternative was that Hansen had left someone outside his home to check if he left the house. There was yet another alternative—that Hoyle had called it in himself, anonymously, possibly saying he was a Good Samaritan, and had seen someone climbing out of a bathroom window.

Dermot wished he could somehow find out whether Hansen had linked him to the bomb girl, or the Geerys, but there was no way he could go there – that was a major can of worms.

"Any word from Gassin?" Dermot asked.

"Funny you should mention him. He's here in the city. Arrived two days ago," Hansen replied.

Dermot was more than surprised; he was shocked. What the hell did this mean? Yet he kept his face as expressionless as possible. "Hey," he said lamely, like a character out of *Friends*. "Is he here because of me?"

"You mean because of Hoyle?"

"Well, sure. I mean Hoyle."

"His investigations were incredible. Managed to follow a trail right up to the Mexican border. Now he's working on the San Diego area, and the south in general. He's like a dog with a bone."

"What about jurisdiction?"

"Oh. That's no problem; he's working for us at the LAPD.

Seconded. As and when we take Hoyle down, the French will want a piece of the action, I guess. Maybe when Hoyle's served thirteen life sentences they'll make him serve another hundred in France. Mind you, he's gonna be mighty old by then."

Dermot smiled but wasn't much amused. There was only going to be one end to this game, and he, Dermot Nolan, would end it himself.

"You say hello to the Commandant for me, okay? Tell him to give me a call and we'll arrange a special dinner. Maybe you can join us?"

"Who knows? Sounds like fun."

Dermot stood – it seemed like an appropriate time to leave; he had a lot to take care of during the rest of the afternoon, not the least of which was an appointment he had with a specialist tailor.

Twenty minutes later he was at the address of Security Pro USA on Westward Boulevard, Suite 17. The rush order was ready.

"This sure is one of a kind, Mr. Beachley," the guy at Security Pro told him as he wrapped the item. "Never made one quite like this before. But considering what you think you could be dealing with, I'd say it fits the bill.

"Let's hope so," Dermot replied with a manufactured easy smile.

Dermot enquired if there was a rear entrance to the building. The tailor gave him a choice of the fire escape to the alley, or a stairwell that led to the side of the building. He'd opted for the stairwell.

"There goes one cautious man, Mr. Beachley," the salesman said with a chuckle as Dermot left.

Outside, Dermot called Neela. She answered almost immediately.

"Neels? It's me. I need you to listen up and then put your faith in me rather than the authorities. This time I know what I'm doing and I'll be safe."

"Please come home, darling. Please," Neela begged. She sounded emotionally exhausted.

"You have to trust me, honey. Just this once. One more day. Twenty-four hours tops."

There was silence her end.

"You got to tell me, honey," Dermot pleaded. "Otherwise I can't do a damned thing properly. So, will you trust me, this one last time?"

"Okay," the word came out like a mixed hiccup and an exhalation. "I'll trust you."

"Great. So now I want you to hang in there. Far as you know, I haven't called you and you don't know where I am. Okay?"

"Okay." She was crying now but attempting to mask it.

"Hansen or anyone else asks, you know nothing. Don't let them spook you by telling you I'm in danger because I know what's going to happen and I'm prepared."

"Okay."

"Hey, don't cry. You just stay safe. And keep Vig safe. By this time tomorrow we can start a whole new life. That's a promise."

"I have to go," Neela said suddenly. "I can hear someone at the door."

The line went dead.

Now he was alone. He knew what he had to do. He just hoped the deck wasn't too badly rigged. A few jokers here and there, that'd be just fine–he could live with them.

66.

Dermot hung out in a Venice movie complex all afternoon, watching movies till it was around nine p.m. Then he walked down to the Axe restaurant and had a dinner of organic soul food.

At around ten he was walking the streets again and happened to pass a building with a neon sign hanging outside. 'Rooms'. He entered. Ten minutes later he had somewhere to stay for the night.

The room was clean and adequate. A bed and a basin. The toilet was down the hallway. What else could he possibly need tonight?

He lay on the bed in an attempt to collect his thoughts – his mind had been a mishmash of images all day; now it was time to calm down and achieve as close a state of Nirvana as possible.

As he glanced at his digital watch he saw the time was eleven minutes past eleven.

11.11.p.m.

This didn't mean anything, did it? No, he didn't believe in fate any more – he, not the stars, would decide the fate of his family; they'd be safe.

Would Hoyle face him in just a few hours? Did the man actually lack the courage to face people without the aid of some means of subduing them? What had been Hoyle's thinking when he sent Dermot on this morning's wild goose chase? Dermot had to presume that it was a safety mechanism;

if the police were considering him seriously as a suspect in the bomb incidents and the Geery gassing, then they'd need to be thrown off the scent. What better way to achieve that end than make Dermot look like he'd had a complete mental breakdown?

What would Hansen make of things when he realized that Dermot hadn't returned home? He'd call Neela for sure, and tell her she had to come clean about everything or risk a charge of impeding an investigation. If she stayed true to her word, she'd keep herself out of things; tell him she had no idea. It was the truth anyway.

So now he'd given Hansen the slip when he'd least suspected it – now they had no idea where he was.

At a few minutes past midnight he rose and walked to the window. There weren't many cars in Abbot Kinney; just a few kids out for the evening together and a few local bag ladies trying to find a doorway for the night.

He stared up at the stars. Did he fear death? Not any more. He'd certainly feared it as he'd lain in his coffin, subsisting on rotting vegetable matter. He thought he'd never see his baby; never again cup Neela's face in his hands and gently kiss her mouth. But since his rebirth, death had not been an issue. He now only feared for the life of his wife and child. He knew he'd willingly lay down his life for them – but would he be able to achieve a positive outcome and still leave Vig with a father and, Neels with a husband? Things had to go right; he knew that.He looked at the package he'd picked up from the tailor and smiled. This time he had his own surprises.

As he lay down on the bed he gave his watch a final glance. It was 12.12. Exactly. Another portent? Nah, he didn't believe in them.

He was master of his own destiny.

67.

The call came in at 1 a.m. Dermot wasn't asleep, just drowsing. He was instantly awake and sitting up.

"That you?" he asked.

"That's me," came the reply. "Now listen to me carefully. First thing you do now is trash that cell phone. Go buy another, there's a Seven Eleven two blocks east from where you are right now. It's easy to set up. The moment you've done that, call me."

He gave a number.

Dermot opened his mouth to ask a question but the line went dead.

If there was a Seven Eleven two blocks east, Hoyle somehow knew where he was. Did the cops? He prayed not. It was clear Hoyle was concerned about the police being able to track him via his cell. Maybe the cops had already tracked him to Abbot Kinney? He'd have to be careful. But Nick had given him his cell phone number, so he was taking a big risk, figuring that Dermot wasn't thinking of calling in the help of the cops, preferring to have his one-on-one. This was the best news he'd had for weeks if not months.

He turned east as he exited the rooming house. He'd left his cell phone under the mattress, figuring that if the cops were using the cell to track him, they'd be happy to think he was still in his room.

The street was deserted, quiet as the grave. Unusual. Sure enough, up ahead two blocks he saw the sign. The all night Seven Eleven.

Inside he selected a cheap phone that came with a card and a twenty dollars of call credits. He then called the number Hoyle had given him. It rang, and then went to messages. A female voice. "I'm afraid I'm not at home right now. Please leave a message at the tone."

That was it.

So Nick hadn't trusted him – not so good.

Then the cell in his hand rang.

"Right. We're good now."

It was Nick.

"You still want to see me? Straighten things out like men? One-on-one?"

"Yes," Dermot replied flatly. "Let's get this thing over with."

"Sounds like you fancy your chances, Übermensch. I like that. Shows spunk."

"When and where?"

"At the end of North Venice Boulevard, cross Pacific Avenue. Hang a right and walk down the Speedway till you get to 17th. Then walk onto the beach. I'll be there at 11 a.m."

"I'll be there."

"You know how good I am at tagging you, so you know I'm watching. How was the night at that slum on Abbot Kinney?"

"I hear what you're saying, Nick."

"Right. Okay. So you'll know I can see you right now. Don't bother to try and spot me. Not if you want to see me at eleven and take your chances."

"I do."

"So it's you and me? No cops?"

"Right."

"That's my boy. Captain Braveheart!"

Dermot heard a chuckle at the end of the line.

"One thing. I don't want you there *before* eleven. That's one of the rules of the game. We both get there the same time – this isn't about one person staking out the spot and waiting for the other."

"Sure," Dermot replied.

"Okay, see you when I see you. Then just one of us walks away, right?"

Before Dermot could reply, Nick rang off.

Dermot knew he did have approximately eleven hours to wait. Where could he hide?

He made his way towards Ventura Boulevard, knowing there'd be a whole bunch of homeless men and women sleeping out on the streets – he'd mingle with them. Much better than being alone. Alone he'd be a target. He wouldn't be sleeping anyway; he'd be biding his time.

He found a spot at the side of a Savon supermarket and sat down, leaning against a wall between an old man clutching a supermarket trolley filled with old clothes, and a younger guy who was lying so still he could easily have overdosed during the night. Either way, he was wedged between two people – if Nick had it in mind to stick him with a syringe before the meet, he'd have to step over a couple of other derelicts, and risk being recognized.

Dawn rose and none of the street people even stirred. What was there for them to get up for?

Dermot had been awake since he sat down; watching, waiting, like a hunted animal. No one had come for him; not

Nick, nor the cops. He hadn't seen anyone who could have been an undercover cop following him.

At 7 a.m. a charity van arrived. One or two of the homeless people rose and took advantage of the tea, coffee and rolls, but most just slept on. Dermot eyes were tiny slits so he could pretend to be asleep yet keep an eye out.

Half an hour later Lincoln Boulevard was solid with traffic. The local Mexican 'hole in the wall' diner was doing brisk business, working men backed up along the sidewalk. The smell of fast food was thick and heady. Finally Dermot gave in and joined the queue, waiting his turn with the Mexican workers, ordering a burrito and a coke. It was one of the best he'd ever tasted, possibly because he hadn't eaten for many hours.

At 8 a.m. he returned to his spot by the wall of the Savon and spent the next two and a half hours priming himself for the meet.

He went through every possible scenario, trick, and hoax that Nick might attempt. For every possible attack, Dermot prepared a counter attack. He knew his life would depend on his wit and skill. It was imperative to be one hundred percent alert. He checked out his clothing. Then he checked out the duct tape on his leg. It was fine. Everything was 'go'.

At twenty minutes to eleven he started walking down North Venice Boulevard. It was shaping up to be another mother of a day. Hot as Hades.

As he crossed Pacific Avenue he checked his digital watch and saw it was six minutes to eleven. Perfect timing. He hung a right and walked down the Speedway till he reached 17th.

The Speedway was busy as ever. Tourists and weird Venice characters of every description. Muscled guys wearing little more than a thong to house their privates and flip flops to guard their feet, old men playing banjos on roller skates, big-breasted teenagers on roller blades lapping up the attention of the old guys who weren't getting any. This was Venice.

Dermot didn't even see these whackos. He was staring out at the beach to his left.

As ever, there weren't too many people sitting on the sand – when it came to the yellow stuff, Venice beach was a poor relation to Acapulco, Bondi or Tahiti Beach in the South of France; the sand hadn't looked truly bright for decades.

Dermot zipped up his jacket and walked across the cement bike track and stepped onto the sand.

He knew he looked kind of weird himself, wearing a jacket on a day as hot as this, but there was no alternative.

The water was a hundred and fifty yards away dead ahead. There were a few people ambling along the water's edge, but he couldn't make out any faces, so he continued walking slowly forward, keeping a very watchful eye out for anyone approaching.

As he neared the water's edge he stopped and looked around again, checking the digital readout of his watch. It was only seconds from 11 a.m.

He watched as the last two seconds ticked by.

Still no Nick.

Was this going to be another trick? Was he playing with him as he'd done yesterday with the pool kid? The thought made his anger so palpable that he spat into the sand. As he did, he noticed what looked like a weird oversized kiddy beach tent twenty-five yards down to his right. It stood twenty or so paces from the water.

It was a two-tone in color; a mixture of cloth and plastic. Looked cute. Any kid in the world would have killed for such a hidey-house. It was shaped like a mini castle, the roof coming to a point. The top was darkish purple, fading to lighter sides. A small flag flew from its tower. Hearts and stars decorated the lighter lilac material.

If Dermot had been thinking of Vig right then rather than

concentrating on Hoyle, he'd have sought out the owner and asked him where he could buy his own tent – it was the perfect way to keep out of the sun; kids cancer safe. And the bonus was it looked as though it came straight out of a *Shrek* movie.

Cute.

He looked at his watch yet again. It was three minutes past eleven. Where the hell was Hoyle? He mentally checked yet again that he was exactly where Hoyle had told him to be.

He was.

The beach was practically empty; just a muscled black guy in the water to his left, his hair beaded in dreadlocks, and a bag lady checking out some clothes a bit further away to his right.

How long to stay? If he knew for sure that Nick was coming he'd stay all day.

But he *didn't* know.

Eleven thirty came and went. Dermot sat on the sand, bitterly disappointed. He'd wait till midday. Then, since he'd promised Neela he'd hand over to the cops if his last trick failed, he'd have to call Hansen.

At that moment the cell phone in his hand vibrated.

Hoyle.

"Dermot?"

"I'm here. What the fuck's the matter with you! Can't you see me? Where the fuck are you?"

"Easy, Tiger. I'm right here."

Dermot looked around. A 360. Just the black guy, the bag lady and the tent. Everyone else was over two hundred yards away.

"No, you're not," Dermot replied, angry.

"I am. Very close to you, as a matter of fact. Come on, it's a game for Christ's sake! Find me."

The line went dead. Dermot stared around him. The black guy? The bag lady? Nick was a master of disguise but this was ridiculous. So where was he?

Jesus! Inside the kiddies tent...

He focused his attention on it. The flap at the front was zipped closed. At the side various brightly colored plastic spades and a bright red play bucket lay in the sand. On the far side of the tent was an oversized sandman. The sculpture was about three foot high and four foot long. Monster-man size. A fuck of a lot of sand! It had shells for eyes, a piece of wood for a nose and a twig for a mouth. Wouldn't win any prizes, but you could see it looked like a big guy.

Checking the beach one last time, Dermot rose from where he'd been sitting.

The tent? Why not? Nick's got to be somewhere, so why not inside the kiddy castle? Or inside the the sculpted sandman, maybe?

He suddenly had a nightmare vision of the sand sculpture exploding and Nick rising out of it; a syringe in his hand!

Don't be ridiculous. That's movie fantasy.

Yet Nick had always managed to maintain the upper hand in the past; he'd always been that bit smarter than anyone else.

Very cautiously, Dermot approached the tent, stopping ten feet or so from the front. A breeze had picked up, and the small triangular flag fluttered like a big butterfly atop the castle turret.

He studied the supine sandman.

Nick's not inside that. No way.

He proded it with his foot and the sand slide to one side. It wasn't hollow. No one inside.

Finally, Dermot's curiosity got the better of him. He *had* to check out the inside of the tent. Then he'd leave.

He stood directly outside the front flap. Apart from the breeze flapping the flag, there wasn't a sound on the beach; just the rippling water, only fifteen or so yards away behind him. The tide was inching in; yet was almost soundless.

Very gently Dermot sank to his knees on the soft sand and unzipped the flap. He looked inside.

The tent was empty. Just a sandy base and a shovel propped against the rear.

Very odd. No kids, no supplies, to towels and stuff. Nothing.

Immediately Dermot sensed a ruse and he whipped his head around sharply, expecting to see Nick standing behind him with a syringe, smiling an evil smile.

But no one was even close.

At that moment he felt a stab in his back, and he knew he'd been had.

Before any drug could kick in, he turned back to face the opening of the tent. Nick was standing in a deep hole he'd dug in the sand. Only his head and shoulders were visible. A piece of laminate measuring about three feet square had been pushed to one side and propped up against one side of the tent. Sand had been sprinkled on top of glue. It had served as a cover, imitating the sandy beach; like some World War Two escape tunnel.

Nick smiled his trademark smile as the muscles in Dermot legs gave way and he sank to his knees.

In seconds Nick was out of the hole and had dragged Dermot inside the tent, zipping the flap closed. Nick was the human reptile, capturing an insect.

Now he had complete privacy.

He pulled hard at Dermot's legs and let them drop over the edge of the hole in the sand, so they hung over the hole. He gently lowered his prey inside.

"Great fit, tough guy. You'll be snug as a bug. Just like before. Only this time, it'll be over more quickly. The tide's coming in, you see. Guess I'm the last of the nice guys, making it quick."

Dermot's lips were slack, his eyes had a vague expression. His body slumped even further down into the pit.

"Well, I guess this is it, Dermot. Game's over. Full time? The referee's just blown the whistle and I guess I won. Same as ever. No surprises."

Dermot continued to stare up at his tormentor.

"You know what?" Nick continued. "I need to find someone who plays a better game. You're not that smart. I need a challenge. Hansen's a muscle bound Neanderthal, not a player. The French detective wasn't too bad. Not in my league, though."

Hoyle crouched down so he was just inches from Dermot's face. "I guess there's not a lot more to say. What I'll do is honor my promise not to go after little Virginia. I'd never kill a child anyway. Maybe that's my Achilles heel. We'll never know. Sure as hell, *you* won't."

It was as Hoyle reached for a shovel propped up against the rear of the tent that Dermot raised the blowpipe and blew as hard as he could. The anesthetic dart shot into Nick's neck, close to the jugular.

"Shit! What the..." was all Hoyle said; a blank look of disbelief on his face. By that time Dermot had grabbed both of

Hoyle's ankles and smacked the shin bones extremely hard against each other.

Hoyle fell heavily.

Almost immediately, Dermot was out of the pit and straddling Nick like a sumo wrestler.

Nick struggled briefly, then the blowpipe's animal anesthetic kicked in and he went limp.

Dermot waited a full minute, unsure whether Nick was pretending to be comatose or not. Then he rose to his knees and studied Nick. Just some eye movement, but little else. Ideal – he wanted Nick to hear everything he had to say.

"Bet you're wondering what went wrong, huh?"

Dermot slowly began unzipping his jacket. "You could have come at me with a gun and I'd still have been fine. But you're a creature of habit, Nick; I figured it'd have to be the syringe again. Take a look here – you're going to love this."

He finished taking off the jacket and showed it to Nick. "Ballistic protection windbreaker. That's what they call it. Bulletproof jacket level 2. Available online thanks to Security Pro. Of course I had them make me a custom job; it doesn't normally come with any arm protection.

"Let's see..." Dermot muttered, studying the fabric carefully, then noticed a pin prick in the back. "There you go! That's where you tried to stick me. Just broke the cloth. Stopped right there. I tell you, the part I enjoyed most was watching you gloat when you thought I was helpless. Well, who's helpless now? Can you hear me? Just a little? Hope so."

Nick's eye flicked from side to side – it looked like he could; just.

"You're probably wondering what I hit you with? Well, I took a leaf from your own book. It's called a gauged projector. Those helpful guys at Pneu-Dart sell them on the Net. Hey, this is America! We have the right to bear just about anything.

This little beauty," he continued holding up the small cylinder, "weighs just 3.2 ounces. Slim as can be. I chose to strap it to the inside of my thigh, right up against my dick in case you frisked me. High strength aluminum alloy; you get over hundred shots per fill volume with this little sucker."

Dermot couldn't help a small chuckle of triumph. The adrenaline was pumping; he'd waited long enough for this moment.

"Guess I'm just a bit more high-tech than you and your little syringe. I tell you one more thing – it won't break the bank; costs just twenty seven fifty!"

He watched Hoyle's eye flick.

Flick, flick, flick.

Yes, it was obvious that Nick could hear and understand everything Dermot was saying.

"I saved the best bit for last. It's recyclable!"

This time Dermot couldn't help himself – he laughed aloud.

"Boy, is revenge sweet or what? To hell with what people tell you about revenge being best served cold – nah, this is electrifying! If there were more people like you around, I think I could *easily* become a serial killer!"

He prodded Hoyle's head with his forefinger. It swayed an inch or two.

"So the idea was to bury me for the second time, then wait for the tide to drown me? Original; but then you're the master of the unusual."

He looked at his watch. "Well, time the winged messenger and all that stuff? It'd tempt fate to hang around here too long. So I think I'll let Mother Nature take her course. And the beauty is this – it won't be me that kills you, it'll be the Nature-Lady. How perfect!"

Dermot glanced around, surveying everything in case he'd forgotten something. "You think I need to fill in the hole around you? Probably not, the stuff in the dart allows time enough for major surgery. But you never know. Better not be lazy, and just do it, eh?"

Dermot reached for the shovel and began digging at the rear of the tent, shoveling the sand in around Hoyle's legs.

"I bet you wondered what was going through my mind all those months underground. Well, this isn't *exactly* the same, but it'll give you *some* idea."

Dermot stopped when the sand was up to Hoyle's shoulders. He patted it down firmly.

"Did you ever get buried in the sand when you were a kid? I did. It was kind of fun, back then. You know something, the weird thing is sand's so heavy – it's damned difficult to shift; even with all your limbs functioning properly!"

He propped the shovel up again against the wall.

"Guess I'm done. I'll leave your head free; you won't be doing any shouting. But just in case, I happened to bring some tape. The tide should be here quite soon."

He pulled some duct tape from his pocket and wound it around Hoyle's head, covering his mouth.

Dermot then stood. "Sayonara!"

Dermot looked back at Nick's head, trying to lock eyes with his former friend, but Nick's eyes stared vaguely into space. It was a disappointment of sorts. A pity.

Dermot turned to leave and slowly unzipped the flap.

"Hold it right there!" the low voice barked loudly.

The strongly muscled legs of the black bather were planted firmly just inches the other side of the flap. Dermot almost fell backwards in shock. Then he looked up. The black guy was holding a service issue Glock – it was pointed at Dermot's chest. A gold shield was now hanging from his bathing shorts.

To his right stood Hansen, to his left Gassin.

It was Gassin who spoke. "We'll take over from here, Mr. Nolan. Thanks for your time and trouble. I'm certain you were about to call us and inform us of Mr. Hoyle's whereabouts. I'm right?"

Dermot nodded weakly. What else could he say?

"You had us worried for a while. How did you manage to avoid the needle stick?"

"Body armor…" Dermot muttered to no one in particular, still in shock.

"Ingenious. We guessed he was in the tent before you did. We thought for a while that you mightn't be curious enough to look inside. That would have been a shame."

"You knew he was inside?" Dermot was incredulous. He'd been staked out like the Judas Goat yet again! "And you did nothing? You just let me take my chances?"

"Yes, I'm afraid we did. It was a joint decision. It was a favor. We didn't want to deny you your…" he grinned, "moment of retribution. You see, given this location, there wasn't much doubt Hoyle had it in mind to bury you again, allowing the Pacific to do the rest. So your life was never in much danger. Possibly *his* life was, but that's another matter; one for conjecture only."

Dermot fingered the miniature .50 cal blowgun in his pocket. The movement wasn't lost on Gassin. "I'd take all your equipment home and destroy it, if I were you. No harm done yet. We've had teams tagging you since you saved the bomb girl's life. My congratulations on that one. Pity you chose not to tell us. Very naughty. Our biggest obstacle was tracking Hoyle. He's in a class of his own when it comes to keeping a low profile. He's like an *apparition*. I think you use the word 'wraith'? Following you was a piece of cake – we knew you'd lead us to him. Eventually. Because he was luring you to him."

The water was now only a few feet from the tent, lapping at Hansen's shoes.

"Go home to your wife and child, Mr. Nolan," Hansen said. There was an unusually severe tone to his voice today. "It's a shame you didn't feel you could rely on us. But hey, that's life." The last thing he was going to tell Dermot was that for the past two days Neela had shared her husband's every move with the LAPD. If she felt like telling him one day, fine. Otherwise…

"Just so you know, we picked you for the Bomb Samaritan as well as the guy who saved the Geerys – well, the truth of it was Commandant Gassin here picked you right away – but we agreed to let you run with the ball. That's kind of funny really – run with the ball? Hoyle called it a game, right?"

Dermot smiled. "Yeah…right."

"Meanwhile I got a man in there I need to dig out. Then I'll read him his rights. Much as I'd prefer to just walk away, that is. But I got a job to do. Can't all play God, can we?"

As Dermot walked away down the beach he saw Hansen and Gassin enter the tent. The black detective stood outside.

He threaded his way through the weird guys and tourists back to the promenade; casting his mind back to the moments he'd just spent gloating inside the tent, relishing his personal vengeance. He'd been about to commit murder and been actually thrilled by the prospect.

He'd been laughing!

What kind of monster had Nick made of him?

How long would prison bars hold a man as cunning as

Hoyle. A year. Ten years. A lifetime?

He knew their paths would meet again with the certainty that the sun would rise the next day.

Scary.

Acknowledgements.

I'd like to thank everyone who helped me deliver the sequel to 'Worst Nightmares.' They have been wonderful enough to keep badgering me to write the sequel.

Laura Blake Peterson, my amazing literary agent at Curtis Brown, who supports me without question – regardless of GFCs.

Scott Citron, of Scott Citron Design, for a magnificent cover.

Melissa Brooks.

Jeffrey Bloom.

The Hotel Buci, my favourite Paris boutique hotel.

Nick and Sheelagh Hippisley Coxe – I'm afraid I treat their house as my own!

Steven Nalevansky and Marti, for simply being my friends.

Beau, Amanda and Josef Nalevansky – ditto.

Rupert, Lizie and Hervé.

Virginia Bates.

Freddy.

Giblet

Wendy.

ABOUT THE AUTHOR

Shane began his theatre and film career in 1971 in London's West End with the play 'Children of the Wolf. He then made four films for Hammer Films and continued to work in London and America playing 'Dorian Gray' for the ABC Network in America. In 1982 he moved to Sydney to make films there.

He has worked with nine academy award winners and as of 2011 has starred in thirty-four films.

In 1995 his first novel was published by Harper Collins – *The Webber Agenda.'* This was followed by *'The Chasen Catalyst,' 'Hitkids,' 'Bite of the Lotus,' Graphic,'* and *'Worst Nightmares,'* which was published in America and Europe.

He lives in Sydney with his wife, Wendy, and their two cats, Giblet and Freddy.

The Dreamhealer online.

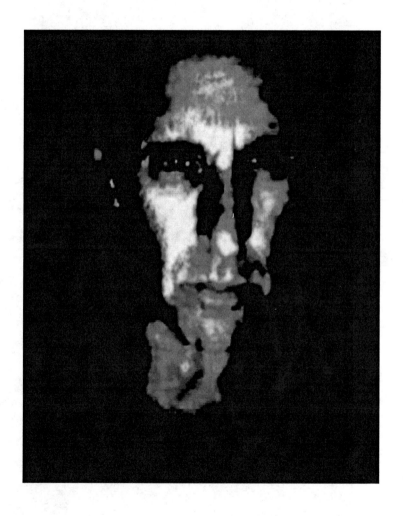

"All the danger, treachery, and suspense a reader could ask for is there, page after page. Shane Briant has the touch. A smashing debut."
—Steve Berry, New York Times bestselling author of The Charlemagne Pursuit

SHANE BRIANT

Worst Nightmares

A NOVEL OF SUSPENSE

'A fascinating international web...to the final intriguing page!' — DI MORRISSEY

DYMOCKS CRITICS CHOICE

BITE OF THE
LOTUS

... just remember to keep breathing.

SHANE BRIANT

German translation.

CPSIA information can be obtained
at www.ICGtesting.com
Printed in the USA
FSOW02n1915151216
28615FS

9 781456 572136